Land of Shadows

Stig Dalager is one of the leading lights of contemporary Danish literature, the author of 51 works of fiction, comprising novels, plays for the theatre, radio, and TV, film scripts, volumes of poetry, and belles-lettres. He is also the editor of a leading cultural magazine. His novel, *Journey in Blue,* was nominated for the Impac Prize 2008, and his docu-drama, *Two Days in July,* proved a major literary triumph in both Denmark and Germany as well as in Britain when it appeared in 2008. Dalager's books and plays have been published and/or staged in 24 countries round the world. "With his novels and plays Dalager has accrued a distinguished reputation in Europe" – Michael Faber, *The Guardian. Land of Shadows* is a powerful book about the 9/11 catastrophe, but the significance of its great strength lies in the author's balance and objectivity in appreciating many conflicting but valid points of view.

Land of Shadows

Stig Dalager

Translated from the Danish
by Frances Østerfelt

Arena Books

First published simultaneously in Great Britain & the USA in 2011 by Arena Books

Arena Books
6 Southgate Green
Bury St. Edmunds
IP33 2BL

www.arenabooks.co.uk

Distributed in America by Ingram International, One Ingram Blvd., PO Box 3 LaVergne, TN
37086-1986, USA.

Dalager, Stig. 1952-
   Land of Shadows
   1.   September 11 Terrorist Attacks, 2001 – Influence -
   Fiction. 2. Jewish lawyer – New York (State) – New York -
   Fiction. 3. Women real estate agents – New York (State) -
   New York – Fiction. 4. Israelis – New York (State) - New
   York – Fiction. 5. Murder – Investigation - Israel
   Fiction. 6. Suspense fiction.
   I.   Title
   839.8'138-dc22

ISBN 978-1-906791-76-6

BIC classifications: FA, FHP, FRD.

Printed & bound by Lightningsource UK

Cover design
By Jon Baxter

Typeset in Times New Roman

 This book is printed on paper adhering to the Forest Stewardship Council™
(FSC®) mixed Credit FSC® C084699.

To Niels and Nina

*"That long black cloud is coming down,
I feel I'm knocking on heaven's door"*

BOB DYLAN

2001

Is memory, as Boris Pasternak writes, a uniquely magical world that looms on the horizon like mountains or a great, distant city? If that city is New York, then memory is hard-bitten, carnal and like a presence that knows no age. Everything happens at the same time, buildings vanish from a street and new ones appear; but haven't they always been there?

He wakes to the sound of a helicopter or was it the noise of tyres screeching around the corner of Second Avenue that woke him, or even something else: the TV downstairs running most of the night with the loud ratatata from the war movies the Puerto Rican never seems to tire of seeing, the Puerto Rican with some shady business in Hell's Kitchen, he's sure of, 'though the Puerto Rican has never really said so.

What is up, what is down? In the darkness enclosing the bed, he reaches out for Eve and under the covers finds the round of her nude shoulder with its dry, warm skin. Here is his refuge. She mumbles something in her sleep, he wants to slip over to her and make love, but feels that he's too tired.

New York by night, even after seven years in the city, Jon's still not gotten used to the cacophony of sounds in the dark from the never slumbering city. Has he ever slept through a single night? In his dreaming, weightless state, cases from Brooklyn's Criminal Court rotate in his mind and are again re-enacted, sometimes angry or sorrowful faces; faces from one case are transformed to faces in another, the condemned are acquitted and sometimes the other way around; clients and convicted wait for him on side streets in Brooklyn or Harlem, places that he's only passed by or heard tell of, but would never be able to find again. His last client, John Carmichael, a businessman living in Boston, charged for killing a colleague and whom he'd gotten acquitted, summoned him in a dream to Coney Island and insisted that he was guilty.

"You didn't do it", he told him, "let it go."

Carmichael bent down in his Armani suit with its broad knotted tie and picked up a handful of sand from the beach, which with a quick thrust suddenly threw into the wind.

"No," he said, "but I could've; it was really touch and go."

High over their heads, seagulls shrieked, the sky was blue velvet, water as far as the eye could see, water in a vast space, greater than he'd ever seen; and he knew it was a dream and that Carmichael wasn't the type who would ever ask him to come to Coney Island to confess. When he again tried to catch Carmichael's eye, the entire beach was peopled with Carmichaels throwing sand into the wind.

Early the next day he took Eve to Coney Island, an August morning, sun shining from a sky with light, ragged clouds. Eve was in a white sleeveless blouse that set off her gleaming black page-boy hair. Hand in hand they walked along the Boardwalk, not many people around; he squeezed her hand in his as they stopped in front of the crumbling Parachute Jump. In the background rose the enormous Wonder Wheel, like a mirage with its spidery patterns and empty covered baskets and he thought a moment of Prater's big wheel, Vienna, Sine and Tobias; and told her about his dream the night before.

"You're just run down, exhausted," she said looking at him anxiously and then at her watch, she had to get back to her office at the World Trade Center; stacks of papers were waiting for her there.

They walked down the beach, which weeks before was wall-to-wall with bathers, each with their own towel; but was now almost void of people. Farther out in the waves they caught a glimpse of a swimmer's white arm and head, the sun's rays reflected out across the Atlantic towards a distant hazy point. It was as if millions of phosphorescent fish teemed in a line moving towards the earth's curve and horizon. He grabbed her shoulders and turned her gently towards him searching for the same distant point in her eyes.

"Find something?" she said with a faint smile before he kissed her.

He nodded and kissed her again; her lips tasted of salt, like her suntanned throat.

In the subway back to Manhattan she asked him why he even took John Carmichael's case when he was so overworked and when so many other more important cases were waiting.

"The case seemed hopeless," he said, "he'd approached several others before coming to me, expensive Manhattan firms; but they refused."

"And you'd play the hero as usual," she said shaking her head, with a faint bitter twist to her lips, telling him that she thought he'd neglected her.

"No ... but it didn't take me long to see a technical, legal solution to his problem, so..."

" So what?"

" So – his situation reminded me of something from my past..."

"You've never been charged for murder," she said and looked at him bewildered as the train glided through the dark tunnel under East River and faces around them in the long, rumbling car paled in the artificial light.

"One thing is to be charged and sentenced; something else is to feel guilty for taking another person's life," he said. "John Carmichael felt guilty, but was acquitted; I've never been charged or sentenced; but it would've helped if I'd been acquitted."

"But, why, for what?"

"Years ago, in Leipzig, I was responsible for another man's death; that is, I felt responsible. He was old, had a heart condition; and maybe he really did deserve to die; but I did nothing to help him when everything came to a head."

"If I know you, your hands are clean," she said taking his hand.

"No one's hands are clean."

Instead of walking straight to the World Trade Center Station Eve left the train with Jon at Grand Central Terminal, and they walked silently up the stairs to the teeming departure hall with the marble steps and the light blue vaulted ceiling with all the constellations. He had to go Uptown by cab to meet a client; but it wasn't like her to follow him to the door.

In the light from the hall's high windows, that always made him feel homeless, her face suddenly became pale and serious, her eyelid trembled as she broke free and stood right in front of him.

"No one 'deserves' to die," she said amidst the din of thousands of voices and steps echoing from the columns, ceiling and marble walls in the great hall.

"What d'you mean?" he asked.

"You said the man in Leipzig, what was his name ...?"

"Wiesbühl, his name was Wiesbühl and was a big wheel in the communist machinery of the DDR."

"You said he deserved to die. No one 'deserves' to die. How can you say that?" She held his glance; but then one and then another passer-by bumped into her.

He was surprised by her insistence, but knew its root, and with the routine he had from hundreds of court trials, he said calmly:

"It was stupid of me; but maybe you'd understand if you knew that the man I spoke of was an ex-*unterscharführer* in the extermination camp Sobibor, who possessed nothing that resembled a guilty conscience."

As grandchild of two who had been murdered in Auschwitz and daughter of a father who'd barely escaped death in the same camp, she was hit at an aching, never healed spot; and from one moment to the next was in a hurry to get the subway downtown and left him with a peck on his cheek amidst the rush in the hall.

Her Israeli father had walled off the pain and she'd inherited the ghosts.

Now, in the middle of the night with the incessant noise of the city, he sits down beside her in bed and lets his hand glide over her hair; but he's restless, gets up, lights a cigarette and walks over to the window and looks out. Second Avenue below is like a hallucination in the yellow light that reaches upward in a brim of light over the neighbourhood and enhances the sense of something that's not there; cars, a Chevrolet, a pick-up, pass but the drivers can't be seen; in the drugstore across the street are customers; he sees some hands rummaging through the goods in the window, but otherwise only shadows. The owner, Mr. Monroe, who's usually behind the counter, is nowhere to be seen, only the drawer with the gun just under the cash register with its shiny handle is in sight. Monroe had often explained to him that it's hidden there "just in case" and that nine years ago he was wounded by two guys on crack that broke into his shop and stole his money, everything he owned, and on that night he'd "looked death right in the face". Café Lucina next door, just closed down for the night, empty white chairs and tables stacked up and in rows phosphoresce in the dark, isn't there someone in white walking through the room? Clairvoyant Studio with its wax figure in the window is alight with its blue neon letters. A police car with black and white stripes drives slowly down the street with its many silhouetted ash trees and their beautifully slender trunks. Music from all sides, muffled rhythms, a woman on the sidewalk walks past the shuttered windows of Indian Curry Makal and Kosher Dish farther down the road with rapid, clicking high-heeled steps, her blue shawl over her shoulders and her blond hair makes him think of Sine. He can see her stopping, turning, as if she'd forgotten something and waving to him in the window, but she walks on and vanishes out of sight.

He's got to pull himself together, how many women can he have in his head at the same time? He's familiar with that kind of exhaustion that makes him long for Vienna and Sine and his son and regret all those years in New York. He's felt it lately, winding himself up into a new vicious spiral of new cases and new fatigue. Just the other day Jim Cartwright showed up at his office on St. Mark's Place to warn him:

"You've got to make up your mind," he said, "are you here in New York or in Vienna?"

"Of course I'm here, got any complaints?"

"It's Eve I'm thinking about," said Cartwright and stood there imposingly in front of his desk stacked with cases, meaning he was serious. It was a habit he had: When something came to a head, no matter whether it was about details in clearing up a murder case or something he'd been brooding about for a while and only had to do with them, Cartwright trooped up and delivered it all standing up. More or less on purpose he played on the effect of surprise and took advantage of his military training and experience as an actor. Behind Cartwright, the door was opened to the rest of the office and to Michele, who from her desk had already looked up and through the glass windows was looking their way. Outside it was raining, raindrops covered the windows facing St. Mark's Place with its still green plantain trees and the Ukrainian bookstore Vaselka across the street; the light outside was grey, even Michele's face was the color rainy weather gives everyone on a late summer day. He got up from his chair behind the desk and walked behind Cartwright to close the door.

"Do you know something I don't know?" he asked walking back to his desk.

Cartwright's suntanned face darkened.

" I just know that she's sad, damned sad; and it's you that makes her sad."

"And how do you know that?"

"I've got eyes in my head. That's what you pay me for, isn't it?"

"Not for you to keep watch on Eve and me."

"She's also confided in me, that sort of thing happens once in a while with adults."

"And what's she said?" he said and could feel at that moment how hurt he was that Eve and Cartwright had apparently built up a trust of which he had no part. Had she called him? Did they meet?

"D' you really want to know?" asked Cartwright and put both hands on the desk, leaning over towards him.

" Sure I do," he said, not really meaning it.

" She said she'd leave you if you didn't wake up to her existence."

"I am awake, I live with her, remember?"

"Could be," said Cartwright and buttoned his jacket, preparing to leave, "but do something…"

Before he could answer, Cartwright was out the door and breezed through the office with a quick nod to Michelle.

That evening, he'd put everything aside just to be with Eve, invited her to dinner under the arches of The Oyster Bar at Grand Central Station. Hand in hand they walked down Fifth Avenue and from there took a cab to Brooklyn Bridge, here at his favourite place with a view of the monolithic city's millions of lights adorning the August night's darkness and vibrating like fireflies, he drew her close and promised that it was just him and her. Her eyes had a new glow beneath him as they made love in the bed in their flat, but even that night he got up to read through a new case, and she surprised him at the computer with her nervous voice that cut through the darkness behind him:

"Why did you leave me in bed … I thought you meant it…"

He turned on his chair towards her standing there in the darkness in a long transparent top, mussed hair and sleepy eyes, somewhere nearby a fire alarm went off, loud laughter was heard in the street.

"I figured you were asleep…"

"I can't sleep when you're not in bed. I dreamed about my dad."

"Yeah?"

"It was so clear. He sat with my mother in the garden in Jerusalem and talked about visiting me in New York, they packed their bags, a dark car came for them, they drove through the arid landscape to the airport in Tel Aviv, checked in, he was happy that he'd finally made up his mind to fly to New York, they walked out into the sunlight, out to the plane. On the steps up to the plane, he suddenly grabbed at his heart and collapsed, my mother shouted for help, there was panic around them, he lay on the steps and died, as he said my name the clouds in the sky reflected in his eyes. And then I woke up and you weren't there."

He walked over to her and held her close. Her body trembled. He led her to the bed, where they sat down. Around them all was quiet, as if the furniture and everything there held their breath: the Modigliani reproduction over their bed of the young nude woman with the kohl-painted eyes and sweet smile was as distant as if it were in another room, a room at sea. In the kitchen the tap dripped.

"What d'you think it means?" she asked, not looking at him.

"Maybe a forewarning…"

"Don't say that…"

"Your father's got a bad heart, he's past 75, you've got to get used to the idea that he won't live forever," he said as calmly as he could.

"I spoke with him a couple of days ago, there was nothing the matter."

"Should I call Jerusalem and hear how things are?" he asked trying once again to calm her, but she went into the living room to make the call herself. When no one answered, she was at a loss and didn't know what to do with herself. They lay in bed awake for hours, typical for them when Eve was worried about bad news from Israel; first she recounted as a sort of incantation everything that had already happened, her grandparents' death and her father's miraculous survival in Auschwitz; she talked about her father's emaciated appearance when the Russians liberated the camp as something she'd been witness to herself, even though she, because of his dogged silence about that part of his life, through books, photos and other's testimony had to construct most of it on her own. Nor did her mother, who'd met him many years after the war and had grown up in Tel Aviv, know much about his bitter experiences in Auschwitz, it was only on rare occasions that he admitted to random events, which he later regretted and made small of. Her mother was in fact a psychologist and worked with children's trauma; and had for a time made great efforts to get her husband to let go of his burdens; but all of this in recent years was overshadowed by a death which came as a shock to the entire family Letterman in Jerusalem and which Eve, also that night returned to: Her older brother, a colonel in the Israeli army, head of an armoured unit operating in Gaza, was hit by a shot from a Palestinian sniper as he was getting out of his vehicle after an operation, he didn't survive his wounds.

"I didn't agree with him," Eve said every time she talked about him, even that night, "but why did he have to die?"

She summed up, she wasn't an attorney for nothing, and said:

"With two parents murdered and a son shot down, God will surely give him some respite."

And then it was his turn to say something:

"You're right, I'm sure your father's time hasn't come yet."

Also that night he was right there and said just what she needed to hear, but perhaps there was something in his voice that was unconvincing, or it might have occurred to Eve, as many times before, that she'd let her father down by staying in New York after her brother was shot and especially, just like her half-sister, who every other weekend went around Jerusalem with peace posters, was opposed to the army's actions in the occupied territories.

"Have I really left him in the lurch?" she asked him.

"No," he said wearily, "you've just taken a stand and said what *you* think."

"Who's it helped?"

"Those who want peace with the Palestinians. Yourself."

"No, not me, absolutely not me, it would've been much easier for me if I'd just stood by my father and brother and stayed in Israel, but I couldn't. I couldn't breathe, I couldn't stand being in a country that's always preparing for war and can't find a way to live in peace with its neighbours."

"There has to be at least two parts to establish peace," he said.

"Yes," she said, "but Israel is the strongest part, and the strongest must give more."

They went on that way through the night until they sank under their covers exhausted, but the next morning – that was yesterday – Eve was more nervous than ever and wanted to stay home from work at her office in the World Trade Center. He convinced her to go.

"Go to work," he said, "it'll distract your thoughts and that's what you need."

"No I need to go to Jerusalem," she said. "And I need to spend more time with you."

They stood in the kitchen, flooded in light from the low-lying sun outside. Rays of sun cast faint shadows of their silhouettes on the white walls, the dark eyes in her unrested face shone; she appealed to him just as she did the first time he saw her, when she came to his office on St. Mark's Place looking for work. She just showed up out of the blue with her experience from a law office on Fifth Avenue and wanted "to try something new" and had happened to hear of him and his office from one of her older colleagues; she wasn't the least in doubt about her own talents and moved around his office with the greatest of ease, as if she already belonged there. She laughed aloud, her head held high in her skirt, black stockings and dark jacket and looked teasingly at him, as if it was he looking for work from her, and yet there was something sad and vulnerable about her that he couldn't quite fathom, and made him want to explore. Was it not a kinship, was it not because it reminded him of something he bore with him, something intangible that made him get up in the morning, and which cast its light on everything he did, both the absurd and the meaningful? He found that quality in certain faces, yes even in the atmosphere of some streets in East Village with their shady ash- and plantain trees or in Tompkins Square Park on a drizzly afternoon, where

Puerto Rican and Afro-American boys were totally absorbed in their acrobat-
ic and stepdancing basketball games. He carried it with him when he con-
ducted a case in one of the lofty courtrooms with polished wooden panelling
in the temple-like courthouse on Schermerhorn Street in Brooklyn or in one
of the crowded, run-down courtrooms in Manhattan's three-winged art deco
courthouse on Centre Street gazing at the twelve jurors who followed his
slightest move with their eyes and in his tone of voice searching for clarity
for their decision, often wavering until the last moment. He knew that tone of
voice was often more important than what he said, that the fate of the accused was decided not only by dry facts and concrete evidence or technicali-
ties, but more by whether he could be inspired and driven by the overwhelming consequence an acquittal would have for the acused. If freedom meant
nothing to him, if it couldn't be heard in his voice, in his manner of speaking,
then why should it mean anything to that man or woman who with baited
breath and a forced demeanor of calm awaited their judgment?

His tone of voice was also decisive yesterday morning when he answered
Eve's question:

"Do you love me?"

He held her close and whispered "yes" in her ear, and he could feel her
body, how a myriad of worries abandoned it; less nervous than before she
asked the next question as she broke free of his embrace and shoved him
slightly away so she could see his face:

"Will you come with me to Jerusalem and visit my father?"

"You mean your family and your father?"

"Yes, all of my family, the one in Tel Aviv and the one in Jerusalem."

He smiled and gazed into her eyes.

"Of course I'll go with you", he said. "When do we leave?"

"Tomorrow!" she said and laughed when she saw his surprise. "I've already booked the tickets!"

"When d'you do that?"

"A week ago."

"Why haven't you said anything …?"

"I wasn't sure where I had you, and was ready to go alone."

He sighed, knowing that he had to disappoint her as he said:

"Tomorrow's the 11th of September and I have my first meeting on White Street with my next client, no good tomorrow, let's do it in a week."

"You'll just have to cancel, the tickets are booked, we've *got to* go!" she said holding his gaze. "My father might not be alive next week."

"I just can't," he said, "it's really tight, my client, a Moslem, owns a service station in Brooklyn, he's charged with first degree murder. I've put off this meeting several times already, but now we have to get a grip on the case. The first trial day is set in three weeks."

"So a Moslem guy from Brooklyn is more important than my father and me!" she replied angrily, turned her back on him and walked into the bedroom, silently he followed. In the bedroom she opened the closet doors, pulled a suitcase down and recklessly threw bits and pieces of clothing into it.

"Aren't you going to work?" he asked.

Still with her back to him she said:

"I'll call and say my father is dying in Jerusalem and I'm going to Israel."

"Just like that?"

"Yeah, just like that. But you wouldn't understand, for you your work and your damned clients always come first."

"Of course they don't," he said, "but I can't just turn my back on a man who's totally depending on me showing up and briefing me on his case."

"You could send Cartwright!"

" Cartwright's good for a lot, but he's no attorney."

"Then send Michelle, give her a chance to take on a bigger case."

"We're talking about a charge of first degree murder, Michelle just doesn't have enough experience."

"Then she could get it!"

He walked over to her, put his hands on her shoulders and gently turned her around; she resisted, but gave in. They stared at each other, she clenching her jaws and provocatively waving the blouse she was holding back and forth.

"Now listen," he said, "I'm going to that meeting tomorrow and will brief
Michelle on the case. We'll work hard for the next week and then she'll take
over together with a colleague and Cartwright while we're in Israel. Today
you call your father and find out if there's really something wrong. What
d'you say?"

She smiled faintly, but wouldn't give in.

"And what if he really is ill?"

"Then you go alone and I'll come as soon as I can."

She looked suspiciously at him, but let the suitcase lie on the floor and the
closet open; then she put on her jacket, scooped up her bag, gave him a kiss,
rushed out through the kitchen to the stairs, a moment later she waved to him
from the sunlit street and disappeared down Second Avenue into the crowd.

He was alone with himself and the papers from Ifrahim Mohammed's proceedings, which filled his briefcase which he'd taken home from the office,
and as he spread a stack of papers out over the dining room table as was his
custom to get the first impression and mentally warm up to delve into yet another mosaic of crime with its register of sorrow, motives for revenge, hyste-
ria and entanglements, the impression of Eve hung in his mind. She'd become a part of him, her changing moods and energy echoed in the back of his
head, and he felt the fear of losing her as a suddenly awakened nightmare,
that darkened his gaze for some seconds and stiffened his movements.

In the window to Monroe's drugstore across the street the moon faintly reflected over Monroe's shadowy contours farther in or perhaps it was just
something he'd imagined, he wondered how old man Monroe got through the
nights standing up behind the counter, and when did he sleep. Many times
during the day he'd seen him walk past his office on St. Mark's Place, in this
city there are millions of lives, and Monroe's and his Irish-born wife occupied almost nothing in the effervescence of the metropolis; they're as light as
the yellowed leaves of the maple tree, which soon would whisk across the
asphalt in Tompkins Square Park when he takes his late evening walks and
Eve can't understand where he's been.

Once he'd given himself away to her that the long-stemmed, ornamental
lamp posts in the park, which in the evening darkness light up like floating

globes and cast a claire-obscure glow through the trees, made him think of similar lamps in Türkenschanz Park in Vienna and his time in Vienna with Sine and Tobias.

"Why walk around Tompkins and yearn for your ex-wife and your son, when you see them every third month?" she'd once asked. "Are you sure that you're not going to move back to them once and for all?"

"I see my son every third month in Vienna, sometimes only once in a half year," he'd answered, "and I'm not yearning for Sine. It's all over between her and me."

Eve doesn't really believe him, but does he believe himself?

Those many visits through the years to the flat on Billrothstrasse in Vienna, where he gathers some father-dignity together with Tobias, and Sine in her own half-retreating, half-direct way makes room for him (many times she's arranged to be completely out of the flat with her "stacks of work" at her office in the UNO building) hasn't made it easier for him.

Hasn't he been a man of complicated paths?

At each visit he has to start from scratch with his son, who is still enshrouded in autism's fog, but has evolved into an equilibristic performer on the piano, playing Mozart and Chopin so that it whistles past the ears of the listener. Sine has gotten him into one of Vienna's many music schools, and fights to inject some vitality into his technically adroit reproduction of other, far older pianists' interpretations; he masters reading notes as if they were street maps, but with his absolute pitch most of it goes through his ears and down to those agile fingers which seem to be those of an angel and gives his playing a particular lightness. When they meet in the flat, Tobias has difficulty recognizing him, but through a series of practiced signals, which go back to their early days in Vienna and their strolls through the parks near Billrothstrasse, he's able to create for himself and for Tobias a sense of presence, which can quickly burst if he unknowingly treads beyond Tobias' acquired habits. Without warning Tobias, now 14, could as they dine together get up from the table and rush to his room, there attired with headphones sit on a chair and rock back and forth for hours. Not only he, but the whole world is lost to him, and in these situations Jon would experience his old dizziness that sometimes grows to nausea. The situation's rescue is to lure Tobias to the piano in the flat or outside on yet another of their many walks, that through the years has taken in all of Vienna, from Schönbrunn's impressive park , past portraits and furnishings in Belvedere's galleries (he never ceases introducing him to history), and to the habitual Türkenschanz Park in all kinds of weather.

After each visit to Vienna he'd return to New York exhausted and saturated with an underlying sense of homecoming and of flight.

He'd been on another planet with an alien from outer space that was his son, yes, a part of himself. When he says good-bye to him in the large vestibule in the old Patrician flat on Billrothstrasse, he's not sure that Tobias understands that he's leaving; perhaps he doesn't even know who he is, even though the word father has long held a mechanical place in Tobias' fragmented mind. That worry he must bear alone, he can't expect Eve to follow him there.

From what is he fleeing? His own inadequacy towards Tobias, his own restlessness, his own defeat in Vienna when he despite collaboration with Wiesenthal could not get Jürgen Menken convicted? But hadn't he long ago convinced himself that by tracking the previous SS-doctor Jürgen Menken down in Vienna with hundreds of Jewish lives on his conscience and ensure his arrest he'd done all that he could? It wasn't his fault that Vienna is a haven for earlier national socialistic war criminals and that the state only reluctantly wants to see them condemned.

He was victim of a letter bomb, almost lost his sight in one eye, was shocked, his son kidnapped, and Sine blamed him that his bad luck had pulled them all down with him.

A kind of fanaticism?

Can he not take blame, is he really so weak? And didn't he just go too far on his strange crusade for justice, and doesn't he still go too far? Who does he think he is?

What shadows are shadowing him when he's shadowing them?

And does he really need the Atlantic Ocean to escape them?

So many questions and so few answers for someone who imagines that he, because he can plead a case in a courtroom and play on the keyboard of law and legal finesse and mood, knows and can do something special.

He can love two women at the same time and make both of them half-way unhappy.

He can neglect his son.

That's what he can.

He pulls away from the window to Second Avenue, stumps out his third cigarette in the ashtray on the windowsill.

Eve's in bed with legs pulled up under her under the blanket like she sometimes does. He gets in next to her in the dark and enfolds her in his arms, an anchor in a floating world. She's sleeping sound and peacefully, from her office at the World Trade Center yesterday she'd finally got in touch with her father: Everything's OK, no ground for panic. They'll fly to Israel next week.

At the edge of sleep the contours of Ifrahim Mohammed's face, as he knows him from a photograph, appear in his mind among many other chance associations and won't leave him in peace.

A face with a light brown taint, a mild countenance and a slightly bewildered gaze, a man in his best years trapped in a machine that is prepared to bury him the next 40 years in a cell the size of a child's room on an electronically monitored corridor in a prison where the prisoners will immediately test his primal strength through rape and forced deals.

A man lacking a killer's eye.

A man who still might have killed.

He'll know much more after his meeting with him after sunrise.

After 13 years as a practicing attorney in New York, it's been his privilege to take on only the larger cases for clients, whose lack of guilt in one way or another seems credible, here his long experience and intuition come in. His love for the difficult and "hopeless" cases for vulnerable or less well-off clients is coupled with a quickly established sense of their "innocence", where the superficial often speaks for their "guilt". Earlier he was, like so many court-appointed attorneys and even defense attorneys with tiny offices, forced to walk on thin ice: The client might be guilty, but I'll work for his acquittal within the framework of the law. What attorney doesn't believe in the words of the law that his client is innocent until the opposite has been proven? Unless money and avarice are everything, what defense attorney in New York doesn't have trouble defending a man whose hands are "dirty"? Sonderheim's unexpected round-handed payment for his work in Vienna helped free him and make him independent.

Even in the pits of sleep, Ifrahim Mohammed's case won't let him go; but his body in the bed is pressed into Eve's, he murmurs incomprehensible half and broken sentences into the darkness of the flat in East Village, dreaming that it is early Sunday morning on Fifth Avenue. The wide street is almost deserted, the skyscrapers cast large shadows under the sun, he and a man resembling Ifrahim Mohammed move in each their own direction on each their own pavement down the street, as he passes him, he discovers that Mohammed has blood on his hands and shouts to him. Mohammed rushes off, he crosses the street in pursuit, he turns a corner down a side street following after, but he's vanished in thin air. The street is empty, but he's no long on Manhattan, in front of him is Lee Avenue in Williamsburg, a weak whimpering voice reaches his ears. He turns towards a window in the nearest shop, a jewelry store with handwritten signs, and walks over to the door. At first he can see nothing for the sun's reflection in the windows of the door, then a silhouette of a man. The man's sitting with his hands tied behind his back on a chair in the back room, around him and in the shop itself are empty flat boxes and cases strewn over the floor. The man is wearing a black coat, hat, down the sides of his cheeks hang two long curls of hair; his long, gray beard slurs his features, his eyes are filled with fright; blood flows from a wound in his breast.

He thinks: "It's him, it's Mr. Ellis Edelstein, the Satmar Jew who Mohammed gunned down", and he grabs the door to get in to him, but it's locked. He desperately heaves and hauls at the knob in vain, but at that moment someone taps him on the shoulder. He turns. Two metres from him stands Ifrahim Mohammed, with a shy smile he hands him a key. His hands are dry and brown.

"What's this?" he asks.

"The key to the door," says Mohammed.

"Where'd you get it?"

"I found it on the street and ran right back to Mr. Edelstein's shop."

"I don't believe you."

"You have to," says Mohammed, "now let's help Mr. Edelstein!"

He turns, key in hand, towards the door and the shop, but it's gone, all of Lee Avenue is gone, there's only the sun from the bright blue sky over the skyscrapers on Fifth Avenue and shadows beneath; he's alone on the amazingly quiet street, which has never been so long and resembles an arid river delta between high mountains of rock and sparkling crystal. His key is gone,too, he looks for it everywhere in his clothes, but can't find it and has the feeling that he must go on, but doesn't know where. He looks at his watch, which he'd bought from a street vendor in Soho years ago, and which with its thin, vibrating second hand has worked perfectly ever since. It's stopped. In the mirror-like glass over its face, the image of Eve fades in, his mouth moves, he wonders how her face can be reduced to that size and what she's trying to say. It's five minutes to five. Still dark outside, they have to get up in two hours.

Up, up, up, effectivity – their middle name.

* * *

It's morning, and what is it about today? How long can summer shove autumn in front of it and keep the sun in the sky? Seldom has he seen such a blue sky over New York in September. A light western breeze blows in over Manhattan's monolithic forest from New Jersey and has carried oxygen to the glittering Hudson River, whose water, called "The Great River," Henry Hudson once passed in his ship "Half Moon" on his journey home to England; before that, driven by a mad dream of finding the Northwest Passage sailed his half-moon ship past Manhattan's staggeringly green, hilly and wooded landscape, home of the Algonquin Indians, and pressed his crew to the farthest point of their energy and capacity.

How many dreamers have not set their name, reputation and life to the building of New York City?

Eve and Jon are up early and barely awake in their flat on Second Avenue, and even though they're in a hurry and used to taking the subway or jumping into a cab, they decide to walk through Washington Square Park and south to their destinations: the office on the 86th floor of the World Trade Center's South Tower and the prison, Manhattan Detention Complex on White Street.

When they, each with their own briefcase, get near the victory arch in the park and walk under it with its view of the many leafy tree crowns, some boys on skateboards are on their way in the opposite direction towards Fifth Avenue, in perfect balance with their bodies. One of them, a black guy steers straight for them and turns skillfully and playfully throws his arms around them in greeting, his laughter hangs in the air around them; Eve drops her bag in fright and bends down to pick it up from the asphalt; at that moment a cab driver wakes up on the driver's seat of his yellow cab somewhere down 21st Street West, here after the night's many criss-cross trips through the town he's fallen asleep and overheard the radio's persistent calls, his eyes meet a pale face, heavy with sleep in the rearview mirror, it must be his, he remembers with a frown that the double bed in his small flat in the Bronx was abandoned by his girlfriend some days ago and he hasn't seen her since; a stockbroker, Mr. Mason, who during a night-long meeting made a good deal in a cigar bar on Seventh Avenue, is in the Marriott-Marquis Hotel on Times Square with its 1911 rooms and 61 suites on his way up in the elevator, through the elevator's glass walls he looks down over the hotel's enormous atrium with its hanging gardens, he gets dizzy, presses all the buttons in vain and can't see an end to his upward flight; in the Chrysler building's lobby, the cleaning lady, Mrs. Dooley, has stopped in front of the elevator shaft, even though she's already tired at the prospect of the many offices she has to clean, she walks slowly with her motorized floor scrubber in hand over the multicolored marble floor and achieves a momentary inner peace in the dark golden light from the angular, glowing art deco lamps, which like lotus flowers in the elevators' inlaid African wood every morning makes her yearn for the peaceful village just outside Nairobi that her family left generations

ago; in the basement under the building, not yet occupied by personnel, re-
sides darkness to the sound of faintly ticking electric meters whose cables
like black arteries run all the way up to the building's spire above its foun-
tain-like top, up here rules light and from here Manhattan's, the Bronx,
Queens and Brooklyn's network of streets, diverse buildings and green parks
like backdrops in a puppet show for a giant's frolicking imagination; like an
invasion of ants, there are hundreds of thousands of commuters in the subway and cars on their way under East River and the Hudson and over the
bridges, Brooklyn Bridge, Queensboro Bridge, Williamsburg Bridge, Manhattan Bridge, towards Manhattan, half awake, half dozing, half dreaming
they let themselves be transported while three addicts who happened to meet
in the damp tunnel under Bowary Station the night before and sneaked their
way on the subway to the Bronx are on the prowl for a pusher and a fix,
wake up under a gray beam in Yankee Stadium's gigantic construction, here,
confused and dead tired sought shelter for the night, now sweating, now
freezing under the sun and have trouble getting to their feet; in an antechamber in the stock market's columned building on Broad Street the young John
Charmer is preparing for the day's hectic activity in the market's 3,500
square meter large gallery, he opens the door of a closet and looks with a
measure of naïve admiration at his smooth face in a mirror and pulls a large-
patterned plaid jacket down from a hanger, the day before he'd slid in some
papers in the middle of the paper bestrewn floor in a crowd of loudly shouting and gesticulating brokers and missed several important notes, today he's
determined to do better and meet his own sky-high goal for success; the security guard Eva Thompson is making her morning rounds in Security Council Chamber in the UN's enormous marble and glass building, the deserted
emptiness around the circular table with its parade of unoccupied chairs enhances the soundproof silence of the room, her ears hum when a door in the
wall is suddenly opened far from her back with an implosive whoosh, she
turns and fumbles for her gun, no one enters; the city wakes, the radio host
Jim McNey, in his packed Greenwich Village studio, as he stares with
gleaming eyes at the microphone suspended in front of him, lets associations
flow and his mouth run in its usual rapping style with magnificent promises

of "sunshine on the walls of the city"; in a stairwell on Fifth Avenue Harlem with a view of the fire tower in the Marcus Garvey Park between 120th and 124th Streets ebony black Marvin Jr. after a night with his mistress on the dry sheets on the narrow bed in her small flat, that smells of cooking oil, can't get enough of her smiles and pulls her in slow motion towards the wall next to the window, lifts up her skirt and inserts his aching shaft, she drives her nails into his neck, he vanishes in her scent and the dark behind his eyes, the fire tower and poplars far below reverberate in the veiled edge of her vision; millions of mobile telephone voices in an inaudible and chaotic chorus cross over Manhattan's skyline, a symphony of fragments of half pronounced or whole longings, wishes, information, meetings, and angry explosions fill the air and find their way to millions of ears like small darts which alter postures in subways, railway stations or cars; in his bed in a two-room flat on Hudson Street Mr. Mann wakes sweaty with pain radiating from his left hand, which was stuck between his head and the headboard while he slept, fearing that he might be out of action for the evening's performance at the Metropolitan Opera, he jumps out of bed, opens a closet, takes out his violin case, opens it and pulls out his violin and bow and starts to play, standing there in bare feet in the middle of the room, at first the tones are uharmonious and his hand stiff, he clenches his jaws, the pain grows, but so do the tones in their depth and fill the room until he, as many times before in the orchestra pit, feels he's floating; six-year-old Latiffa, has a fever, eyes glazed, gets out of her bed in a run-down house with a rusty fire escape on Lafayette Street and looks for her doll with the peach-colored muslin dress and corkscrew curls and suddenly feels that she's alone in the flat, she starts shouting but is drowned out by the noise from a TV in the next room, that with its incessant ads rolling over the screen showing the newest Toyota offroader in the Rocky Mountains' silvery landscape; Tony Viscaro has after many dark deliberations walked onto the footpath on the Brooklyn Bridge, here under the spidery web of cable and with a view over the Financial District's gray monoliths in the astronomically blue sky's sun crawls over the railing and gets up onto the edge with a drawing sensation towards the East River's mirror-like water below, he stands there like a shabby wing-shot bird and spreads his arms out to make an end to his big city solitude, but is suddenly grabbed from behind by two arms belonging to Joy Silver, who's out on her usual morning jog across the bridge; 82 year-old Mama Luc from Trinidad, has layed awake since 4 in the morning and with her cane found her way to Cathedral Church of St. John the Divine on Amerstam Avenue bends forward on a pew in prayer beneath the arches and Gothic vaults that reach towards heaven, the brilliant light from the circular rosette window at the end of the grand nave captures her gaze and a sense of the joy of being and having given birth to seven children fills her small, nimble and wiry body; the city wakes, also Jim Forster, who's been sentenced for shooting his neighbor in a condemned tenement in Bronx South in an act of jealousy, wakes up in his 3 x 3 meter small cell in the James A. Thomas Center prison on Riker's Island, where he, because of unruly behavior, spends 22 hours a day, stab wounds in his hip that he'd gotten from another prisoner three months ago because he'd "squealed" to a prison warden about that prisoner's rape of him in the prison's shower room, still hurt, he doesn't feel like getting up from the hard bed and lays there listening in the prison's echochamber for familiar steps and voices and suddenly remembers the scent of the large forest of tsuga pines in the New York Botanical Garden in the Bronx that his stepmother took him to when he was seven; the beaches along Long Island's southern coast this morning lie open and deserted up against the firmament, millions of brittle, white mussel shells light up from the dry sandy plains, which send the sight on a refreshing journey towards infinitely distant meridians on the horizon; that same morning 342 years ago a group of Algonquin Indians passed the coast with their bows made of ash and quivers of arrows and arrowheads of fishbone fastened behind their sweaty dark backs, one of them laughed to the sun at the promise of a bountiful hunt, their footprints long vanished in the sand; but in the subway tunnel on Third Avenue on Manhattan Mr. John Marcosse with a long-dead Dakota chief's necklace under the tie of his suit rushes down the steps, now underground a human swarm closes in around him and spreads out in the wide passages that smell of electric current and sweat; a nether world evolves with prison-like net walls, long rows of steel columns, enclosed entrance ways and ticking turnstiles that tick on in the subconscious of the hundreds of thousands that pass them at stations called Cypress Hills, Rockaway Avenue, Jack?son Avenue, Castle Hill Avenue, Brighton Bridge; gum chewing, banana eating with headphones, hats, scarves, turbans, kippas or bald, thick hair with shiny shoes, boots or bare legged, perfumed, tattooed or drugged smelly and sitting or standing the human mass moves in the trains at 90 kilometres per hour through the darkness in the narrow, contorted tunnels under ground; an air conditioner cools down the body, but the darkness and artificial lighting and speed enhance dizziness and the sense of a random fling towards an unknown fate; unexpected and passing shafts of dreams and memories open for the hundreds of thousands of drowsy and half-asleep, soon they are in a long-forgotten shack, in a field, soon they inhale the scent of pines or the sounds of birds, face to face in the belly of the train they once again are in kitchens or stairways or shady passageways where they once spent a couple minutes of their time, and where faces that had meant something live anew; images from space odyssees on film mix with thoughts of love, sex and eruption and sudden liberation from captivity under ground; New York awakens, weary poker players leave after many wins and losses the green table at The Players Club on Second Avenue after a long night's game and surge toward the avenue to wave down a yellow cab, cattle are slaughtered in anonymous halls, rats run frightened for their life from the tracks in front of the subway train's lights, dogs stretch in their baskets in the brownstone houses in Brooklyn Heights or wander thin and hungry in the burned down tenements in the Bronx, cats lie in the sun on the grass at the edge of the shady elms on Bowling Green; in a painting by Edward Hopper that hangs on a white wall in a peaceful room in the Whitney Museum of Americans, a nude woman stands in the midst of a sunbeam, a lit cigarette that she'd just had in her mouth sends a faint veil of smoke from where it's resting between the fingers of her right hand, a faint smile appears under the introspective, sorrowful eyes, how far she is from others and from the deserted landscape behind the house with its soft green hillocks and their brilliant carpet of wild flowers and the dauntingly blue sky above, the bed behind her is still warm and unmade with the white covers just thrown back under the black bedspread, there she dreamt about a brand new day, and the sun comes to her in greeting just as it does when Eve that morning in Washington Square Park pulls up her bag and for a few seconds looks up at it.

"Something wrong?" Jon asks, also stopping.

"No, it's just the sun," she says, "I wish we could stay here in the park and enjoy it a couple of hours."

"I can't," says Jon with a faint smile, looking her deep in her eyes as he wraps his arm around her, "my client's waiting for me."

"Oh yeah, your clients, how could I ever forget?" she says with an ironic twist that he knows all to well.

They stand a moment pressed close to each other in the center of the square (he senses a spicy scent from the cream she's rubbed on from her throat and her barely visible breasts beneath her open shirt under her jacket), he raises his arm with his briefcase behind her back and looks at his watch, lets her go and starts walking towards La Guardia Place. She follows; together they pass the stairs up to the university, where small groups of chatting students have already gathered and pass the busy Houston Street and hand in hand continue down West Broadway with the many shops and galleries. His thoughts amidst the stream of sounds from the motley street have raced ahead and are taken up by Ifrahim Mohammed and the first impression he'll make on him. As always before the first personal meeting with a client he tries in his own way to "cleanse" himself of prejudice and bring himself in a mental state of willing openness, but because of his restless sleep and dream he has trouble relaxing and evoking a clear image of his client. In fact, his inner unrest grows the closer he comes to White Street and the prison and the corner with the coffee shop on West Broadway where he must take leave of Eve.

As they stand in front of the coffee shop with its many customers, and she once again with a faint smile grumbles something about them still not going to Israel, and her dark pageboy hair and eyes and her way of moistening her lips with the tip of her tongue in front of the mass of scurrying people brings him back into the present and reminds him how much he loves her, he can't leave her and says:

"Tomorrow we go to Jerusalem!"

"Really?"

"Yeah, as soon as I can I'll put Michelle and a colleague on the case, you book the flight and we're off."

"I thought this case was important."

"You're more important," he says.

She looks at him for a moment as he stands there amidst all the passers by with his intense gaze, shadows from the coffee shop's multicolored awning with its dusty windows cover half of his sunburned face with his blue eyes, the other half is in the sun. Amid his mania for work and his ability to make quick decisions and defend pointed issues is a quaint softness. He continues to amaze her, isn't that why she can never get enough of him?

"Thank you," she whispers and kisses him and quickly turns and hurries on down West Broadway with its myriads of cars and pedestrians and the Twin Towers' gray and massive vertical buildings so close that they seem to pull the blue sky down.

For some reason he remains standing there following her with his eyes until she's vanishes from sight under the grandiose silhouette of the towers.

He feels like running after her and bringing her back, but why? He'll see her again this evening.

He hurries down White Street and through the automatic door in the glass front of the Manhattan Detention Complex, "the graves"; an armed guard silently lets him pass slowly through the metal detector and continues deeper into the building to "the tower" with its many high security cells and video-monitored corridors. From here he takes the stairs up to the second floor and again through a security check and past wide awake, staring eyes, until a guard whom he's met many times before and who acknowledges him with a nod, guides him through a massive barred door that automatically opens with a screech. The officer leads him into a narrow passage with:

"Good weather we're havin', Mr. Baeksgaard, how much time d'you need?"

They stop in front of the door into the interrogation room, but for rows of sparkling white teeth, in the dimly lit corridor the guard's black meaty face is strangely blurred.

"Two hours," he says looking at his watch.

"It's eight thirty now," says the officer looking at his watch and shuffling on his heavy body. "So we'll come back for the accused at ten thirty, okay?"

He nods as the guard through his walkie-talkie has the prisoner brought in.

The officer opens a door to the closest vacant room with reinforced plexiglass windows facing the city and a camera monitor mounted just under the ceiling; the sun's rays illuminate the room and reveal the grain of the wooden table, and the two chairs placed in the centre of the room. The air's stagnant, the guard turns on a fan and goes back to the door to the hallway, he turns and looks towards another door, breathing heavily in a uniform that's at least one size too small that makes him sweat. Jon pulls out one of the chairs, places his briefcase on the table and walks over to the window and stares out over the streets and rooftops of Manhattan South, veiled in a haze.

What's wrong with him, where's his usual energy? Maybe he really is burned out? A new case is waiting, new proceedings, new legal feints and finesses and a new – could be – reluctant judge who just wants to be done with it in a hurry. Cases on an assembly line, and he's on the assembly line…

"When the prisoner comes, I'll leave and lock the door," says the guard behind him. "You've done this before, and you know how to get hold of me if something's wrong."

"Yeah, sure," he says turning towards the guard, remembering another episode a couple of years earlier when a client under the influence of crack assaulted him and forced his face down against the edge of the table, demanding that he be released immediately. For that reason he feels safest when his clients are handcuffed at their first meeting.

"They're takin' their time, Mr. Baeksgaard," says the guard again checking his watch, he nods, and at that moment the door opens, a man of average height, dark hair, regular facial features and an embarrassed gaze comes in followed by a female guard. The man wears a blue uniform, on his wrists two handcuffs, his eyes beneath his sweaty brown forehead squint at the sunshine, as if he'd been brought up from subterranean darkness. He immediately recognizes Ifrahim Mohammed from the photo. Unsure of what to do, Mohammed remains standing just inside the door as the female guard announces his name; with a nod to the other guard she quickly retreats and closes the door behind her.

And the first guard turns on his heels and leaves the room. He's now alone with Ifrahim Mohammed.

Jon introduces himself, walks over to him and offers his hand. Despite difficulties caused by the handcuffs, Mohammed returns the handshake with surprising strength.

"You're not afraid of me?" he says with in a dry voice and accent that gives away his Arabic tongue.

"No," says Jon,"should I be?"

Mohammed looks him straight in the eyes.

"They treat me here like I was a crook, like a dog, but I haven't done anything, I'm father to four children, a peaceful man."

For a few moments they take stock of each other, one from on low, the other from the clouds. Jon had the apparent advantage, a free man and can leave the room whenever he choses, he knows that on one hand he must underplay his role and at the same time evoke a sense of trust and safety by speaking openly and sometimes very direct. Ifrahim Mohammed appeared nervous and stiff below his superficial calm, but it could be due to stress from the case itself and incarceration, which knocks the wind out of most, it could be a sign of his innocence or the reverse. His dark eyes reflected sorrow or sadness in the sun's light, neither aggressive nor glaring, something he noticed immediately, and which from the start, almost without closer reflection, gave him a certain trust in the man. He was quick to assess his clients, and was seldom wrong, but when he was his professionalism usually "saved" him and the case, but to whose advantage? One of the mistakes he'd never forgiven himself was a guard in a highrise in New Jersey, charged with killing two fourteen-year-old girls in Brooklyn Heights, whose bodies never were found; he'd agreed to defend him pro bono because his alibi seemed watertight and his calm demeanour immediately woke his sympathy. He couldn't see the "killer" in him and got him acquitted despite strong evidence against him. But the man was psychopathic and killed yet another fourteen year-old three weeks after his acquittal, on a "vacation" to Florida. Both his talent and misjudgement could be his greatest opponents in a case.

"Sit down and we'll run through your case point by point," as Jon pulled out the chair for Mohammed. Mohammed moves reluctantly towards the chair, and Jon sits down in his place and takes a small tape recorder from his bag, tests it and is ready to jot down Mohammed's statement; he does all this automatically, practically in his sleep; and only when he returns his gaze to Mohammed does he see that Mohammed is still standing behind his chair.

"I asked you to sit down so we can get started, there's a lot we have to get through today," as Jon tries to hold his glance.

"But first I've got to know whether you really believe I could shoot a man in cold blood?" says Mohammed holding both hands out in front of him, revealing the handcuffs on his wrists.

"When I take a case, I assume my client is innocent, and that includes you," he says. "In your case, it looks like the district attorney has some good cards in his hand. You've been pointed out in a line-up by a witness who's sure it was you leaving Mr. Ellis Edelstein's shop in Williamsburg shortly after he was found shot in the backroom."

"But I wasn't even there," says Mohammed showing emotion for the first time. "I've never been in Williamsburg, why should I, the Jewish neighborhood?"

"One of your acquaintances, a Mr. Benzir Zawawi, says different."

"He's lying," says Mohammed, "as Allah's my witness!"

"We'll look at all of that," says Jon, "sit down now!

"Do you believe me when I tell you he's lying?" says Mohammed sitting down at the table, eyes glassy, doesn't know what to do with his hands. In the window behind Mohammed one can faintly discern the contour of the World Trade Center's towers and for a moment Jon wonders what Eve's doing and whether she's as tired as he is.

"For a start, I believe you, but I need to have something to put it in," says Jon. "I won't try to get you acquitted, I won't even take on the case if I'm not one hundred per cent sure that I can trust you. Can I?"

"I swear by Allah that you can. There's no blood on my hands."

"But they've found blood on one of your shirts, blood from the victim."

"It's Zawawi and his gang that're behind this," says Mohammed. "They want to get back at me because I know something I shouldn't."

"Something worth killing for?'

"Yes, that's it, I can tell you everything, but d'you believe me?"

"I believe you," he repeated,"but tell me now exactly what you did that day…"

Mohammed sighs, there's sweat on his brow, he squirms restlessly on the chair's hard seat and finally recounts in detail that fateful day in his life, where he presumably should have killed another man for the sake of some jewelry. His voice is shaky, as if from the start he expects to be chopped to pieces. How many times has he already mapped out that day for New York State Police's chief interrogator, and how many times have they doubted his testimony?

*

In the meantime Eve's gotten past the global fountain on World Trade Plaza and gone in through the automatic sliding doors to the spacious lobby of the World Trade Center's South Tower. There are days when she feels that she totally vanishes to nothing, when she walks in that rectangular hall with its enormous windows and trees in huge pots and glass inlaid railings, days like this when the sun shines and her body protests against being a small, insignificant link in 50,000 peoples' activities in two materialized figments of imagination each with their 110 stories. Hasn't her father, an architect who for the past 40 years has built houses which reach only to the tops of the cedars and cypresses in Israel, wondered why she wanted to be so high up, "Americans think that they can reach heaven, but we know that heaven is to be found at the foot of the eucalyptus or at the Wailing Wall", he's said, and she knows what he means.

And yet, she had come to New York, seventeen years ago, not just to study, but also to come away from those ancient trees, walls, prayers and suffering and from everything that in her imagination had become symbols: war, struggle for survival, fanaticism and suppression of the truth. In New York all the walls were new, here was no fear of the Tower of Babel, there was at least one on every corner, here was no victim mentality, here she wasn't first and foremost daughter of a Polish-born Jew with trauma from Auschwitz and a void in his soul, but a young student that mixed in with many other young students with a wide variety of skin colors, background and mentalities. Here she experienced being more of what she said and did than at her starting point, here in the first years she became more American than Israeli. Everything was new and accessible and open in a surprising and liberating way, even the big city's anonymity, to be able to frolic in the masses on Fifth Avenue was stimulating, seductive as was the city's energy, which was illustrated by the rappers on street corners or the quick meetings and decisions and movements of people or the nightclubs' churning, melancholy or rhythmic music. She couldn't get enough of Harlem, Greenwich Village or the Lower East Side, small towns within the city, and she squeezed into a one-and-a-half room flat in Greenwich Village with a boyfriend from Columbia University, where she studied. Her family in Israel, thought she was just visiting the USA and would come back with a degree in law, was convinced that Israel was not only the greatest place on earth, but that it was every Israeli's duty, had coaxed her many time to "come home soon"; hadn't she, through generous scholarships "donated" to her by the Israeli state and funds "loaned" to her by her family, something she should come back to and square off? But the more they cajoled her, the more she was determined to prove that she'd made the right choice, and that in a city of so many workaholics she not only studied hard, but took extra jobs at restaurants to make her economically independent, and she did it, with an impressive exam she was hired as an apprentice in one of the notable law offices on Fifth Avenue. Now she could send the "borrowed" money back to her father, who, too proud to accept them, "returned" them when she'd visited the him and the family in Jerusalem.

It occurred to him that his daughter was just as much a survivor and just as stubborn as himself, maybe she'd even inherited some of his trauma, but her way out of them was different than his. She flew on wings while he was earthbound, she had to journey to the other side of the world to a city of Babel to find herself, sometimes he drove for the same reason to the Negev Desert to absorb the cleansing silence. But the joy of Arabian music, the glorious colours, the mysticism and the Jewish shops in the labyrinthian old Jerusalem, that is what they shared, since she was small, had taken her around in a world of sukhs, haggling, kippas, veils, scarves, prayer and many tongues, and it was the atmosphere from here that with the years brought a greater yearning and she became more and more alienated with New York.

Where was the mysticism? Where was the history? Didn't most of the people here float on a blue balloon deafened by TV and film and shows and monetary transactions, and were the skyscraping, faceless and smooth buildings not a symbol of this? Perhaps she was unfair to the city, perhaps she'd just landed in the wrong place, in a firm for real estate transaction; all these real estate agents that criss-crossed the city, and who agitated both the buyers and sellers, she was fed up with it. She had to get away from Bengols & Betermann and their air conditioned lounge and "luscious" offices with a skyview on the 86th floor, but where to?

In a dream, which repeated itself in many variations, she'd seen the back of the neck and a halo of blond hair of a man in the crowd in one of the narrow passages in old Jerusalen's Arab quarters; she wanted to follow him, but the crowds of people around her were too tight, she shoved and pushed her way forward and tried to edge through. Many shoved back and became angry, some actually blocked her path, she fell and knocked over a stall with oranges that practically buried her, and when she finally got back on her feet, the man ahead of her had vanished. She still kept on through the crowd and tired and as if asleep she passed the one shop and stall after the other with everything from cameras, overcoats, books and sweets to weapons and musical instruments, there was no end. At an intersection, where the sunlight could come through, she realized that she'd lost her sense of direction, she turned to go back, but there in the half-shadow and in striped prison pyjamas stood her emaciated young father, as she knew him only from photographs of others just as emaciated prisoners; she tried to move towards him, but was bolted to the spot and had the feeling of not being recognized. For some reason he raised his hand and pointed to something behind her, she turned and through a large pane of glass, that reflected her at different ages, she saw the man with the blond hair. He was seated on a chair up against a wall beside a row of empty chairs in a tobacco shop and was being waited on by an employee who with his back to the window handed him a metal tray with a teacup. A wailing note from a lute streamed out to her from a loudspeaker in the shop, she stepped onto one of the many woven, crimson carpets with zigzag patterns that led to the shop and walked over to the mand with the blond hair, it was Jon, but Jon at different ages, at once a boy, at once a youth, at once old, all in a single movement. "What took you so long?" he asked. "I only just saw you," she said. "I couldn't come for the crowd." "I can't understand," he said, "I've had this shop many years, how could you be so mistaken?" She was hurt, angry and said, " But why didn't you look for me?" He smiled and said: "But I have, every day I kept watch for all the faces in the passage, I've sat here and looked for you, but of all the thousands of faces there was not one that looked like you. Once in a while a man would come in and say that he was your father, but nor did he know where you were. We played chess together, we drank tea together, but I couldn't cheer him up. I don't know who of us has waited for you more." Her gaze glided past his mouth and face to a clock on the wall behind his head, the hair now gray. But the face of the clock had no hands; it looked like the moon over Ararat, full, orange, distant. And no one knew what time it was, nor did the Palestinian employee. She looked at her watch; it was two minutes past twelve.

In the World Trade Center lobby, when she reaches one of the three high speed elevators and waits in a small group of "suits" until the door automatically opens, she glances at her watch, it's eight thirty-two. If she doesn't hurry she'll be late again for the usual staff meeting ten minutes to nine with all that's waiting for her in her office, and Betermann will again from his place at the head of the table squint and send her an unmistakably irritated look over the heads of the others; but how and when will she explain to him that she can't go on, that his "prize attorney", whom he two months ago gave a bonus because she made the firm an unexpected profit of one million dollars, rather would go back to her husband's modest law firm on St. Mark's place with pro bono cases for the oppressed and seriously charged clients the kind of which Betermann wouldn't touch with a ten-foot pole?

Finally the doors open to an empty elevator, she hurries in under the soft light in the elevator followed by a knot of employees which has grown significantly in number and quickly fills the car. There are men of all sizes, skin color and hair color, but almost all of them are wearing the same gray or dark suit and are holding identical briefcases. Their have the same moderated expression that makes them look alike, only the soft colours of the women's skirts or jackets delineate them form the others. She notes – as every morning in the elevator the odeur from a mixture of spicy and sweet perfumes, after-shaves and deodorants, as she half turns and with some difficulty guides her hand past several smooth jackets and over to the button for the 86th floor.

A man smiles discreetly at her, but she doesn't respond.

With a jolt and a sharp upsurge as in a helicopter making a sudden vertical take-off the elevator surges upwards and in a matter of seconds was many stories up in the building, the first phantom ascent always making her dizzy, she knows that the others feel the same, but silence prevails, and as usual no one shows any sign of unease. When she started working in the tower she enjoyed this dizziness and the rapid ascent and took it as a sign that she'd really landed in the city and had become a newyorker, and that there was no limit to how far she could rise, but now the dizziness in the elevator every morning makes her feel vulnerable, even though it's often over before she's again steady on her feet.

With some stops on the way, they reach the 86th floor and she hurries into the vestibule with the many pop art pictures and the smooth, shiny floor, faintly shadowing her body; a slight nod to the receptionist and brief greetings to familiar colleagues that breeze past her on her flight through the many corridors on the way to her office. Finally she reaches her office, opens the door with her cardkey, walks into the sharp light from the two windows facing west and the Hudson River, puts down her bag, sits down at the computer, turns it on and waits for the icons to appear on the screen.

It crosses her mind that she has to get hold of Betermann and tell him she's leaving the firm, but first she has to book the flight to Israel and check

through some details for a new real estate deal. He probably won't understand, might even offer her a raise to keep her, and when he finally realizes
that she means it, might even just kick her out at fast as he can.

She opens the file for the deal, absent mindedly skims it, prints it out, closes the computer and walks over to the printer to gather the papers. Papers in
hand she turns in her own thoughts and looks out the window.

The sky's amazingly clear and blue, far beyond the network of roads, highrises and houses runs the Hudson River's aquamarine water towards the endless. The gray monolithic North Tower with its enormous sheet of glass
shines in the sun.

She sees it, but doesn't believe what she see: An airplane appearing in the
sunlight like a phantasmagoric, shadowy bird with stiffly outstretched wings,
is flying towards the North Tower and vanishes into it with an enormous
roar; at almost the same instant, a fire ignites in the upper part of the building, spewing out flames and clouds of smoke. Her legs tremble beneath her
as she stares at the unreal scene, it takes some seconds before she realizes
that what she'd seen is real, and that the North Tower, not far from her, is in
flames and hit by an airplane that has torn a gigantic hole in the upper floors.
Smoke, white, gray and black, increasingly black, pours out of the hole in
clouds of increasing force and is enfolding all the floors at the top, like a colossal burning candle in a landscape of stone. She breathes quickly, turns,
takes a couple of steps back to her desk, grabs the receiver of the security
phone and tries to call the lobby to warn them, but the line is blocked and she
hangs up. She's frozen on the spot and in doubt as to what to do: Should she
go to the scheduled meeting, should she leave the building? The sense of unreality returns. She walks out to the dimly lit corridor, farther down the hall a
small group from the firm are standing and discussing in muffled voices, she
can't hear what they're saying. One of them shouts to her:

"Did you see it, did you see it?"

"Yeah," she shouts back and starts walking towards them, but suddenly
remembers her bag and goes back to her office to get it. Once there she picks
up her bag from her chair, pauses a moment and moves once more towards
the window as a voice is heard from a loudspeaker in the hallway and office.

"There's been an accident in the North Tower," says the voice, "the necessary measures will be taken. South Tower is secure, stay where you are or return to your office or flat. I repeat: South Tower is secure, stay where you are or return to your office or flat!"

The voice has a soothing tone, but outside her window, some hundred metres away black smoke pours out into the sunny blue sky from a gaping hole in North Tower's shiny façade, and a feeling of fear and forboding invades her, two shadowy forms have just come into view on a ledge outside the burning hole on the floor just under the crater and holding each other's hand cast themselves out into the void like two wing shot birds crashing to the ground.

She closes her eyes, breathes slowly, thousands of thoughts rush chaotically through her head, but only two take form: She must get out of the building, and then: Maybe she can even help some of them caught in the other tower, hasn't she – long ago - served in the Israeli army, doesn't she know something about rescuing people?

Bag in hand she rushes out to the hallway towards the elevator. On her way she passes small groups of people who she urges to follow her down, but most of them wave her away, one she knows from the staff shakes his head and shouts:

"No grounds for panic, you heard what security said …"

As she gets to the vestibule about ten people from the firm, including Betermann, have gathered in front of the elevator and are waiting impatiently for it to get to the 86th floor.

"Horrible," says Betermann with an ashen face, hand on the knot of his tie, "that kind of situation hasn't been considered. I've got to go down to the lobby and talk to security, the telephone net is overloaded, we can't call."

"There's nothing to be afraid of," says the vice director Mr. Normack, standing next to the group and not intending to go down, "we're not hit and there's no way the fire can spread here."

"How d'you know?" she asks and is amazed at his self-confidence.

"There's hardly any wind and this building won't burn because of some black clouds of smoke," he says adjusting his tie.

"And what about the victims over there?" she asks. "Hundreds must be dead by now; I saw two jump from a burning office."

"… awful …" mumbles Betermann as unrest spreads through the group. Several have taken their cell phones to make quick, hectic calls.

"What are we going to do? What should we do? " says Betermann's secretary, a young woman with heavy lipstick and glazed eyes staring into the vestibule's great vacant room, brightly alit by the sun and with an open view of the blue sky. For some reason the receptionist has left her place, a small group hurries across the shiny floor in the direction indicated by a civilian security guard. From an elevator on its way up a new group stream out, some of them stop and loudly discuss the accident. Others walk calmly towards their offices.

"We can't do anything, it's something for the fire department and police," says Normack and emphatically crosses his arms. The blue eyes in his aged face melt in with the celestial panorama far behind him.

At that moment the doors to the elevator open, Eve steps in together with Betermann and nine-ten others, and as she calls Jon on her cell phone and just before the doors close, she sees the security guard's tense face close up, his gaze directed to Betermann:

"It's best you stay up here, Mr. Betermann, and wait further instructions …"

They go down, at the sky lobby on the 44th floor the elevator stops and more people come in, the elevator continues its dive further down into the abyss. Her cell phone's dead in the elevator, but when the doors open and light from the bright, sunlit lobby streams in and she's practically thrown out onto the floor, it buzzes with its usual fanfare; she takes it and hears Jon's voice:

"North Tower's burning, what's happening? Fire engines, police, everything and everyone down the street are prepared for action…"

"Aplane's crashed into the tower," she says, " I saw it. I'm in the lobby of South Tower. Where are you"

"On Broadway," he says, "I stopped my meeting with my client and am on my way to you. Are you OK?"

"Yeah, we're safe here," she says and glances at Betermann, who after talking to the uniformed chief of security with controlled gestures, waves to the staff that they should get back to work. "We're going up again."

"Are you sure that's wise?" says Jon in his cell phone, as the hollow sounds of cars on Broadway reach her.

She hesitates a moment and halfway follows the group back towards the elevator.

Betermann's now close to her, his thinning hair glistens on his sweaty brow, she asks him what the security chief said.

"No danger. It's best if we stay calm and resume our work, avoid panic," he says and smiles faintly. His usual demonstration of self confidence is gone, the expression in his pale face is still composed, but fear is in his eyes, something she's never seen before. He briefly places a hand on her arm to calm her and himself as well.

"I'm going up," she says to Jon in the phone, "and will try to pursuade some of the staff to come down to the plaza and help where we can."

"No, that won't do," says Betermann, "the security chief expressly asked us to stay far away from the plaza, it could be dangerous!"

"I'm on my way and will come up to you," says Jon. "Take care of yourself. Okay?"

"Okay," she says, turns off the phone and follows Betermann into the elevator.

The car is packed, more have come from the lobby and go from one elevator to the other trying to get in. The doors close leaving a larger group waiting in the lobby. The elevator sets off, with a small jolt it's already on its way up and accelerating quickly, she gets dizzy and is hit by a wave of claustrophobia; suddenly she has no idea why she's gone up again. She's wedged in the deepest corner of the elevator and must lean her head against the wall with eyes closed, the image of the two plunging from the flaming North Tower flashes across her mind, a scream rises from the depths of her being, but never reaches her lips; the elevator glides to a stop. She opens her eyes, the doors glide open, light floods in, the elevator half empties and she again can breathe and feel steady on her feet, and looking to her left she finds Be-

termann standing there with a handkerchief up against his cheek and anxiously looks at her.

"Anything wrong?" he asks, drying his forehead.

"I felt ill," she said. "I'm ok now."

"Damned situation", he says. "I'll get our people together when we get
back, so we can discuss what to do. I'm for a day off, maybe more. But for
every day off, there's more money lost."

The elevator starts again and sends them on in the sluice, where the laws of
gravity temporarily repealed.

"You can't expect people to work with a disaster just outside their windows," she says.

"No, of course not," says Betermann, "but I'll get an emergency staff together to keep the business going the next couple of days, I can count on you,
can't I?"

"No, I'm going to Israel and quitting my job," she wants to say; but instead she says:

"Yeah, sure."

Betermann nods satisfied and like the others in the elevator turns his gaze
towards the doors, for a few moments loose fragments of conversation about
the accident stop, the elevator stops, the doors open. Across the vestibule,
people with small groups of workers, some waiting, others talking, others silent, some with light over clothes, others in shirt sleeves as if they'd merely
been interrupted in their work, through the windows she sees a broad band of
black smoke crossing the expansive blue sky. The atmosphere is nervous, but
on the surface calm. Two civilian security guards in gray uniforms with
calming smiles circulate amongst the groups. The typical, newyorkish feeling
of invincibility is written on their faces and in their tone of voice.

Betermann's already on his way towards the receptionist and her microphone to call the staff to a meeting in the vestibule when a distinct yet calm
voice is heard in the loudspeaker through the hallways and offices, restaurants, shops and flats in the whole of the towering construction. It evaporates
all worry and fear of an added rise in heat among the thousands that have ei-

ther spent the night or met early to work in the building that morning and
each in his own way has considered or processed the "accident" or "fire".

For some, especially those whose windows face south or east, the "accident" is still just a rumour that's reached them through short, undramatic
messages in the loudspeaker, like others that are part of a fire drill or the like.
Some have turned over in their beds and fallen into a deeper sleep or gotten
up without dressing and have turned on the taps for their morning shower as
they try to figure out what they should think about something they've only
just heard about. Isn't it too improbable to be true? Maybe it's like what we'd
once heard about with the Empire State Building – just a small aircraft off
course? Pity, but those things can happen. Others have switched on their TV
and take several minutes to comprehend that images of the burning North
Tower are not scenes from a film, yet another disaster film, but images from
the naked, unadorned truth, not from the past, but now right around the corner. Some call or have called 911, most of them with the promise of a return
call, a call that never comes. Again others, especially those employed in the
jungle of engineering, insurance, investment, bank, cable-tv, and law firms
with names like Agricor Commodities, Asahi Bank, Bellard, China Resource,
Dongwon Securities, First Liberty, Guy Carpenter, Kanebo Informations, In-
fotech, Golden King have dismissed the uncertainty and lack of information
and have gone to their officees, counters, meeting rooms, gyms blinded by
the force of habit and start their day. Aren't piles of jobs waiting for them?
Shouldn't they get their hair cut? Isn't this what they're paid to do? On the
83rd floor insurance agents Mr. Goldwinn and Mr. Kausuak meet at the wash
basins in the large lavatory with soft lighting and quiet music in the loudspeakers and exchange small jokes about the other's dress.

As the two wash their hands and fleetingly observe themselves in the mirror above the basin, and uneasy workers and residents have gathered in the
sky lobbies on the 44th and 78th floors, the Arab-born Fayez Banihammad,
Ahmed al-Ghamdi and Hamza al- Ghamdi are the so-called "strong men"
that hold the passengers and personnel in check on United Airlines flight
175's huge machine, which after a zigzag course from take-off from Logan
Airport earlier in the morning in the blue sky is on its way towards the Hud-

son corridor and New York City, and not to Los Angeles as planned. Fifteen minutes after take-off from Logan, Hamza al-Ghamdi and Mohand al-Shehri, who are now in the cockpit together with the leader of the plane Marwan al Shehhi, forced their way into the cockpit and forced the seatbelted pilots with blows to the neck and threats of death underscored by raised Swiss army knives away from their seats and to the rear of the cockpit, where the senior pilot who'd resisted was knifed down and still lies bleeding on the floor. The co-pilot is shoved out of the cockpit to the passengers in first class and is ordered seated in the second row, which Marwan al Shehhi had just left to enter the cockpit and take over command and control of the plane, which was set on automatic and sailed through the air like a beautiful blinking kite. Everything's gone according to the plan (or almost) that was worked out in rented rooms and hotels in Florida and Newton by Mohammed Atta, leader of American Airlines flight 1, which by now is also on course towards New York City: At the same time that Hamza al-Ghamdi and Mohand al-Shehri broke in to the cockpit, Fayer and Ahmed al-Ghamdi takes advantage of the effect of surprise and gets up – not being very impressive in height – from their seats in first class. In full view and with a bomb-like dummy andwith flashing knives they bully in Arabic-sounding English the passengers to complete silence with the threat that they would like "cowardly dogs suffer a deserving death in the name of Allah and his prophet Mohammed" "This is a bomb," said Fayez Banihammad, flaunting again and again an object wrapped in black cloth in front of the passengers, as if demonstrating an article on sale, his eyes gleaming in excitement and self-intoxication. "Don't move or we'll kill you!" A steward tries behind his back to force his way into the cabin; but Hamza al-ghamdi, who'd returned to protect al-Shehhi, who'd taken his place in the first pilot's seat and had switched off the autopilot and was navigating manually, dragged him out, pushing him backwards into the narrow pantry, where he stabbed him several times with his knife, until he with arms raised in defense and with a faint cry falls bleeding to the floor. Hamza al-Ghamdi lets him lie, leaves the pantry and goes further into the plane, a stewardesse, who the highjackers have not yet seen, finds the murdered steward in a pool of blood and resolutely locks herself in the toilet adjoinin the pantry, where she with her cell phone telephones a warning to the flight leaders on the ground. When she leaves the toilet and stands over the body of her colleague, Hamza al-Ghamdi again enters the pantry, she freezes and her eyes meet those of the young Hamza al-Ghamdi horrified over what he'd done; but there's no meeting in the disturbed gaze. He holds the knife, still bloody, up at her and shouts words, half Arabic, half English, which she doesn't understand; he points with his free, trembling hand at her cell phone, which she clutches tightly, until he tears it away from her, hurtles it to the floor and crushes it under foot, turns his back on her and vanishes into the plane leaving a cloud of fear.

Fear rules, from reports in the plane's loudspeaker system, which Mohand al-Shehri had forced another stewardess to make from an already prepared declaration, all of the 65 passengers now know the life-threatening danger they are in. Some faint, others pray, others think about resisting, but the threatening figures pacing up and down the aisles displaying items that re- semble bombs ready to detonate, keep them from action. Passengers who just after take off from Logan Airport had sat alienated from their neighbor, some with laptops, others with music in their ears from cd players, others absorbed in accounts or minutes from a business meeting, open up quietly to each oth- er: What do these madmen want? Who are they? Are they flying the plane themselves? Where is the plane going? Maybe the plane's being highjacked and will land somewhere en route to the Middle East, hasn't this happened before? They're probably Palestinians, no, Arabian terrorists, no, it's … Many try to get through with their cell phones, few get through, some with heartbreaking messages and whispering cries for help in answering machines in deserted flats on the ground, others with fragments of sentences that reveal fear, highjacking, farewell or eternal love to astonished and shocked recipi- ents, who incoherently call back from a flat, a car or a street in Detroit, New York or Phoenix and involuntarily stare up or out towards the sunfilled sky, where there's nothing to see besides the void, distant heaven itself. Here and there was no mercy, only a buzzing in the ears that smack of darkness; sud- denly an ordinary Tuesday becomes a plunge into a mill of extinction, where appointments, deadlines, calculations, plans and visions mean nothing, but where repressed moments of closeness and times of endearment with a loved one or playing with a child on a chance day long past mean everything.

Marwan al-Shehhi, who only in April had completed his training for flying the big jets in a Boeing 737 simulator at Huffmann, Florida, and two years earlier had signed a declaration of martyrdom in al-Qaeda's camp al Faraq, in Afghanistan, after completion of "recruit training" there, had with sweaty hands and brow steered the heavy Boeing 767 perfectly on its final course towards New York Manhattan and had disconnected all communication to control towers. He's now alone at the wheel in front of the windows at the head of the plane and has the outskirts of Manhattan in New York State southwest below him and he turns the tremendous rumbling body of a machine, with reduced speed steadily decreasing altitude in a large arch so that its course is directed towards Manhattan and its gray monoliths, that fade in far in the distance, becoming increasingly visible like rectangular giant screens on a drawing board.

Shehhi is about one minute from voluntary extinction and is already at one with death. In hotel rooms in Coral Springs, Florida, or more recently in Newton, he's many times in dreams and waking imagined these final moments , where he in the great wahhabitic martyrs' footsteps is in the vanguard breaching the heretics' world with an act of jihad, of which the entire world will speak. In a dream, the very Osama bin Laden has received him like a white-clad sheik in his residence in Kandahar and presented him with his own kalashnikov as a sign of recognition and led him out to the jubilation of thousands of Muhajedin warriors, who with shots fired into the air show him special honor. In another dream, also a waking fantasy, he's stepped unscathed and whole out of the astronomically huge buildings' sea of flames directly into a celestial palace with running water and fountains and shady palm groves surrounded and attended by lush and beautiful women in colourful saris, that hide nothing of their bodies' forms. They drug him with their bodies' fragrance when they wash his feet and lead him to the bath, slowly applying balsams and to lovemaking, everything he never achieved on the other side of paradise. Sometimes he's awakened at night in fearful sweat for the darkness that will enfold him and the agony that he'll meet when the plane with great speed ploughs into the building. He's repressed it, is silent and then suddenly – by day – aggressive and incontrollable, as when he and Atta literally came to grips with the aviation instructor in Sarasota, Florida, in their attempt to take control of the plane on their training flights, or when they both failed instrument flying at the same place. Like Atta's family in Egypt, Shehhi's family knows nothing of his total surrender to martyrdom and his extreme disgust for western lifestyle, which since his studies in Hamburg he's superficially been a part of; up to the last evening in the hotel in Newton, Atta time and again has reminded him, yes, everyone in the group of the hollowness and emptiness in the western world's materialism and greed for money. When he'd visited Atta's father and mother in Egypt to get Atta's international driver's license and was confronted with his father's disappointment over Atta's "pause" in his city planning studies in Hamburg, he was on the brink of revealing their plans, which would guarantee both Atta and himself "eternal honor" among the "believers", but their jihad shouldn't be shattered and was until the Day only for the initiated. Only on that day, will it shock the world and their families with amazement. Shehhi doesn't hear in his adrenalin surge and blindingly total concentration on the panorama before him the shouts, the mumbled prayers and tears of fear from the passengers in the cabin, here many can sense from the machine's loss of altitude and view out of the windows to the buildings and road net and fields on Staten Island, where it will all end. A cloud of black smoke rises surrealistically over the familiar Manhattan landscape in the distance.

The toxic smoke pours in steadily greater formations out of the gaping and red hot holes in the North Tower, like ethereal lava; waves brush the windows on several stories of the South Tower as a voice from the loudspeakers throughout the building announces:

"A security message to all in the World Trade Center's South Tower. Due to the accident in the North Tower, an orderly evacuation of the South Tower is advised, conditions permitting. I repeat: An orderly evacuation of the South Tower is advised, conditions permitting."

With the increasingly alarming smoke, hundreds of people have already descended to the sky lobby on the 78th floor, and the announcement increases the crowding in front of and in the elevators that stop and continue down. Many try in vain to press their bodies in the already packed elevators as the doors slide open; panic spreads as many are caught in the doors and are pushed out by hands from inside and out against the wall of those trying to get in.

In the large ground floor lobby people are rushing to get out of the elevators, in the midst of the rush Jon gets in to one of the vacant elevators together with two fire guards and a couple of civilian security guards, the doors slide closed, the elevator quickly accelerates upwards. Two-three minutes ago he passed the North Tower, and the sight of the molested tower with its flaming clouds of smoke and the fire engines, ambulances and the hectic activity on the plaza around the gigantic building, which from above was covered by glowing, collapsed scraps of material, wouldn't leave him.He clenches his jaws and his eyes survey the elevator until it stops at one of the fire guards, a muscular young man with an open face, who takes a step towards him and says:

"You're going the wrong way, the right way isn't up, but down!"

"My girlfriend is up on the 86th floor," he says succinctly.

"I'm sure that she'll find her way down by herself," the guard replies with a faint smile. "The fewer that are on the way up, there are more that can come down. Get off at the sky lobby on the 44th and ride down again!"

A moment later the doors slide open to the lobby on the 44th floor; they're surprised by a group of workers with briefcases and cell phones, crowding in front of the elevator to ride down. They're so eager to get in that they don't see that the elevator's on the way up and force themselves in and quickly fill it up; he pushes through the group and steps out onto the floor of the lobby. The doors slide closed and he figures that he'll take the stairs down.

On the 86th floor Eve and Betermann and many of the staff from Bengols & Betermann wait for the elevator's arrival from above. The mood amongst them is more tense than it was before, many are unable to hide their nervousness and wander restlessly from elevator to elevator in preparation to throw themselves in the first opening; others talk incessantly, most in their cell phones. At one end of the foyer the view is obscured by a black cloud of smoke setting the room in a surrealistic claire-obscure: sundrenched day on one side and dark night on the other. Eve can't make contact with Jon on his cell phone and worries where he is. She turns towards Betermann, who reluctantly has given up trying to herd the personnel and is standing a few paces away from her with his eyes peeled on the blinking floor number by one of the elevators.

"Stupid that we came up again," says Betermann, "there's neither head nor tail to anything."

"My boyfriend is on his way up to me," she says.

"He's not, is he? "

"Or he's waiting for me down there, I hope…"

"He's that outstanding defense attorney from East Village, isn't he?"

Waiting just behind them, the vice director Normack is arguing with a colleague about some real estate deal on Long Island that should've been home, but now seems lost.

At that moment the buildings on South Manhattan have grown to enormous mountains in front of the tip of the United Airlines plane that Shehhi is steering and with some 800 kilometres per hour is on its way towards South Tower. Both Shehhi and many of the passengers register the enormous fire in the wreck of the building behind it. In the cabin passengers scream, others bend over into the darkness between the seats; others reach out with sweaty, trembling hands. Hamza al-Ghamdi senses that the last moment is near, gives up controlling the passengers and runs in to Shehhi in the cockpit. The sun reflecting from the windows in the enormous wall before them jolt them, al-Ghamdi places his trembling hand on Shehhi's shoulder.

"Allahu Akbar!" they both shout.

With a deafening roar the plane's enormous body crashes into the gigantic building's south face of steel and concrete between the 77th and 85th floors like a projectile at a scewed angle and penetrates well in towards the north wall. The violent blow from the impact between walls and plane kill almost all in the airplane instanteously, the last still living are blown to pieces by the furious explosion that follows, as the 90,000 litres of fuel from the plane's tank begin to leak and burst into flames.

Most of the hundreds of people waiting in the sky lobby on the 78th floor and at the point of impact are killed on the spot, few miraculously escape, others are thrown over and are seriously injured by the penetrating airplane's metal construction, that like a monster in a nightmare transforms the floors between the 77th and 85th into a gigantic demolition site, where plane wings, cables, walls, screen, installations, furniture from one moment to the next are whirled together. The smell of jet fuel is so strong that it's impossible for the survivors to breathe; all lights go out, elevators stop working and leave passengers imprisoned in the darkness, and the flames from the impact begin to heat up everything.

In the sky lobby on the 44th floor, Jon and others feel the impact throughout the building, like being on an ocean going vessel, where the deck rocks from side to side; on the 86th floor, Eve's, Betermann's and the others waiting in the foyer had their legs knocked out from under them, and the deafening explosion is still in her ears as she shocked tries to get up from the lightly swaying floor and she discovers that her forehead's bleeding when her head hit the floor. She's dizzy, standing up with furniture and panels and people in a chaos around her, some quietly getting up, others still on the floor. Some have already begun trying to find a way to come out, either up or down in the building and are trying switches and doors in the foyer and hallways all in vain. She goes up to Betermann and gives him a helping hand so that he slowly and shakingly gets to his feet; someone else shouts:

"Fire! Smoke in the elevator, smoke in the elevator!"

And a moment later another shouts:

"Smoke in Stairway B, smoke in Stairway B!"

Everyone's now on their feet in the vestibule, two have to be helped, they're about twenty and gather in the middle of the floor in the vestibule and begin from one to the other to discuss what's happened – "another plane", "another disaster" – and how they'll get out. Some call 911 and are told that they should stay where they are, help is on the way.

"They've confirmed that we've also been hit by a plane," says one of them, a young programmer from California, who'd just been employed in the firm and switches off his phone, "the floor below is on fire!"

They look silently at each other.

"We can't just stand here and wait to be roasted alive," says vice director Normack, turning his back on them and vanishing down a hall.

The smoke rises up outside both sides of the building and closes them in a drab darkness, below it's boiling and rumbling. They're paralyzed and all fear that there's no way out, or that help will come too late; one weeps, others support each other, some clutch to their neighbors, but no one speaks aloud about fear. Betermann hands Eve his handkerchief and she dries the blood from her forehead. His face is deathly pale and he gazes at her with a look that makes her think of Jon.

"Let's get out, let's get out of here!" shouts a voice suddenly, "Stairway A is open."

A civilian security guard appears from one of the hallways and points down the hall from which he's just come.

They follow him, Eve takes hold of one of Carter's arms, one of the injured, an accountant in the firm, who's limping on one leg after the fall, and helps him forward together with a colleague, her own wound is only superficial, and her dizziness is gone. Many doors are open into the offices they pass, through the windows thick, black smoke envelopes the building, ominously dangerous; but still there's no panic, the presence of the security guard and a feeling that there's a way out gives calm and hope.

Stairway A is in total darkness. As one of the last ones to step out onto the stairway with the limping Carter by her side, she's momentarily blinded by the darkness and senses immediately the smoke and heat from below, without being able to see anything she follows the stream downwards and fumbles onward on the stairs. Carter trips, but both she and her colleague manage to prevent his fall by holding onto his arms; they stand there a moment on the step, and only then they eye the self-illuminating strips on the steps and panelling. This detail, which had never meant much to her, but which she'd quickly skimmed in the safety manual she'd been given when she'd been hired, had long since been forgotten, because she like the other 50,000 in the World Trade Center had lived in a stupor of safety – wasn't New York one of the wealthiest and invulnerable cities? – now meant everything to her and raised her hopes of survival.

They continue their descent, calmly, silent and in a group; the smoke burns in their nostrils and the heat increases, but the strange silence in the shaft embraces them and makes them feel safe as does the light from the security guard's flashlight in front of them.

In the meantime on the 44th floor Jon has wandered the halls and found, together with a smaller group, the same intact Stairway A. A call to 911 has informed them that South Tower was also hit by a plane. Where they are is light and no smoke, and as the rest of the group disappears down the illuminated stairs, he remains standing looking upward into the vacant stairwell. Farther up he hears voices and people's steps on their way down, but he can't see them. Could it be something he's dreaming? He breathes deeply, calls Eve's cell phone, but only reaches her voice mail. Hearing her voice, at once both near and remotely anonymous, reinforces a new fear deep inside that he'll never see her again.

"I'm on the 44th floor," he says trying to sound as composed as possible, "I'm on Stairway A and am on the way up to you now. I love you."

As he with rapid steps works his way up, a door opens onto the darkness of the stairwell just at the point where Eve and the employees from Bengols & Betermann are standing, a man stumbles out and shouts:

"Fire, fire!"

In the next moment he collapses, falls down the stairs onto the landing. The security guard rushes down the stairs with his flashlight, others follow and try to lift him; half of his face is severely burned, his jacket is in tatters and smells of smoke. When they lift his head from the floor, blood streams from his neck. He whispers:

"Hell … I don't want to die."

"You're not going to die," says the guard, "We're taking you with us."

In the flashlight's spot a faint smile flashes across his face; but it's as if his eyes are focused at something inevitable and frightening in the distance, something that only he can see. A jolt runs through his body, his gaze freezes and he's gone.

The security guard feels for the man's pulse, looks up, gets to his feet.

"He's dead," he says, "We've got to get moving."

"We can't just leave him here," says a voice. The others are momentarily transfixed.

"He's dead," repeats the guard, his face hidden in the darkness, turns and starts down the stairs.

"He's right, we've got to move on," says another voice; and they resume their descent. The smoke grows stronger, burning their eyes. Eve and her helper have trouble holding on to the injured, who'se started coughing in the darkness. From somewhere in the building they hear screams and a huge crash from something collapsing, the stairs tremble beneath them.

"Let me go," says Carter and stands on the steps and pulls his arms tightly around his body, "save yourselves!" But they don't listen, again grab each an arm and lead him on step by step like a big, lame mechanical puppet.

She's lost her sense of time, hasn't she always been claustrophic with pitch darkness? She stares at the self-illuminated strips in front of her and thinks them an unending track, a signal that they'll never get out. They sag increasingly behind the others, farther down the dark shaft agitated voices can be heard and the sound of impact against a hard object. She can distinguish Betermann's and the guard's voices from the others.

"I can't," says the guard, "it's locked!"

"You've got to have a key, how can you be a security guard and not have a key!" says Betermann.

"The fire doors close by themselves, sir, we weren't prepared for this kind of situation," says the guard.

As they approach, the smoke increases, many cough and gasp for breath, and the security guard tries to pursuade them that they should go back, up to the open air on the roof. She recognizes many of the voices, and it occurs to her that some of them are trying to break through the fire door, one of them batters it with a fire extinguisher. Just as they reach them, she's blinded by the guard's light.

"Step aside," he says, "we're going up!"

The older security guard, once a marine and used to having "control of the situation", now seems desperate, he rushes past her and from a position higher up on the stairs shouts commands down to the group:

"Let's get moving, get your asses in gear, now!"

And people, whose faces and voices she knows only remotely from the firm, almost topple her, her helper and the injured man as they rush past.

She hears Betermann's voice close to her ear:

"Come on, Eve, you don't have a chance here."

"Carter can't make it," she hears herself say.

The smoke envelopes them, Carter buckles over coughing, and suddenly it crosses her mind that one of the employees one day broke out laughing that he'd gotten lost in one of the stairwells and its many side passages, she lets go of Carter and runs down to the fire door and from that to a hallway to the right. Like a nightmare, another corridor, another door, she sees neither door or knob as she gropes with her hands along the wall and reaches them; she grabs the door knob, turns it and the door reluctantly opens up to a new darkness and even greater heat. Again there's a cry far in the building and a rustling as from a gigantic swarm of locusts. Sweat pours from her, her body screams for water, but she must go back and get the others.

When by calling out she returns to the place where she'd left Carter, Betermann and her helper, whose name she never got, Betermann's taken over and is supporting Carter, but her helper's disappeared.

"He ran off," says Betermann, "and I didn't think you'd come back."

Together they lead Carter through the smoke and darkness and into the hallway and arrive at the open door leading to yet another stairway and heat. For whatever reason, the smoke isn't as dense on this stairway, and with the self illuminating strips as a guide they begin their new, slow descent.

The violent blaze in the crater of the building devours its way up and down and spreads, like a Moloch, death and destruction; clouds of smoke grow into mighty dark formations and torches several hundred meters in breadth around both of the flaming towers and spread over Manhattan and the East River. The surrealistic nightmare transforms day to night; thousands of firefighters and policemen are in action, in large and small groups or single-handed, and at the risk of their own lives, breach the flames into the buildings. A storm of metre long red hot metal fragments and pieces of construction materials descend over the plaza and the surrounding streets, also people jumping to their deaths from the towers, forced out of the windows by smoke, flames and the extreme heat, crash like heavy projectiles down over the rescue crews killing many of them; they're forced away from South Tower's main entrance on Liberty Street and find another way into the tower, often through the Marriott Hotel, or they must remain on West Street or Church Street and wave the survivors and their helpers to the intermistic field hospitals which gradually appear on the pavement outside the towers. In the subsequent chaos from the disaster, New York's traffic police are busy closing the subway stations close to the World Trade Center and evacuating civilians, also the bridges and tunnels to Manhattan are being closed; throughout the city the New York police are clearing the main thoroughfares so that only emergency vehicles, ambulances and fire trucks can get through. The entire inner core of the metropolis is, in the course of 45 minutes, set in a state of emergency that resembles siege or war, but a war started by an unseen enemy, and President Bush, who after a visit to an elementary school in Sarasota, Florida, is with his entourage on their way to Air Force One for take-off from Florida to Washington, announces through a spokesman in the media, that the World Trade Center has been the apparent target of a terrorist attack. No one has any information on the perpetrators, who seem to have literally appeared out of the blue as nightmarish figures from a Hollywood movie, everything is just speculation. No one was prepared for the apocalyptic attack, even though top secret reports sent to the President's office through the summer should have gotten all red alarm lamps blinking, and the President's Advisor on Terror, Clarke, had done what he could to mobilize the government. In The White House, Vice President Cheney, watching television, when at 9:03 AM it is announced that an airplane has crashed into South Tower and that North Tower is in flames, explodes: "How the hell can a plane crash into the World Trade Center?" He's now on his way, together with Security Advisor Condoleezza Rice and Clarke to a video conference on the nation's security in a bombshelter under The White House.

Throughout the North and South Towers people are trapped in elevators and await their fate; above the site of impact, people are getting lost in the stairwells or are forced back by smoke and invading flames in the stairways or offices and apartments. The automatically locked fire doors up to the roof prevent a path of escape in that direction, but the 911 operators aren't informed and can't warn callers against this last desperate solution. Within the first fifteen minutes after the plane's impact with the tower, Stairways A and B above the burning crater are filled with rising, suffocating and toxic smoke, and flames rise from floor to floor, but miraculously Stairway A and parts of Stairway B as well as several side stairways are open and free of flames far up in South Tower. Firemen with ladders and oxygen masks and tanks are on their way up just as Jon and a few other civilians who, instead of going down, are committed to helping injured colleagues higher up in the building. Alone the sight of firemen on the illuminated stairs a bit below the site of impact is enough to calm the many employees and residents, who in large and small groups are on their way down. On the 22nd floor, a security guard and fireman free a group who for over a half hour had been caught in the elevator out to the lobby.

Eve, Betermann and Carter are still groping their way down through the darkness in the side stairway to Stairway A not far from the burning crater, on their way down they stumble over a body of yet another who'd been severely burned and who had sought shelter from the burning inferno in his office and found his last refuge on the stairs, not able to go further. Betermann falls against the wall and bangs his shoulder, but Eve's able to hold on to Carter before he buckles over.

"Just go on, *for Chris'sake*, and let me stay here," says the exhausted Carter and dumps down next to the body as Eve in the darkness helps Betermann back on his feet.

"We're taking you with us no matter what!" says Betermann stepping up to him not minding his aching shoulder. The heat is unbearable and Betermann gasps loudly.

Eve reaches out for her bag, which she's had over her shoulder to find her cell phone, but discovers that it's gone. In the sweltering heat and darkness she hasn't the strength to search for it, nor to try identifying the body. She takes some steps up, and together with Betermann they pull Carter up from the stairs, and they continue downwards more weakened than before, a new obstacle would throw them totally off course.

The self illuminating strips in front of them blur before her eyes and delivers her back to a night with fireflies at Lake Genesareth, where she held her father's hand on the water's edge; she's assaulted by an almost overpowering urge to let Carter go and remain in the darkness and sleep and hears in the distance a whispering voice that reminds her of Jon's; at that moment she bites her tongue – a trick she'd learned during her duty in the Israeli army – and regains consciousness only to see flames rise up towards them ten meters farther down. The flames seem neither large nor dangerous, but Carter, who's also seen them, freezes and refuses to go farther. They talk to him, try to pull him farther down the stairs, but with almost superhuman strength he firmly clutches the railing.

"You've got to come now, it's now or never!" shouts Betermann in surrender and leans exhausted against the hot wall, but immediately pulls away, sweat pouring from him, he removes his jacket and dries his face with it.

"I'm not going through fire, I can't walk," says Carter.

"We can get through together," says Eve, "but it has to be now before it spreads."

"It's already spread, I'm done for; and if you don't go now, you're finished, too."

They can see their outlines and for a few seconds say nothing. Smoke from the fire has now reached them, growing in strength, lapping the walls five meters below. She tries to pry Carter's hand free of the railing, but he shoves her away, Betermann is already on his way down the stairs, she follows after him. They're now close to the fire, he turns, throws his jacket over her and tramps his way through, she closes the jacket over her head and moves forward. It's inhumanly hot, something's stabbing at her like knives, but she continues forward at the same time beating the fire away from her legs. From somewhere she hears a cry and someone falling to the floor, maybe Betermann, maybe something else, she's dizzy and suddenly hits her head on something hard. With her last strength, she gets up and seeks towards the left, towards darkness, here there's no fire, here the flames cease. The noxious smoke makes her vomit in the flameless corridor, she pushes herself forward on all fours all the way to the end and reaches a door, but hasn't the power to get up.

When will the flames reach her, where is Betermann, Carter?

Her hands and legs hurt, the pain numbs her, again with her father by Lake Genesareth, and the fireflies dancing in the darkness overhead, sleep, just sleep, that's what she wants. He lifts her up in his arms and carries her along the shore, so light she is, a little girl again; the fireflies vanish, darkness envelopes them, it's night, Damascus Port opens for them, she's now in his arms in old Jerusalem's narrow, deserted alleys, from shops and stalls Arab and Jewish dressed figures silently watch them, like shadows; tones from a sorrowful droning man's voice hangs in the air and at the end of the alleyway in something like a tobacconist a door opens to a synagogue; they go forward towards a coffin, in the mirror in her father's eyes she sees who's lying in the coffin: Herself.

An uproar, a spark of life forces her up on her knees in front of the door, she gropes for the door knob; she turns it slowly, it feels like hundreds of years. The door opens into yet another darkness; she crawls out onto a stairway, the door slams shut behind her. She tries to get up on the ledge, but the effort is too great, she falls back to the floor and remains lying there.

On his way up in the illuminated shaft, Jon has chanced to meet people on their way down; somewhere he stops in front of a casualty who without assistance can go no further; he rings to 911 and is promised that help's on the way, he gives the message to the injured with some comforting words and continues upward with an unpleasant taste in his mouth, as when one passes over one person and chooses to help another. Everything's happened so quickly, almost mechanically, as if he's two: the man on his way up and the man who's already arrived and seen the worst.

In reality, his senses and his body have made the choice for him, long before he'd stepped into this hell, which becomes more tangible the farther up he ascends and is passed by firemen, who open doors to floors in whose ravaged and burning rooms are people still screaming and fighting for their lives. His body summons Eve, but the sudden darkness in the stairwell is the only response he gets. The heat hits him and a toxic, thin, invisible smoke burns his eyes, he senses that familiar dizziness, but still goes on.

*

Exhausted he's now 30 flights up from the 44th floor where he'd begun, the last 4 floors in total darkness; it rumbles and roars in the colossal construction around him, like a half insane fanatic he's prepared to go to his death for a greater cause. His mind's devoid of all thought, overmanned by fantasies of rising up through the flames, and is not amazed to be entirely alone in the darkness, not meeting others on their way down; only one driving thought: Upward, upward!

He gets to a landing on the 75th floor and trips over something on the floor, when he gets up and turns and kneels and feels the object, he realizes that the object's a body and that it's still barely alive. From far away a signal, a tangy fragrance reaching his nostrils and the faint contours of a woman's face beneath him. His hand trembles as his fingertips explore the woman's neck to find a small depression there. But it can't be her or …

"Eve," he says, it buzzes in his ears, but the woman doesn't reply.

Not noticing, the smoke has grown denser; his eyes burn, the more he tries to clear them with his jacket, the more blurred they become.

He gropes his way forward over the woman's charred arm and with his fingertips finds her scorched pulse, still beating; the woman suddenly moans and whispers something in her delirium, but he can't understand what she's saying.

"Eve," he says, "Eve, is it you?"

The woman doesn't answer, but he cautiously shoves his arm under her and lifts her up and almost stumbles as he's stands with all of her weight in his arms and takes the first step down.

A door opens somewhere behind him, a cry for help and an oppressive heat invades the stairwell, but he doesn't have the strength to look back or turn around; another shout, but weaker, that peculiar blend of burnt clothing and the pungent fragrance from the woman coupled with her weak respiration drives him forward and downward. A haze before his eyes, the darkness, exhaustion makes him feel that he's nailed to the spot; a light suddenly floats up the stairs from below, he hears footsteps, and someone soon points a light in his face. Behind the light the contours of a man in protective gear and helmet.

The cone of light hits the woman's face, he's jolted when in a fog sees Eve's ravaged face.

"She's bad off," says the fireman, "can you manage?"

"Yeah," says Jon.

"Hurry down, there's light two floors below."

"There are more farther up …" says Jon, the fireman is already on his way past him, the light gone, he's again left to the darkness and the self illuminating strips.

The knowledge that it really is Eve he's holding in his arms is mixed with the concern that she might not have much time.

"We'll make it," he whispers as he keeps going down, down until he reaches the light and can go faster and steadier.

They meet only a few people on their way down, mostly firemen on their way up, the shaft at times is empty. From somewhere sounds of insistent pounding, but under Eve's weight he grows more and more tired and hears it only as a distant echo. On his way, he's forced to lay Eve on a landing and gather his strength and stretch his tense and overloaded arms; his vision is still blurred, the wounds in the scorched holes on her arms and stockings swim double before his eyes, small jerks in her body and feverish mumblings give him hope.

Totally exhausted he gets down to the lobby on Liberty Street with Eve, even here it's strangely deserted or the people here seem like shadows to him. Despite the light in the ceiling, a dirty, surrealistic darkness from the smoke outside the building prevails. A group of firemen with ladders pass and vanish up the stairs behind him, two casualties are guided towards the main door by a security guard and a policeman holding them up under their arms, outside a storm of fireballs and dark objects rains down over the street. He carries Eve to the main door, it slides open, several officers shout to him and point to the sky, one approaches him, he moves along the lobby. The scream of sirens and flames up in the building deafen him; he feels as if his legs will buckle under him, the officer is now close by in his dark uniform.

"Let me take her!" he says with an authority that spreads all the way out to his fingertips, and the officer at that moment is the brother he's never had. He hands Eve over to him and leans against the window facing the lobby.

"I'll get a doctor for her. Are you ok?" says the officer.

He nods, but it darkens before his eyes.

"Follow me," says the voice amidst the din.

But when he again opens his eyes and has come to himself, the officer's gone. Confused he walks along the wall and out onto Liberty Street and finds himself standing between two fire trucks and buildings that are smoking from their roofs, the windows higher up reflected the fire in South Tower and give the impression that there's fire everywhere. A group of firemen are on their way to North Tower, somewhere down the street two ambulances drive off, objects fall down from the darkened sky and hit the pavement heavily. The officer and Eve are nowhere to be seen.

He follows the walls of houses down the street and for the first time succumbs to his instinct: to save himself. He hurries around the corner and north. At that moment a supernatural roar is heard behind him, and like a house of cards the steel skeleton of the South Tower collapses to the ground under the extreme heat, and a skypump avalanche of metal, elements and concrete sink the flaming inferno to the ground. The ground trembles beneath him, he starts running not looking back, he runs and runs as do others close by, a man with a briefcase, a woman in high heel shoes that trip her, and like the others he's assaulted from behind by a rolling torrent of dust and soot that escalates under the enormous pressure and fills the streets radiating from the fallen tower.

He falls on the asphalt and gets up again, in the storm of white dust he he pulls the shadowy man beside him, who's also fallen, back up to his feet and goes forward. He can't see anything, everything around him is white and, like a blind man, he shuffles towards a wall, falls again, gets up and lets himself be blown by the force until it slowly dies down, and suddenly without being able to see finds himself on a side street to West Broadway, where a little man, who calls himself Bodigliami takes hold of his hand and leads him through a group of people and into something that resembles a de-peopled pizzeria, all the time speaking soothingly to him:

"Come here with me, you'll make it, you look like a snowman, but we'll figure it out, it's ok, now I'll get you a towel and something to drink."

Bodigliami steers him out to a small backyard behind the kitchen where he seats him on a chair, a moment later he's returned and sets something on the table in front of him, a brush, a glass of water, a cloth and a towel.

"It's a disaster, they're making war against us, but we won't be knocked out," says Bodigliami handing him the glass of water, which he promply drains, then Bodigliami pulls him up from the chair and starts brushing the dust from him.

The sky is dark over head, in the kitchen window he sees his white reflection, but is too weak and dizzy to react; for some moments everything seems unreal, and he's in doubt whether he's even survived.

"I've got to go," he says, "I've got to find Eve."

"I don't know where you've come from," says Bodigliami, as he washes his face with the damp cloth, "I don't know Eve, but I can see that you can't go anywhere right now."

"I've got to go," repeats Jon mechanically, "where am I?"

"In my pizzeria, my customers've disappeared, the city's been attacked, on TV they say it's terrorists, but who knows, maybe they'll come back, but I'm not leaving my pizzeria, it's taken me 10 years to build it up…"

Bodigliami's nervous flood of words goes on; he's getting a constant stream of impressions from the little man, but can't read his face. Bodigliami now dries his face with the towel and seems satisfied with what he sees.

"Now you look human again, and not like a ghost," says Bodigliami and giggles, and before he knows it Bodigliami has gotten a shaving mirror and holds it up for him: But before him are two faces and can't see himself in either; he shoves the mirror aside and gets up.

"Where're you're going?" asks Bodigliami.

"I've got to look for her, don't you understand …" he says and tries to get to the door of the pizzeria.

"Who is she?"

"My girlfriend. She got away from me, she's hurt, she's …"

"Gimme her name and your telephone number and I'll help call around and find her."

"She might be dead," he says and stops.

It darkens before his eyes.

"Listen to me," says Bodigliami, "I've got a car, I'll drive you home and you rest, and I'll try finding your girlfriend. OK?"

"Will you?" he says and doesn't believe his own ears.

"Sure," says Bodigliami, "You'd do the same for me, wouldn't you?"

They get to the car, it's parked farther down the street, he sags down in the seat next to Bodigliami and can hardly stay awake as the car drives through the streets and out of the darkness. Bodigliami's talking to him, the car radio's switched on and reporting even more macabre news, another plane's hit the Pentagon; shadows of people on street corners, gesticulating. He hears and sees it all from a distance through a filter of overwhelming fatigue and tries with all his might to find a key to what's happened, and by the time they've gotten to the flat on Second Avenue in blinding sunlight, Bodigliami's written down Eve's full name and all their telephone numbers and in his own particular nervous and comforting way has promised to ring and takes leave of him. With his last ounce of strength, Jon grabs a photo of Eve and his cell phone and calls her number, getting nothing more than a whining in his ear. The whining cuts like a knife, he goes out to the bathroom and starts undressing, but gets no farther than the dusty, still-white jacket before he turns around and as in a fog stumbles towards the bed, crashes and immediately falls asleep.

*

As he sleeps in his bed in the flat on Second Avenue and vanishes into shafts of sleep, where new doors open to airy, white, over-exposed rooms, through which he's lead by a constant sense of unease (in his dream, the walls are painted with arrows pointing in contradictory directions, warning signs are written in hieroglyphics), the smouldering North Tower also crashes in an avalanche of smoke and dust, carrying with it nearby buildings and sending waves of dust rolling through the streets. Hundreds of thousands of stumps of material from the tower are strewn down over the plaza, the burning crater which was the South Tower and the nearest streets, and hundreds of people, the employees who'd gotten lost or had been injured in the upper part of the tower or are on their way down, firemen, in the midst of their rescue missions in the tower, policemen guiding folk out of the building, all are mercilessly buried in the ruins of what looks like an earthquake, a natural disaster, but which is a monstrous act of inhumanity and mass annihilation.

Tens of thousands of new yorkers and chance visitors are evacuated and are walking and running and in cars, fleeing from the smoking, crater-like South Manhattan across bridges to Brooklyn, Queens and New Jersey and roads going north; terrorized mothers and fathers leave their homes and work and fetch their children from schools and nursery schools across all of New York City to bring them to something that resembles safety, but what is safe? In this city, from one day to the next this word has lost its substance; schools, universities, courthouses, airports, and systems of public transport are closed down, UN's headquarters is evacuated, personnel are called on emergency duty at the city's hospitals and the mayor's office, relations from all over the country to the potential victims of the disaster call New York's police and fire authorities as well as the hospitals in a feverish search for information and certainty. False or hysterical alarms are mixed with the many calls from cell phones on the street and overload the telephone net. The buzzing, nervous pursuit of certainty by hundreds of thousands of voices sometimes make the network break down, and the void leaves many with fear or desperation, left as they are to the TV's minutely detailed reports and images from the city's destroyed and still burning centre and the Pentagon's ravaged and smoking buildings. Many small ethnic groups – Vietnamese, Albanians, Rus-

sians, Chinese – who speak neither English nor Spanish – are left in the dark
about what's happened and think that New York has been bombed or attacked by anthrax as in the Lower East Side, where evacuation of the UN
headquarters has been by rumoured or misinterpreted by obscure radio stations as the result of a terrorist attack.

By the end of the morning, a fourth plane highjacked by terrorists, a Boeing 757 from United Airlines, has crashed near Pittsburgh, Pennsylvania, after intense hand-to-hand combat among the passengers and the high jackers
and is deflected from its set target: Capitol Hill. By the end of the day, the
Saudi Arabian leader of the terrorist group al-Qaeda, Osama bin Laden, has
been presented in the media by unspecified top politicians in the US administration as chief suspect behind the attacks, and a third building, 47 floors
high, in the World Trade Center has collapsed along with a fourth building,
One Liberty Plaza, with its 54 floors, in a cloud of dusk, bricks and soot. In
his television address, Præsident Bush has confirmed that thousands are dead
and has assured Americans and the world that the USA will pursue terrorists
as well as the countries that shelter them. Government leaders around the
world send declarations of sympathy for the families of victims and support
to the American people and the American government.

By nine o'clock in the evening, darkness has fallen over the glowing New
York City, and while buildings are still burning in the vicinity of the barricaded, smoking ruins left by the collapse of the North and South Towers, and
rescue workers search the wreckage for possible survivors, and families desperately search for their missing at its outskirts, the telephone rings in Eve
and Jon's flat on Second Avenue in East Village where Jon is still asleep. Far
off, in a dream, he's alone in a church for Polish immigrants on a side street
to Fifth Avenue, where he's sought shelter with many other refugees from
south Manhattan, he recognizes the church as a place where he 16 years ago
confessed to a Catholic father in connection with Wiesbühl's death in Leipzig several years before, but hadn't been there since, and now neither priests
nor choir boys can be seen. Sticks of incense send a bluish smoke up from
the main altar in front of a large painting of the Virgin Mary's ascension and
diffuse their scent; hosts, vestments, even shoes are scattered on the floor be-

fore the altar, and before two side altars burn thousands of candels; a tape recorded chant can be heard from the loudspeakers and echo in the church's void. He has the feeling of taking part in a church service, which everyone has suddenly abandoned; his legs and eyes burn. A curtain blows behind him, he turns and notices a crucifix, from which the wooden face of a martyred Christ looks mournfully up towards the sky; a wind blows through the church and a bell strikes from the church tower. He walks towards the exit and looks in the direction of Fifth Avenue, but there are no people, everything is deserted, in the show windows of a department store, the wax mannequins look out at him, one of them has Eve's head and short, black hair; church bells and fire alarms sound across the city and mix with the telephone's incessant ringing. He opens his eyes and for a few seconds in the darkness of his flat doesn't know where he is, then still drowned in sleep, gets out of bed, rushes to the living room facing Second Avuenue and grabs the receiver.

"Bodigliami here," says the voice.

"Who, what?"

"I've found her, your Eve!"

"She's alive?"

"Yeah, but ..."

"But what?" with his heart in his throat.

"She's been badly burned, she's very weak, she ..."

"She's what?"

"She's not quite conscious, I'm really sorry, for both of you. But you better go see her yourself. I couldn't see her, just talked to a doctor, was very busy ..."

"Where is she?"

Bodigliami gives him the address of a hospital uptown.

"Thanks," he says,"I don't know how I can thank you."

"You already have. Just get over there."

He hangs up, turns on the light, walks out to the bathroom, jumps out of his dirty clothes, turns on the shower and lets the water flood over him, but no matter how much he scrubs, he feels that the dust and soot is glued to him, and when he hurredly glances in the mirror, he's met with a ghostly sight that quickly blurs. His old eye injury from the attack in Vienna has re-awakened, stabbing pains pierce his eye, is barely able to focus as he hunts for clean clothes in the dark closet.

His body and fingers are tense, it takes forever to button his shirt and then his jacket and tie his shoe laces before he closes the door behind him, rushes to the street and hails a cab; but even though his body's already on its way down Second Avenue, and he feels the soot in the air over the city, his mind is elsewhere, his thoughts are diffuse, uncollected. He's forgotten the paper on which he jotted down the hospital's address and has to go back to the flat to get it and then all the way back to Second Avenue and the peculiar silence there to find a cab.

In the cab, which he jumps into from the curb, the radio's running full blast; an agitated voice reports on the still burning buildings at the World Trade Center complex and the many deaths. The driver, an older man, whose eyes and face he sees only in the rear view mirror and whose broad, muscular shoulders and crew cut sit diagonally in front of him, steps on the gas without a word as soon as he gets the address and for some time is silent, seemingly absorbed by the voice in the radio as the car approaches Central Park. En route they drive by street corners with small or large groups of people in lively discussion, some of them pointing up to the sky or to the south. He takes it all in in short glimpses, sometimes sight from the one eye is blacked out, at others he's blinded by a glare from a shop window or a blinking neon light; he raises a hand to his eyes to lessen the pain.

"Something wrong, mister?" asks the driver.

"No, no problem, I'm fine."

"Nothing today's fine," says the driver. "Those goddammed Moslems have set the town on fire, and the only thing to do is bomb them out."

"No one knows for sure who's behind the attack," he says.

"Man, don't you hear the radio, or watch TV? It's that bin Laden, he's crazy, a terrorist, and if I wasn't wounded 'Nam, I'd go to Afghanistan myself or where the hell he is and get him. Y' got me?"

Jon doesn't answer, he's trying to collect his thoughts about Eve, but the driver's worked up and won't leave him in peace on the back seat.

The car rushes past the first stand of trees in Central Park. The driver stares at him in the mirror.

"You're not one of those sympathizers are you?" he says suddenly, turning down the radio.

"Sympathize … with whom?"

"Bin Laden and his mob…"

"No, why should I?"

"You look like one of those guys who can't take sides …"

"Look," he says leaning forward, "I'm not on his side, but right now I've got other things on my mind."

The driver gesticulates, turns up the radio and speeds on; soon they've reached the driveway to Memorial Hospital's large illuminated buildings. The car stops at the main entrance, he pays the driver, and as he walks through the automatic doors into the dimly lit vestibule, buzzing with activity, things swim before his eyes. He stops a few paces from the receptionist and her monitors to recover, his hand stroking his eyes. A voice calls him to the counter; he walks over and finds himself looking into the face of an attractive Asian woman who's asked him something several times before he can find the answer.

"I'm looking for Eve Letterman," he says several times.

"I understand," she says and asks him to spell her name.

She punches the name in on the screen and runs back and forth with the mouse.

"She's not here?" he asks nervously.

"There're two with that name," she says with a worried look. "One of them…"

"Yeah …?"

"Either she's been discharged to day or…"

"Or what?"

"Her bed's been removed, I'm sorry, but it could mean…"

"Oh no…" he says, not knowing what to do with himself.

"Wait a minute, give me your Eve Letterman's address and I'll check another file."

"He stutters her address.

A moment later, "I'm so sorry, I was wrong. Your Eve Letterman's still here. We don't have her address, just her citizenship. Israeli, isn't she?"

"Yes."

"She's in the burn department. Just a minute; I'll get a doctor."

From one minute to the next he'd feared that Eve was dead, and it seems that today everything around him was crumbling; he knows that he's not his normal self, that his body's working on its last reserves, but he's got to get through, walk the line to where he's convinced that Eve will make it even if he has to stay there all night. He finds a chair in the corner of the vestibule, closes his eyes, delves deep in himself and refuses to be overpowered by the anxious fantasies of Eve's condition: Of course she'll make it! His right hand trembles and tries to calm it with his other hand; even as he follows a Dr. Walcott up in the elevator to the burn department, it trembles slightly and he presses it against his stomach under his jacket.

Dr. Walcott stops in front of a door with a round window and focuses on him with a muffled voice:

"She's in there, on morphine because of the pain, and must have complete rest," he says pursing his lips in his tired face.

"I have to see her," says Jon and walks up to the window looking in, but apart from the dimly lit lamp in the room behind the door, his sight again fails him.

"I can't let you in," says Dr. Walcott, "She's not up to any emotions, has a high fever and is delirious."

"What d'you mean?"

"She's barely conscious and because of the morphine she couldn't recognize you, if she comes to."

"If ...?"

"I mean: if she wakes up now," says Dr. Walcott correcting himself tensely. Just then his beeper goes off; he takes it out of his pocket and looks at it.

"It's important, I'm afraid I have to go."

"But ... you've gotto tell me ..."

"It's urgent, I've got to go, we've got a lot of patients," says Walcott no longer able to hide his irritation.

"Will she survive, what're her chances?" Jon hears himself say.

"Her prognosis is relatively good, but to be honest, she's been severely burned, so we can't be sure for some days…"

He holds Walcott's glance for a few seconds, but now it's a closed void, Walcott turns and walks down the hall.

"Find your way out, call us tomorrow!" shouts Walcott, already far down the dimly lit hall, and gone 'round the next corner.

He's alone. Hasn't he been so many times before?

He looks for the elevator, but stops halfway and turns around. Two nurses pass him in the hall but don't notice; soon he's back at Eve's door and a moment later by her side. In the narrow dark room he walks carefully towards her bed, it takes a while for his eyes to focus in the dim light.

She's lying flat on her back and both of her arms, over the covers, are wrapped in gauze bandages from wrist to shoulder.

She breathes heavily, her face perspired, and her mouth moving wordlessly, a plastic tube leads from her mouth down to her throat.

His vision's doubled again, but reaches out to stroke her hair.

"Eve," he says, his hand no longer trembling.

She opens her eyes and looks at him with a leaden gaze.

"Eve," he repeats.

A faint smile crosses her lips, but her eyes close heavily again, hiding the dark pupils.

Did she see him? Did she recognize him?

He wants to touch her again and stands a while to capture the least movement, but the stabbing pains in his eye again overpower him and he must leave the room and then the hospital without speaking to anyone.

A half hour later, back in the empty flat on Second Avenue, it all seems like something he's dreamed and could again awake from if only he could fall asleep, and again it would be morning with a new September sun over New York City.

But why is he afraid of sleeping and why is he just as afraid that he can't?

Without turning on the light he searches for some sleeping pills, but finds none.

He stumbles over to the telephone and calls Cartwright (why hadn't he thought of him before?), gets only his voice in his voice mail, leaves a message, but a moment later can't remember what he'd said.

Is Cartwright alive?

"Cartwright's alive", he murmurs to himself and walks to the kitchen, moistens a cloth, takes it with him to bed and without undressing, goes to bed and places the cloth over the painful eye.

Eve's alive, Cartwright's alive, and his son and Sine are alive.

When he finally falls asleep, he dreams of Tobias sitting at the piano in the next room and filling the darkened flat with tones from some music he's never before heard.

The music spreads like a soothing breeze through the streets of East Village and out into the city, it lifts Eve from her bed in Memorial Hospital, soon she's with him, isn't she already laying by his side in bed?

His hand searches mechanically for her under the quilt next to him, luckily he sleeps on.

Being is like a stream in a river, and one can never twice descend into the same river, so says Heraclitus, but once one has stepped into a river, the stream there reminds one of a stream in another. And every river flows into yet another or into the sea. Where does the one start and where does the other end?

As she lies in the bed at Memorial Hospital, Eve sees close to her the contours of a man whom she thinks she knows, maybe Jon? At first it was dark, then it was light and he was there and then again darkness, and in the darkness he was transformed to a lemon yellow butterfly that she chased across Bowling Green in the red summer dress her mother had bought her years ago in Jerusalem. Her thoughts flutter like its wings and dive down into a pool of light and shadow; soon she's in the blue translucent water at the sundrenched beach in Tel Aviv with all of its white parasols and can't find her way in to the coast; soon she's standing at her brother's gravestone at the cemetery in Jerusalem with the sun beating down on the back of her head and would place a stone on it, but the small stone is too heavy; soon she's standing in front of the poster in her office in the South Tower with a photograph of construction workers several hundred meters up on a cross beam of the Empire State Building and vanishes into it; now it's she balancing on the beam giddily high above the streets far below her; the wind whistles in her ears and grabs her, it gets dark, something hits her throat and it gets light; above her a face and a pair of gray eyes, someone's pointing a light down on her: She touches her mouth and feels a tube.

"Don't..." says the face with the gray eyes.

"Am I dead?" she asks.

"No, you're not dead, you're alive, but don't move, lie perfectly still, you've been injured."

"Where am I?" she asks.

"Memorial Hospital," says the face, "and I'm Dr. Walcott."

She'd ask more, but words won't come, the face is transformed to a sun that vanishes into a black wall and suddenly resembles a paper moon like the ones on the wall paper next to her crib in Jerusalem. The moon becomes many and they move away from each other, she reaches out, first with the hand of a child, then with the hand of a woman, but only darkness remains.

She sleeps.

*

Two weeks pass, but nothing's normal, whether rain or shine everything seems to be dusk, and the hole where the towers once stood with its rubble of bricks and shattered fragments of facade and steel, which slowly have been removed (where in the first days survivors buried there were miraculously uncovered) threaten to be a magnetizing black hole not only for the life of the inner city but also himself. Gone is the hectic dynamism and President

Bush's televised speech where he vows retribution and war against terror and pursuit of the criminals to the very last man, pass him by as a message from a distant planet. It is only the desperate relatives who still search for their lost ones, whose images occasionally appear on his TV screen in the flat, with whom he can relate; he's either there or holed up in his office or at Memorial Hospital still waiting for Eve to recover.

Her condition improves slightly day to day, he's moved into her small room and can sit for hours holding her hand (his in rubber gloves for fear of risk of infection), when her mind suddenly clears and can exchange a few words with him. Those moments where she recognizes him, her faint smile and the gleam in her eyes, which most often are closed or half-closed or veiled in a fog of morphine because of the still intense pain - those are the moments he lives for. As soon as he's no longer in touch with her, his life is a prison, alive but somewhere else beyond real time and space. Not only his body but his consciousness is often paralyzed by a crippling fatigue; he sometimes falls asleep next to Eve in her bed or in the cab shuttling between his flat and the hospital, his eyes still hurt despite a soothing salve and the pain killers he's gotten from Dr. Walcott, who's shown increasing interest in him and has also referred him to a colleague at the hospital.

"Your eye's intact," says Walcott one day calling him into the hallway outside Eve's room, "There are some pinpoint hemorrhages and a minute scar from a previous injury, but otherwise nothing to see."

"But why the double vision in light or darkness, and why the pain?" he asks.

"My colleague is the specialist and says that there could be a pinched nerve somewhere near the eye, but it's hard to localize, and it could calm down by itself. But you've got to accept that you've gotten a shock, the best would be to see a psychologist."

But he has no strength to see a psychologist, and the many maybe's exhaust him, and when Cartwright finally calls him at his flat on Second Avenue to hear about him and Eve and arrange a meeting in his flat because of the case against Ifrahim Mohammed, he's happy to hear his voice again, but hasn't the energy to see him.

"Let's make it next week," he says, "I'll be on top again after all this, and then we'll talk about our client. Where were you on the 11th?"

"Visiting my sister in Chicago," says Cartwright, "but I thought about you and Eve and couldn't get through to you. It was hell. What happened in the Tower? How bad was it?"

"Eve's recovering, and I'm managing," he says evasively and can't remember how much he'd already told him.

"I can hear that it wasn't good," says Cartwright.

"It wasn't good for anyone in New York, but let's not talk about it right now," he says.

"OK," says Cartwright, "but you've got to make some quick decisions about Ifrahim Mohammed, the legal machinery is still running, they've reopened all cases and won't wait for us. The man needs a good defense, especially now when everyone's sure that all Arabs and Moslems are potential terrorists."

"Get hold of one of my colleagues and Michelle, and I'm on next week," he says hanging up with the feeling that someone's tied lead weights to his arms and legs.

He takes the papers for the case, stacks them on his desk, but the letters dance before his eyes, and after 10 minutes he gives up; goes to bed and when he awakes hours later in darkness, he decides to call Vienna to hear if Sine and Tobias are alive.

"Of course we're alive," says Sine from her office phone at the UNO building on the Donau-Insel, after several attempts where he'd dialed the wrong number and finally had gotten hold of her, "it's the third time you've called to ask."

"I'm sorry," he says, "have I really called three times?"

"Don't worry, we're fine, it's peaceful here. I go to work and Tobias goes to school, I'm more worried about you."

"I'll make it," he says mechanically echoing a sentence that has been his mantra the past couple of weeks.

"I'm not sure. You've never really been good at taking care of yourself; and something's happened, hasn't it?"

"Yeah," he says and can't find focus in the darkness of the flat.

"Something awful?"

"Yeah, New York's been hit by terrorists."

"I know," she says as she breathes rapidly in the receiver, "The whole world knows, but where were you when it happened?"

"Near by," he says, "but forget it. Everything's OK."

"You've already said that, but I don't believe you; I don't think it's OK, Jon."

He's suddenly on the verge of tears, but collects himself, a long pause to get his voice in control. But it's shaky.

"For Godssake forget it , I'll manage. Say hi to Tobias and tell him I'm thinking of him and will visit him soon."

"It won't be soon," she says with a muffled voice, that briefly reveals all her disappointment with him and his departure from Vienna, that she'd never serious confronted him with, but through the many years has lurked under the surface of their conversations about Tobias. He'd hidden it behind a locked door within himself, or he'd sometimes taken it out like a case file that one finds in a drawer or a filing cabinet. Still it's always there when he thinks of her or just hears her voice in the phone.

"As soon as I can," he says and hangs up.

What's he to do with himself? He puts on his jacket and walks through the streets that are more subdued than ever, and reaches the silent Tompkins Square Park with its oriental plantains and American elms whose crowns are like flowing canopies in the darkness. Their shadows wave in the lights of the street lamps like small lakes over the deserted square in its midst; his body and mind are awakened by the cool quiet, and he finds himself standing in front of an eroded obelisk commemorating the thousands of victims lost when the steamship "General Slocum" burned, which he normally never gave a thought. A ship went down, oblivion ruled, faces vanished in the East River and lost their form in the mill of history, maybe just something someone dreamed?

There are dead many places – and the accused. What meaning do his small steps on Earth have? A man with too many nerves on edge.

To plead a case in Criminal Court in the near future seems overwhelming; even so when he returns to his flat he finds the papers. He turns on the lights throughout the flat and makes himself read through all the documents once more, he even listens to the tape recording of Ifrahim Mohammed's testimony from the morning of September 11th. His experienced routine carries him through, the more he recognizes and comprehends the greater his strength and by morning he has command of the case.

Hasn't he just won a small victory over the darkness?

*

That same afternoon he calls a meeting at his office on St. Mark's Place with Cartwright, his colleague Ben Johnson, Michelle and Dan Williams, Cartwright's assistant, to plan their strategy for the Ifrahim Mohammed case. They're all astonished to find him fit for fight, without visible scars, at three o'clock sharp at his usual place at the head of the long table in the office.

"Yes," he says anticipating their queries, "I was up in the Tower when it burned; and yes I got Eve down; and yes she's recovering; so let's stick to Ifrahim Mohammed, we've already lost a lot of time."

But he couldn't escape their congratulations or a package from Cartwright that he placed on the table in front of him, and which he reluctantly unwraps: A twenty-year-old shiny New York Fire Department fire helmet from an antique dealer in Soho.

"Next time remember to put on your helmet," says Cartwright laughing in his usual hoarse manner.

Everyone around the table is momentarily moved and laughs as Cartwright reaches across the table and places the helmet on his head, a perfect fit. He embraces Cartwright and puts the helmet away. There's something special in the fellowship they have, as if the day of the disaster had reinforced it, like darkness underscoring light. Laughter releases something deep inside; and for the first time in ages laughs with them, but the pain in his eye returns. He figures, "it'll go away", "it has to go away", "in a little while it'll be gone", "I've got to pull myself together", and even though their faces and bodies fade out of view, he remains standing behind his chair at the head of the table and even though it's as if he's sunken down in a subterranean tunnel, dimly lit, or the next moment one with the rain pounding on the windows facing St. Mark's Place, he presents them with his thoughts: Ifrahim Mohammed is most likely not guilty of the charge of premeditated murder, there's neither a confession nor probable motive, Ifrahim Mohammed has no criminal record nor has he ever been accused of crimes of enrichment; the police have on the basis of a witness and particularly of an informer in the Moslem environment around Al Farook mosque on Atlantic Street in Brooklyn worked only to hang him up on the murder of Ellis Edelstein and have neglected to turn all stones; Ifrahim Mohammed is most likely a scapegoat for a conspiracy in the Moslem milieu because he knows too much about people there, who in one way or another are remotely involved in the attack on the World Trade Center or some other planned attack or something entirely different. Before he was charged for murder, there were those who tried in vain to threaten Mohammed to silence; and now, where he's cited for murder, he's afraid of naming names, even though he knows that it's his one chance to free himself of the charge. The only name he'll deliver is Benzir Zawavi, the name of the man who's informed on him, but his name is already part of the case, so for the moment the conspiracy's succeeded in silencing him because he knows that with the charge of murder they're serious about their threats and are prepared to do whatever necessary to keep him quiet, even "cool him down" in prison if need be. On the other hand: If he's first sentenced for murder, there's no one who'd believe him, so it's crucial that we make him talk now.

"But haven't you already talked to him?" asks the thick set Ben Johnson, who was his colleague at his first law office on the Lower East Side, before he went to Vienna. Johnson seems turned on and "for real" and is wearing his usual dark jacket that's a size or two too small.

"Yeah, on the day of the attack at World Trade," he says. "It's crazy when I think about it: sitting with a man in the "graves" who's fantasizing about an attack, which he apparently knew something about, at least knew something about the people who in some way were connected to it, and at the same time looking through the windows facing Manhattan South and seeing North

Tower smoking. A guard came in and said that an "accident" happened down there and that I'd have to end the meeting…"

"So you never found out exactly what attack or other our client knows something about?" asks Johnson wryly.

"No,"he says,"nor *how much* he knows…"

"With what's just happened, it should be a case for the FBI," says Michelle and looks inquisitively around the table.

"If we let the FBI in now, then it's good bye to our defense, they'll take over entirely, put us on the sidelines and frighten everyone away from saying anything," says Johnson, brushing it away with his arm.

"But this could end up being bigger than a murder in Williamsburg," says Michelle.

"Yeah, maybe," says Jon, "but it's not clear what Mohammed really knows, probably only that something was in the works. He only mentioned "attack" once, and I'd practically forgotten about it until I replayed my tapes. That part of the case, about an attack, could well be a case for the FBI, and I'll contact them myself. I'll talk to Mohammed as soon as possible and try to get him to give me some names; but for the moment, let's work on it as a criminal case. The most important thing for us right now is to get into the "milieu" and prove that Mohammed's telling the truth when he says that it's all a set-up and that he's never been at the scene of the crime and for that matter has never set foot in Williamsburg. We've got to build up his alibi, got to get hold of his family, friends, relatives, colleagues. According to him he was repairing a car at the time the murder occurred.

"Where?" asks Cartwright, looking at him with his dark eyes.

"At his service station on Atlantic Street. And according to Mohammed, his cousin, who worked for him, was working on another car that same day; but according to the police report, the cousin hasn't confirmed his alibi. Maybe he won't, maybe he doesn't dare, or maybe he can't.

"Dan and I'll take care of that," says Cartwright. "But d'you have any theories about the murder?"

"Yeah," he says sunking exhausted onto the chair at the head of the table. It blackens momentarily before his eyes. Michelle gets up to fetch a glass of water.

"You're white as a sheet," says Cartwright. "Let's stop until tomorrow."

He drains the glass and looks at the faces around the table. They float past each other, Michelle's and Cartwright's deeply tanned, Johnson's and Dan William's fair skin; suddenly he's back in the Tower and closes his eyes.

"They must have set it all up," he says ignoring Cartwright. "The killer must look so much like Ifrahim Mohammed that they could pin the murder on him. If we could find someone in Mohammed's circles who, for whatever reason, was willing to betray him and to kill, then we might have a clue. Mohammed has several brothers …"

"Could it be one of them" asks Williams.

"It's a shot in the dark here, but let's get hold of some photos of Mohammed's family …"

"I'll take care of that," says Williams.

They keep on talking, even about the limited wages he's able to pay them for this case until Cartwright insists that he go home and lay down before he falls down. And before he knows it, he's out in the rain in front of his office on St. Mark's Place and says good bye to them there, Williams and Johnson with a warm handshake and Cartwright and Michelle with a quick hug. He rushes towards Second Avenue to catch a cab in the direction of Memorial Hospital and Eve.

He hadn't thought about her for almost an hour, but now –drenched in the rain, with his back to a shop with a sign "Himalayan Visions" and an arm waving at the yellow colors amidst the various cars – he senses that she's waiting for him.

*

When he finally gets to Eve in her small room and closed the door behind him, she surprises him by her presence and greater clarity than when he last sat by her on her bed – she's angry with him, but with tears in her eyes.

"Why're you so late?"she reprimands and the next minute:

"I don't understand that you're here, I don't understand that I'm alive."

Wearing plastic gloves he takes her hand and smiles silently and wearily at her. Her eyes shine, but not in that unnerving way and she proudly raises her arm slowly, apparently without much pain. In the dim light shadows darken her face, he removes the glove and strokes her smooth, thick hair with his hand, something he'd done so often in his dreams.

"You're alive because you were brave..."

"No, I was desperate, I fought for my life..."

"You must've gone through the fire and it must've been tough where you were."

Tears come to her eyes, she turns her head away and at the next moment catches his glance.

"I wasn't alone," she says, " I was with Carter and Betermann."

"They helped you through?"

"Not Carter, he was so weak, he refused to go on, he ..."

"Yeah?"

"The flames and smoke must've gotten him, and Betermann, he..."

"What about Betermann?" he asks as she clenches his hand firmly.

"He gave me his jacket, and ..."

She stops, closes her eyes and is back in the claustrophobic room where Betermann's face is illuminated in the darkness by the flames from below. Her face is white on the white pillow, she purses her lips together.

"You don't have to talk about it now," he says; but she's not listening.

"He gave me his jacket, I remember that now, now I remember ..."

"And ...?"

"I couldn't see anything, I had his jacket over my head, I went through the fire, I was almost strangled by the smoke, and then I heard a thump ..."

"A thump?"

"Like someone falling or something that fell ... Oh God, it must've been him ..."

She falls silent, looks at him with a darkened gaze, a tear runs down her cheek, he wipes it away with his hand.

"He's dead," she says.

He nods.

"Why him and not me?"

"Don't think about it now," he says.

"I could've helped him, Carter couldn't be helped ..."

"You couldn't've done anything," he says.

"How d'you know?"

"You almost died yourself ..."

"He gave me his jacket, I gave him nothing," she says turning her face away.

"You did what you could," he says.

She sees Betermann's frightened eyes before her and suddenly: all the shapes on the darkened Stairway A on the way up.

"And the others, all of them, what's happened to them?"

"Who?"

"We were about 20 from the firm that went down, most of them went up again, where are they?"

"If they went up then they couldn't've survived," he says holding her hand tightly, but she pulls it away.

"How can you say that?"

"Because I think that's how it is," he says, "and because the Tower collapsed."

"But you don't know? You haven't checked?"

"No," he says, "I was too tired and I've gotten started on Ifrahim Mohammed's case."

"How can you do that now," she says without looking at him.

"The trial's coming up in a couple of weeks, and he's my client," he says, "and I think that I can clear him. That's how."

"But you don't even know how many from my firm died ..."

"No," he says, "I'll check, I'll try to find out if it means that much to you."

"They're dead," she says, "they're dead, couldn't you ...?" she says and becomes distant.

"What?" he says and carefully turns her head slightly so he can see her face.

"They're dead," she repeats, her gaze veiled, her voice fails her and she murmurs some incomprehensible words.

He gets up, pulls the covers over her shoulders, sits down again, takes her hand, she groans, closes her eyes, suddenly tries to get up in bed.

"I've got to call Betermann's wife, I need a phone," she says and stares at him like an utter stranger.

"Eve, lie down ...," he says pressing her gently towards the bed, but she resists and sits up again.

"Eve, it's me, Jon," he says, " lie down, you need to sleep."

She keeps on staring at a point far behind him, a dark point that frightens her and is speechless, but he finally presses her back on the pillows. Her forehead's feverish and damp; she finally calms down and falls asleep.

After sitting with her a while and drying her forehead, he gets up and walks out into the hallway to get some air and recover. He paces back and forth down the long corridor with closed or half-closed doors in to the many wards with patients. The corridor is dark and dimly lit from lights in the ceiling, a gray light from the rain outside is seen at the end, several nurses and a few visitors pass without him noticing. He sits down on a hard chair not far from Eve's ward and stares towards the light outside.

Nausea creeps up on him. How to handle so many dead? No one can, not even Eve, especially not Eve right now.

He had to call Betermann's wife.

He had to calm Eve.

He had to arrange a meeting with Ifrahim Mohammed tomorrow.

He had to do something with this exhaustion that constantly overwhelms him.

He had to, he had to ...

He fishes his cell phone from his jacket pocket, gets up, walks down the hallway and calls the switchboard at the Manhattan Detention Complex; he gets through to the jail. As he's making an appointment, he notices Walcott on his way down the hall and waves him over to him with his free hand.

Walcott walks towards him with a faint smile on his pale face.

"Eve's better now, we've changed her bandages, the burns are healing - slowly but surely," he says without change in tone. "Have you seen her?"

"Yeah," he says, "But she's very agitated."

"Agitated, how?"

"It's only now that she's realized what happened."

"We've reduced her morphine now that the pain's less," says Walcott candidly. "That means that everything she's been through will come back to her. As soon as she can, it would be a good idea if she spoke with one of our crisis psychologists. As far as the burns go, I think she can be discharged in a couple of weeks."

"I don't know if she's ready to talk to a psychologist," he says and can feel how tired he is. "Right now it's as if she needs a sedative."

"I'll try talking to her myself," says Walcott reaching for the breast pocket of his smock, for his beeper; he looks at it quickly and then at him as for the first time. "What really happened to her at the World Trade Center? Does someone know?"

"She almost died ..."

"Yeah, that much I know," says Walcott. "But how'd she get out?"

"She fought her way out on one of the upper floors, that's where I found her..."

"You?" says Walcott looking at him amazed.

"Yeah. I was lucky, found my way up the only stairway that was intact in the Tower."

"You don't look the firefighter type."

"No, probably not," he says defensively, "but I'd really appreciate it if you'd give Eve a sedative."

"I'll look into it and send a psychologist. Okay?"

"No, she needs something to calm her as soon as she wakes up, she might already be awake. I know her, I know what's she's been through, she's upset..."

"I'm the doctor here," says Walcott clenching his jaws.

"Yeah, but I have to deal with her desperation."

"Here at the Memorial we don't pump our patients with medicine."

"Do as you like, I'm wasting my time," he says leaving Walcott in the middle of the hallway to go to Eve.

The room seems darker than before, someone had turned down the lights; her face is lit by a faint ray of light. Only one side of her face can be seen, or maybe it's his eyes that are failing him again?

He sags down onto the chair next to Eve's bed. The room starts spinning, her breathing is close to his ear, he breathes rapidly, hectically in tact with her, unbuttons his shirt, a door opens, but is there a door behind him or a door to Stairway A?

He gets up, looks behind, but there's no one and the door's closed. Where is he?

Someone's moving; it's Eve:

"My father ... have you called Jerusalem?"

It occurs to him where he is.

"No, not yet, Eve," he says and sits down on the chair.

"You've got to call him, hasn't he called us?"

"Probably, but I haven't checked the voice mail in quite a while."

"I don't understand what you're doing…"

"I'm here most of the time," he says.

"You've got to call my father, find out how he is and calm him," she says staring at him. "Promise?"

"I'll call your family tonight," he says trying to catch her gaze, but her thoughts are already elsewhere and she's again looking at something behind him, something far away and yet close by."

"He shouted ..." she says.

"Who?"

"Betermann ..."

"She raises her bandaged arms and puts her hands to her ears.

"Calm down," he says and takes hold of one of her hands. But she keeps on seeing images from the burning tower, and it takes some time to calm her down so he can leave her. It's a cool evening outside and the trees in Central Park are a parade of dark silhouettes as he again sits in a cab en route to Second Avenue. Behind the glass in the quickly moving car he's suddenly struck by the illuminated streets' unreal busy-ness, as if he's on the bank of a river looking into it and all the cars with their bright headlights on their way to places of entertainment and distraction.

Like a wounded giant, the city again is about to get on its feet, but isn't there a strange sort of quiet amidst all of it – behind the noise, the sounds of sirens, the blinking lights, motion and the laughing faces?

In the dark flat on Second Avenue, without taking off his coat, he walks straight to the telephone, to Eve's address book, turns on a lamp, looks up the number for Eve's parents and calls.

After some time, he gets the sleepy woman's voice in the receiver and guesses that it's Eve's mother, he's never met her and only greeted her on the phone a couple of times. He introduces himself several times with his full name before she realizes who it is and she switches from Hebrew to English.

"Is it you? Is it really you? We've called several times … How's Eve? Nothing's happened to her? She wasn't at work that day?"

"She's at the hospital, Memorial Hospital in New York, but ..."

"Don't tell me, my husband's ill, he couldn't bear to hear ..."

"Eve's been burned, but she's recovering …"

"She's alive, recovering?"

"Yes, she's in good hands."

The voice vanishes from the receiver and he can hear the woman talking to someone else and guesses that it's Eve's father. Now it's back:

"Say it again: She's alive and recovering?!"

He repeats the words. The woman starts to cry but collects herself.

"I feared the worst, imagined she was dead," she said, "but I couldn't say anything to my husband."

"She's not dead, she's alive," he says. "Tell Mr. Lettermann."

He's about to collapse, but has to repeat the sentence many times and regrets that he didn't have the presence of mind to call sooner.

The phone call goes on and on, he tries to hang up, promises to call again, but again and again has to tell how Eve and he got out of the tower; his voice fails in the end, the receiver suddenly falls out of his sweaty hand and hangs by the cord near the floor; and when he picks it up and listens, the line's dead. He pulls off his jacket, drops his trousers and shirt on the floor, stumbles towards the bed and creeps under the covers, but in a restless slumber he keeps on hearing telephones ring and voices churning, he sees his son's face and hears his voice and is bent over him by his bed on Billrothstrasse in Vienna, no they're not in Vienna, and the boy beneath him has dark hair and is perspiring (is it his son?) in the cot; his face is pale and lean, and his dark eyes stare back at him. They're on a small boat, a barge, it's dark, the ship rocks back and forth, outside a mild breeze can be heard, cold and damp sieve in from below, into their bones; next to him on the deck lies two others sick, Adam Moore and Michael Butt, packed in pea jackets and thin covers, and the lame Syracke Fanner has crept into a corner and sings to himself half mad; outside Thomas Woodhouse and Arnold Ludlow are rowing and the carpenter Philip Staffe is at the rudder, but why are they getting nowhere? Maybe they've dozed off, maybe they have no more strength, maybe they've given up? He's got to get to them and take over, but hasn't the energy, can't take more cold on an empty, tormented stomach and more wind in his ears. The boy beneath him is talking to him, it's John, his son, no doubt about that, John's saying:

"Will we get home? Will we make it to Limehouse in London?"

"Yes," he says, "we'll make it to Limehouse and to your mother and brothers."

"Will we find something to eat?"

"Tomorrow we'll catch some fish," he says. "Tomorrow the sun'll shine."

"Will I get up?"

"Yes," he says, "you've got fever, but you'll get up."

John falls back again on the cot, and he wraps himself in his coat, in the moonlit darkness that can be glimpsed through the cow eye, to sleep, but can find no peace. He hears Staffe curse and swear outside and calls the two others to work, and finally feels the barge move, but they have neither compass, oil lamp, quadrant, Stella Maris or log line; only the North Star to guide them when it's clear and the sun by day when it's out.

Three days have past since they last had two fishes on their lines and had to eat them raw, it's been five days since Arnold Ludlow was lucky with his pistol and shot a gull, but the current was so strong that they couldn't fish it up. If only they could reach land and gather some moss, frogs and birds' eggs and make a fire, but the ice, the current and cliffs prevent them from getting close to the shore. God only knows where they'll end in this labyrinth. Will James Bay and its deep blue water and ice be the last they see in this world?

Six days ago, early morning, the mutineers from "Discovery" put them off in James Bay and let them sail their own sea, six days ago they attacked him, Captain Henry Hudson, in his cabin and dragged him out on deck and tied his hands behind his back, led by Henry Green, the son of a nobleman, who had a way with words, and whom he'd housed in London and taken with him at his own expense. Among the leaders was also the first mate Robert Juet, whom he'd hired for his third voyage and counted as his confidante, but who since the hard winds off Greenland and the broken mast, had laid plans against him and tried to pursuade the crew to keep their swords and muskets at the ready in their cabins. He'd been too mild, he'd courtmartialed him, but had pardoned him and when after thirty days they'd hacked their way through the ice in the great bay with the tide and strong easterly current without finding their way, and when they were forced to winter in James Bay on its southernmost point and live off frogs and moss and the small fry they might catch and dead birds, and the dark and cold rode them like an ape, and scurvy was rife, he knew what was in store for him from that sceptical man, who no longer shared his dream of finding the Northwest Passage, but would be "master" of the ship like that upstart Henry Green.

And what was the charge: They were trapped in the ice under the sun in the middle of James Bay and felt that they could do it better, but no one had ever before doubted his ability in running a ship! They wanted to go home and he wanted to go northwest, but wasn't that the purpose of the expedition! Why should he give up his dream? They were starving and there was only provisions for fourteen days, but hadn't he ordered that all food be collected and tearfully divided it amongst them in equal portions?

"You bragged that we'd be on Bantam (Java) before Christmas Eve, through the Northwest Passage," said Robert Juet to him on the deck, surrounded by all the mutineers and spitted at his feet, "but here we are now, up to our necks in ice with three men more dead than alive and one stone dead. Get on your barge and find your passage and take all the sick ones with you!"

The cook Bennett Mathius and head seaman Robert Blylot, who'd attacked him and disarmed the boatswain King, mocked him, but he said:

"If you ever get to London, the gallows will be waiting for you."

Henry Green, firy and thin of hunger, shoved him on the deck so he fell and shouted:

"You're mad, you're misfortune isn't ours, we no longer need you!"

When they were all on board the barge with their clothes and blankets and about to be hoisted down, the carpenter Philip Staffe stepped forward and insisted on following his captain. They begged Staffe to stay as they needed his services, but he turned his back on them and voluntarily boarded the barge. He saw that Staffe's loyalty had made an impression on many of them. Before hoisting them down, they were given a pistol, some gunpowder, a couple of cartridges, an iron pot, some flour and a box with carpentry tools. That was all the mutineers let them have, they figured that it would be a sure voyage towards death.

The day came when "Discovery" broke free of the ice and pulled the barge with it; when they were some distance out in open sea, the mutineers cut the line to their ship and set the main sail to catch the wind and sail from them. They were four in the barge that pursued "Discovery"; he, too, rowed with all his might, but when the mutineers saw them close in on the ship, they lowered the sail and caught more wind and sailed away.

He stood at the barge's stern and saw his ship vanish towards the northeast, towards the white horizon of ice floes farther ahead; he cried to himself all the while bitter.

How had it gotten this far? Hadn't he led "Hopewell" farther north than anyone else had been, past the snow covered Greenland through the galling southerlies and often with frozen rigging and almost nil visibilty up to Svalbard, hadn't he mapped and named areas never before seen by the human eye? In the "Northeast Land" he'd found an island covered with flowers, in the midnight sun south of the "New Land" and close to the pole he'd encircled the great whales and had not the ice closed in on "Hopewell" he would have reached the "New Land" that lay before them on the horizon? He had on his second voyage with "Hopewell" in search of the Northeast Passage north of Russia reached the islands Novaya Zemlya and was again stopped by ice and floating icebergs that threatened to crush the ship, and had he not in his sorrow at having been held back by fate from the easterly route to Asia journeyed with "Half Moon" and had come farther northwest up "The Great River" to Manhattan and its long funnel than any white man before him? Captain John Smith had written to him from Jamestown about this great river, which according to the Indians led north towards a "pacific sea", and hadn't throngs of them greeted him and the crew in their boats from the hilly and green Manhattan country and traded grain and tobacco with them? An entire flotilla of 28 canoes with men, women and children in feather covered leather garments sailed out to the ship at the northern tip of Manhattan and only his and the crew's suspicion of this great flock kept them from going on board; but they traded foodstuffs with them and smoked their red copper pipes and gave them knives, axes and glass beads in return.

At the wonderful and wide Tappan Zee he'd thought that he'd finally found the passage to the northwest, and here on the coast his suspicions about the natives was brought to shame when they helped him haul the "Half Moon" free of ground and the village's chief received him and his mates as guests of honor in his house. It was like a dream: The round house with the vaulted ceiling built up of oak bark, mats were laid out for them to sit upon and food served in carved wooden bowls, around the house were other houses and fields were filled with cultivated corn and great heaps of corn laid out to dry, enough to fill three ships. Oaks with wildly branching crowns, great pine trees and trees with flamboyant scarlet blossomed crowns which he'd never seen before were spread through the fertile landscape. Young Indians with quivers of arrows and bows strapped to their bodies brought them freshly shot doves, young women in leather garments and men with bare chests painted in their honor in colors of the rainbow danced laughingly to the rhythm of drums and paid homage to him as a "white" chief. He'd gotten"high" on the tobacco in the red copper pipes that wandered between the chief and his people and to them and back again. They couldn't converse, but exchanged words by pointing at items and colors and using sign language and interpreting eyes and faces, especially the silence and the old native men's gracious gestures and goodness when they realized that he would return to the ship for the night: They assumed that they were afraid of their weapons and bows and broke their arrows into pieces and cast them into the fire.

All this he'd seen up "The Great River" – thousands of miles from London and Amsterdam - long before the others and written it down in his log books, he'd also wondered about who these Indians were and whether they were in the hands of God, for there were with them as it was with his own crew and in his own mind the suspicious and the hostile *and* the friendly and good. One day he'd sent his boatswain Colman and four others in a boat up the river about 12 miles away, but Colman never returned, Indians in two canoes had attacked them and shot an arrow through Colman's throat, two of the other four that returned were seriously wounded and bleeding and only with the greatest arguments had kept them from taking revenge. But occasionally he had trouble controlling himself and the crew, they took Indians captive on their ship, they stole their boats or their provisions or cheated them in trade; and when the crew threatened mutiny at the prospect of spending the winter near Manhattan and a continued search for the Northwest Passage, he decided to sail back to London and release them from their commission. On their way south across "The Great River" they were attacked from Manhattan's shores by Indians in many canoes; the Indians howled and their bodies were painted for war. They shot their arrows over the ship and sailed towards them, and he gave orders to fire back with their muskets and pistols, in that way many Indians were killed and their blood stained the water.

Was it an omen of evil times that would catch up with him and of the account that he must settle with his Lord and Maker?

His son calls to him in his feverish delirium from the cot in the barge. Throwing his covers aside, he gets up heavily in the boat, the boat tips and is alive beneath his feet as he walks over to him. His son's face glows and his feverish eyes search for him. His son has little time left, he moistens his lips with his own spittle.

Beneath them is the icy, dark water, above them the cold starlit sky and the shimmering moon. The two ill sailors on the deck don't move, their faces stiff from the cold as are their arms and hands spread-eagled from their bodies. The third, Syracke Fanner, starts singing deliriously from his dark corner: "Fare thee well, Fare they well."

So many dreams to get so far.

What went wrong?

A voice calls him, is it his son's, or from the dark heavens?

Jon wakes up, it's still night in the flat on Second Avenue, his hands search for Eve in the bed, had he heard her voice?

He gets out of bed but feels the ground beneath reel, for reasons unknown to him, he starts searching for her in the flat.

Alone in the empty kitchen with its view onto the backyard of the coffee shop and the orange rim of light from the city, he realizes how hungry he is; when had he eaten last? The eyes of a cat gleam from the lid of a garbage can in the alley, its fur melts in with the darkness of the night.

*

Early the next day, before the meeting with Ifrahim Mohammed at the detention center on White Street, he tracks down Betermann's telephone number through information and calls from his flat. Outside the sky is gray, a cool breeze blows through the window that's opened out to Second Avenue, clouds are faintly reflected in the windows across the street. A woman in a red dressing gown stands in one of them looking down on the street; he tries hard to collect his thoughts, but hadn't he promised Eve he'd call?

"Mary Betermann speaking," says a sonorous voice in the phone.

He quickly explains who he is and that he's calling on behalf of Eve.

"Yes, Eve Lettermann," says the voice, "my husband liked her..."

"Liked?" he says sensing what was coming.

"My husband's dead, gone, I can't believe it..."

"I'm so sorry," he says closing his eyes to lessen the pain in his left eye.

"That day there was a message for us on our voice mail from him at the office at World Trade that everything was ok and that we shouldn't worry about him, that's the last we heard..."

"I'm so sorry," he repeats, reeling slightly on his feet, "it's a great loss."

"I've played that message over and over," says Mary Betermann's now broken voice, "but I don't know where to start. Everything's in ruins and a gaping hole. I've stood there and looked out over the chasm, I don't even know if he's there under the rubble..."

"Maybe Eve knows something," he says as his gaze meets the woman's in the flat on the other side of Second Avenue, once more closing his eyes.

"Eve's alive? Does she know anything about Amos?" says Mary Betermann, he no longer hearing her breathing.

"Yes, Eve's alive," he says thinking how unreal the sentence sounds. "She knows that you won't be happy, but Eve's probably the last one who saw him alive..."

"I'd like to talk to her, I ..." says Mary Betermann, her voice breaking, fighting back the tears, and he suddenly wishes that he could hold this unknown woman close and lessen her sorrow.

"Tell me where you live and I'll come for you..."

"Would you?" she says.

"Yeah, I'll come this afternoon if you're home. Where d'you live?"

"Park Avenue," she says explaining where he can stop.

"I'll be there," he says, "but I've got to run now."

"That's ok," she says, "what was your name?"

He repeats his name and hangs up, taking his hands to his eyes.

Again fog, how'll he manage it all?

What'll Eve say?

She might not like it, maybe she's not ready?

He dons his trenchcoat without jacket, grabs his briefcase and hurries down to the windy Second Avenue, where Monroe greets him with a nod behind the window of his drugstore, as if time's stood still. He returns the greeting, but the cars and noise beneath the leaden sky seem alien to him, the only reality seems to be the scent of sulphur hanging in the air, and, instead of hailing a cab, he walks towards Washington Square Park with its Victory Arch, skating boys and trees with their bright yellow and red leaves, his eyes searching for Eve, even though he knows where she is. In the broad gray horizon beyond the heavily trafficked West Broadway, there's a silence as if things are moving in slow motion, the World Trade Center's towers and many of the surrounding buildings are strangely absent, and he feels hit by a twilight and stripped of an arm. Is New York really so much his town that he can't escape the feeling of a void in his soul? Fifteen years he's lived here, but hasn't he always thought that he was just passing through and merely stopped there for a while?

The perpetual wanderer.

But perhaps New York is the perfect hiding place for his ilk? Maybe that's why he can't quit the city even though his hiding place is threatened?

He devours two quick sandwiches and a cup of coffee in a small coffee shop on Broadway, that from the outside looks like it's on the verge of extinction and like the coffee shop on the Lower East Side where he worked as a dishwasher when he first arrived from Denmark with a law degree and a broken marriage to Sine in his baggage. The walls are bare and yellow in the neon light, the doors and benches brown and worn and the hired Puerto Ricans and customers, straight from the cold street, candid and alone, even when they laugh. Here there's no guise and he feels himself at home but has to rush off to White Street and the detention centre with its glass front that makes it look like a bank and effectively hides its secrets. One of which is the prisoners and their silent cries for escape.

He walks past the guards and the many security precautions, is led into an interrogation room by a policeman he hadn't seen before and who religiously follows the rules. As from a cage, Ifrahim Mohammed is let in to him. Despite his olive complexion, with the light handcuffs on his wrists and the blue prison uniform, he seems even paler and bent than before and casts a weary glance at him as he moves towards the chair by the table in the middle of the room that he's pulled out for him. He asks the tall, young guard, who's still in the room, to unlock Mohammed's handcuffs, and only after he'd consulted a superior through his walkie-talkie and void of any expression, takes out a key and frees Mohammed from the cuffs.

Mohammed silently lets his fingers stroke his tender wrist, puts his hand out to Jon and thanks him as the guard retreats and stands stiffly in front of the door.

"I thought you'd given up on me after what happened in the city," says Mohammed looking at him sceptically.

"No, but things have been delayed for some time. I haven't given up on you," he says smiling lightly.

Mohammed glances in the direction of the guard by the door and bends over towards him.

"You've got to get me out, it's been hell after what's happened," he says.

Jon feels his warm breath close by and pulls back slightly.

"How so?"

"The other prisoners shout, one of them spat at me, another kicked me, they blame me for what happened and hate all Moslems, the guards just look the other way."

"I'll see what I can do," says Jon, "but you'll have to be patient, the mood isn't good right now, I'm sure it'll change when people realize that there's a difference between religious fanatics and ordinary American Moslems…"

Ifrahim Mohammed shakes his head.

"Mr. Bush will probably attack Afghanistan, I saw it on TV, it'll be worse, I haven't got a chance, I'm already convicted, if Allah doesn't protect me."

"Not as long as I'm here," says Jon, taken aback by Mohammed's pessimism. "But now I want you to answer all of my questions precisely, got it?"

Mohammed nods, sits up in the chair and Jon looks from his notes and back to Mohammed. The gray light from the window falls on his face, that within these few weeks seems to have aged, and his dark eyes at their first meeting seemed calm now are bloodshot and nervous; he presses his hands together.

"Do you have a twin brother?" he asks.

Mohammed's speechless.

"How'd you know?"

"I don't; but what happened was that you, on August 14th, at 7:15 PM were in your service station on Atlantic Avenue with your cousin," says Jon. "You were repairing two cars. At the same time Ellis Edelstein was murdered in his shop in Williamsburg by a man who presumably was you. Since it's physically impossible to be at two places at the same time, I assume that the man that hogtied Mr. Edelstein and killed him must be someone who resembles you closely, may even have worn some of your clothes. He might even have done something to be noticed that evening, anyway you were picked out in the line-up and mistaken for him, identified as him by a witness who's sure she'd seen you."

"Yeah, but my brother's living in London, he's a mullah and our paths separated many years ago, it couldn't be him," says Mohammed reluctantly.

"He's never been in New York?"

"Yes, twice."

"Then we can't ignore him in connection with the killing. Why won't your cousin give you an alibi?"

"Benzir Zawawi's probably shut him up."

"Why should he?"

"Because he's already lied for me once, when he said that I was in Williamsburg and that I know something about him that I shouldn't know."

"You've said that before, but what exactly do you know?"

Mohammed's attitude changes with the question; hands to his head, he looks nervously towards the guard and becomes silent. Jon gets up and asks the officer with the smooth face to leave the room; at first he's reluctant and again has to consult his boss through his walkie-talkie, then says – holding tightly on his holstered revolver:

"It's at your own risk."

"Of course it is; but I'm not afraid of my own client."

The young guard looks suspiciously at Mohammed and stands there a moment marking his fragile authority, then turns on his heel and walks out the door, closing it behind him.

Jon turns towards the window and, not wanting to, looks for the towers' silhouettes in the landscape of skyscrapers and streets of southern Manhattan beneath the leaden sky. Time stands still, he hears someone shout, becomes dizzy and closes his eyes, but when he again opens them and walks towards the table and Mohammed, besides the distant buzz from traffic on the street, they're surrounded by silence. He takes a piece of paper and a pen out of his bag and places them in front of Mohammed.

"If you feel safer, you can write your answers on the paper so that you know that I'm the only one who sees them. Got it?"

Mohammed nods.

He sits down on the chair and stares into Mohammed's eyes.

"What exactly do you know that's put you in so much danger?"

Mohammed looks at him for a long time, as if his eyes sought the door he should open and then grasps the pen and writes something. It takes some time, he crosses out and writes again and then suddenly hands him the paper. Jon reads and re-reads the sentences written in Mohammed's shaky hand. It reads: "Benzir Zawawi and two others who come to the mosque on Atlantic Avenue planned an attack on one or more subway stations near 8th Avenue."

Jon folds the paper and puts it in a plastic folder with the other documents from the case.

"We won't speak directly about what's on the paper," he says, "but only on your source of this information and what it means. Okay?"

Mohammed nods again.

"So – where'd you get this information?"

"From video recordings and my CCTV-camera."

He's amazed.

"How so?"

"For many years I've had my service station under closed circuit surveillance because of so many break-ins…"

"There's also a sound recorder?"

"Yeah, one of the break-ins happened at night and the insurance company advised me to have sound recording, it was expensive finding the right equipment…"

"You don't normally sit and look through hours of recordings…"

"No, but that night, when Ben Zawawi and the two others were recorded, there was a break-in so I went through the tape the next morning."

"Then it was just by chance that you learned that Ben Zawawi, the two others and your cousin had talked about "the case" in your own service station?"

"Yes."

"Why haven't you told this to the police?"

"I've already told you," says Mohammed in frustration, looking at him wearily.

"You were afraid of the consequences?"

"Scared – more scared than you can imagine!"

"What did you do right after you'd seen the tape from your service station and knew what it meant?"

"I couldn't believe my ears, but looked at it again and warned my cousin that I'd go to the police. And then everything started going wrong."

"How?" he asks and they talk about the threats that Mohammed received when he visited the mosque on Atlantic Avenue, an anonymously written letter with threats was stuck in his pocket as he bent over in prayer with hundreds of other worshippers; a telephone rang at his service station and when he picked it up an unfamiliar voice threatened him and his family with "violent revenge" in the name of Allah if he "told"; his cousin, who knew nothing about the tapes and nothing about where he'd gotten his information "played innocent and ignorant" but came in to him daily asking him to change his attitude. Still Mohammed wanted to stand firm, he'd go to the police; and to salve his conscience went to one of the imams at the mosque for advice, who encouraged him to do the same when he'd"thought it over" and could do so with sufficient"caution" so that the reputation of the mosque didn't suffer; but he'd talked about the case in veiled reference without naming names. And then there was the killing in Williamsburg and the next day he was arrested in a larger police action and later the same day questioned with the rights of an acused.

"That was on August 16th, only a week before the attacks were to take place."

"But nothing happened a week after the 16th?" says Jon.

"No, but they must've been set on it – otherwise why'd they get me caged up and brought to the edge of hell?"

Mohammed holds his hands to his eyes and sighs deeply.

Jon looks at his watch, his time is pretty much gone, the face of the watch is faintly double and the second hand invisible. "Is there anyone besides yourself that's seen the tape or knows of its existence?" he asks.

"No and yes," says Mohammed letting his hands fall.

"Meaning what?"

"No one's seen it, but my cousin might know something about it."

"How?"

"The camera's well hidden, but I think I might have talked out of place when I threatened to go to the police and expose them."

"Then you're not sure that Zawawi and his"friends" know nothing about the tape?"

"Can anyone be sure of anything in this world?" says Mohammed and sighs again.

"I'd really like to see it."

"It won't be easy…"

"Why?" he asks, getting up and packing his bag.

"I've hidden it in a safe place."

"I've got to have it; it could be crucial proof that you're telling the truth."

"You're not going to use it at the trial?" says Mohammed.

"I don't know yet," he says. "But if I can't confirm your alibi, I'll have to go other ways."

Mohammed clenches his hands tightly to his body.

"It's dangerous for me if you use the tape," he says. "Don't you understand?"

"I'll try not to," he says. "But it could even more dangerous for you if I don't have the chance to do it. I'd advise you to tell me where it is."

Mohammed slowly shakes his head; his frightened eyes can find no fix point in the room.

"Those people have already done you enough harm, and I understand that you're afraid of their next move," he says sitting down again on the chair, " but if they can scare you into not delivering the tape then I might not be able to help you at all and then they've won completely."

"Won?"

"Yeah, not only do they get away with murder and have gotten you charged for premeditated killing, but it'll go on. Next time – and there'll be a next time – it'll be at the price of others. Is that really what you want?"

Mohammed stares at his hands.

"Okay," he says. "You'll get your way."

"Write the address here," says Jon and pulls a notebook out of the inner pocket of his jacket, opens it and puts it down in front of him, a moment later he hands him a pen.

Mohammed scribbles something down on one of the pages and hands him the book, his eyes seem dead, as if all colour and gloss had left them. At that moment the side door opens and a female guard enters, her face expressionless, it's impossible to read her thoughts, maybe she's just thinking about keeping the rules, maybe about a boyfriend in New York, maybe about what TV show she'd see that evening when her routine tasks among criminals and murderers are finished. The meeting with his client is over within the established frame, Mohammed once again is placed in handcuffs and guided back to his cell and the shouts and the fears that unfold at night like a black flower on that slippery cell floor. Before he goes out the door, Mohammed turns and says:

"Say hello to my wife, I haven't talked with her since…"

The words hang in his throat, the officer gives him a slight shove, mechanically he turns around and is now holding his cuffed hands down in front of his body and disappears out through the open door.

Jon walks out to the young guard who accompanies him down some flights, he continues through the security control at the entrance hall, but has second thoughts, asks for the chief warden and is again accompanied down a whitewashed hallway adorned with framed photographs of uniformed police officers leading to the chief warden's office. He waits outside the office and is admitted by a secretary and is in the chief warden's office who's in the process of telephoning and with a wave of his hand motions him to a chair in front of his desk.

The corpulent officer, with his uniform jacket slung over the back of his chair, takes his time – in his crisp white shirt – moving the phone conversation between the jovial and the harsh, as he casts an assessing glance Jon's way. He finally hangs up with a self-satisfied smirk and immediately looks at him.

"What can I do for you, you are …?" he says and reads a small handwritten note.

"Ifrahim Mohammed's attorney," he says calmly.

"Oh yeah - Jon Baeksgaard, now I remember, we've met before…"

" Several times in fact..."

"You're the one who takes on the impossible cases," says the chief warden laughingly.

"Where've you heard that?"

"That's what they say about you."

"Do they also say what I get out of them?" but the chief warden ignores him.

"This time I think you've overestimated yourself. As far as I've heard your client has killed a Jewish jeweler and there are solid witnesses, are you trying to commit harakiri?"

"I'm not here to discuss the case with you, but to file a complaint on behalf of my client."

The expression in the man's perspired face changes.

"There's nothing to complain about. Ifrahim Mohammed's being treated like everyone else here: by the book."

"He's complained to me that the guards look the other way when the other prisoners spit at him, kick him or curse him."

"There is a freer language here inside, everyone knows that…"

"But kicking, spitting and threats?"

"I don't know anything about threats, I'm sure that my guards would report that sort of thing to me, but you've got to understand folk's feelings…"

"Meaning what?"

"The prisoners are only human and Americans, no matter what their crime…"

"Please be more precise …"

The chief warden bends heavily over his desk, pulls a white kleenex out of the box and dries his suntanned brow. His thin, greasy hair is combed back from the forehead exposing remarkably high temples. He dries them, too, with his kleenex.

"Think about what happened here in this city only 4 weeks ago," he says and crumples the kleenex in his meaty hand. "Folk're frustrated, Moslems aren't exactly popular for the moment in New York.

"In other words: Let them spit on my client!"

"Don't you go putting words in my mouth with your fancy lawyer talk!" says the chief warden and suddenly reaches behind his back for his jacket and starts putting it on, but as he doesn't succeed, he gets up, turns his back, apparently ignoring him as buttons his jacket and retrieves his cap from a closet.

Jon, too, gets up and takes his briefcase. A moment of silence between them.

"I assume that you'll take my client's complaint seriously."

"You're still here?" says the chief warden and without looking at him starts searching for something in a desk drawer.

"Am I to understand that you won't take my client's complaint seriously?"

"You're to understand that here we follow rules by the book, and if you have something to complain about, don't waste my time but file a written complaint."

"You'll have it tomorrow."

"Do what the hell you want," says the chief warden waving him out.

*

Park Avenue in wind and rain, Park Avenue with Chase Manhattan's and Met Life's tall, gray buildings, that by day with their thousands of small windows in the petrified facade resemble oversized feudal towers, but by night, in the November darkness are sowed with scattered lights that glimmer like random images in a frozen memory. He drives there by cab as he phones Cartwright about his meeting with Ifrahim Mohammed and asks him to go to the address in Brooklyn get Mohammed's video.

"D'you have a name at the address?" Cartwrights asks.

"No, no name, just an address."

"I'll look into it," says Cartwright who apologizes for not yet being able to track down Mohammed's cousin.

"What about Zawawi?"

"I got his number and called; but the voice in the phone just kept on speaking Arabic, pretending not to understand what I said."

"You better go to Zawawi's address," he says.

"That's my plan," says Cartwright with his rusty voice, ending their conversation.

The cab turns off Park Avenue and drives in to a small side street with autumn yellow trees that light up beneath the dark and rainy sky and tall old buildings that ends blind at the foot of Met Life's closed skyscraping buildings.

He arrives punctually and just as he gets out of the cab, a slight woman wearing a tight black raincoat leaves the building and walks towards the car. Guessing that it must be Mary Betermann, he waves her to the door he holds open for her. She smiles faintly as she walks past him with her already rain-soaked hair and gets in.

On their way through the city's traffic towards Memorial Hospital, they exchange a few sentences behind the car's rainy glass that encloses them in a time capsule; once she silently turned her face towards him and seemed to search for some sort of sign, but only when they leave the cab in front of Memorial Hospital's grayish buildings and in the rain they hurry into the vestibule to the elevator to the second floor, can he in the corridor light see her

martyred face and how affected she is. She leaves him to find something to
dry off with and he goes in to Eve to prepare her for Mary Betermann's visit.

Eve is wide awake and has waited impatiently for him, she's eager to show
him how she can sit up in bed and from the edge of the bed get up; a moment
later she's standing on the floor and teeters from side to side and won't take
his hand when he offers her it.

"It hurts and I get dizzy, but I can do it myself," she says with a strained
smile falling back on the bed.

He helps her sit up, kisses her and says.

"I've brought a guest."

"A guest?" she says guardedly.

"Yeah, someone who wants to see you, she's out in the hall, Mary Betermann."

" Mary Betermann," she says, repeating the name several times, as if suddenly in a trance. In the dim light her face is again pale, and it occurs to him
that he might've made a mistake. Still he says:

"Try talking to her, it might help you both."

"I don't know if I'm ready," she says.

"If you're not, I'll explain and take her back to Park Avenue. But I did as
you asked, called her and now there's something she'd like to know…"

"Yeah …," says Eve and is silent.

"Is that a yes or a no?" he asks, to be sure.

"Yes," she repeats and he turns and leaves to fetch Mary Betermann, but in
the dimly lit hallway he can't see her, only when he's turned a corner he sees
her sitting by a table across from two patients, with whom she has no contact.

When he taps her on the shoulder she gets up immediately, nervously
smoothes her hair that's gathered with a shiny barret at the nape of her neck.

"I'm not sure I can handle this," she says.

"I think you can," he says.

She searches for something in his eyes.

"I hope you're right," she says as they walk down the hall and he opens the
door to Eve. He'd leave them in peace, but Eve asks him to stay. Only now

he notices a light in the ceiling and turns it on; but the light's too sharp and he quickly turns it off.

Semidarkness embraces them, Eve and Mary Betermann begin talking, at first haltingly and then more direct. They're like two passengers in a train through a tunnel with faint flickering light through the window, and he's the conductor who's just punched their tickets and can't make up his mind to go.

"We were on our way down in the tower," says Eve, "Your husband on one side of Mr. Carter and me on the other…"

"Typical Amos, people often misjudged him…"

"When we were above the flames, they came in from all sides, he threw his jacket over me, he …"

"Yes?"

"I ran through them, he must've been behind me …"

"And? "

"I couldn't see anything, the toxic fumes were blinding and I heard a bump and someone shouting…"

"Amos?"

"It was an inferno, sometimes you'd hear a cry in the dark and you didn't from where, I thought I was gone, I only thought about saving myself, but it must've been him. It was close by, as far as I recall, very close …"

Mary Betermann sags down in the chair in front of her bed, Eve reaches out to her, but Mary straightens up. Jon fills a glass with water and brings it to her, she stares at him, his hand slightly shaking, takes the glass and empties it. One of her eyes is a dark spot in the dusk.

"So that's how he died," she says, "I've searched for him in my thoughts, I've had dreams that he'd thrown himself out of the tower, I've thought of following him just because I didn't know where he was. Our two sons couldn't help me. Oh God, it was a terrible death, but now I know where he was."

"I should've gone back …" says Eve.

"You couldn't, you can't blame yourself. Amos is gone and won't return, but you're still here," says Mary Betermann, reaching her hand out and thanking her for letting her come; but now she must leave, she says, go home and try to find herself again. There are days when she doesn't want to see anyone and must hide, she doesn't answer the phone, not even her sons, she doesn't know who or what she's hiding from, maybe herself, she afraid, maybe the void after Amos. She wakes up at night and doesn't understand why he's not beside her in bed, she starts looking for him in their big flat with so many rooms, she imagines he must be in his office with so many files and books and the Chesterfield leather armchair that he always sat in when he read or saw TV. She goes into his room and is sure she'll find him there, he's probably just gotten up like he's done before in the middle of the night when he for one reason or another couldn't sleep, because there was a big contract that bothered him or something entirely different that he couldn't put into words, it could've been his big brother's and father's fate during the war in Europe, they vanished, he heard nothing from them, but he and his mother were saved in time, out of Munich by a rich uncle who had warned the whole family and saw it coming. Amos spent a lot of time when he was younger searching for them in the German archives from the concentration camps or the extermination camps' lists, when he was older he never missed a chance to ask the American or German authorities, but in vain. Now, where he too has vanished, it's as if he's moved over to his father and brother's vast darkness and she's taken his place, chasing shadows and finding nothing. The other night she discovered a pack of photographs at the bottom of a closet from his youth, his early years in New York, ones she'd never seen before. In them he looks both happy but also confused, like a big boy who's landed on the moon. That same night she found their old wedding pictures; here he looks more at peace and also happy. This is how she wants to remember him because she was afraid that when she closed her eyes she couldn't remember his face as it was that morning when he disappeared. The last ten years they'd grown farther and farther apart, money and property transactions took more of his time. Mary Betermann tells them these things as she stands on her way out of Eve's room, as if they were things she didn't want to say, had probably never told anyone, perhaps totally unexpected on her part, but suddenly it all poured out.

When she quickly takes leave of Eve and in a cab he drives her back to the bright Park Avenue, where there's no longer wind or rain, and gives her his hand outside her flat, color has returned to her cheeks, her eyes shine and he can't decide whether she's relieved or even more saddened or maybe both at the same time. She insists that the three of them should meet again and that they should try to gather more of the relatives to the victims from Bengols & Betermann.

"Did you know that John Bengols has already started reconstructing the company at a new address downtown and has asked me if he could still use my husband's name?" she asks as he stands with one foot on the stairs up to her flat and her hand on the doorknob.

"What did you say?" he asks.

"There are other and more important ways to remember my husband by."

He drives on by cab to their flat on Second Avenue and exhausted falls on the cool sheets of their double bed; Eve won't sleep at the hospital and misses him; but what's to be of their life together when the shadow from the tower washes over it and he's already started on a new case before he's even ready? He doesn't think she's notices his nervousness and the eyes that some days are veiled that he closes when they're the most painful. Is it that she doesn't see anything about him, even when she's not able to see clearly and is plagued by her own exhaustion and pain? Just one glance at his rundown face, no longer tanned but wintery white. Just hearing his ragged voice, touching his trembling hand when he reaches for her smiling as if he's on top of it all and will make her safe. How strange that this man, whom she's known for years, how strange that he with his vulnerability has put his life at stake for her and keeps on showing up at her room, as if he'd nothing else to do. Who is he? And why her? How can she ever live up to it? When she thinks about him, she's consumed by great tenderness; but when he's there, in her room, she can't shake the feeling that there's something wrong with her, or is it that he just can't accept it? Is it his exhaustion? His restlessness? There's something new and alien about him, something she doesn't understand, maybe something she shouldn't understand? She reminds him of a boy that she was with in Jerusalem, she didn't even know where he lived, just that it was close to the old town. When he showed up – out of the blue – eve-rything around them was so intense, smells, sounds, voices, faces, they went long walks through the divided city, they visited the Temple Mountain, the graves, yeah – even Al-Aqsa mosque, there was no one who stopped them and they imagined a life in the time of the Second Temple and of the future, he wanted to go to Europe and she to America and that they would live to-gether even though he was Palestinian and she a Jew. The intervals grew longer; she never knew when he'd show up suddenly in the sunlight in front of their house and she'd run out to him. One day she realized he'd come no more, she was disconsolate, she searched for him for days, but couldn't find him, and as the years passed it was as if it had all been a dream. Until she met Jon. He became an unexpected part of her life, but wouldn't he just as unexpectedly vanish again? Where is he? Is he at all in their flat, maybe he's with Mary Betermann, maybe he thinks her more "interesting" even though she's a good deal older than he. Isn't Mary Betermann intact, without scars on her hands, legs and body, ugly burns that heal slowly? Hasn't Dr. Walcott told her: "You've been badly burned, you were minutes from dying, unbe-lievable that your body withstood it, but I can't guarantee you won't be marked, don't expect the impossible, we might have to graft the worst plac-es."

Will she ever get her body back, her mobility; will things ever be the same? Will she be able to stay in New York; won't she always be afraid of walking the city's streets or going up in a tower? Could Jon still like her body, could she?

Her singed hair, her branded body.

When she closes her eyes, can she not still smell the smoke and ash?

Oh, those images racing through her being of burning walls and tormented shadows.

She won't be locked up in a room in Memorial Hospital, she can't stand being alone, she wants to go home, but she can't walk.

She wants to walk, she can walk.

In the semi-darkness of the small room she inches her body to the edge of the bed and gets up. Slowly and by leaning on the bed and the bedside table she moves forward towards the door. The bandages around her legs make them stiff and inflexible and it hurts; but her arms under the bandages are more pliant and she reaches the doorknob with one hand and opens it out to the dimly lit hall. She takes a step forward, but she's overcome by dizziness from behind, it's as if her wounds are aflame, walls, carpeting, the window at the end of the hall illuminated by the street lights outside dissolve, again she's in the tower, behind her she hears the flames, the noxious fumes are about to reach her, darkness. Her swaddled arms reach out for a solid point, her stiff legs will no longer bear her, but she's got to get away, away. Instead she falls forward and her bandaged body hits the floor; she crawls a short distance and lies there. The lights have vanished.

Ten minutes later a nurse and doctor who happen to be on their way down the long hallway on the second floor find Eve lying on the floor. The doctor bends over her and immediately checks her pulse and can confirm that she's alive. She's breathing rapidly and in small gasps; when they lift her up from the floor, she opens her eyes.

"Easy, easy," says the doctor looking down into her frightened eyes, "You're in safe hands."

"It's burning," says Eve…

"You're in the Memorial Hospital in New York," says the older nurse as they carry her back to her room, "it's not on fire."

"I can smell the flames," says Eve.

"There's no fire her," says the nurse and wonders about the woman's fantasies and her determined resistance to return to her room.

They get her back into bed and place the covers over her; the doctor who'd just come to the hospital and is on one of his first duties is in doubt as to what to do, he checks her heart that's now racing frantically and decides to give her a sedative.

"Strange condition" he murmurs getting some tablets and a glass of water and makes Eve swallow them.

Eve in her delirium keeps talking about a fire, and the nurse who's seated at her bedside watching over her, even though she's from another unit, suddenly remembers rumours that've gone through the hospital: in the burns unit are several victims of 9/11.

"I know what she's ranting about," she says and turns towards the young resident, who for his entire duty has appeared uncertain and overly controlled, but he's not there. He's already gone.

The nurse sighs, looks at her watch, how long can she sit there? She'll have to get back to the cancer ward soon and assist in an operation. It's midnight and there are too many operations, too many that can't be saved, yet are tried to save.

She glances at the woman with the feverish face and closed eyes. Gets up, carefully shoves the pillow up under the woman's heavy head and neck so that she can breathe more easily. Is there more she can do? She'll give her ten minutes more.

As through a crack, Eve sees the nurse's dusky Indian-like countenance with its graying hair; she'd say something to her, but the strong sedative has already taken effect and sent her imagination journeying to places that only a show with photos and yellowing documents in an attic in Brooklyn had given her faint knowledge of. Since she'd seen the exhibit– two years ago – about the lives of the Cheyenne and Arapaho Indians on their reservation in Kansas and Colorado on the vast southwestern prairie, she went 'round with the impression of their alternating freedom of movement, passionate faces and their contradictory imprisoned being and downward glance. Then, she'd said to Jon that the way they in the winter landscapes and large groups of prisoners in front of the palisades and wall were photographed with primitive blankets thrown over their shoulders and with well-nourished, self-confident uniformed gunmen at their side reminded her of something her father had reluctantly told her from a collection camp – the last one – before extinction and from before his own father and mother disappeared.

Now, in the heat of fantasy beneath the surface of her virtually paralyzed body, the nurse's mahogany brown and aged countenance draws her into the flames that she continues to see; but the flames are a bonfire within a cold teepee hung with antlers and insignias and with buffalo skins and blankets on the ground. In the flickering glow of the fire, Medicine Woman Later's, her mother, countenance, floats before her as she speaks with Black Kettle, her father. It's late evening in their small teepee village of 40 tents at that branch of the Washita River where they've made camp for the winter. Outside the teepee in the enveloping darkness blows a cold wind from the south and sweeps drifts of snow through the camp and out over the frozen river delta to the north. Restless whinnies are heard through the wind from some of the 800 horses and mules corralled in the windbreak in the snowy landscape. Most of the tribe's elders are gathered in the chief's teepee with a white flag of peace waving at its tip, but Medicine Woman Later has her eyes glued on Black Kettle, when they're not closed and the whole of her energy is focused on the visions coming to her: Nine times she's been wounded, when the white chaplain John Chivington and his madmen like a pack of jackals attacked their camp at Sand Creek and slaughtered women and children so blood flowed, and they severed arms and heads from bodies and rode off from the camp with the heads as trophies, but Wakatanka willed Black Kettle to ride back and save her and their daughter Blue Dove without the use of firearms or arrows. Many have been wounded and many have died and far have they journeyed, but Black Kettle wants only peace with the White Man, does he not stand in league with the Ancestors of the Pipe and adhere to the Four Rules: Faith, Truth, Humility and Respect? Had he not returned after sunset two days ago to their home from the White Man's Fort Cobbe seeking protection for his people from General Hazen, but the white general sent him out in the wind and cold without giving audience. Now there are shadows around the camp, the Evil Spirits are in the wind and will take their lives, she can see and hear their horses and their bloodlust, their rifles are at the ready and in their eyes is Death.

Medicine Woman Later gets to her feet.

"We must break camp in the shelter of the night, we must move," she says and in her exhaustion she again sits down.

The wind howls and grows in strength as all around the fire speak of the evil omen, also she, Blue Dove, is heard as the daughter of Black Kettle and Medicine Woman Later, and she speaks for a quick decampment in the shelter of the night, but even though no one doubts Medicine Woman Later's divining arts, and all fear what will come, most are inclined to wait. Now it is Black Kettle who must decide; and all look his way. As is his custom, he's long sat silent, wrapped in his skins of chamis and beaver and listened to the voices of the council, his long hair plaited, miraculously still black as ebony and his walnut brown face with its broad mouth, thin lips and sharp nose glistens in the flickering light of the fire, as do his calm, dark eyes that have seen too much. Many young warriors have in the last four years left him and the tribe because he believes too much in the White Man and has gotten calamity in return, as at Sand Creek, and his camp is largely populated with old men, women and children.

"Many good voices have spoken after Medicine Woman Later's vision," he says, "and we must break camp, we must journey closer to our brothers farther down the river, we must protect our men, women and children against attacks from the white men. We are too few in our camp and have not the power to strike back, and I will not have war. General Sheridan has promised us peace and we must believe in what he says, he will give us a chance to prove our will for peace before he attacks. We must await dawn before breaking camp and getting to safety, the night is too dark and cold, the winter to strong and many will get lost and end in confusion if there are white men around us and we are ridden by fear. At dawn everything will be clearer and we can journey calmly with provisions and animals. But fear not, General Sheridan knows our willingness for peace.

Black Kettle's calm, droning voice is convincing, none contest his words, quickly folk leave the teepee and once again they are alone, she and her elderly parents who she helps into their fur bags for the night, and when she'd put more wood on the fire, she, too, falls asleep to the song of the wind and with the fire's smoke in her nostrils and a longing for her husband who was cut down in front of their teepee at Sand Creek and the children whom she hadn't seen since. She imagines that they live at another place, a place beyond the realm of earth, a place on the horizon, there at the eternal hunting grounds, but each time she dwells too long on these thoughts she becomes madly insane and only Medicine Woman Later's herbs and medicine can calm her.

She lies awake most of the night, the wind no longer sings, the fire's gone out, the stillness overcomes her, even the horses and mules are silent, her hands and face freeze. Medicine Woman Later suddenly starts talking in her sleep about Washita and shadows sailing down the river and she creeps out of her bag, removes the blankets and looks out through the opening towards the black, starry sky and the moon shining down on the row of teepees around them and the deserted, hilly landscape with the many snow clad trees. She loves that sky and the peace that makes her forget herself and heals the madness surging within her, but now she's afraid and the anxiety that has long kept her awake makes her drop exhausted in the shadows of the teepee.

She doesn't hear the wind's return at dawn in the snow covered landscape around the frozen Washita River, the snow whirls in cascades from the skies and drifts along the river's curving shore and icy banks, it blows through the Arapaho's, the Cheyenne's and the Kiowa's camps farther down the river with their six thousand sleeping folk. She doesn't see the cohort of Colonel Custer's 800 cavalry and Osage scouts, who after four days' journey from Sheridan's camp – Camp Supply – in the north through the newly fallen snow in the silent night have invaded the Washita valley and like silent animals, in the shelter of night, creap in to their prey, have taken their positions in a four-pointed formation covering all points on the compass – Captain Elliot's sharpshooters by the river, Myer's men from the east, Thompson's riders south and Custer's cavalry from the west – awaiting Custer's signal to attack with rifles and revolvers. The cold snow and wind before dawn excites the hero from Waynesboro, Dinwiddie Court House, Four Forks and Gettysburg, leader of the 7th Cavalry, George Custer, in his saddle, haven't they unjustly suspended him from his commission and charged him for neglecting his men, even for neglect of duty and brutality; but his old comrade in arms General Sheridan knows what he's worth and his brilliant talents in the field, isn't he the most photographed and written about because of these? Isn't he the most perfect man to punish those dogs of Indians with their raids against settlers and railroads and their thirst for blood – after crime follows punishment, as Sheridan says – now he has the chance to prove it?

There are no Indians in sight outside or between the teepees only 200 meters ahead, only the snow and a white flag waving above a teepee in the endless darkness. Custer senses the tense unrest from the hundreds of silent men
and their horses behind him and feels exaulted, with a familiar gesture his
gloved hands press his white hat tighter down on his forehead, brushes the
snow from his scarf at the neck of his chamis jacket and draws his revolver
from its holster on his belt. The thick winter jackets have, at his orders, already been piled in a stack behind them to ensure the men's maneuverability.
Custer raises his arm and starts singing, the hundreds of men behind him
draw their weapons and join in the song "Gary Owen", a dance tune, that
grows in strength and is carried ahead by the howl of the wind and the brass
instruments that threaten to freeze on the players' lips; the horses are spurred
and come in motion, now the song can be heard from all corners around the
camp and the horses' hooves thunder over the earth, the shadows close in. In
the teepees, men, women and children awake, some grab their weapons,
knives or rifles and rush into the darkness; shots and loud screams tear
through the night as the few guard posts and stray men who resist outside the
teepees are shot down by the invading cavalry coming from all sides; from
many teepees desperate cries are hear as the riders shoot in through the tent
cloth as they ride by, children, women and men flee in panic in bare feet out
into the snow and cold and wind, some crossing down to the frozen river are
hit by a shower of bullets from the sharpshooters, the ice is stained red with
blood; others hide behind trees or in the rocks and are either passed by, captured or shot down, it's like a hunt for frightened animals; she, too, Blue
Dove, and Black Kettle and Medicine Woman Later have long since awakened and in the tumult from the shots and cries run towards the horses. Many
horses fall around them, shot, but with a life on horseback behind him, Black
Kettle jumps up on an unsaddled horse and in the next moment pulls the light
Medicine Woman Later up in front of him; she, too, Blue Dove, in a leap is
on a horse and forward into the darkness and down towards the river past
dead animals and people and horses whinnying in panic.

A few long moments of freedom on horseback and in the desperate belief
of yet again to escape the dark blue men's bullets as the three gallop with the

horses' hooves thundering beneath them through the newly fallen snow on the way towards the frozen river and the windswept river bank; is it not as if the sky and the moon, again visible between the dark clouds, are coming to meet them? But in the moonlight and its reflection in the snow, they, too, are visible to their pursuers and sharpshooters by the river. A shower of bullets hit Black Kettle, Medicine Woman Later and their horse and it crashes down and lies there with a groan that reaches her ears just before her horse too crashes down and she in confusion lies there in the snow. She half rises, kneeling in the snow, the small group of pursuers advances towards her, two of Custer's Osage warriors are already past her and jump off their horses, pull their knives, bend down over her father and mother and take their scalps that they lift howling to the sky. She turns and sees this just before she's roped with a lasso from behind. She turns her head; a cavalrist has hauled her in, tightens the rope and is on his way through the snow to her. She gets up and tries to free herself of the rope, but he pulls her to him. She trips over her feet and stares up at the sky. As his head and his clenched jaws and flaming eyes fill her horizon, she screams and he reels back in fear.

"Easy, easy," says the nurse with the dark face by her bed, taking her hand; Eve doesn't know where she is. The nurse gets up, moistens a cloth in the washbasin, comes back to her to dry her forehead.

"Where am I?" asks Eve.

"At Memorial, and I'm Cheyenne, you've been far away, you screamed."

"Have you been here all along?"

"No, I just got back after a major operation, I figured you'd wake up. There are too few nurses here at night, so I wanted to see to you myself. But my watch is over, it's almost morning."

"Morning? "

"Isn't there anyone we can call?"

"Why?" asks Eve and can't take her eyes away from Cheyenne's dark face with its wrinkled brow and vibrant eyes.

"It's best you're not alone just now."

"My boyfriend's coming later today."

"When?" asks Cheyenne getting up.

"He's usually here in the afternoon."

"Get him to come earlier!" says Cheyenne with a faint smile, stands there a moment returning her glance. Then she turns on her heel and is gone.

The most damnable of all is being afraid, says William Faulkner, and when the day is done and the sun has yet again shone on your face, thoughts of those things that frighten you have still not left you. A door remains ajar, but to what?

There are faces and voices that seem insecure and unconvincing, simply because they seem to be without flaws and are mostly edified by and appeal to strength; that's how he felt about Nixon's face and voice on the TV, that's how he feels about President Bush's unreal likeness on TV that morning as he's about to put on his trousers and jacket and from time to time watches the screen as it churns in the flat. He remembers Bush smiling, energetic but fumbling on the screen during the election campaign against his stiff, unproven opponent Al Gore and later, when elected president, as a lacklustre political figure – surrounded by his ex-president father's older, dominating supporters, who in a bumpkin sort of way livened up when talking about golf clubs, cattle breeding and horses; in short, a father's favorite son, who according to rumours in the press was guided through Yale and various director posts in minor oil companies and had encountered a wall of fiascos that led him to the bottle. Living in Daddy's shadow is never easy, but his meeting with the female librarian from Texas, a confirmed Baptist, had apparently inspired him to new faith; and as a re-born Christian he'd found the way to the post as Governor of Texas and with that as his platform and supported by a surge of many Americans towards conservative religious values, he was elected President, with just as many against him as for.

Now he's grabbed his political chance thanks to the terrorist attack on the World Trade Center and Pentagon and has stepped into character, he's become the focal point for the entire nation, as all presidents dream of being, but seldom have the opportunity, at least not for very long. His arsenal of punchlines, inspired by Wild West mythology and religious rhetoric has grown considerably – "you're either with us or against us" or "we'll hunt them down to the last man" – and his talk of "a crusade" and not least "a war against terror" together with his stage talent in personifying Americans' "retribution for the cowardly and criminal acts against the country" are valid for the moment. Still there's something frivolous and for Jon frightening in this transformation against aggression, this running monologue on war, met by standing ovations and shouts from the Congress.

When has war ever been the solution?

Doesn't this have to do with criminals and mass murderers who must be tracked down and arrested as quickly as possible?

He discusses this with Cartwright at their meeting at the office on St. Mark's Place to decide what they'll do with the still missing video tape.

"You're lying to yourself how angry you really are," says Cartwright pacing back and forth in front of his desk in his dark jacket as pale rays of sun from the window to the street shine on his tan. "You can't fool me, you were in the Tower, Eve's still out of it, you must feel like stringing these guys up from a lamppost!"

"I've never felt like stringing anyone up," he says, "and even if I did, I'm not a lawyer for nothing. No matter how crazy people are, they have a right to a trial."

"Turn the other cheek and give notorious mass murderers something they'd never in their wildest dreams would give us?" says Cartwright standing in front of his desk in his favourite pose: slightly spread legs and arms crossed.

"We've got to show them what civilization is," he says. "We can't compromise our ideals and come down to their level. They want war, they want aggression, they want to show the world how barbaric and "godless" we are, but we won't walk into the trap!"

"You're naïve," says Cartwright laughingly, "Americans want revenge, al-Qaeda and bin Laden have humiliated the whole nation, and if their President doesn't meet them there, he's finished, they'll throw him out."

He looks out from behind his desk through the glass to Michelle, in the front office waving to him that someone on the phone wants to talk to him, 10 minutes she says with her fingers. He lights a cigarette and gazes intensely at Cartwright, who demonstratively with a shake of his head says he's waiting for an answer; their usual game: Cartwright shooting from the hips and him thinking, considering his stand and the case from all sides. Occasionally their roles change and he takes the stand of the devil's advocate. To manage a case, he needs Cartwright's provocations; through the years Cartwright's brought him back to earth many times; but here he's in doubt.

"I spent almost a year of my life – actually several years – to get the Nazi killer Menken arrested," he says, "Should we have hung him, too? And what about Zawawi and his gang if it turns out, like Ifrahim Mohammed claims, that they planned a bomb attack on a subway station here in the city, should we hang them as well?"

"Even if you're right in standing staunchly by the law, we're talking about premeditated murder of civilians on a large scale," says Cartwright walking up to his desk. "And you'll have to admit that that sort of thing can't always be handled in a court of law. People become primitive when they see their countrymen succumb in flames, and al-Qaeda's people will never surrender."

"We'll have to force them to …"

"Yeah, but how, if we don't make war on them?"

"The same way that the police in the USA do when they arrest suspected killers and lock them up for a trial."

"Afghanistan's not USA; and bin Laden isn't your run-of-the-mill criminal!"

"In some ways he's not much different from other criminals; and we've got to try to catch him and bring him to justice. In a court-room we can confront him with his deeds. On that point he's not different from Dr. Menken. He should still have the chance to defend himself, the court system should be able to acuse him. As Wiesenthal said: "It's not about revenge, it's about justice."

"Wiesenthal's gone to your head," says Cartwright shrugging his shoulders in surrender. "This isn't Vienna, but New York, and even inVienna they wouldn't try Dr. Menken. You put your son's life on the line for that case and did a lot of work for nothing. Where was justice then?"

"Should I not have, should we just let the mass murderer Menken walk away to enjoy a "well-earned old age"?"

"Of course not," says Cartwright. "But sometimes fine principles and justice don't do much good, and then you have to make short work of it. Personally I wouldn't mind finishing Mr. bin Laden off myself. You can bet on it, that as long as he's alive, there'll be mobs of people dying around the world."

"And you can bet on it, that if America starts wars against all the Middle Eastern countries that might house – or just indirectly support – him, there'll be a lot more of his kind!"

They look at each other with a combination of doubt and warmth, they've had this kind of debate many times before; but this time it's different, Jon *was* in the Tower. As they talk, darkness returns; but he feels no anger, just a kind of mourning he's never known before. Right now he's stunned, no longer hearing what Cartwright's saying, he sags silently into himself on his chair behind the desk.

"You OK?" Cartwright asks concerned.

He sees him, but still doesn't hear what he's saying.

"You're white as a ghost, what's wrong?" says Cartwright, leaving the office and soon returning with a paper cup with water. "Drink this!"

He unbuttons his collar and swallows the water in the cup, crumples it and tosses it into the waste basket.

"I felt faint," he says smiling weakly. "I'm ok now, let's continue."

"You don't look ok," says Cartwright. "Why don't you go home and rest? It's too much for you and you're probably the only one who doesn't see it."

"No, I'm all right and we've got to get on," he says stubbornly, smiling; and without transition, they talk about the video and the address in Fairfield, which Cartwright hasn't been able to get – where a supposed Moslem professor in mathematics will neither let him in nor had any idea what he was talking about.

"Maybe he really didn't know what I was talking about," says Cartwright. "But he looked more like a man who just pretended to be disoriented and wouldn't get involved. He didn't even give me a chance to explain. As soon as he heard Mohammed's name he brushed me off and shut the door.

"We'll go there together," says Jon. "This time you stay in the car and I'll try to get the man to talk. What's his name?"

"Fakir Annan, professor at Columbia. I've checked him out."

"How long's it take to drive to Fairfield?"

"About an hour", says Cartwright.

"Let's go," he says getting up from his chair and grabbing his trenchcoat.

"Now?"

"Yeah, now!"

Cartwright smilingly shakes his head and tucks his overcoat under his arm opening the door for him in an exaggerated gesture of servility that makes both of them laugh and they walk through the front office. Only when he sees Michelle he remembers the phone call, he gets the number from her and they walk out onto the cool, sunny St. Mark's Place with its cafés, shops, yellow leafed trees and pedestrians. Also here there's a sort of vacuum and fewer people than usual on a sunny November day. They quickly find Cart-wright's shiny four-door light blue Ford Costumline from 1955, get in and Cartwright sets course toward Brooklyn as he expounds on its outstanding driving qualities and how he enjoyed restoring it from the old wreck it was.

With a view to the East River's murky water, a cloudless sky and Brooklyn Bridge's spider web-like suspension Jon calls the number and reaches a nurse at the Memorial Hospital, and soon after has Eve on the receiver with the shaking voice he remembers from her first days of consciousness at the hospital. His hand holding the phone perspires as he senses her fragmentary, non-sequitor sentences he has difficulty following.

"Are you on pills?" he asks cautiously.

She grows silent, he hears her rapid breathing.

"Have they given you something strong? Has something happened?" he asks again.

"It was a dream. They were killed ..." she says.

"Who?" he says feeling the bridge swaying beneath the car, he looks at Cartwright who's placed both hands on the top of the steering wheel and seems calm, practically half asleep as the car keeps on.

"Indians, I was one of them, I can't stand it ..."

"What?"

"I want to come home to you, but I collapsed in the hall. Can't you come now?"

"Take it easy, where are you?"

"In my room, they brought a phone in to me, can't you come?"

"I'm on my way to Fairfield," he says.

"What're you doing there?" she asks.

"Something about my client, I'll tell you about it when I come..."

"When?"

"This afternoon."

"When this afternoon?"

"Early, take care 'til then."

They say good-by but he's not sure Eve's understood him and feels guilty, as his gaze follows the highway in front of them with its few scattered cars and over the abandoned and delapidated factory buildings and warehouses along East River on the Brooklyn side where they unremarkably have landed. Cartwright speeds up on the wide gray road with its unsightly concrete lathing.

The enormous blue firmament above seems to grow down to them as an endless row of anonymous houses on both sides of the street is replaced, after twenty minutes' driving, by a view of Long Island Sound on one side with its open horizon and a glittering blue-gray sea and beach.

Dusk dissolves into a great light and a calmness falls over him as the one magnificent villa enframed by trees along the shore is followed by the next. Like leaving an oppressive open prison on a sunny day and take an unexpected break from suppressed emotions; and he thinks of nothing, dozes finally forgetting where he is, until Cartwright's rusty voice and the sight of Fairfield's ramrod roads with their monotonous wooden houses, lawns, garages and trees jolt him back to reality.

"We're here," says Cartwright and stops the car outside a black house with its manicured lawn and white picket fence. A dark blue Toyota with two Arab-looking men drive by them and continue some distance down the deserted street with the many identical houses.

Fakir Annan's gray painted house is diagonally across the street; and as they agreed Cartwright stays in the car as he in his trenchcoat walks over to the house and rings the bell. Some time passes, a couple of cars drive by him, also the dark blue Toyota with the two men; one man, thin, sinuous, unshaved in a dark duffel coat, sends him a long look; he looks towards Cartwright, who's also noticed the Toyota and jots something down. Just then the door is opened and a heavy-set slightly subservient man in a white shirt and tie with combed-back graying hair stares in hostility at him.

"What d'you want here?" he asks.

"I'd like to talk to you about my client Ifrahim Mohammed," he says and shows him his card.

"He doesn't live here, see the sign on the door, that's not his name," says Fakir Anna squinting up at the sun.

"I have reason to believe that you know him."

"I don't know what you're talking about, I'm not getting involved in anything," says Fakir Annan, already starting to close the door.

"You can choose to speak with me here or I can have you summoned to court," he says raising his voice. "And then you'll be forced to speak under oath. What'll it be?"

Fakir Annan looks nervously past him and over to the neighbouring house with the shiny reflecting windows, breathing heavily as he noticeably considers his situation; suddenly he opens the door and quickly admits Jon into the entrance. He carefully closes the door behind him and gestures him to follow into a larger room filled with furniture swathed in white sheets. On the waxed floor are rolls of carpets and moving crates stacked up in the corners; a small, solitary cashmere blue prayer rug is on the floor pointing to a wall, a framed, slightly dusty photograph of hoards of tens of thousands of pilgrims dressed in white around the Kaaba mosque in Mecca leans against a box. Fakir Annan points with clenched lips towards the only table in the room and they both sit down by it.

"I don't have much time," says Annan now in a more friendly tone, glancing at his watch. "As you can see, we're about to move, my wife and children have already landed in Riyadh, and I'll soon be joining them, the movers are coming in the afternoon. Everything'll be in a container. I'm winding everything down. I've quit my job …"

"I'll only ask you one thing," he says calmly with a smile.

"It's impossible to stay here," says Annan apparently not hearing him. "The mood has turned against people like me, people no longer greet me in Fairfield, my children are bullied at school; even at the university I sense this. The authorities have closed in on me, I've taught mathematics five years, but suddenly they treat me as if I walk around with a bomb in my bag…"

"I'm sorry to hear this," he says.

"Are you?" says Annan looking at him in amazement, but quickly continues. "I know why you're here, I'm hiding something for my cousin, he was desperate, but I should never have said yes to him, it's kept me awake nights. How should I know that they'd charge him for premeditated murder of a Jew?"

"Do you know what it is you're hiding?"

"I told Ifrahim that I didn't want to know. I won't get involved in anything, I don't really know Ifrahim that well, but he appealed to my sense of family. I promised to take care of it, and that's what I've done, and he promised to come get it again, but he hasn't, of course he can't…"

"No; and that's why I'm here."

Annan quickly gets up from his chair, walks over to the framed photo of the Kaaba mosque in Mecca, bends down, shoves it aside and picks up a brown parcel from the floor. He turns, takes a few steps towards him and hands him the package.

"Now it's yours," says Annan apparently relieved. "I'm actually happy to be rid of it; I had no idea what to do with it now that I'm leaving. I hope it can help Ifrahim in some way."

Jon, too, gets up and thanks him for the package, but remains standing. The tumult of moving, the sun's bright light from the large shiny windows, Annan's melancholy eyes and the ghostlike atmosphere in the virtually abandoned house has taken hold of him but won't focus.

"Has anyone else been here to ask for the package?" he asks.

"A man came a few days ago, didn't say who he was, so I didn't let him in. He drove away."

"Did you see his car?"

"An old model, light blue…"

"No one else?"

"No."

"D'you know anything about Ifrahim Mohammed's brother?"

"Which one?" says Annan looking impatiently at his watch.

"As far as I know, a priest at a mosque in London."

"Only distantly, our family and relations are widely branched, the last I heard was that he was a member of a Moslem brotherhood. That was at least 15-20 years ago."

"Then he was radical…"

"Maybe then, like so many Saudis, enraged over the occupation of Afghanistan by Soviet troops."

"Did he go to Afghanistan?"

"Maybe, maybe not."

"Could he have had anything to do with bin Laden?"

Annan's dark eyes are charged with sudden terror.

"Don't ask me anything else, I've already said that I don't want to get messed up in anything," he says and lashes out in irritation towards the entrance.

Jon follows Annan to the front door and offers his hand.

"What'll you do in Riyadh?" he says.

Annan opens the door to the street, the sunlight revealing how tired he is, he smiles for the first time.

"Do what I'm best at," replies Annan.

"And that is?"

"Teaching and researching mathematics. Mathematics has its own beauty, and if the world followed that, it would look much different."

Jon walks over to the waiting Cartwright and gets in. Cartwright starts the car, they're quickly out of Fairfield and soon again on the coast road along Long Island Sound, whose bright sunlight again overwhelms him. In the rearview mirror Cartwright keeps watch, there's no sign of the blue Toyota on the gently sloping terrain, and they agree that the car must've shown up by chance on the way to Fairfield, but as they turn into a gas station and when Cartwright's filled the tank and enters a slightly dilapidated cafeteria surrounded by several parked trucks to pay for the gas, the blue Toyota suddenly appears out of nowhere and drives up to the pump just next to the Ford Costumline, where Jon's sitting. The paved area around the pumps is bare and wide open and bathed in sun, and in the shadows under the half-roof over them, because of the reflected sun rays in the windshield, he's unable to identify the faces of the two men, who now get out of the car and together stride towards him and the Ford's hood. Without moving his torso, with his right hand he hides the brown package under his seat and grabs the door to get out of the car, but the sinuous man in the duffel coat has already reached his door, guesses his plan. Just then the other man opens the driver's door and grabs him. He's caught between the two. The man in the duffel coat rips the door open and he falls halfway out of the car, momentarily hanging out with his feet caught in front of his seat; the men are now holding him from both sides.

"Give us the tape!" says the man in the duffel coat pressing his thumb against Jon's throat. Above him is a sinuous, unshaved face under the vast blue sky and he can barely breathe.

"There is no tape," he stammers, only to get a fist in his stomach by the other, heavier man in the light jacket who's sitting halfway in over him and shouting something in Arabic.

"You've got a package!" says the face above him as the pressure on this throat increases, he's gasping for breath and is sure he'll die; in the distance he hears a voice, someone shouting, maybe Cartwright? And then a shot, the pressure on his throat is suddenly gone; gone, too, is the weight on his lower torso, he falls out of the car laying on the asphalt, and as he dizzily gets up he sees Cart-wright 20 meters from the gas pumps with a drawn pistol pointing first at the one and then the other man, both on their way into the blue Toyota. In the car, they slam the doors, the man in the duffel coat feverishly starts the car and drives towards Cartwright holding his gun aimed at the car's windshield, shouting: "Stop!"

For some seconds it feels as if it's totally quiet; the rusty hinges on the door to the cafeteria squeal; a truck driver with Goodyear painted across his chest walks carelessly out to his truck and stops dead in his tracks at the sight of what's taking place under the half-roof; a dog barks in the distance; the blue Toyota gets closer to Cartwright; but just before it hits him with his raised pistol, he steps aside and lowers the gun.

The car speeds up onto the highway, Cartwright runs over to him and grabs his arm.

"You ok?"

"Yeah," he says and holds on to his arm with his free hand. The space floats in front of his eyes. Cartwright looks at him in concern and helps him over to the car, opens the door and helps him in.

"Did they get the pack?" Cartwright asks as he gets into the driver's seat and starts the car.

He shakes his head, not able to say a word.

The Ford drives out on the highway; the rhythm of the humming motor gradually brings them calm and he slowly becomes himself with a slight headache and awakens to the light over the bay and the many colours.

"Sure you want to go on with the case?" says Cartwright.

"I've given Mohammed my word," he says.

"Yeah, but you haven't promised him to risk your life for it," says Cartwright looking sharply at him.

"Are we going to stop now that we have the tape?" he says.

"Think it over," says Cartwright hoarsely.

"Ben Johnson and Michelle can take over with the grand jury, but first we've got to see the tape. Get them to the office tomorrow morning, will you?"

"Sure," says Cartwright, but he senses that Cartwright would rather drop the case.

"And then we've somehow got to get hold of Mohammed's wife."

"I'll try again this afternoon," says Cartwright.

The first gray high rises in Queens appear on the horizon. His throat's dry, and his Adam's apple hurts.

"Tell me something," he says.

"Yeah?"

"I heard a shot, who'd you shoot at?"

"I shot in the air, no one was hit."

"No, but you probably saved my life. Thanks."

"No problem," says Cartwright sitting silent as he speeds up the car.

*

At the Memorial Hospital Eve's still upset, rambling and exhausted, still insisting on going home. He's at his wits' end, but promises to speak to Dr. Walcott and walks to the desk in the hall to find him; after some time Dr. Walcott finally appears. In the midst of the constant activity with patients, relatives and personnel around the counter, they find a niche with a table and a couple of chairs and sit down face to face.

"I wouldn't advise discharging her now," says Walcott momentarily present after leafing through a sheaf of papers.

"Why not?"

"Her condition isn't good, neither physically nor mentally. Last night she fell in the hallway on the second floor."

"Why aren't there personnel around her?"

Dr. Walcott looks at him with a plaintive smile.

"We lack personnel; it's hard getting folks for the heavy night shifts."

"Admission here costs enough," he says.

Walcott smiles ironically, sighs, runs his hand through his crewcut:

"You're welcome to find another hospital for Eve, but maybe you should first consider spending a bit more time here yourself. Eve needs you."

"I do what I can," taken aback by Walcott's directness.

"I don't doubt that," says Walcott, "but I told you before, you're in a kind of shock. It could be you think you've gotten off, but no one can go into a burning tower and come out unscathed. It must've been like being at war."

"What d'you mean?"

"As a green young doctor I was in a warzone during the Golf War. When you've driven on the Highway of Death, between Kuwait and Iraq and seen charred bodies and burning oil fields in the horizon, there's not much that surprises you except that it takes a helluva long time to put it in perspective. I thought that I could just go home and relax and then start fresh in New York. But I couldn't."

Walcott's beeper sounds, but he ignores it, puts his papers on the table and for the first time seems like a person with enough time. He stares with moistened eyes at his broad hands and then catches Jon's eyes with a peculiar vibrating glance of people who for all too long have gone around with something suppressed.

"What happened?" Jon asks.

"It's not me we're talking about; it's Eve – and you."

"I want to hear what happened," insists Jon.

Walcott's face pales, he looks for something in the pocket of his white smock, which he doesn't find and looks at his watch.

"They kept on bombing the long retreat of Iraqi troops and civilians from the air, they were dropping like flies, that's what happened and that's what I saw," he says reluctantly. "No one talks about it, everyone seems to have forgotten, but it's there somewhere in my head and I can't get rid of it. Everything I learned as a doctor was without meaning, what d'you do with charred corpses and burned out cars? Some months after landing in New York, everything came back, it haunted me in my dreams, I couldn't sleep or be anywhere. One night I went amok in my flat in New Jersey 'cause I thought I was back. My girlfriend was shocked and actually afraid of me and left. I would've done the same; in fact, I was ready to leave myself. By day, I was "normal" and concentrated on my work at the hospital and that was probably what saved me – and years of therapy. When I see photos of myself from then, I look like a dead man walking. I wonder how I could function at all. Maybe it's a picture of how the whole country functioned with the Vietnam War and others, you've got to repress. But what happened here in September is harder to get rid of, it happened on our turf, hit us in our solar plexis. I really don't understand how you keep on going."

"When Eve's down, I've got to try to stay up ... don't I?" he says surprised by Walcott's outburst.

Walcott smiles wearily, his beeper demands his attention; and this time he collects his papers, gets up, stands, shuffling his feet.

"Duty calls," he says.

"And what about Eve?"

"In a week, she'll be ready to go home," says Walcott. "That's my advice – take it or leave it."

He nods, but Walcott's already turned on his way to the stairs. He follows on his way to Eve.

It'll be a long afternoon and evening. On his way up the stairs he rehearses how he best can explain that it's too early for her to return to the empty flat on Second Avenue, where he virtually doesn't live, just sleeps.

*

Only when late in the evening he gets back from Eve and the Memorial Hospital to the darkened flat on Second Avenue does he admit the danger he's still in because of the tape. If it was Benzir Zawawi who somehow stood behind the attack at the gas station, then he and his men have already picked him out and it's only a matter of time before they strike again. Maybe they'll pass him by on the street, or break into the flat, if only because of this he has to try to conclude the case as fast as possible and at the same time keep Eve from the flat. But what can he say to her when because of her condition he can't tell her what's happening?

And how can he conclude a complicated case quickly when he's daily drained of energy and lives on the edge of exhaustion?

He doesn't have time for closer analysis, the phone rings; he reaches for it and picks up the receiver. Not recognizing the voice at the other end, he first thinks it a wrong number or perhaps harassment. The voice is weak and he's about to hang up when it says:

"I'm Paul Carter's daughter; my mother gave me the number, is Eve Lettermann home?"

"No, Eve's not home," he replies." But who is Paul Carter?"

The receiver is silent, the girl, whom he judges to be around 15-16 years old, coughs nervously.

"My father worked in the same company as Eve…"

In a flash he sees the connection and suddenly remembers what Eve had told him about Carter, whom he'd never met.

"I think I know why you're calling," he says. "What's your name?"

"Alice," says the voice. "My mother couldn't ring, so I told her I would."

"That's ok," he says as his eyes search for a fix point in the room, where two lamps are shining in the dark and the lights flicker softly in the darkness through the windows out on the street on one of the walls.

"We're searching for information about my father," says Alice. "Do you think that Eve might know something?"

"Yes," he says holding his breath. "But Eve's in bad shape right now, so I don't know …"

"He's dead, my father's dead, I know that, but maybe you know something?"

"Only the little that Eve told me…"

"That's better than nothing."

"Yes," he says and is about to offer to share his knowledge with her, but she asks first.

"Can I come by?"

"Ok," he says reluctantly.

"Can I come now; I live at Battery Park, it's not so far?"

"Then come, we're on the third floor on Second Avenue, you've got the address and my name?"

"Yes," she says with a grateful voice quickly replaced by a long drawn out dut-dut in the receiver. She's already hung up, where ever she is, he tries imagining her with his inner eye as he wanders 'round the flat turning on lights; a girl in a frangible state of mind – maybe just what he doesn't have the energy to handle right now.

He realizes that he hasn't cleaned house in more than a month and that he has nothing to offer to eat or drink. He removes his jacket, gets the vacuum cleaner out of the hallway closet and vacuums the entire flat, room by room. He then rushes down to the drugstore across from him on Second Avenue to buy coffee and wine. He's dizzy when he crosses the street and eyes the contours of thick-set Monroe through the drugstore window. Doesn't he look like a shadow?

Mr. Monroe's alone in the shop when he sees him enter. Monroe follows him with his eyes as he walks under the harsh lighting among the many scents of spices, fruits and vegetables, heaving a bag of coffee and a bottle of wine from the shelves, in passing he also snatches a loaf of bread and approaches Monroe, who as usual is seated behind the counter by the cash register.

"It's been a long time," says Monroe with a worried smile on his broad, ruddy face, getting up to punch the price of the goods into the old cash register.

"I've had a lot to see to," he says taking the goods in a brown paper bag.

"You look beat. Rumours have it that you and Eve were in the Tower when it happened?"

"What rumours?"

"Aw, you know, people in the neighborhood talk," says Monroe spreading his arms.

"Let them talk," he says and would turn to go, but stops. "Yeah, we were in South Tower, Eve's in the Memorial Hospital, we're trying to get through."

Monroe nods and holds his gaze.

"If there's anything I can to do help, just say the word."

"Thanks," he says and walks towards the door to the street, but Monroe's voice stops him.

"By the way," says Monroe, "there was a guy here this afternoon, spoke broken English …"

"Yeah?"

"He asked for you, knew your name and wanted to know whether you lived across the street and how often you come home."

"What'd you tell him?"

"I said I didn't know anything. Mean anything to you?"

"Maybe," he says.

"He was nosing around by your door, I had customers, but a little later when I looked he was gone and I haven't seen him since."

"If you see him again, let me know," he says walking towards the counter and handing Monroes a card with his phone number.

"Even late at night?"Monroe asks.

"Day or night," he says smiling tired, carrying his bag out into the cool evening street that he's crossed hundreds of times before; but dizziness again overtakes him and he finds himself standing in the middle of the street in front of a braking car; the black guy in the car clenches the steering wheel in shock, then gets out onto the street and starts shouting at him. As more and more cars drive up in front of and behind them, horns honking, he stares uncomprehendingly at the angry face like something beyond his reality. The next moment he offers the black man his hand, apologizes and is soon by his door, where he unlocks it and slowly goes up the dark stairway.

Just as he unlocks the door to his flat and opens it, the door telephone on the wall rings; he momentarily considers not answering, but lifts it anyway with his free hand and recognizes Alice's voice; he presses the button to the street door and hurries into the flat with the bag, but he's not sure where he is and what he's to do with the wine, bread and bag of coffee. In a strange confusion he walks into the kitchen and puts the brown bag on the counter next to the sink.

He can barely breathe, hyperventilating as he stares into the white kitchen wall and feels that his legs are about to buckle under him.

"Pull yourself together, together, *for Christ's sake"*, says a voice in his head.

"Is anyone there?" shouts another voice far away, maybe something in his imagination, maybe a voice from the flat or the street, he's not sure, but soon after he hears someone knocking on a door behind him and turns to find a blonde girl in jeans and a white jacket, somewhat confused, standing at the threshold to the murky kitchen. She's tall and slim, smiles shyly.

"Sorry," she says. "The door was open and I just came in …"

"You must be Alice," he says. "Go into the living room, I'll be right there."

She nods and disappears; he straightens up, pours a glass of water for himself and drains it quickly, dries his mouth, closes his eyes to collect his thoughts and walks into the room to the girl. She's standing with her back to him looking down on the street, turns when she hears him, but as he feels unsteady on his feet he walks over to the coffee table and sits down.

"Come over here?" he says trying unsuccessfully to smile.

"Something the matter?" she asks as she sits down by the table.

"Exhaustion, that's the matter," he says, "but don't think about it."

"Should I not've come?"

"No," he says, "it's just me; I seem to overestimate my own strength."

"Just like my dad, he worked way too much."

"Paul Carter?"

"Yeah, Paul Carter. He was an accountant for Bengols & Betermann, but had other jobs, too. He came from Ohio and wanted to prove to himself that he could manage in New York, I think. He was proud that he could afford a flat in New York and we always had to have the latest of everything."

She looks searchingly at him trying to find an open door. Her pretty face is marked by dark circles under her eyes, and as she speaks her hand nervously gesticulates in front of her throat.

"Why isn't it your mother who's called or come?" he asks.

"She couldn't," she says wrapping her arms around herself swaying to and fro in the chair.

"Is she ill?"

"She drinks, she's started drinking," says Alice, "drinking all sorts of hard liquor and I don't know what to do. She's mad and sad all the time."

"You've got to get hold of a doctor."

"I have, but he just writes prescriptions, which she takes and drinks at the same time, so ..."

He sighs.

"Don't you have family ...?"

"Yeah, in Ohio, but they won't come to New York," says Alice. "And when one of them came, her own brother, he didn't know what to do. She practically threw him out of our flat."

"Let me see what I can do," he says. "There must be something ..."

"Will you?"

"Yeah," he says, "I'll get one of my people at the office to look into it. We'll figure something out."

"Are you sure?"

"We'll try anyway," he says and feels a piercing pain in his eye as if someone stood and poked it. The room expands and he feels as if he's seated in a vast hall with no beginning and no end.

"What do you know about my father?" asks Alice.

"Not much," he says. "But are you sure you really want to know what I know?"

"That's why I'm here," she says with sudden candour, straightening up in her chair.

"I know he was injured when the plane hit South Tower, he had trouble walking, but Eve and a colleague from the firm supported him some way down Stairway A until Mr. Betermann took over and together with Eve helped him farther down ..."

"Is that all?"

"No," he says having difficulty going on. He gets up and walks to the window out towards Second Avenue, some guys run across the street, one of them making faces at the driver of a car and dancing in front of its hood, the others laugh; a couple are leaving the half-empty café with the white tables and lit faces; the yellow rim of light from Midtown, swallows the white light from the street lamps and lamps in the rectangular windows of the houses vibrates up towards the total blackness of the sky. He turns to her.

"I want to hear everything," she says.

"It was an inferno," he says not really believing her, "and your father couldn't and wouldn't go on. In the midst of the smoke and darkness he insisted that Eve and Betermann go on without him."

"Did they?"

"Eve tried to change his mind, but …"

"But what?"

"It was burning below them, it was a matter of minutes, and he didn't want to … be a burden for them. He held on to the railing and Eve could do nothing."

Alice hides her face in her hands saying nothing.

"Do you really want me to believe that?" she says suddenly getting up from the chair, walking over to him.

"You better, that's what Eve told me."

"That he just gave up?"

She clenches her hand and he can see that she'd like to hit him.

"Your father didn't give up … in a way he gave his life to the two others," he says. "That's entirely different."

"No! He gave up and now my mother's giving up!"

"None of them have given up, they were struck by an accident, something greater than themselves; and your father made a decision. He was probably scared, scared to death and exhausted; but the others helped him the best they could and in the midst of all that he decided to set them free."

"Just like my father," she says, "why didn't he think about us, Mom and me?"

"Who says he didn't?"

"He didn't!" she says walking towards him and thrashing out, but he catches her arms and holds them tight.

"I'm telling you: He did what he could. I'm sure that you were the first and the last he thought about."

She stares disbelievingly at him, he holds her glance. The twisted and contrary look in her young face dissolves; resistance in her arms and body grows less, her body sags. She starts sobbing and turns half away; carefully he pulls her close and holds her in his arms.

Words no longer have meaning. He lets her go and offers a cup of coffee, a glass of wine, but she shakes her head, is somewhere far away, he can feel some of the way, a doubt or anger or bitterness or maybe it all, all at once, something she can't handle, something unexpected has entered that short life that is hers and that is faced to the future.

A cold wall was waiting for her and she's already older than her age.

He follows her out to the entrance and suggests that she meet Eve as soon as she's up to it and maybe Mary Betermann as well. She nods, but isn't there, her hand is cool. When she'd taken a few steps out into the darkened hall, she turns abruptly amid a dull noise from the TV from the neighbour downstairs and faces him.What is a face? Hers has not yet fully unfolded but already has a shadow across it; she turns her back to him with a faint smile and is soon gone in the streets with their many over dimensioned buildings and strongly illuminated show windows and the rush of other faces that for a few seconds chance to come close to hers.

He closes the door to the stairway and again is alone with himself.

Under the dark celestial vault, New York City is the city of lights and shadows and Fifth Avenue a valley of sharp and flickering shadows under the hectically blinking lights; the headlights of yellow cabs glide around the corners of highrise hotels,office buildings and shopping malls that stand with vast, vacant patches of light and are suddenly seeing eyes in the long drawn perspective of the streets by night; an electric heart on Times Square pumps the letters of Sony's and Coca Cola's white names out on lit red squares; millions of fireflies rush in the cities black silhouettes, office buildings tower up from the streets like shimmering penants in a dream, but on Manhattan

South there's a mega-hole in the asphalt, the place of Ground Zero. Sirens draw long threads through the night. Eve and Jon are spun in them, sleeping in each their own bed. The city sleeps and is awake in a broken dream.

It's a gray November day; the tans have left their faces and thy're sitting together with him at his office on St. Mark's Place, Ben Johnson, Cartwright, Michelle and an interpreter to look through Ifrahim Mohammed's video on a TV. The tape is black and white. A long stretch is uneventful, in the small workshop with gray stone walls, a matte window at the end of the room is a source of light from outside, and a dark floor with a well for getting under the cars in the center, Mohammed's cousin's standing with his tools bent over the raised hood of a high, four-wheel drive safari vehicle changing some parts. Sounds from his movements and tools are clear and monotonous, even his irritated grunts and groans when he gets in the vehicle and tries starting it in vain. It's hard to stay focused, they get up from their chairs and talk amongst themselves about the various aspects of the case and not least the scheduled grand jury hearing, that they've now agreed that Ben Johnson and Michelle should handle together with Mohammed, who for the first time will give his version to a larger audience.

"Something's happening!" says Michelle from her chair in front of the TV, turns and shhh's those present, who again gather in a circle around the small screen. Cartwright steps over to the interpretor, a young dark-skinned student from New York University with Syrian background, who all the while has been glued to the screen, and says:

"No matter what they're saying, we've got to hear it."

On the TV's image of the workshop, the light from the matte window is gone and a neon light in the ceiling has been turned on, making Mohammed's cousin, Hamsal's face, who's now under the car, that's been driven halfway over the well, to seem extraordinarily pale. Also the three people now in the workshop, all in dark, light weight jackets, two with their backs to the camera and the third with his eyes on a small office, seem pale as in an overexposed movie, when they call Hamsal up from the well, and from the start in a slightly aggressive tone remind him of the task he, in the name of the Prophet, has accepted.

"I must think of my wife and child," says the lean Hamsal in his dirty work clothes, not looking directly at the thickset shorter man, whom they immediately recognize as Ben Zawawi. Zawawi goes in a rage and starts out shouting the others and abusing Hamsal. Hamsal walks away from them over to a sink on the wall, he turns his back to the three, moistens a rag with turpentine and tensely cleans his hands of oil, but Zawawi has followed him and grabs his arm, threatening "revenge" if he doesn't do what they've already agreed.

"If we have to, we can take care of you," he says gesturing the two others to come.

"It's a calamity for me. Don't make me do it," says Hamsal. "I've never killed anyone before."

"You're not going to kill anyone or make the bomb," says Zawawi, "You just go down to the platform on Jay Street Station, like we planned, and on your mobile phone will report when the coast is clear and we'll do the rest. It's easy – there are four tracks and two platforms. Show him the drawing again!"

One of the two takes a piece of paper from the inner pocket of his jacket; reluctantly Hamsal is led over to the car, on the hood of which the paper is laid out. Zawawi starts explaining the action and points to the entrance on Eighth Avenue that Hamsal should use and the platform he'll stand on, and gives him the time where the A train would be in. Five minutes before that he's to report coast clear.

"If a policeman does show up, then just get him talking."

Hamsal takes his hands to his head, the others nod conspiratorily to each other.

"But why?" says Hamsal.

"We've said it again and again," says Zawawi impatiently, "you've signed up in the name of the Prophet, it's too late to back out."

"A lot of people will die …" says Hamsal weakly.

"Yes, Inshallah, hundreds of nonbelievers in a country that together with Israel occupies Palestine and has soldiers in our motherland, isn't that enough for you? What more do you want? You're Moslem, now it's your chance to prove your faith."

Hamsal is about to give in, he's silent, his pale face shines, he looks from one to the other.

"My wife must know nothing, no one must know."

"No, no one'll know anything, everything's secret," says Zawawi placing a hand on his shoulder. "Then we can count on you?"

"Yes," says Hamsal and leans on the hood of the car.

"Then you're one of us, brother of the faith?"

"Yes."

"We're counting on seeing you tomorrow – at my place?"

"Yes, I'll be there."

"Allahu Akbar," says Zawawi looking up.

"Allahu Akbar," repeats the two.

They repeat Allah's praise several times, Hamsal joins in, they embrace one another, Hamsal cautiously, and a moment later, apart from Hamsal, they move out of the picture. Hamsal's left alone next to the car staring at them. He nervously rubs his hands together. His face is void.

"Enough," says Jon,"let's stop here."

Cartwright turns off the player and TV, none react, everyone's affected by what they've seen, also the young interpreter, who mumbles something in Arabic; and when Jon asks him what he'd said, he replies:

"They're criminals and dangerous, they go against everything Islam represents."

"And what's that?"

"Mercy, peace. But they're cynical, when they recruit followers, they refer to the so-called verse of the sword in the Koran, where the Prophet commands all to combat those not believing in the true religion. And the true religion is of course Islam."

"Then the Koran itself has opened a door to violence?"

"Yes and no; there are more than 100 verses in the Koran that say something else, it depends on the eyes reading it."

"How d'you know?"

"The tradition of the sword goes far back in time, this isn't out of the blue; bin Laden also uses it, you can read Al Qaeda's declarations on internet."

"Could you translate some of their declarations for us?"

The interpreter nods and packs his things, he has classes at NYU; Jon thanks him for his help and they start discussing how best to proceed.

"The tapes confirm what Ifrahim Mohammed has said all along," he says, "but we still don't have the necessary material against the charge of premeditated murder. The grand jury is basically a formality. More the reason to prepare the case for the trial itself in January."

"It doesn't give us much time," says Ben Johnson as he moves a chair and wedges his large body down in it. "We haven't confirmed Zawawi's identity, we don't even know if he's still in the country, and what about his two accomplices?"

"We don't know anything about them either," says Cartwright. "This was the first time I saw one of them, the other looks identical to one of the two that assaulted Jon at the gas station on Long Island Sound. But Dan's tracked down Hamsal, he's working at another service station in Brooklyn. Now that we have the tape and know what's on it, it's likely that we can pressure him to give Mohammed an alibi and witness for him in the case."

"We're really playing with fire," says Michelle. "Those people are ready to do anything …"

"I think we should take advantage of our upper hand now that we have the tape," says Cartwright.

"I agree," says Johnson. "Our weak link is that we still don't have an alibi for Mohammed."

"Yeah, if we can get that," says Jon, "then the case will fall apart for the district attorney, and now with what we have on the tape, we can build a strong defense."

"You're all out of your minds," says Michelle agitated, getting up from the table they're seated around. With a trained gesture, she brushes her long black bangs from her eyes. "You're so set on winning this case that you just won't see the danger we're putting ourselves in if we walk the line and put Hamsal or any of the others under pressure. They've already been after Jon, they're obsessed with getting hold of the tape, they know perfectly well what this is about, and what about our client's safety? He's totally dependent on what we do. I'm not as experienced as you, but I think that this case is too big for us; we've got to get the FBI involved in some way or other.

Michelle looks from one to the other, Jon clenches his jaws, Cartwright shrugs his shoulders. Just then the telephone in the front office rings, she'd go out to take it, but Jon waves her away, it'll just have to ring. They all turn towards it as if expecting a signal from outside, something that can dissolve their tension and he feels the sound still hanging somewhere in his head. Behind him is someone who looks like him calling him away.

"We've had this discussion on the FBI before", says Johnson annoyed, "Zawawi and the other criminals didn't actually do anything at Jay Street Station. We don't know why, but probably because of the tape and the fear of being exposed. I think we should handle the case only as a charge of murder and keep the FBI out …"

"And use our advantage!" interjects Cartwright with a long glance towards Michelle, now seated at the table.

"Yeah and take the risk of danger in the bargain," says Johnson laconically.

"It's easy for you to say, you've neither wife nor children!" says Michelle shaking her head.

"Why've you changed your mind?" asks Jon.

"What d'you mean?" says Cartwright.

"You asked me to consider dropping the case because it was dangerous, remember?"

"It's simple," says Cartwright: "After seeing the tape, I'm convinced that Hamsal is the weak link and that we can "break him" to our client's advantage. He can't run from the testimony on the tape."

Jon looks over the small contingent around the table: Slim Cartwright in his black jacket and squint in the long face where his cheekbones are pronounced, the heavy set Johnson with the wrinkled blue jacket who's for the moment fallen in a trance and doodles small curleyqueues on note paper with his pen, dark Michelle who, still upset, searches his eyes for support.

"I think you're right," he says to a smiling Cartwright, "but it has to be discreet. D'you think you and Dan can contact him and "arrange" a meeting with him and me?"

"Sure," says Cartwright, "but it'll take a couple of days, and in the meantime, I'd suggest that you find another place to stay."

"I'll think it over," he says, and they talk for hours, gradually planning most, delegating jobs, and he feeling relieved not being responsible for the grand jury hearing, maybe he could even take a half day off while he's waiting to hear from Cartwright and drive out to Long Island?

When they adjourn the meeting in the middle of the afternoon and Cartwright and Johnson have gone and he's on his way out of the office with his briefcase to visit Eve and the yellow light from the round lamps in the ceiling mix with the gray light from the windows facing St. Mark's Place, Michelle places her hand on his arm.

"You can stay with me," she says. "My husband's gone for the week."

"Thanks," he says, "but it's safer for you if I get a hotel."

"You need someone to take care of you now that Eve's in the hospital. I've never seen you like this before."

"He notices a vibrating point in her dark eyes.

"What d'you mean?"

"You were already exhausted when all of this happened. You've grown paler and thinner for each time I've seen you, sometimes your hands actually shake. I don't understand how you stay together."

"Maybe I don't," he says with a faint smile.

"Do you ever sleep?"

"Yeah, but not much."

Hesitatingly they stand there face to face, he in his trenchcoat, briefcase in hand, she in her black turtleneck pullover, at least fifteen years his junior, but who's hit a tender spot.

"Why not drop the case?"

"You know I can't, not now when we're so close."

"What if we're not close, what if it turns out that we're up against powers we can't handle?"

"Then we go to the FBI"

"Has it ever occurred to you that it might be too late? Or are you able to see past more than one day at a time?"

He knows she's right, but won't give in.

"Right now, I've got to see Eve," he says opening the street door. "Let's talk about it in the morning."

"Not tomorrow, tonight, you know where I live!"

"I'll call," he says and is out the door.

*

His senses cry that Eve's recovering, but when he sees her lying in bed in the darkened room at the Memorial Hospital with a tube in her mouth and feverish forehead and veiled eyes and her black hair in tangles on the pillow and goes out to the hall to find Walcott, who has little to say other than that several of the burns have become infected and that he was unprepared for it, he sinks down in a chair by her bed and watches. Gone are all his thoughts about when she'd come home (weren't they going to spend the first evening looking at the trees in Tompkins Square Park and return to the flat and make love?). The talks in the office that morning, yes, all the plans for the case no longer have meaning and resemble flight. As she lies there in bed, far away from him and him not knowing what he'll do with himself or her, he just wants to take over her fever, and when she finally says anything comprehensible, it's:

"Don't go."

And he doesn't go, he sits by her bed for hours as the darkness fills the window and covers the walls, ceiling, door, machinery, even the lamp with the orange light and her face with a new veil and transforms him and her to shadows and he hears the tap dripping and her staccato breathing and doesn't know whether he's awake or hallucinating.

Nor does he know when, but the door opens, light comes in from the hall and an older nurse with a dark face and graying hair, called Cheyenne, comes

in with a tray with hot soup and takes his place, and as he eats and partly recovers, she suggests that he go home.

"You can't do more right now," she says.

"It's serious, isn't it?"

"She's gotten fresh bandages, Dr. Walcott's good, he'll get her back on her
feet," she says.

Not realizing what he's saying, he asks her the same question over and
over, and each time she answers quietly:

"I know Eve, I've talked with her many times, she won't give up even
though it's gotten worse."

For whatever reason, maybe her calm, maybe his need to believe, he takes
her word and leaves the hospital, and only when he's sitting in a taxi and is
on his way to the empty flat on Second Avenue that he decides to see
Michelle and has the taxi drive to her flat in Upper West by Central Park. He
calls her from the cab and says he's coming and after being put down in front
of the high brick buildings with thousands of small and large flats in a complex with sports' facilities and baths, lying deserted, illuminated by long neon lights, he walks in the cool night air and with ground crunching beneath
his shoes towards the hard asphalt, to the stairwell and gets an elevator up to
the seventh floor.

A young man passes him in the long, dim hallway, looking right through
him, as Jon looks for Michelle's name plate on the many doors; he doesn't
find it and goes back and discovers that he's gotten off on the eighth floor. A
veil of unreality envelopes his senses; he has the feeling that he could keep
on walking 'round in the building without finding the right door. When he
takes the garishly lit stairway down, he passes a man of his own age, slightly
bent over, he only catches a glimpse of the light, bearded face with its dark,
staring eyes, and when he gets to the next floor and starts looking for the
door, he realizes that there was something familiar about the man's face. He
turns and rushes back to the stairs and is soon on the eighth floor with the
hall with its yellowing, bare walls that seems even longer than before and is
now completely deserted. He stands there a minute lost with his gaze into the
faintly lit darkness, a door opens farther down the hall and a young couple

walks kissing and laughing slowly towards him and glides past without noticing him. Again on his way down the stairs to the seventh floor he stops and
notices his hands sweating, he puts his briefcase down and takes off his coat.
No, the man couldn't be Ifrahim Mohammed; it's not possible, what's wrong
with him?

He hurries down the stairs and some distance down the hallway and stops
and looks back when he hears steps on the stairs and sees an older woman on
her way down. Finally he finds the name plate: Paul Beauxchamp, Michelle
Beauxchamp on a green door and knocks. Michelle opens the door, dressed
in a black skirt and blouse and a surprised smile and leads him into the in-
credibly large flat with a view – from an open kitchen with soft lighting from
several lamps – on to Central Park's enormous dark areas and illuminated
paths and the distant high rises on Fifth Avenue. He drops his briefcase,
standing a moment, taking in the view.

"Y'know Eve's lying somewhere out there, behind the buildings along the
park, at the Memorial?" he says without turning.

"How is she?" she asks just behind him, he turns half 'round and takes the
glass of wine she offers. For a few seconds, Eve's face fades over Michelle's,
he raises his free hand to his forehead, cold chills flood over him.

"Not good," he says and walks unsteadily to the closest chair and sits
down.

"What's the matter," she says, "you want to lie down?"

"I'm starting to hallucinate …"

"Hallucinate?"

"I was sure that I saw Ifrahim Mohammed on the stairs."

"Where?"

"Just outside."

"It must be someone who looks like him, there're a lot of Arabs in the
complex."

He smiles weakly, agrees and sips his wine, they talk about details for her
and Johnson's preparations for the grand jury hearing, Michelle is visibly set
on getting a handle on it all and has her own ideas. He takes another glass,
which he quickly drains and under its influence, finally relaxes, even though

his thoughts still revolve around the glowering eyes on the stairs. Once in a while Michelle disappears into her study, returning with new papers and new questions, he answers absentmindedly and notices an entire wall in the room covered with miniature heads of dragons, masks, calligraphy and framed photos of sites and street scenes from Saigon, Beijing and Hanoi. From somewhere is heard low, piercing Chinese music; only when Michelle walks over to change the cd does he realize it's coming from there.

"Paul's grown up with that kind of music and I've learned to enjoy it," she says pulling a leather armchair up next to his and sits down.

"Where?"

"In Saigon, his father was a diplomat with the French embassy. They had a house in the French quarter of the city, he went to school there and learned the language, Vietnamese and English, that's why he does so well in the Foreign Service. When he was seventeen, he and his family and a lot of Americans were evacuated by helicopter from Saigon, for his father it was a defeat, for Paul it meant a new life in New York, Hanoi, Beijing, Washington, round trip, I don't see much of him …"

"Are you sorry?"

"I don't even know if there are other women, I don't know him any more. We still have something when he's home, but I don't trust him …"

She shrugs her shoulders and holds on to his glance, but he's much too affected by Eve's condition to have any thoughts about her candour.

"Why don't you ask him what's happening?"

"I know what's happening. When the Americans closed Saigon and fled, the French embassy was also evacuated, but Paul and his father and mother didn't make it. At the last minute they got hold of a diplomatic car and drove through Saigon, it was evening, gangs ravaged the city, the city was paralyzed by fear of the communists approaching from the north, and the South Vietnamese soldiers were bitter over the Americans and French because they just gave up. On a street corner their car was stopped by two South Vietnamese soldiers ordering them out, they shouted and screamed into the car as Paul's father clenched the steering wheel and wouldn't give in. He drove forward and hit one of the soldiers, the other shot into the car and hit Paul's mother, she sank down on the seat, and when they reached the American embassy and wanted to drive past the barred gate, it was besieged by a crowd of South Vietnamese who were desperate because they were left in the city and feared that their cooperation with the Americans was the same as a death sentence when the communists got hold of them. They attacked the car, pulled Paul's mother out and he hasn't seen her since. That's what's happening."

"How did Paul and his father get through?"

"The American soldiers on the other side of the bars intervened, opened the gate, shot warning shots under howls and shouts of protest. For many years, you wouldn't notice anything about Paul, he got the best degrees, assimilated, made a lightning career. When I met him, he was already in the Foreign Service and really on the way "up", and if he came in the door now, you'd probably think him charming, a "great guy"."

"Yeah, why not?"

"He speaks English with a slight French twist that people like."

"Yeah?"

"But in some way, he's lost. He keeps on travelling out there to find her, he keeps on searching for his dead mother, but he'll never find her, no matter how many women he … has. And I can no longer reach him, he doesn't understand it himself."

"Probably not," says Jon wondering how they could rub shoulders for the past two years in the office on St. Mark's Place without knowing more about each other. "Who is she?" he thinks and again is caught in the gaze of her dark eyes and light, nervous smile, that at the same time reminds him all too much of Eve's.

He'd get up and go, but stays seated. He even takes another glass of wine, and the light from the lamps opens for the many moods that constantly change in her face. At one moment she's laughing and the next is sad, he can't follow her and finally gets up from the chair and walks over to the window to get his bag.

"Where'll you go?" she asks also getting up.

"I'll find a hotel," he says. "This won't do."

"What won't?" she asks.

"You know perfectly well," he says with a smile finding his way to the entrance where he's left his coat.

She follows him out.

"Don't treat me like a child," she says.

"I'm not," he says putting on his coat. "We're attracted to each other and that would be great some other time and place. Right now I'm thinking about Eve and your safety as well."

"Then why'd you come?"

He looks at her searching for an answer, but at that moment the door's broken in, someone out in the hall breaks it in. He steps back into the darkness of the entrance almost falling over Michelle who's shouting; it happens so quickly that he has no time to think before he's standing face to face with the broad shouldered Zawawi and the man who he'd mistaken for Ifrahim Mohammed.

For some seconds there's total silence, he senses Michelle's tense body behind his; "no, no" she says grabbing his arm, when he sees that the man resembling Mohammed is holding a gun pointed at him with an ice cold look.

"Where's the tape, give us the tape!" snarls Zawawi.

"What tape?" he says.

"You know what I mean," says Zawawi, "If we don't get it, you're done for."

He bends down to open the briefcase, there's ringing in his ears, his hands fumble in the semi-darkness of the hallway through the papers in his case and finds the cassette. He pulls it out and with throbbing temples stands two meters from the two with the tape in his hand. Michelle's still holding his arm, half hiding behind him, he feels her heart pounding against his back. Whether it's the cold eyes before him staring right into his or the feeling of imprisonment, fear, he's revolted when it occurs to him that Edelstein's killer is standing in front of him; he takes a couple of steps forward and hands the tape towards Zawawi to the right, and just as Zawawi with a crooked, self-confident sneer reaches out to take the tape, he kicks Mohammed's twin brother firmly on his shin. His gun goes off hitting Michelle, who collapses with a faint shriek. Mohammed's brother hops backwards, out into the hall-way while he whiningly holds his leg. Zawawi is momentarily confused and strikes weakly out at him and takes a few steps backwards to pick the gun up from the floor. In the confusion of the moment Jon's able to get out into the hallway where he starts running for the stairs, but the hallway seems endless. A shot is heard, a bullet whistles past him. Finally he reaches the stairway, never has he run so fast, seldom has he been so afraid, and when the cold air meets him outside the building, his body is driven forward by an inner panic towards the trees and darkness of Central Park.

Only when he's in the park, breathless seeking refuge in the bushes behind some tall pines, does he look for his possible pursuers, but the park ahead is deserted in the moonlight. Now with shaky hands he takes his phone from his coat pocket and to report the episode to the closest police station, but in his exhaustion and muddled state of mind he can't remember where it is and in-stead presses the number for New York State Police.

"What is this about?" says a terse voice moments later.

"A possible homicide," he says giving the address. "You've got to come now, a woman's been shot."

"What's the woman's name?"

He gives Michelle's full name and again looks across the deserted park with its tall dark pines and ash trees that project vague, gaudy shadows in the moonlight over the hoarfrosted lawns.

"And your name and address?"

He hesitates a moment then gives his name and address.

"Where are you now?"

"In Central Park, there are two men after me, one with a gun; you've got to send people now!"

"Where in Central Park? "

"I'm not exactly sure, in some bushes, somewhere near Belvedere Lake, I think."

"We're on the way," says the voice. "Stay where you are!"

Freezing, he stands there staring out from his hiding place across the slop-ing lawn in the pale darkness, a man suddenly appears and moves along one of the footpaths under trees farther away. The distance is too great, and he can't see him clearly, but makes up his mind that he's homeless pulling a small trolley behind him. Gradually his alarm preparedness abates and the sound of Michelle's cry when the bullet hit forces itself upon him and he feels more and more that it is he who was hit and feels himself exposed and captured where he stands, accustomed as he is to moving freely. He tries in vain to collect his thoughts, his hyper-awareness of all sounds and everything moving close by comes in the way. He now hears police sirens and recognizes the sounds of an ambulance coming closer, and without thinking clearly he starts walking across the vast lawn in the direction of one of the park exits towards Park Avenue West.

Three officers, one with a dog and other two with raised pistols appear at the other exit, one of them sees him and signals the others, and they now move towards him. He raises his hand and sets his course towards them, but one of the officers shouts and he raises his arms over his head and remains there with his hands up until they're close by, pistols still aimed at him.

"Who are you, what're you doing here?" says the officer with the dog, beginning to search his body for weapons, finding the video cassette in his trenchcoat pocket, pulling it out.

"Jon Baeksgaard, I was the one who called …"

"What's this?" he says holding the tape up in front of him.

"A cassette, a videotape. I called for you; my colleague's been shot in her flat on Park Avenue West."

"And what're you doing here?" asks one of the other officers, lowering his gun as the third officer holds his gun ready farther away.

"I was hiding in the park," he says and shows them his attorney-ID card. "It was me they were after, if I hadn't run, I would've been shot, too."

The officers look at each other, one of them, a tall, muscular man, whose sergeant stripes shine in the dark, shakes his head staring at him.

"Might be you're telling the truth, but that's for my colleagues to decide …"

"I've got to have the tape," he says. "It's important material for a case I'm handling …"

The officer ignores him, turns his back, letting him stand there as he walks a few metres away on the lawn, talking in his walkie-talkie. The other officer keeps a silent eye on him, also speaking in his walkie-talkie with the third officer who's vanished from view and now shows up between some of the pines with his dog, pulling and jerking on its lead. In the harvest moonlight, beneath its darkly yellowish sky, it all seems unreal. Distant sounds from the city reach them and he doesn't understand that from one half hour to the next is part of it.

The tall sergeant returns a moment later standing in front of him in his dark uniform with slightly spread legs. Beneath the vast starlit sky the sergeant's face is in the shadows, but one eye clearly visible, and Jon now sees his broad mouth, moving.

"Are you familiar with a woman by the name of Michelle Beauxchamp? "

"Yes," he says, "she works for me, I was visiting her …"

"She's just been declared dead, shot at close range."

"Oh no!" he says hiding his face in his hands.

"I'm sorry, but I have to ask you to come with me and identify her, and then get a statement."

"A statement? "

"As an attorney, you know what this is about."

He looks out into the darkness, he sees only contours of the trees, bushes, somewhere a bench is illuminated.

"Where were you when you called us?" asks a voice, the sergeant's.

He turns and points towards the bushes some metres away.

"We'll go back there and show me exactly where you were standing. You're sure you weren't carrying any weapons?"

"Of course, you don't think that I shot her?"

"I don't think anything. A woman's been murdered on Park Avenue West, you say you know her and had just visited her, so we're checking whether you had a weapon on you."

"Why aren't you searching for the two killers who shot Michelle?" he says.

"According to my colleagues, there's no sign of criminals in the building on Park Avenue. What'd they look like?"

He describes Zawawi and Ifrahim Mohammed's twin brother. One of the other officers joins them and jots the information down on a pad.

"And you have only the name of one of them?" says the tall sergeant impatiently.

"Yes," he says naming Benzir Zawawi.

"An Arab!?" says the officer with the notepad.

"From Saudi Arabia," he says.

His information illicits a reaction from the sergeant, again walking away and talking in his walkie-talkie, and when he returns soon after, he searches the bushes, where all three officers meticulously search for the assumed weapon which refuses to materialize.

The cool of the night penetrates to his bones, he wraps his trench coat tightly around his body as he stands there watching the three policemen, moving in an ever greater radius from the bushes and out between the dark trunks of the pines. All possible images cross his mind, but one in particular keeps returning: Michelle's frightened look when the entrance door was broken down, and from the one minute to the next is powerless, and as he turns his gaze towards the outermost edges of the park and again sets eyes on the homeless man pulling the trolley after him, he admits that it's his carelessness and presence in her flat that cost her her life. Wasn't it she that warned them that the case was too big, too dangerous? And now …

He pulls out his phone, turns his back to the officers and calls Cartwright who soon answers in a sleep-drenched voice.

"Cartwright here, d'you know what time it is?"

"I'm in Central Park …"

"What's happened?"

"The worst possible," he says. "Michelle's dead, and I'm standing here with three policemen, searching for a weapon they think I had …"

"Michelle, dead? How?"

"Shot, in her flat, it was Zawawi and Mohammed's brother, I escaped by chance, it's winding up to a hearing and I'll have to put my cards on the table, but you've got to get me Zawawi's and Hamsal's addresses …"

"Sure, of course, I'll use your mobile voice mail. Should I come?"

"Maybe later, I'll call when it's over."

"I've talked to Hamsal, under pressure he'll meet with you. It was the opening we've been waiting for."

"Yeah, but now anything can happen, if the anti-terror corps first gets hold of Hamsal and scares the shit out of him, then it's good-bye to Mohammed's alibi."

"You must feel like hell, keep cool. Try to keep Hamsal's name out of this. D'you still have the tape?"

"They confiscated it …"

"Shit …"

The sergeant's on his way over to him in the dark with an oversized flash-light whose broad cone of light makes it impossible to see his face. He walks feather light across the grass.

"If I'm not in action tomorrow, go out to Hamsal yourself, first thing, and see if you can't make him give you the alibi, remember to tape it …"

He finishes the call and slips the phone back into his coat pocket, the light from the torch wanders up over his body and face.

"No more phone calls," says the sergeant coolly.

"As long as I'm not under arrest, you can't stop me from talking to whom-ever I want," he says calmly.

"I'll put it another way: if you don't drop your phone, then you'll be ar-rested!"

"For what?"

"I don't care about your lawyer talk, just follow me," says the sergeant and lets the light rest a bit too long on his face. With a superior gesture the ser-geant turns and calls the two others out of the park and they all start walking towards the exit.

*

It might be the cold, or the reality of Michelle's death, maybe he's reached a turning point on a path where almost everything has towered up around him – didn't he used to be most certain when he had his back to the wall? This night and at this moment he feels himself clear and ready to take anything come what may. They drive him to the police station on West 96th Street, where after a preliminary hearing by a local deputy detective, who quickly realizes that there's more than a murder involved, he's driven to the massive and strongly guarded headquarters for New York Police, Police Plaza One on Park Row.

After a long wait in one over-illuminated front office after the other high in the cold building, where he senses hectic activity around him – uniformed and plain clothed police pass him many times with closed faces and efficient – he's finally brought into a large office with cabinets, book shelves with ringbinders, panelling and an oversized metal desk with a glass top. He's barely stepped across the threshold to the softly lit room with large windows onto the night and East River accompanied by an officer, who constantly keeps an eye on him, when a side door opens and three people walk in, all stonefaced: a uniformed male senior officer, a plain-dressed male Afro-American detective and a woman about forty in white blouse and black skirt with papers and something else in her hand. To his surprise, it's the woman who sits down in the leather chair behind the desk and promptly presents the two others:

"I'm Louise Black, head of the Anti-terror Corps, to my right is Police Captain Donaldson and to my left is Detective John Smith from my department. Please be seated."

They all three take their seats, the two policemen on either side of Louise Black, he on a chair which the officer has silently placed in front of the desk.

Both the older Donaldson and the younger Smith observe him in silence with a neutral gaze while Louise Black looks through her papers; at that moment he realizes that the dark item next to her papers is a video cassette.

"Let me get straight to the point," says Louise Black holding up the video cassette, "I think you know that you're up to your neck in trouble."

"How's that?" he asks.

"A cassette that documents a planned terrorist attack on Jay Street Station in Brooklyn, I don't know if you're aware of what happened in New York on September 11th?"

"Yes," he says, "better than most."

But Louise Black, waving the cassette back and forth ignores him.

"Three officers find you in Central Park with this cassette in your possession and near a flat where one of your employees, Michelle Beauxchamp, was shot at close range. We know you were in the flat a half hour earlier, and that you maintain that two men, one named of Arabian origins killed her while you were in the flat."

"Yes, that's what happened."

"And by a miracle you escaped unharmed from the flat even though you maintain that the two Arabs were after you?"

"No, not by a miracle, I kicked the gunman in the shins and got away."

"From two cold-blooded killers with a gun?" interrupts Donaldson shaking his head. "Not very likely."

"I'm sitting here," he says. "I got away."

"Yeah, maybe from them, but not from us!" says Donaldson leaning forward towards him with a self-confident look.

"What d'you mean by that?" says Jon controlling his anger.

"What if I told you," says Louise Black not moving in her chair, "that the most likely is that in one way or another you were in cahoots with the two killers and the three others on the tape. What do you say to that?"

"That's crazy," he says. "I'm about to clear up a case for my client Ifrahim Mohammed …"

"A Moslem, accused of premeditated murder of an Hasidic Jew!" interrupts John Smith.

"Yeah an American with a Moslem background also has the right to a defense."

"You yourself have a foreign background, don't you think it's strange this interest and association with residing Moslems?" says Louise Black brushing a hair from her pale face.

"How do you know my background?"

"I'm not at liberty to say."

He breathes deeply, the three in front of him eye his every move, every detail in his face, but he senses with his long experience that they're groping in the dark and professionally hide their irritation that they've unexpectedly fallen over a tape, that while the entire nation's arming for a war against terror and are at a loss what to do about not having avoided a catastrophe that could give some sort of signal. But he won't be part of that signal; he won't be mixed in with the flushing out of "all evil powers." And instead of questioning his detention and the character of the meeting he proceeds – despite many interruptions – to explain the true elements of the case. Trained as he is in procedure, he gets to his feet, paces back and forth in front of the desk, turns and uses his hands to underscore his points, all improvised and semiconscious, and the closer he gets to the conclusion – his presence in Central Park – the more his fear dissolves, and when he again sits down and has said the last word for the moment, Louise Black, Donaldson and Smith sit silent long, casting poorly disguised glances to each other.

"Your explanation puts things in a new light," says Louise Black and smiles slightly for the first time. "But there are still some unanswered questions. Some of them we'll have to return to, but here's one: Why didn't you come to us immediately with your suspicions and the video tape?"

"Because I only knew and was sure about the tape's contents since yesterday," he says evasively.

"Yes, but suspicion must've been there after your first meeting with your client!"

"At that time I wasn't sure about what it implied and yesterday I figured that I needed a couple more days to press one of the involved with the cassette. Of course it was a mistake, a huge mistake."

"Your misjudgment probably cost Michelle Beauxchamp her life," says Louise Black holding his gaze. "For as long as you had the cassette or a copy, you and your closest will be a target, if your story is true."

"I know," he says, "I know that now, but …"

"What?"

"I was thinking first and foremost about my client."

"And what about the many New Yorkers, who were and are in danger if that gang of terrorists led by that Arab …" says Donaldson searching for the name.

"Zawawi!" says Smith.

"What if this Zawawi and his Arabian gang had succeeded in blowing up Jay Street Station?" says Donaldson correcting himself.

"They didn't," he says "and an important reason for that was that the tape revealed their plans and my client had seen the tape."

Donaldson angrily gets to his feet.

"You apparently don't understand shit. You haven't gotten it – how those criminals think, these Arabs and Moslems are prepared for anything. What guarantee do you have that your client isn't a part of the entire conspiracy, too!?"

"The tape is my guarantee," he says. "And by the way, you'll get no where if you put all Moslems in one box. You've got to consider each situation by itself, the same for people."

"Free me of your sermons! They're fucking not human, but mad dogs the bunch of them."

"Even Bush has managed to separate the majority of peaceful Moslems from the few violent fanatics …"

"Bush, Mr. Bush ..." says the increasingly choleric Donaldson, barely getting the words out, "that college boy, I'll tell you one thing: Mr. Bush is a pansy, if it hadn't been for Cheney and Rumsfeld, America wouldn't be standing!"

Louise Black sternly waves Donaldson back to his seat, more questions follow and she finally makes it clear to Jon that she'd like to quickly start an investigation, and that she expects that he neither talk about the case to anyone nor do anything without consulting her department.

"I can promise silence to others and also to keep in touch with your department," he says, "but I have a client to defend, a man accused of premeditated murder on false pretenses!"

"He just doesn't stop!" says Donaldson annoyed.

Louise Black looks at him with cold eyes. He can't decide whether there's something behind the face, an empathy, sympathy or whether she's long ago buried her senses in the police state's efficient machinery.

"If you want, we can close the case on Ifrahim Mohammed indefinitely, it's a question of higher priorities, we could call it state security. Give me a reason why we should let you keep your case."

"I can get my client acquitted on a solid alibi, that alibi one of the small fry in the case gets my client, if you give me one day to establish it."

"And how will you do that?"

"If you get the District Attorney to accept that I offer him a reduced sentence in exchange for giving my client the alibi, signed and witnessed. And if you don't send an army to arrest him in Brooklyn tonight or tomorrow morning, but let it happen discreetly, I can do it. In return, you get his address. His name is Hamsal."

From the inner pocket of his jacket he takes a piece of paper and hands it over the glazed desk to Louise Black, who scans it briefly and passes it on to Smith.

In the windows behind them stretches the dark evening sky endlessly, distant lights on the other side of East River are small dots in an unreal tableau. It's as if the building floats through the night, he momentarily sees Eve's feverish face and veiled, dark eyes, almost unbearable fatigue overpowers him. He holds on to the arm-rests of the chair vaguely hearing Louise Black.

"I can meet you concerning the District Attorney and a deal, but we can't risk not arresting your man for a few days. He could get away and that risk I won't take. You have until tomorrow afternoon and have to accept that Smith and my people are right on your back and will do whatever's necessary as soon as you've talked to him. Are you sure that he's even at his address?"

"Yes," he says distantly.

"We'll keep him under observation from tonight," says Louise Black motioning that the meeting is at an end.

Donaldson quickly gets to his feet and leaves the room, Smith walks over to him, and Louise Black is already on the phone pressing some numbers. He tries to get up from the chair, but only when Smith with a slight smile gives him a helping hand does he get to his feet.

"Thanks," he says observing the eyes in Smith's young, dark, smooth face. "Only a boy," he thinks as Smith leads him out of the office and a moment later in the sharply lit and deserted front office and offers him a lift by police car to Second Avenue.

"Rather a cab," he says, "and I'm not going back to my flat."

"Where to?"

"A hotel."

"Good idea with two killers running around town after you."

"Then you believe my "story"?"

"If my boss does, then …" says Smith and fishes his phone out of his jacket and calls a taxi.

With difficulty Jon puts on his coat.

"The cab's waiting some way down Park Row – because of all our security," says Smith a moment later, giving him a pass and following him to the elevator in the gray hallway now devoid of people.

"It's best if you find a small anonymous hotel," he adds.

"Hotel Chelsea Inn, 17th Street."

"OK, I'll have one of our cars keep an eye on the hotel tonight, but we can't guarantee your safety."

"I haven't asked you to," he says entering the elevator, whose doors have just opened. When he turns towards Smith, his eyes meet his own ghostlike image in the long, narrow mirror.

"Depending on our success, there'll probably be witness protection later," says Smith reaching into the elevator to press a button. "Under no circumstances, don't leave the country."

In his daze of fatigue, Smith's black face is transformed to that of a doll's, the doors slide closed automatically and he's staring into a shiny gray wall reflecting the blindingly sharp light. Something starts moving and he discovers that he's on the way down. Down, down …

*

Twenty minutes later the cab lets him off in the darkness of 17th Street in front of a dimly lit four-story redstone from the 1800's with bay windows, squeezed between larger and newer buildings on either side – Hotel Chelsea

Inn. Many tries on the bell and the sleepy porter finally lets him in, but informs him that there are no vacancies and he must use the last of his powers of persuasion to get a small guest room on the first floor. He goes up the steep, crooked and creaking stairway in the kitsch hotel and dizzily arrives at the room with framed flower drawings and 19th century etchings of sailing ships on the walls and a yellowed curtain over the door to the balcony facing the backyard. He's previously had reason to hide out at the hotel, when relatives to clients or the condemned crowded him and kept him from doing his job, but this time he doesn't feel safe and considers, as he slowly undresses and creeps under the covers, all the possibilities the two killers have to hide in the city. Even intensely wanted criminals can hide for years under an assumed name, in disguise or at false addresses in New York, like an ocean for shady fish.

He's barely fallen asleep before he once again is back in the dark, moonlit Central Park with its black tree trunks, hills, statues, mirrored lakes and figures. Something forces him forward, like a plaintive voice, but he can't identify it, maybe the voice of a woman, maybe something coming from himself; a homeless man suddenly appears next to him begging for money, he empties his pockets and hands him what he has and goes on in the direction of the sound, which gradually becomes more clear and full. Two tall maples tower up in front of him, and as he walks between them he sees far away a woman on a bench at the edge of the park. She's wearing a yellow cloak, her face and bare arms are chalky white. On her breast is a red spot, utter motionless as in a tableau, she's holding one hand up against her equally white throat. From the black hair and the plaintive voice he recognizes Michelle and calls to her as his moves in her direction, but at that moment her voice is overpowered by another's, and the woman turns her gaze towards him, catches his glance as she grabs her throat and he can see that it's Eve.

He awakes in panic with a hand on his throat gasping for air, steps onto the floor and for a few seconds doesn't know where he is. Quickly he remembers that he's in a hotel room. He turns on a lamp and finds his phone and presses the number to the Memorial Hospital. Through several channels he reaches a nurse in the burns unit.

"I've got to know something about Eve Letterman," he says.

"What do you want to know?"

"Her condition," he says. "The last time I saw her it was very poor."

"Just a minute," says the voice and then silence at the other end. He stares at the yellowing curtain and thinks he hears sounds from the backyard.

"Anyone there?" he calls into the receiver.

"According to Dr. Walcott she's recovering slightly, in the right direction …"

"Are you sure?" he asks sensing his relief.

"Yes, she's been asking for you. You can visit her tomorrow."

He thanks her and hangs up. Stands a moment listening to the darkness, then turns off the lamp and walks to the balcony door, lifts the curtain and looks down into the yard. Beneath a high, slim ash still with some leaves, the yard is filled with junk and white garden furniture. One part of the yard is dimly lit by a lamp over the gate; the other part leading to a second gate is dark. The high walls around the yard are peeling and massive. Isn't a man standing there staring up at his window? From the yard an iron stairway leads up to a shed roof with a small balustrade, and from the roof there's only a few metres to the French balcony with cast iron bars in front of the doors to his room. How easy it would be to climb up to him and …

He gulps and feels utterly unprotected as his eyes again seek the staring glance in the yard's black corner. Suddenly the eyes are gone and a cat races across the light patch in the yard and vanishes between a couple of planks.

That's what it was; only now he sees the contours of the garbage can in the darkness where it must've been sitting.

A cat with yellow eyes. Is he going mad?

Tomorrow early he's got to get hold of Cartwright before he does anything stupid. It's four AM, he sets his watch for seven and again dives under the covers to a heavy, uneasy sleep that takes him to the snow-clad Türkenschanzpark in Vienna and to Tobias with a sled, Tobias turns his back on him at the top of a hill, sits down on the sled and disappears down the hill that seems without end. The next moment he's in a crowd on Fifth Avenue in the middle of the day, some distance in front of him, between many faces, appears the brother of Ifrahim Mohammed in a dark suit with a case under his arm; he ducks his head and goes to the side, opening a door between two show windows into a room that surprisingly is a mosque with red carpets spread on the floor and Arabic calligraphy on the walls. About one hundred followers stand gathered around a pulpit, and from that pulpit Ifrahim Mohammed's brother is speaking garbed in burnus and skull cap.

"Fight for God against those who fight against you," he says holding a copy of the Koran up before the group. "If they turn their backs on you, grab them and kill them, wherever they are. Allah is great!"

The group repeats his words as Mohammed's brother stares self -assured over them, their eyes meeting. He stiffens momentarily, Mohammed's brother points in his direction and now most in the group turn towards him. He turns, runs to the door, but can't open it, already feels the breath of many on their way towards him. The door opens and he staggers into the daylight of Fifth Avenue, the buildings shimmering in the sun.

In fear we are confronted with our own death, says Heidegger, but if we combat fear, is it with our life at stake?

The first he sees when his watch wakes him at 7 in bed in the weak morning light from the window is Ifrahim Mohammed's peaceful and sad face, but when he again closes his eyes half asleep the face of his twin brother with the glowering eyes glides over. He shivers and quickly gets to his feet, pulls on his trousers and with a small piece of wrapped soap and a fragrant, fresh towel goes down the hallway with the white painted doors to the narrow bathroom with sink and shower. He steps naked under the shower, stands there long and lets the lukewarm water flow down over his hair, head and body to wake up. It's long since he feels as relaxed as now and suddenly longs to hold his son in his arms or just see him again. Maybe Tobias could relate to him, maybe he's even gotten a language that they could share, wasn't that what Sine had suggested in their last con-

versation? An expert in autism had assessed him to lie on the border of As-
perger's syndrome …

Thousands of kilometres away, on the other side of the Atlantic, his son's
walking around, seeing the world in a special, splintered way, that's his, and
that he'd like to share with him.

But what's he doing in New York City, is there anything here that's more
important than his son, that sphinx in his life, whom he'd left behind because
he couldn't figure out how to live with his mother?

Not even Eve understood him on that point, "I'd never have left my child",
she told him one evening as they lay in bed in their flat on Second Avenue
smoking cigarettes after making love.

"If I hadn't come back to New York, we'd never have met," he surprisingly said to her. "Has that occurred to you?"

"You didn't know we'd meet," said Eve and looked at him in her own candid way. "Your starting point was that you left your son and your girlfriend.
A girlfriend can be left, but not a son."

He turns off the shower and dries his body with the fresh towel and feels
how little time he's had to just think and how much he misses Eve's candour.

Already on his way back through the hall to his room his body tenses and
as he quickly puts on his shirt and the next minute reaches for his phone to
call Cartwright, he's again that person he's dreamed of being, but who's been
carried away by unexpected events and more alien to himself because everything's happened too quickly.

"Cartwright here," says Cartwright's sleep-drenched voice in the phone.

"You awake?"

"Sure I am, but I still can't understand Michelle's dead."

"Me, too."

"Have you talked with her husband?"

"Not yet, he's away and I assume the police are trying to find him," he
says and sketches the night's events for him.

"Then you've made a deal with the police?" says Cartwright skeptically.

"Yeah, we've got 24 hours to get an alibi for Mohammed from Hamsal, you've got to get hold of him and arrange a meeting today; we'll both drive out to Brooklyn."

"Maybe he's flown the coop, have you considered that?"

"No, his address is being watched by the police's anti-terror corps, so he doesn't have a chance to run."

"And if he tries?"

"They'll be on his heels."

"Since when do you trust the police?"

"In this case we've no choice, and I want my client acquitted before it's all blacked out."

"Fine, I'll call Hamsal ..."

"And you call me back right away?"

"Sure," says Cartwright hanging up.

He puts on his jacket and walks out into the hall with its framed flower pictures and down the crooked stairs, past the porter who distractly nods to him and out on the street where its cold and damp and down to the basement where a young, smiling woman in jeans and shirt takes his coupon for a continental breakfast and hands him a bag with a danish, butter and juice and a closed cup of hot coffee. But by the time he turns to go back to the hotel and climb the stairs his phone rings, he gets it out of his pocket with his free hand and presses it open as he continues up the stairs. At the hall, his dizziness returns, the white doors blind him and at first he doesn't hear what the voice is saying. Only when he's found his way into the room and sits down on the bed does he realize that it's Smith asking him to come to Police Plaza One to identify Michelle's body.

"We've gotten 'til the day after tomorrow and I'm expecting a call from my colleague," he says. "It can't be now."

"Sometime today, latest tomorrow," says Smith abruptly. "We've gotto get on with the case."

"I figure we'll pay Hamsal a visit sometime today, ASAP."

"I'm going out there myself in a half hour; in the meantime I have my people in position close by. There's a flat on the second floor of Atlantic Avenue with stairs opening to the street. When you come out, wave your right arm, if everything's OK we'll move in and arrest the man. It'll be discreet as promised."

"Have you postponed the grand jury hearing?"

"No problem, but there's something else ..."

"Yeah?"

"We want our money's worth."

"What d'you mean?"

"If you get your alibi for your client and Hamsal gets a reduced sentence, then you've got to persuade Hamsal to promise to witness against his collaborators ..."

"That's not my job, that's yours," he says and turns his gaze towards the sallow daylight through the yellowing curtain.

"If I was you, I'd listen ..."

"What d'you mean?"

"Your attitude could easily be misinterpreted."

"How?" he says already sensing where Smith is going.

"Do I need to spell it out?"

"Yeah," he says.

"Right now the only thing that matters in this country: Are you for or against Moslem terrorists?"

"I don't have to answer. You already know."

"Exactly. Therefore we're expecting you to do your duty."

"I do what I can as an attorney," he says. "I can't promise more. My job is keeping my client out of prison for something he didn't do; and if at the same time I can help you arrest a suspected terrorist, then I'll do that."

"I'm not sure you have a choice."

"Are you threatening me?"

"Call it what you like," says Smith.

"That's what I call it," he says and hangs up.

He remains seated on the bed and feels he's surrounded by quicksand. He starts eating and drinking the hot coffee, the phone rings, it's Cartwright who's arranged a meeting with Hamsal at 10 the same day and will pick Jon up in his car in half an hour.

"Did he understand what it's about?" he asks.

"I'm not sure," says Cartwright. "He seems scared to death."

"Did you tell him anything about the tape?"

"Yeah, but I had to promise not to go to the police with it, it was his condition for meeting us."

"So did you?"

"What else could I do?" says Cartwright.

"No, OK," he says and turns off the phone.

He gets up from the bed and walks over to the window, pulls the curtain aside and looks out as he eats the danish. When was the last time he ate anything that tasted good?

The scene outside the balcony door is totally changed, the ash trees tall dark trunks leading up to its many branches with sporadic green leaves glistens in the gray diserted yard. He stands there staring at the leaves dangling from the branches in the faint breeze and will soon fall.

Why does he have the feeling of something soon over?

Oh yeah, he's almost forgotten. Michelle is dead and wasn't it him that had brought Death to her? She'd invited him and he was stupid enough to accept, because he needed someone to talk to, no, because he was attracted to her or maybe a little of both.

His idiotic thoughtlessness is to blame for her death.

He's got to find her killer, not be afraid, abandon his lawyer jacket, ally himself with Smith or the Devil himself and pump Hamsal for everything he knows.

But is that him? Can he do it?

Also not having happiness can – as seen from heaven – be happiness, says Wolfgang Koeppen. But if one doesn't know what happiness is, how how can it ever be found, heavenly or worldly? Does one not first get a sense of it when it already has paid a visit and left the house empty?

Cartwright's waiting for him in his light blue Ford Costumline in front of the hotel when he a comes down the crooked stairs a half an hour later and walks onto 17th Street, where several orthodox Jews in their traditional dark dress and crisp white shirts are gathered in front of a door on the other side of the hotel. One of them crushes a cigarette out under his dark shoes, two others smilingly greet each other, a fourth looks guardedly in his direction holding on to his black hat that's almost almost blown away by a sudden gust of wind through the street. As he gets in the car and Cartwright quickly pulls out from the curb and down the street towards the pulsating Fifth Avenue, which the next moment lies open like a gray shaft before them, the smell of sulphur and burning hanging everywhere in the air is in his nostrils and deep in his consciousness there's the image of the hogtied and deathly stiff Edelstein in the office of his jewelry store in Williamsburg.

How many more deaths are waiting for them in this case, that already seems to be one of those without an end?

Uncommonly mute and tight-lipped, Cartwright pilots the car onto the road under Brooklyn Bridge's mycelium of iron wires and a formless leaden sky; a couple of prams are seen far out on the foggy horizon past the East River. Only when they land with the Ford humming on the Brooklyn side and turn north along the deserted and filthy warehouses and factories, does Cartwright speak:

"We were wrong trying to handle the case ourselves, we were unprepared. Michelle warned us and now she's dead. I'll never forgive myself."

"Same here," he says. "Let's try getting as much as we can out of Hamsal and then decide what we'll do."

"I'm ready to go all the way," says Cartwright quickly looking over to him.

"And what's that for you?" he asks.

"*All* the fucking way," says Cartwright, as he takes a short cut to Atlantic Avenue turning the car to the right between two highrise apartment complexes.

"Also with the anti-terror corps?"

"With or without the police. This time we know what we're up against, we've got to find those killers. And detective work is what we're good at. Remember what you did in Vienna."

"That was seven years ago," he says, "I'm not sure I'm up to the pressure again, not to mention Eve."

"You're not alone ...," says Cartwright and again is silent.

Some time later they drive onto the busy Atlantic Avenue and park the car a few blocks from the address and walk the last stretch past the many businesses and shops, coming to a shabby five-story brick building, the front door locked with a small intercom and button device, but no names of the residents.

"It's the third floor to the left," says Cartwright, pressing the button to the third floor.

They stand waiting in the cold as people pass them on the pavement; he presses again looking around at the buildings nearby to catch a glimpse of Smith, but to no avail. Time passes; then a voice with a touch of Arabian saying.

"Who's there?"

He gives his name.

"Are you with anyone?" says the frightened voice in the scratchy loudspeaker.

" Cartwright, my assistant."

"No one else?"

"No."

"How can I be sure?"

"You'll have to trust me."

Noisely the front door is pressed open and they enter the narrow, murky stairwell, that smells of oil and garlic, the steps beneath them creak as they quickly make their way up. They get to a flaking door on the third floor, he knocks; a moment later it opens halfway and a nervous, pale, unshaven face looks questioningly at them from a dimly lit entrance. He recognizes Hamsal, who's in a white shirt, dark trousers and stocking feet, as if he's on his way to a wedding. For a few seconds he feels some sympathy with the thin man's visible nervosity and remembers so clearly Zawawi's coercion from the video in the service station. From his awkwardly stooping movements as he leads them into the plainly furnished living room with carpeting, framed calligraphy on the walls, shelves with photos of his family, a soft, worn velvet sofa, a portable TV and a small, low table with a dusty fruit bowl and ashtray, he sees immediately how weak he is and how easily he could break if they push him too hard. If he knew that his flat was under surveillance by people who were waiting to arrest him and lock him up for a long time, he'd probably do something desperate.

So they'll have to deceive him on that point and slowly lift the veil of the inevitable and at the same time get the necessary information before it's too late – for him, a hair-fine balance and a game of cat and mouse.

And for that reason it's Cartwright who has the first word as they take off their coats and shoes and are seated across from Hamsal by the table, each with their cup of sweet, hot chai that his young wife with black head covering has brought to them on a metal tray. Cartwright turns on a small tape recorder and says:

"We've talked several times on the phone, and you know we want you to confirm that your cousin Ifrahim Mohammed was at his service station here on Atlantic Avenue on August 14th at 7:15 PM, that is, at the time that he is charged with having killed Mr. Edelstein in Williamsburg.

"Turn that off," says Hamsal pointing to the tape recorder as he inhales smoke from his cigarette.

"We want your testimony on tape," says Cartwright, smiling slightly.

"Turn it off!" Hamsal repeats, his eyes searching Jon's, who bends over towards the table and turns off the recorder.

"I have a paper here that says about the same," he says taking a folded sheet out of the inner pocket of his jacket and smoothing it out on the table in front of Hamsal. "You have only to sign it."

"I can't", says Hamsal taking a deeper drag from his cigarette and with tense fingers stubs it out in the ashtry on the table.

"Why not?" says Cartwright hissing.

"I can't remember exactly what I did that evening. I told the police."

They look suspiciously at him, but his eyes glide away, the next moment he pulls a pack of cigarettes out of the breast pocket of his shirt, takes a new cigarette, and with a trained hand, pulls a lighter out of his trouser pocket and lights it.

"We have a tape, you know which tape, the tape made at your cousins' service station, that tape seriously incriminates you," says Jon.

"I don't know anything about a tape," says Hamsal shaking his head.

"Sure you do," says Cartwright. "According to your cousin, who's now charged with premeditated murder, you know exactly what tape."

"He's lying!"

"We're certain he's telling the truth."

"I don't know anything about a tape," says Hamsal.

"Listen," says Jon, "we'll give you a chance."

"No you can't, no one can."

"Listen to us: The police know everything about you, they know that you were prepared to be part of a bomb attack on Jay Street Station, it's all on that tape that they have. You can be sure of that."

"How'd they know?" says Hamsal getting to his feet and staring at him. "You've told the police."

He clenches his hands, white in the face.

"We haven't told anyone, one of my colleagues was shot last night. You know who shot her."

"I don't know anything."

"The police confiscated the tape, they've seen it, and they're ready to make a deal with you if you give Mohammed an alibi and witness against Zawawi and Mohammed's brother."

"You're working for the police!"

"No, but I've gotten their word that you'll get a reduced sentence if you give me that alibi and cooperate with them. You stand to be charged for some serious crimes that could send you to prison without any chance of parole for the rest of your life. If you value your life, your wife's, your child's, then think it over. I don't think you'll get another chance."

Hamsal sits a moment, looking from one to the other, trying to find a way in to himself through their eyes, but he sees only two strangers whom he frankly doesn't understand and fights with himself to trust. His young wife opens the door to the lounge with a baby in her arms and asks him something in Arabic; he's confused and waves her out of the room, gets up from the table, walks to the window and looks down to the street. His shoulders move upward, he's still holding the cigarette in one hand, but no longer smokes, the other hand rubbing his neck, he sighs. The long ash on the cigarette drops down to the floor.

Perhaps it was decided there, or he might've decided several hours earlier, but in a frightened, blurred state of mind; at 3 o'clock that morning, Zawawi phoned him from an unknown place in the city, agitated and shouting because he hadn't, as planned, come to Mohammed's service station on Atlantic Avenue and drove with them to "that woman on Central Park Avenue" to guard him and Laban Mohammed in their search for the tape and the "laughable lawyer" who'd stolen it and would bring them trouble; it was his fault that they hadn't gotten that "laughable lawyer", he got away and now the woman's dead and they had to hide from the police; he must come right away to their hiding place, that was the least he could do and if he told anyone, he knew what they'd do, he wouldn't see his child or wife again; maybe they'd seek revenge anyway because he'd let them down, Laban Mohammed tolerated no betrayal. Zawawi kept shouting in the phone until he gave him an address where they could hide and slammed down the receiver. The rest of the night Hamsal wandered restlessly through the flat, pacing to and fro in the lounge in an ambivalent nervous state of mind not able to collect his thoughts. His young wife, whom he'd married last year in a mosque on Atlantic Avenue and has a child with; she'd come from Saudi Arabia not knowing anything about American life, came in to him and was worried, but he couldn't talk to her. How could he ever confide in her what he'd gotten messed up in because they always pressured him? At first he - alone as he was – had been attracted by the thought of their special Moslem fellowship. Zawawi had introduced him to the world of the Koran and named names of sheiks that he'd never heard before. Five-six Moslem men, searching as himself, had met regularly in Zawawi's flat, and there, the meeting with Laban Mohammed, who could talk your ears off on the West's godlessness and the corruption of money and the Americans' satanic hangup to subjugate the entire Moslem world and enter into alliances with despotic regimes, had been a revelation for him. They also helped him with money and a flat on Atlantic Avenue instead of the miserable room he'd lived in for years on the South Side. But when he realized what they wanted of him, and he secretly regretted, there was no way out, he was swept along by sweet persuasion, threats and force, something great would happen in New York that would make the entire world open their eyes to the Moslems' cause and would prove Moslem superiority, and he would be play a small, but important role at Jay Street Station, he could be part of the small breeze that augured the storm. But instead of a breeze, it was a murder with a gun and now another, and he also had a gun in his tool box in the kitchen closet which he'd not yet gotten rid of because he wasn't sure whether he needed it. Now he does.

Now he's decided. He'll liberate his wife and child and cousin. For once in his life he'd do something that means something for someone.

He turns towards Jon and Cartwright and suddenly appears collected.

"I'll sign," he says and walks to the table, picks up the paper and reads it slowly.

"You're absolutely certain what you're signing?" says Jon surprised handing him a pen.

"Yes," says Hamsal. "I'm signing that Ifrahim was in the service station together with me at the time when the murder took place in Williamsburg."

"You're also signing that your alibi for Mohammed is given freely and without any form of coercion."

"Yes," says Hamsal and sits down by the table and writes his name with large, clear letters on the paper.

"Are you prepared to witness against Laban Mohammed and Ben Zawawi in a possible court trial?"

"Yes," say Hamsal smiling a tired smile as he runs his hand across his pale face.

"Do you mind confirming that with a new signature?" asks Cartwright handing a piece of paper to Jon.

"No," he says. "Just give me the paper and then leave me in peace. OK?"

Jon quickly composes the statement on the paper and hands it to Hamsal, who signs without reading.

Then they get up, Jon folds the papers and sticks them in the inner pocket of his jacket.

Hamsal smiles again cautiously, his gaze dreamy, as if he sees something far away.

As they walk across the soft carpeting towards the entrance and the brown painted door to the stairs and crouch down to put on their shoes, Hamsal follows; from a room on the other side of the living room a child's cries are heard. Hamsal listens calmly, his body relaxed and he even jokes about the smell of garlic throughout the building. He's another person.

Suddenly he says off handedly:

"I have an address for you, take it as a gift."

And he says a street name and house number in New Jersey.

"What'll we do with this address?" asks Cartwright.

"Keep an eye on the flat on the first floor, then you'll see."

Jon's put on his trench coat and takes a step towards Hamsal, the dark eyes in his pale face still have a strange gleam. Something tells him that this is the last time he'll see him, or has he really underestimated him?

"I assume you know …"

"Know what?"

"Who shot Mr. Edelstein?"

"You know that yourself," says Hamsal.

"Could be, but I'd like to hear it from you."

"Look at Laban Mohammed's little finger …"

"What d'you mean?"

"There's no more time, please go," says Hamsal and opens the door for them.

They nod to him, leave the flat and mystified walk down the stairs, first when they're standing in front of the door to street they stop and look at each other in silence. They've gotten everything they asked for, but something's wrong. He turns and runs up to the third floor and rings the bell, no one opens. It's completely quiet, his temples are pulsing. In the hall, a cry is heard through the door to the flat.

"Allahu Akbar!"

It's Hamsal's falsetto voice. A shot is heard, its echo hangs in the air and is followed by a dull thud like a heavy body falling against something hard. He tries pushing the door in, a few seconds elapse, a woman screams from the flat, a child cries, he hears steps behind him, he turns expecting to see Cartwright, but it's Smith and two other unknowns with raised pistols and padded bulletproof vests on the way up to him. Smith shoves him aside, and before he knows what's happened, the two others have broken down the door with tools they'd brought with them and are already in the flat from which the woman's cries and shouts get louder.

"Don't touch anything!" he shouts; now Cartwright's on the third floor.

"What's happened?" says Cartwright putting his hand on Jon's shoulder; shocked, Jon shakes his head and leans against the wall in the hallway. Cartwright looks enquiringly at him and disappears in the flat. Someone's closed the door, sounds of the men's voices from inside mix with the woman's and the child's crying, like from a large conch, he'd get away, down the stairs to the street, but for some minutes he's frozen to the spot.

When he's halfway down, Cartwright's caught up with him, but can't capture the eyes in Cartwright's tense face.

"Hamsal's shot himself, there's a helluva lot of blood, the whole kitchen's covered, even the windows. Good you didn't see it."

"But you did," he says putting a hand on his shoulder.

"I've seen a lot in my time," says Cartwright closing his eyes. "But this wasn't necessary; the guy has a wife and child. What was he thinking?"

"They must've put a noose around his neck," he says. "backed him into a corner, I don't know. Right now, I can't take any more, I can't think, I'm going to be sick..."

They look at each other in defeat, they go down towards the street door, it seems forever. Before they reach the door they hear the sharp, enervating sound of an ambulance's siren and when they open the door to the teeming Atlantic Avenue with its sea of neon signs, burger bars, delicatessens and clothing stores, movies, green grocers, coffee shops, banks, renovated house fronts and ugly houses in the gray light of day, he can still hear the woman's screams deep in his head. The sky is impenetrable somewhere farther up than he'll ever reach.

A yellow ambulance stops in front of the door, two men in antiseptic green overalls rush out, one of them with a folded stretcher in hand. An instant later they've disappeared up the stairs, he'd go back up with them, maybe there is something he can do; but Cartwright grabs him on the sidewalk before he reaches the door.

"There's nothing you can do right now," he says smiling weakly.

Cartwright knows him too well. Sometimes that's an advantage.

*

Eve's sitting up in bed when he arrives a half an hour later, still shaken, at her room on the second floor of the Memorial Hospital, where Cartwright's dropped him off. Cartwright's waiting for him in his car to drive them to Police Plaza One and a "talk" with Smith, who's been in telephone contact with him several times.

"What's happened? You look awful," she says when he sits down beside her and silently takes her hand trying to smile, searching for something in her dark eyes in the room with its open curtains that is surprisingly bright in the daylight, like her skin.

He doesn't reply, doesn't know where to start or end. Instead he says:

"We'll talk about it later. What matters now is you."

"No, I want to know what's happening," she says squeezing his hand.

"You're looking better," he says.

"I've gotten lots of pills and can't stand it any more. I just want to get well. But what's wrong?"

"I've been worried about you, think about you all the time."

"That's not it, I know you. Something's really wrong," she says and puts both of her hands on his.

He pulls his hand away, gets up and walks over to the window. The trees outside dissolve in a fog. Through a crack between two apartment buildings he falls into a revery at the sight of the yellow leaved plantains in Central Park. It's as if they form a portal to something he's long sought. He turns towards her.

"You're crying," she says.

Confused he wipes the tears away with his hand and sits down on the chair by her bed.

"Michelle's dead."

"Dead ... ?!"

"Not just Michelle, also a man, a cousin to my client, an hour ago ..."

"What is it you're saying?"

He takes her hand and tries to recount what's happened in the many weeks where he hadn't been able to talk to her, but he doesn't quite succeed, he confuses days and his words seem to run into a blank wall.

"I knew there was something," she says, "I could feel it, it must've been horrible."

"Not so much for me, but for the two and their families ... Michelle's husband doesn't even know yet."

"And for you. You've got to drop the case, we've got to get away from this city," she says and he sees how tired she's become. He helps her lie down flat on the bed. The burns on her legs still hurt, but they finally find a position where she can rest.

"There's a nurse here who looks in on me every day," she says smiling.

"Cheyenne?"

"You've met her?"

"I've talked to her on the phone."

"She's amazing."

"Those kind of people do exist," he says thinking then how hard it'll be when she moves back into the flat on Second Avenue with Laban Mohammed and Zawawi still at large in the city. What'll he say to her? Hasn't he said enough for one day?

He can't find peace with himself and catches himself wanting to get up. He looks at his watch regretting it as he does; her face is lovely, but it's like looking at something that he can't hold fast, something that's become strange to him, and he doesn't know what to do with the feeling and is suddenly afraid of himself. She senses his unease and sees a strange pain in his face which she doesn't know. His clothing seems different, his gaze is out of tune, his gestures awkward, is he at all here, can she reach him?

"You've got to drop all of it," she says, "it's killing you."

"I can't," he says, "there's too much at stake."

"What?"

"Among other things, two fanatics who could do anything."

"That's a job for the police."

"It's mine, too. I owe it to Michelle."

"And what about me?"

"What d'you mean?"

"What's happening to you also affects me."

"Try to understand: I'm forbidden to leave the city, I have to witness in the trial against these two when they're found, and as long as they're still at large, in one way or another I'll be in mortal danger."

"Then the police have to protect you!"

"They'll do that first if I witness in the trial against the two…"

She stares at him.

"Cartwright's helping you?"

"Yeah."

"When I get on my feet, I'll help, too …"

"It's too dangerous …"

"No," she says and would say more, but her voice fails and she closes her eyes and dozes off.

He draws the curtains, sits some time by her side making sure that she's asleep. He kisses her and leaves the room, goes into the hall, down the stairs

and through the noisy vestibule with the many patient arrivals and out to the
waiting car in the blinding light of day.

*

Tel Aviv. Eve's back, she dreams: The palms and their long fanlike shadows
beneath the burning sun on the road in front of the low white buildings with
their rounded portals on the Tel Aviv University campus; the white beach
with sunchairs and the hundreds of sunbathers and bathers in the blue
Mediterranean water and the endless horizon; Yarqon Park with the red flowers in the botanical garden, the cedars, Rokah Boulevard and the Yarqon
River's opaque water; the clamour of the many pedestrians on Sheinkin
Street, the coolness of Azrieli Center's smooth marble floor, the white Bau-
haus houses with small windows and balconies on the shady side that she
passed with Ben when they walked so many evenings to their little one-and-
a-half room flat in Ramat Aviv. Now she's walking next to him, but it's so
dark that she can barely see his face, not even when they walk under the light
from the street lamps and she's not even sure it is that young man of 25 she
fled headlong from when she was the same age, just as she abandoned her
law studies at Tel Aviv University and Israel and came to New York. She
reaches out for his hand, but it's stiff and cold when she holds it in hers, and
thus they walk a long time, like two strangers hand in hand, down street after
street until they suddenly find themselves at one of the small artificial lakes
in Yarqon Park, where he in the glow of moonlight reflected in the water
lights a cigarette and silently hands the pack to her.

She'd ask him why, after pursuing her "madly", couldn't "get enough of
her" and absolutely wanted them to live together, that he began neglecting
her until one day she happened to see him with another woman on Sheinkin
Street, something he first denied, but later admitted, when she saw them together again. She was unprepared for his betrayal, after her initial resistance
to involvement had given herself utterly to him, but how could he know that
trust for her was more important than the daily bread, when she herself didn't
know? Hadn't she hundreds of times played free and independent, when after

some compulsory years in the army had left her family in Jerusalem and gone to Tel Aviv to live her own life and to study? She wasn't bound to anyone or anything, not to mention what happened so many years ago in Europe with her family and father, she looked forward, would be a lawyer and earn money to live "comfortably" and journey out to see the world. Wasn't that how she was, the seemingly unencumbered young woman of 25 in loose fitting modern clothes, that she in her dream can barely recognize because she's back in her emotions of then and at the same time sees herself from outside, just as she also sees Ben with his smooth, brown face and those dark eyes, as what he was then, but experiences that he in his reactions are somewhere else than she was then. Maybe he was somewhere else most of the time, but she couldn't see it before it was too late? Maybe he just pursued the woman she wanted to be or thought she was until he discovered that she was far more insecure and complicated than he cared for?

She went blank when she again saw him with the other woman, it was on the Tel Aviv University campus, he embraced her, kissed her in the shadows of some cedars on one of the sprawling lawns, maybe he figured there was no one to see them together, particularly her, maybe in a strange way he didn't care or really hoped someone would see them?

In her dream, this, too, she would ask him, but because she's at once afraid of his answer and that she's come farther and no longer need worry about something that happened so many years ago, she remains silent as she smokes her cigarette by his side and looks out over the lake and into the park's moonlit darkness that quivers ghostlike across the trees and bushes. Only when he without reason gets up to leave and has already turned his back on her and is on his way away along the edge of the lake she says:

"Why?"

She says it almost to herself, but he hears it anyway and turns.

"You were beautiful, seemed self-confident, but there were too many problems and they bored me."

"What d'you mean?"

"A woman who wakes up at night and talks about her dead grandparents!"

"All Jews know what that's about."

"I wanted to be Israeli and couldn't live with a daughter of an Auschwitz Jew. I tried, but it was too hard, all the emotional outbursts and the melancholy!"

"You tried nine months!"

"That was enough," says Ben apologetically throwing out his arms. He then turns his back on her and continues along the edge of the water in the silvery darkness. Eve wakes up and stares into the curtains in front of the windows separated by a crack of sunlight from outside. Where's Jon? Wasn't he just here?

*

On their way in the light blue Ford to NYC Police Headquarters' massive block of a building Jon and Cartwright are tense; gone is their usual relaxed confidentiality. Cartwright asks casually about Eve's condition; dusk has invaded their relationship.

"Have you considered that Eve isn't sure where she is?" asks Cartwright out of the blue as he drives on to Park Row and the red building with all its barriers comes in view a few hundred metres ahead.

"Yeah," he says annoyed. "But what d'you want me to do about it?"

"Ask Smith to put up a guard, of course."

"One minute you're against closer collaboration with the police and the next, you're for. I won't get a guard at the Memorial before I commit myself even more to the anti-terror group, and I'm not sure I want to."

"Not even it means Eve's safety?"

"I'm not sure she'd feel safer if I threw myself in the arms of the anti-terror folk. They have their own agenda, and they're only interested in us as long as we fit in. Right now we're at a point of mutual suspicion."

"What d'you mean by that?"

"I have no illusions that we enjoy their trust."

"Why not?"

"You haven't met them yet …"

Cartwright stops the car at the curb some distance away from the first police barricade in front of the headquarters. On their way into the building they pass several check-points before they get to the fifth floor under the garish ceiling light and are received by Smith and a senior detective whom Smith with a quick wave of his hand presents as Ralph Kennedy. Ralph Kennedy is a head taller than the black Smith, and in his crisp white shirt, his red hair perfectly parted and his dark suit and tie shines in the light as do his faint blue, almost colorless eyes.

Instead of taking them into his office as they expected, Smith leads them into what looks like an interrogation room with a large mirror on an end wall. They'd barely sat down at a large table in the centre of the room and Smith's closed the soundproof door, when Kennedy asks them the first question.

"How are we to understand that a suspected terrorist takes his own life just after you've been in contact with him?"

"On that point I can't help you," says Jon. "It came just as much as a surprise as it did for you. But what's this all about? Are we being interrogated …?"

"Let's just say that we're asking you some questions," says Smith sorting some papers in front of him.

"Are we charged, or have you thought of charging us for something?"

"Just answer our questions," says Smith lifting his gaze. "If you haven't done anything wrong, then you can't give wrong answers, can you?"

"We did exactly as promised."

"With a dead man in return …?"

"That wasn't our fault," says Cartwright.

"Not ours either," says Kennedy. "Something must've gone wrong, and we're gonna find out what."

"You've robbed us of our chief witness in our fight against terror in New York City," says Smith holding his pen in the air. "I'll make it 100 per cent clear …"

"We haven't robbed you of anything, a man probably hard pressed by his collaborators or something else, was desperate enough to take his own life, that's what happened," says Jon holding Smith's gaze.

"Call it what the hell you like, but we've got a problem," says Kennedy suddenly unsettled, getting up from his chair.

"Is this being taped?" asks Jon.

"Damned right it's being taped," says Kennedy half shouting.

"You can't."

"We can do what we like," says Smith with a stiff smile waving Kennedy back in his chair.

"We're neither detained nor charged with anything."

"We're talking about national security and the new Patriot Act, signed by the President on October 26th," says Smith with his eyes on the papers in front of him. "We've been authorized to interrogate anyone without warning if we have the least suspicion of collaboration with terrorists or obstruction of our investigations into terror."

"Collaboration ... obstruction?" says Cartwright. "You're mad."

"OK, prove it! We're all ears" And we've got all day!"

"We don't have to prove anything," says Jon with controlled calm. "It's you who have to prove ..."

"No, under extenuating circumstances you have the burden of proof."

"Then charge us."

"We just might," says Smith clenching his jaws. The whites spring out of his eyes.

"On what grounds?"

"It depends on your explanation. It's all up to you. How may times do I have to tell you?"

"You've absolutely no grounds to suspect our behaviour," says Jon, still calm and takes the two folded papers with Hamsal's signature from his pocket, unfolds them so that Smith and Kennedy can read them, as he slowly and meticulously explains the entire course of their visit in Hamsal's flat. When he's finished he senses with his experience eye that his move has had some effect and adds:

"And if there are more questions, just ask."

But he miscalculated.

"That you've gotten the alibi you wanted and in your own interests got the suspected terrorist to sign that he'd witness against the two other terror suspects proves very little," says Smith cooly. "In fact, it only proves that Hamsal was out to save his own neck."

"Who wouldn't be?" says Cartwright.

"Yeah, but why even give him that chance? We're talking about a man who's ready to blow up a subway station, and I've always wondered why neither Mr. Baeksgaard here nor you have expressed any antagonism to this man."

"The witness statement is primarily to your advantage, I don't understand what you're getting at," says Jon. "And with respect to our antagonism to this man, we don't have to keep on protesting terrorism."

"It would be a help if you did it just once."

"Yeah, just once," reiterates Kennedy. "And we still haven't gotten shit about what made the terrorist shoot himself. You must've said or done something ...?"

He's silent and grows more uncomfortable and looks at Kennedy's face, his pale cheeks ruddy with agitation. Kennedy gets up again from his chair and paces in front of the mirror. How many are sitting and listening behind it? How many eyes and ears in this room?

"What should we have done, tell us what you suspect us of?" says Cartwright losing his patience. "I just won't sit here and listen to that I'm not against terror."

Kennedy stares straight at him.

"You're an ex-marine infanterist, aren't you?"

"Yeah," says Cartwright in amazement.

"In your papers, it says that you don't care for American society."

"That's a lie."

"Didn't you leave the army like a bat out of hell after an argument with your superior officer about wasted resources on the American defense?"

"I thought that Reagan's idea of "star wars defense" was idiotic and I was tired of the army ..."

"And of America, and now you're working for a lawyer who enjoys defending murderous Moslems, who are directly related to real terrorists. Can't you see the point?"

"There's only one good point, my assistant does something good for society, for the law, for the rights of the individual, it's an excellent point," interrupts Jon waving his hands.

"Also running around at a gas station on Long Island threatening folk with a gun?" says Kennedy, pounding his hands on the table and leaning across it towards Cartwright.

"What happened that afternoon has nothing to do with Hamsal," says Cartwright. "We were assaulted by two madmen."

"Or two terrorist sympathizers that wanted revenge for an internal affair?!"

Cartwright looks from one to the other sighing deeply, but Kennedy sensing that he's gotten his knife in, goes on, still staring at Cartwright:

"Why don't you just admit that it was you who shot Hamsal?"

"Why in the world would he shoot Hamsal?" says Jon.

Kennedy nods several times mutely and self-assured, retreats slightly from the table, removes his dark jacket and hangs it on the back of his chair and wipes his forehead with a white handkerchief. All four are silent; Smith sitting and waving his pen as he intensely keeps his eyes first on Jon's face and then Cartwright's posture; Jon closes his eyes and seems distant, as he spreads his fingers on the dark tabletop; Cartwright, who's suddenly and unexpectedly become midpoint feels the heat rise from under his collar and that his forehead is ready to boil over; Kennedy reaches for a plastic bottle of mineral water on the table and nods conspiratorily to Smith, who turns his dark, skeptical gaze towards him. With a jolt, Smith, face totally neutral, confronts Jon:

"We're not saying that Cartwright shot the suspect, we're saying that he could've had reason to or that you had grounds to make him shoot himself."

"Why? It's without meaning."

"No, not at all. Look at it this way: You got Hamsal to give you his signature promising that he'd get a reduced sentence. When he fell into the trap, you told him that we were waiting for him down on the street and that you wouldn't keep your promise and he was done for. It all had to do with you were afraid of what he could tell about your part in or sympathy with the terror plans. He protested, you threatened him with his own gun, maybe you shot him and rushed out, maybe he shot himself."

"And what about Michelle?"

"How could a terrorist, who's used to handling weapons, shoot the wrong one at close range? How could he not hit you if you really were, as you claim, his actual target?"

"Because at the moment he shot I kicked him over the shins and now this madness has to stop," says Jon.

"What madness?" says Smith. "There's only the madness you've brought yourself into."

"Where'd you get it into your heads that we sympathize with terrorist? You've got nothing on us that'll hold up in court, no evidence, no witness, it's all guessing ..."

"There're big holes in your testimony and who's talking about a court of law?"

"I'm talking about a court of law," he says. "'Cause regardless of the Patriot Act, you'll have to try the case sometime."

"Yeah, sometime, but that could have long prospects and in the meantime ..."

"What?"

"We can keep you as long as we want. Sooner or later you'll come up with the right answer. Just think of this as the first test. We could drive you somewhere else, there're lots of possibilities."

"One of them is that you let us go ..."

"Never," says Kennedy laughing mockingly as he holds a cup of water out before him.

Jon first looks at Kennedy and then at Smith and tries assessing them, he's tired, he's eyes again hurt, aren't there two men behind them holding them up while he has just himself and Cartwright, but Cartwright's eyes are frightened. In the sterile and murky room, where everything's plastic and synthetic, Smith's and Kennedy's faces show up in the mirror, his own face a shadow and the room stretches towards something floating and unpredictable, without any meaning.

"I've got a suggestion," Jon says catching Smith's eyes.

Kennedy's already protesting, but Smith holds his gaze, maybe he's testing him again, maybe he's just curious for how far he'll go. Small beads of sweat cover Smith's dark brow, isn't he, too; tired of not getting anywhere?

"And it is?"

"You haven't a chance of finding Zawawi and Laban Mohammed, but if you let us go then you'll get a reliable tip from us where they are in return."

"You mean, where your terrorist friends are?" says Kennedy shaking his head.

"No, I mean where the killers Zawawi and Laban Mohammed are hiding."

"And why should we believe you?" asks Smith.

"Because that was the last Hamsal told us before we left his flat and took his own life, and because in that way it proves why he took his own life: It was his way of getting even, yeah - getting revenge and taking leave of them. He just couldn't take any more."

Smith holds his gaze, breathing deeply.

"Hell, you don't believe him and all his fancy tricks?" says Kennedy.

"You stay here," says Smith getting up with a jolt. He turns to Kennedy and whispers something in his ear. Kennedy shakes his head, but reluctantly follows him to the door and leaves. The safety door closes behind them with a sigh. They're alone.

There's utter silence, he hears Cartwright's rapid breathing. Cartwright silently places his hand on his arm and gives it a small squeeze; he sags slightly bringing his hands to his face; Cartwright gets up and starts pacing the room. When he again looks up he sees Cartwright's shadow back and forth in the mirror.

They're being watched, can say nothing to each other.

How long must they wait?

The minutes go, ten, twenty, once in a while they send the other a confidential glance, but upon what is this confidentiality built? Cartwright seems harried, he'd never seen him like this before, slightly drooping, perspiring with a veiled gaze, is he already on the verge of breakdown? Have they hit his solar plexus? Is he afraid of being locked away?

He tries to figure out Smith's and Kennedy's strategy, but maybe they don't have any, maybe they're just treading water and maybe because together with Mrs. Black they're just fumbling in the dark?

Will he really have to find Zawawi and Laban Mohammed himself, just like he found Dr. Jürgen Menken in Vienna? If they ever let him out …

"No, let it lie, he's got to concentrate on Eve, he's got to …

He doesn't even see them come, Smith and – to his amazement – Louise Black, who with a nod, greets Cartwright and walks straight over to him in a long, dark skirt, black jacket and her brown hair pulled back from her pale face in a soft bun. With yet another nod she remains standing in front of him by the table as Smith and Cartwright are seated.

"I understand that you know where the suspected terrorists are hiding?" she says, her face seemingly frozen.

"Yes, if Hamsal's information is reliable," he says.

"Are there grounds to believe so?"

"Yes, his signatures on the two papers prove that he clearly wanted to distance himself from them."

"Why haven't we gotten the address of these two already?"

"Because your people were so busy suspecting us that it seemed meaningless to go on in the case."

"I'll take that up with them later, right now I want that address!" says Louise Black quickly shaking her head. There's something tense and rigid in the way she stands that makes her seem older than she is. Could be a trick of the light, her full, shiny lips confuse him.

"And we very much want to get out of here!" he says.

She retreats a step pausing a moment.

"You can, under certain conditions."

"And they are?"

"You sign a statement that none of what's been said ever gets out to the public and that you've come and gone on your own free will. This meeting has never taken place the way it has and that you know nothing about

Zawawi or Laban Mohammed. Furthermore you're committed to keeping us informed of your whereabouts and you're not to leave the country? Understood?"

He looks at Cartwright, who nods wearily.

"We understand," he says.

"Now - that address!"

He looks for a piece of paper. Smith hands him one and he writes the New Jersey address holding it up in front of Louise Black, who tears it out of his hand and reads.

"First floor? To the right or left?" she says stiffly already on her way out of the room.

"First floor … that was what Hamsal said."

Louise Black is at the door and her hand slips from the knob in her eagerness to leave the room, she curses loudly. Smith jumps to his feet to help, but before he's there she's opened the door and is gone.

Also Smith leaves the room, they again sit and wait in the diffusely lit room until he returns with a paper with the agreed conditions for what mustn't be called their release; there's no release because they've neither been arrested or questioned, but merely voluntarily met for a talk whose contents cannot be disclosed.

What's happened hasn't happened and even though it had, will be denied. They've been part of a non-happening and have spoken with people who officially don't exist.

But Michelle's body exists. After signing the paper, they follow Smith in the elevator down to the building's main lobby, where a distraught Cartwright leaves them to find his car on Park Row; and the elevator takes them farther down to the coroner's unit and the coolers for storage of bodies.

With his card Smith silently opens the door to the shiny white and totally silent room with drawers for the bodies, he follows him in to the neon lit, clinical room where the soles of their shoes click softly on the stone floor. Smith dons a pair of rubber gloves before walking up to the drawer and releasing a button on the wall. A half transparent bodybag comes into view with a smudge of black hair at the end.

With a trained gesture Smith opens the zipper to expose the body's head.

"Can you confirm that this is Michelle Beauxchamp?" he says calmly fastening his gaze on Jon's face studying its reaction to the sight of the body.

He stares some long moments at the yellowed, slightly dissolved face of a woman who's facial expression is frozen in fear and recognizes Michelle from a matrix that's half disfigured and shattered. With a macabre mask of something she'd once been, she lies there in front of him, but yet it's not she. Not only has death halted everything within her and transformed her, from what days ago went around so vital with bright eyes, to a heavy piece of flesh, but because it hit her with such shocking speed and in a state of fear, her face has become a mask of fear itself.

He senses once again Michelle's tense, warm body behind his own.

At that moment he feels more than ever convinced that he himself - if no one else can – must track down her killers.

*

Four days pass with a weak November sun shining over New York, where much seems to be going in the right direction, and where he's able to put the enervating focus of Zawawi and Laban Mohammed behind him in the belief that the police's anti-terror corps will get the two and put an end to the shadows that have swelled around him and the people closest to him.

Eve recovers quickly, her bandages have either been removed or replaced by lightweight plastic so that her skin can breathe and she's able to take short walks around the halls of the Memorial Hospital without serious pain as he supports her. The re-training of her muscles and joints has begun and she's gotten telephone messages from Jerusalem that her father's condition is stable, maybe even so good that he and her mother can visit her in New York. It's now just a question of time before he can take her home to their flat on Second Avenue, to which he's also returned.

He refuses to be a victim of fear, as does she.

Also in the case of Ifrahim Mohammed, there's progress, though unclear whether it's due to a helping hand from Louise Black, but the District Attorney, on the basis of the signed testimony from Hamsal, who established a solid alibi for Ifrahim Mohammed for the time of the murder, has begun negotiations with Johnson about possibly giving up the grand jury hearing and ultimately a trial becuse of the doubtful quality of the evidence.

At a meeting he had with Ifrahim Mohammed in the "graves" on White Street he was able to give him the good news personally. Ifrahim who arrived depressed and in handcuffs, was pleased and before the handcuffs were removed pressed Jon's hands cordially for several minutes promising him "eternal friendship". And when the handcuffs were finally gone, he embraced him with tears in his eyes, then five minutes later confronted with Michelle's murder, his cousin's suicide and that Zawawi was still at large and probably hiding somewhere in the city.

But Ifrahim Mohammed is really shocked when hearing for the first time that his brother not only shot Michelle, but is most likely the man who ended Edelstein's life in his jewelry store in Williamsburg.

"It can't be, can't be, the Prophet forbids it," he says hiding his face in his hands.

"I'm sorry," says Jon placing hand on his shoulder," but it can't be anyone else. It was me he was after when Michelle was hit; and Edelstein was shot with a gun of the same calibre."

"How d'you know that?" he says looking despairingly at him.

"I've talked to the police, as recently as today, and it fits, also the pattern of the crime. Your brother's been involved from the start, including the bombing of Jay Street Station."

"Are you sure?"

"Yes, but I have no solid proof. That's the police's job. Right now, your brother's on the run, maybe still in New York, maybe somewhere else."

"And what about me?" says Ifrahim. "As long as he's free, I'm not safe."

"I don't think you matter to him or Zawawi any longer," he says trying to calm him. "They've figured out that the police already have the tape and know what's been going on, so they have other things to think about than you."

But Ifrahim remains darkened in the clear daylight coming in to them from the windows. Outside the sky is blue like the day they met for the first time, and it hurts when he for a few seconds closes his eyes and unwillingly recalls the sight from the window of the North Tower in flames. Somehow he suddenly smells sulphur and something burnt in the interrogation room, but pushes the thought aside and gets up.

"You don't know how these people think," says Ifrahim staring at him.

"I'm finding out, but do you?"

"In their eyes I'm a traitor and at some time they'll come for me. For them everything is justified by their "sacred goal". They're blind, a sort of sickness, but they believe that they see more clearly than all others."

Jon walks over to the window. From here he looks down on the tall gray, red and white buildings on Manhattan South that are now lit by the sun; his eyes search there where the two tallest had been; a wave of nausea rolls over him.

To escape it he abruptly turns towards Ifrahim.

"How do you know so much about how 'they' think?"

Ifrahim looks surprised and shrinks in his chair.

"Nothing can be hidden from you ..." he says.

"Have you something to hide?"

And now Ifrahim tells him about when he in the early 1990's came with his family from Jedda to New York and settled in Brooklyn and bought his small service station on Atlantic Avenue for some of the money he'd brought with him; then his brother also lived in Brooklyn and had only one goal: to be imam in the new country. He was strongly religious, started wearing a burnus and kefije and was educated at the imam school in Riyadh; as he despised physical labor, he was supported by him, Ifrahim; at nights they went to a local English school, but by day his brother floated around, his life had no direction before he started frequenting the al-Kifah Refugee Center in an anonymous flat above a Chinese merchant. In the course of one month he was transformed, it was as if he'd had a vision, he couldn't speak of anything else than the blind sheik Omar Abdul Rahmane and got Ifrahim, who'd never really been religious to come to a prayer meeting at the centre. Here he heard the sheik preach in a room where only ten were gathered; the sheik spoke flammingly about the Great Satan USA and all its crimes against Islam and the Moslems in Palestine and Iran and Egypt and about its false handshakes with the royal family in Saudi Arabia. Just as wrathful as he was when he preached, he could be as friendly afterwards when he greeted and offered his hand and praised his brother for his orthodoxy. He encouraged him to follow in his brother's footsteps; but Ifrahim glided away, he wasn't called to a strong belief and had a family to support. His brother didn't understand, became more and more remote, stopped visiting his family and became more secretive; through the grapevine he'd heard that his brother had left for Afghanistan to take part in the muhajedines' fight against communism there, but he'd closed his eyes. Ifrahim saw him as a man who'd gotten lost, and only when sheik Omark Abdul Rahmane was arrested in connection with the attack on the World Trade Center in 1993 could he see how blind and dangerous the men were that his brother, Laban, had been in contact with in Brooklyn. He prayed that he'd never see him again, even though he was his brother.

"But when did you hear from him again?" asks Jon.

"Many years later. I wish it never happened, it was a nightmare, like a bolt of lightning. Some years ago I suddenly saw him on the street in Brooklyn, not far from my service station. He didn't see me, but it was like seeing myself in someone else's clothing, he looked exactly like me and was in ordinary American clothing, jacket, trousers, no beard, short hair. I thought I was mistaken, but it was him. I asked about him in the mosque on Atlantic Avenue, but no one there had seen him, maybe he was going under a different name? I'd heard rumors that he's been here several times, I've never greeted him, I won't greet him, but they say he's imam in London, he lives there. I don't know."

"I'm sure it's him I've stood before," says Jon. "It's his eyes I looked into and it's he that instead of shooting me, shot Michelle my colleague."

"How can you be so sure?"

"Because he looks exactly like you and because Hamsal has met him and knows him by his name Laban Mohammed."

"It's a curse, he's possessed, my own brother, who so many times was so ill at home, a shy boy whom my mother and father always sheltered and had great plans for. My father proudly called him the "little Prophet". He always had a better memory than the rest of us, read books, many books and knew the Koran backwards and forwards."

They keep talking, but he can't avoid the inevitable; Ifrahim again must be handcuffed and led back to his cell, and he leaves him with a bitter taste in his mouth filled by the impression of Laban Mohammed.

That afternoon he sits down at his pc in the flat on Second Avenue and prints out everything for Omar Abdul Rahmane, Osama bin Laden and al-Qaeda and starts reading. Late afternoon the telephone rings, he takes it, it's Cartwright with his rusty voice apologizing for "biting the dust" during the interrogation at New York Police Plaza One.

"You're not used to questioning," he says conciliatorily. "It's not your beat; I know it from the both sides."

"But with everything you've been up against, I should've done better."

"Not when they roll out information from your time in the army, they were really ready for 'the big one.'"

"I'm glad you're taking it that way."

"Sure," he says. "Think about all the times you've helped me."

They both know there are topics that couldn't be discussed on the phone; so they avoid Zawawi and Laban Mohammed and the anti-terror corps' search for the two; but he senses that Cartwright still has something on his mind, he just says:

"Let's see what happens and meet in a couple of days."

"Where?"

"My office on St. Mark's Place."

"Monday?"

"Yeah, Monday morning."

"How's it with Eve?"

"Better and better."

"Will she be coming home soon?"

"Yeah, that's one of the things I want to talk to you about."

"Okay."

"Talk to you later."

"Take care," says Cartwright just as he hangs up. He stands there looking around the flat at the soft lamps shining like small moons in the darkness. A stupor of fatigue from the many months of almost constant tension assaults him; he undresses and crawls under the covers of the unmade bed. But fatigue is too great, his body can't find repose, he gets up, puts on a bathrobe, takes a glass of whisky , wraps the covers around him, sits down on the armchair in front of the TV and takes the remote and zaps between the many channels to find a film to fall asleep to. Unexpectedly – on an English station – the face of Osama bin Laden appears, he's seen photos of him, but no live pictures and lets the TV run. The tall, dark, long-bearded man in camouflage jacket and a white turban on his head, whose one hand as a guerilla hangs out of the jacket, a Kalashnikov rifle at his side in front of a promontory holds a microphone up to his mouth, as he with a magnetic, gentle look speaks austerely to the camera. There is something electrifying and at the same time hypnotic about his voice and gaze, as if he unaffected by the world around him speaks from a space of insight and pain, but the words, that in the English translation run across the screen beneath him, increasingly contradict the staged calm. From an imam-like blessing of the perpetrators of the terrorist attack on the World Trade Center, which fills him with joy, and which Allah by his desire would ensure the chosen a place in heaven, bin Laden speaks of a chain of mortal terrorist attacks that have divided the world into two camps and that the time has come for every Moslem to defend his religion against Israelis and the fallen, heretical rulers in Saudi Arabia, Syria and Jordan, these "killers who play with Moslems' blood, honor and shrines."

The face with the woeful and hallucinating gaze has only disgust for America and President Bush as "the leader of the heathens of the world" and can only see a reflection of vanity on behalf of the men and warring powers in the operation the American military has inaugurated against him and that in its wake has drawn many countries, those countries that believe in Islam, into its shadow. At no point does the apparent self-assuredness and self-satisfaction leave bin Laden's face, not even when he swears by Allah that

America will never live in peace before peace rules in Palestine and before the heretical forces abandon Muhammed's land.

A paler, spectacled man without the same charisma, dressed in a cape and turban, whom he recognizes as bin Laden's closest comrade, the previous Egyptian physician Ayman al-Zawahiri, charged for conspiracy in the assassination of the Egyptian President Sadat and founder of Islamic Jihad, also appears on the screen. His speech is less musical and mere direct, and his voice bordering on the hysterical when he says, "By creating Israel whose ongoing crime for 50 years has America made itself the leader of all criminals. The Moslem nation will not accept this crime." Some aggressive words fall from a third, dark and long-bearded person in burnus and turban, Muhammed Atef, the man who is rumoured to be the military organizer behind the attack on New York and Pentagon, and perhaps also him who got the idea; but in Jon's exhaustion, what remains in his mind is bin Laden's numbed yet flaming eyes and his mesmerizing gaze.

When he falls asleep soon after in the armchair, that gaze still haunts the face of a man all in a white Arabian costume on a sun-drenched terrace surrounded by wedding guests. It's the son's wedding, the guests listen smilingly to the white dressed's recitation of verse that mocks the American military's fiasco when it would protect the warship USS Cole in the harbor in Aden, Yemen, but was caught by an heroic and mortal revenge in Allah's name: A bomb blew a hole in their false sense of security, "pieces of the heretics' bodies flew in the air like dust. Had you seen it with your own eyes, your heart would've been filled with joy!" The white-dressed man resembles bin Laden, in dreams, nothing is really certain, not even when the boy Osama walks around in mother Hamida's house in Jedda, given to her by the father Mohammed bin Laden as the tenth wife, and finds his way to her through rooms with heavy statues of gold, antique carpets and Venetian candelabras, this dark-haired beauty from Syria, who has refused to wear a burka and stands before the mirror in her dressing room wearing her Chanel slacks bought in Paris and is preparing for yet another journey. He stands in the doorway and admires her uncomfortably from afar and doesn't understand why she, his mother, has been ostracized by the 23 other wives; her extrava-

gant habits are whispered about, about her western dress, her trips to Paris
and London, hasn't she taken a new husband, his step-father Muhammad al-
Attas, who works for his father and in whose house he lives? Why hasn't she
followed the rules? Should he be ashamed of her as are the others? Has he
not a strange hard feeling in his gut because they call her "slave wife", neither a Saudi or a Wahhabi, but a Syrian who reads unholy books and has
opinions on this and that. He's asked her what he is if she's a slave-wife, is
he perhaps the son of the slave-wife and not the son of his father, whom he's
seen only occasionally, when he asks him about his Koran reading and behaviour and has impressed him about discipline, oh yes, he who was friend to
King Abdul Aziz al-Saud, and who'd built great roads and restored the holy
mosques in Mecca, Medina and Jerusalem, he saved the King and the country with his money and was just a poor mason when he came to Jedda from
Yemen, him he'd like to know. He has some time talked to him like a grown
man and had given him the feeling of being something on earth, he'd be like
him, great in the king's and the others' eyes, but his father is dead, a helicopter that landed wrong and his mother just laughs when he asks her: "Am I
still the son of a slave wife or of my father who's dead?" She hasn't time for
him and where can he find a new father who will see him? He must find a
way, by himself, he'll show them, is he not wiser than his 52 siblings, he can
lay out roads, build great buildings and be a holy man. He'll shrug shame
from his back like his father threw rocks and baggage from his when he was
only a porter in the harbour in Jedda.

And he builds himself up, this courteous, shy and quick boy, this lovely
and soft and confused and homeless boy, this boy who is mute until he's
asked and always knows and has dark waters within, this boy who mirrors
himself in the greats, his wealth gives him the best teachers and the best
schools, like Al-Thagher Model School in Jedda with its vast grounds planted with rows of eucalyptus, whose branches are bent by the winds of the Red
Sea. Here in a modern two-story concrete and stone edifice with a view of an
inner court-yard and in shadowed halls with air conditioned classrooms he's
taught together with young princes from the Saudi royal family and rich
men's families by teachers from England and Ireland in English, mathemat-

ics and the natural sciences and is brought up with the rituals of Islam. Every morning they're lined up in military fashion in their English-inspired uniforms, on a chair sits the rector with a whip prepared to punish the disorderly under their bare feet, in the middle of the day they kneel together to pray zuhren, the afternoon prayer.

He's among the best and will achieve more than just studies, and isn't it as if luck smiles upon him when the young and popular Syrian and physically well-trained sports' teacher hand picks him and a few others for an Islamic study group after school hours and opens the door for him to Islamic Jihad? It's like an initiation, giving direction to the confusion and effervescence to the dark water within. Year after year, afternoon after afternoon they gather around the teacher in his office on the second floor and recite suras by heart from the Koran until they've gotten through the entire book. Occasionally they play soccer for distraction on the green lawn outside the building (he's the tall forward who scores goals), but intensity increases when they read and discuss hadiths. It's not just stories about the Prophet's life; the young Syrian with the persuasive voice goes farther: Sharia must be implemented in all Arab countries, one cannot just sit and wait for it to happen, Moslem judges must populate the courtrooms and governing councils, pure Islamic law must again be installed, nothing must stand in the way for Islam and brothers in Islam, in every house, in every family must Islam be the cornerstone and be made free as in the time of the Prophet; but how far must one go?

One should be prepared to go all the way, like with the boy, the just boy who found Allah. He wished to please Allah, but his father stood in the way. His father pulled the carpet out from under his feet, he found all sorts of things to distract him from the path he should take. In the beginning, the good boy was confused like he who stood between his father and Allah, but a voice, ancient and deep, told him what he must do. His father had a rifle, hidden in a large closet in the father's bedroom. The boy laid a plan for how he undiscovered could get the key to the closet and the rifle and cartridges; when he succeeded, he practiced loading the rifle and found a place where he could undiscovered shoot at targets. Then he laid a plan for how he could shoot his father. He went forward step by step until an early morning he could surprise his father, when his father unsuspecting came into his office. He aimed the barrel at him and pressed the trigger, the father fell forward, hit in the chest, and Allah be praised, Islam was liberated in that home!

They sit with mouths agape and digest the teacher's story, and bin Laden doesn't forget it, neither consequence nor direction. He has it with him all the way, both when he with a new beard, shortened trousers and unironed shirt agitates the others in the schoolyard about the absolute necessity of resurrecting Islam in the entire Arab world and at Abdul Aziz University in Jedda. Here Professor Muhammed Quth confirms for him the importance of the Moslem Brotherhood and opens his eyes for brother Sayyid Qutb's work, *Milestones* and his ideas about the indivisibility of Islam in an Islamic and a fallen, heretical split world and an anti-occidental jihad, that once and for all will eliminate the world partition, eliminate corrupting western thoughts and its carriers in the world and resurrect an Islamic state based on Islam's holy texts. In Jedda the Islamic dissidents rage, in mosques and on mattresses they preach about the decadence of the West and on Islam's purity that must be protected; bin Laden takes it all in, reads and prays, discusses the Koran at the university; but the Palestinian Abdullah Azzam's violent voice, that he has on tape, and that he listens to over and over again, penetrates deeper than all else. Here's an anger that gathers and purges all feeling of shame from him, his own feeling of shame, the Moslems' humiliations: the West is not only decadent, but criminal, violence is necessary; are the true Moslems not those, who with weapons in their grasp besiege Mecca and demand theocracy and purity and are prepared to give their own lives, even if they wade in blood? Weapons must speak, weapons against the domestic and foreign enemies, and is he not the man who can work to cleanse the world; can he not be the flying, the worthy warrior who can deliver Islam? In Iran, they're on the way and now the time has come for Afghanistan, where the Soviet communist troops ravage.

In dreams one doesn't really know, like the 22 year-old multi-millionaire in Peshawar among spies, drug dealers, Afghan refugees, exiled journalists and thousands of Moslem sympathizers with the muhajedins look at him in meticulously tailoured shalwar kameez and handsewn English boots, not yet looking like a mountain guerilla, good intentions but still soft. But together with his role models, the experienced organizer and founder of the Hamas guerilla group on the West Bank, Abdullah Azzam, he's quick and takes everything in. Soon he's here, there and everywhere: He's in steady movement between money collections among his rich brothers and old school mates in Saudi Arabia and the wounded warriors at the city's hospitals; he writes cheques to their families; he builds trenches and tunnels to which he brings his own bulldozers; he establishes training camps; he works at his newly established office in support of the muhajedin and Arabian volunteers; he's teaching muhajedin warriors in Arabic; he has long nightly discussions in his villa on the Syed Jalaluddin Afghan road with muhajedin warriors about his anger with the historical English attacks against the Arab countries after the First World War; he's flying. Rumours know him already as the young, generous Saudi Arabian sheik who lives and sleeps under Spartan conditions and on the hard floor in his offices with freedom fighters and gives lectures on Sura Yasin, where the Prophet reveals his message and the task Allah has laid out for him.

He talks of Salehuddin and the great Islamic warriors, and soon he's also in the Jaji region with a contingent of fifty Arab warriors, shot at from the air by Russian bombers and by Scud missiles from the ground; he's lightly wounded in direct close combat with Russian soldiers; he's hit by shrapnel from a grenade in the battle for the airport in Jalalabad; in the Jaji region a Scud missile explodes close to him but he survives, is this not a sign from Allah? And should he fear death? The Russians and Americans fear death, they're like small mice. Everything succeeds for him, he's the relentless warrior (isn't this how they describe him through the Arab world) and the billionaire who heaves huge contracts home in the progressive Bin Laden Brothers Contracting for the restoration of the holy places in Medina and Mecca, even King Fahd is said to be impressed by him, he's a hero, is he not already greater than his father? But he wants more, jihad has only just begun, jihad for the whole world and he's the spearhead, he creates his own organization, al-Qaeda, the base that recruits and trains Islamic warriors to continue the holy war; but when he returns to Riyadh and should harvest the fruits of his heroism in Afghanistan and desires support to the continued fight and offers the king to be at the front for the expulsion of Saddam Hussein's invasion forces in Kuwait, his offer is refused. Instead the king entrusts the Americans, the heretics, in protecting Islam's holy places. Three hundred thousand American soldiers arrive in Saudi Arabia with their dominance and Colas, their bases and sunbathing; he's humiliated, he preaches, he protests, he sends thousands of tapes to mosques across the country with his warnings and refers to the Prophet's own warnings against Jews and Christians in the Holy Land. Prince Abdullah invites him and his Afghan veterans to his beautifully furnished lounge in Riyadh; will he receive him, will he give him and his warriors the place they deserve and support their fight in Afghanistan? Prince Abdullah places his soft hand on his shoulder, smiles and talks about friendship and loyalty, his words are polished, but he senses the underlying threat: "Family Mohammed bin Laden has always been loyal subjects in our kingdom and has helped us magnanimously in the time of need. We are convinced that nothing will be permitted to destroy our good relations to them." They nod in respect to the prince, but he's seething inside, a no, a rejection.

Yet again has shame touched him, he re-recruits his army and sends 400 men to training camps in Afghanistan, who do they think he is, son of a slavewife or of the great, untouchable Mohammed bin Laden? They're corrupt, bought by Americans, they have no legitimacy and their Wahabbitic faith dishonest. They search his house, through his brothers they bait him, they threaten him, but he is inflexible, and now they turn their backs, even his family, even his brothers. They ostracize them, but he's wiser than they, he's greater than they, he can't use them for anything, he has his own funds, he'll go his own way, the way of jihad, in the Prophet's footsteps. Is he not flying, is he not the rebel?

He will create something they've never seen, he'll unite the Sunis and Shiites, have they not already broken the Russian communists, now he'll break the neck of the Americans, he'll write himself into history. And is it not what he, Allah be praised, has already done? As he lies there on his soft bed, wrapped in covers in a locality the name of which he doesn't even know, and where his men have led him along mountain paths in the White Mountains in Afghanistan and looks into the darkness and listens to the silence – is there not water dripping somewhere out ther? - comes doubt upon him, or perhaps it's the darkness between the mountains, that from outside rises up in him and makes his hands and back freeze? They've searched for him and haven't found him; they've made the greatest efforts, the entire world has searched for him and hasn't found him. Is that not proof of his significance? Many times they've tried to take his life, but they won't get him, he's too fast, too smart for them.

He remembers the time in Sudan where he created a string of companies and earned millions of dollars in export and import and grand contracting companies and expanded al-Qaeda and together with Zawahiri who lobbied for global jihad, made plans for coming actions. And what about the great time under Taliban in Afghanistan, where the flower of terror in the name of the Prophet slowly but surely unfolded? They played on internet and the media like a grand piano and all the time got their messages out, they spread fear among the Americans and the disbelievers like hail from the heavens, and each time that Islam's enemies thought themselves safe, they struck again, unpredictably, like a tiger. Oh yes, he keeps count on a grand scale: There was the attack on the World Trade Center in 1993 and on the American troops in Mogadishu the same year, the car bomb in Riyadh in 1995, his fatwa in the name of "The World Front for Jihad against Jews and Crusaders" where they declared it every Moslem's duty to kill Americans and their allies. There were the bombings against the American embassy in Kenya in 1998 and against the American embassy in Tanzania the same year; the misled Americans sent cruiser missiles against his camp in Afghanistan in 1998, but again to no avail; he struck against the USS Cole in Aden's harbor in 2000 and pulverized yet more enemies. He was here, there and everywhere and exposed their weakness and fear. Did he not stand in June in a video transmitted by al-Jazeera in front of a map of the world and promise spectacular events in the near future? And yet his and Atef's and Zawahiri's masterpiece came like a bolt of lightening from the sky for them.

With their masterpiece in New York and Washington, they'd demonstrated their strength, not alone had they hit their target, but hadn't he calculated in advance where they should hit to sink these satanic towers? They shouted about morality when they saw the bodies of their own, but in war there is no morality. The worst thrives in today's world, and the worst terrorists are the Americans. Has he not shown that terrorism targeted against tyrants and the enemies of Allah is the only one valid? Has he not shown that he doesn't fear death, but on the contrary wishes it for the sake of Allah? But the godless don't understand him, they think that they with their bombs and missiles and machine guns can hunt him like an animal, they don't understand that he's not afraid, that he's already won over them by exposing their fear, hate and confusion. They fear his next move, and it will be of the same size as their fear: Ten Boeings and Airbusses will burn up over the Atlantic and the next again will be like a mighty tower of fear. What did not succeed for his warriors at the Olympics in Sydney: to detonate a nuclear power plant; it will succeed, it's just a matter of time, and they'll never get him, they'll never find him because his spirit floats over water and mountains, and that they'll never reach.

He turns on his soft bed and again looks into the darkness, but the darkness is impenetrable. Wasn't there someone out there? Wasn't there the sound of steps, or just the wind, the cold wind? His bones and wound hurt, he freezes, no matter how many camel hair covers he has around him, he's captured by the cold and cannot sleep. He shouts to one of his guards, but the shadows of his guards have long since vanished in the darkness. The cave is hard and vacant, just like the world that's hidden in his heart and the innermost of his mind. The stone grew up in his darkness and became a heart of stone.

Jon wakes up in the armchair in front of the weakly illuminated phosphorescent screen showing nothing in the flat on Second Avenue, clutches his heart and stares into the darkness of the room with the moon-like lamps lit. His heart hurts and he's forgotten to turn off the TV and the lamps. Where is he? Is there anything really wrong with him? He gets up scared and breathes heavily as he holds his hand on his shirt over his heart. Now he remembers: bin Laden, pictures of bin Laden on the screen … Everything that he knows about him has gathered within him, he's even dreamed of him, can he escape him?

He stands some minutes entirely still on the floor and slowly regains himself. His heart's beating easier, but the jagging pain has not completely left him. He turns off the TV and moves around the flat and ends at one of the windows looking out at the dark night sky above the city and the illuminated Second Avenue, here he looks down on the street where several cars with bright headlights race past.

He'll first escape bin Laden when he's found Laban Mohammed and Ben Zawawi. Won't he?

No, he'll escape bin Laden when he concentrates one hundred per cent on Eve and tries to live a normal life. But can he?

Has he ever led a normal life?

What is a normal life?

It's not a life in bin Laden's shadow.

I declare that I in sleep experience states of euphoria which I don't know when awake, because they demand that one completely forgets oneself, writes Simone de Beavoir, but what if forgetting one self is to tread in angst like the ship in the breaking sea sailing with an empty place on the bridge where the mate has stood?

Almost a week passes, it's December, the cold is seen on the faces of the thousands in their close fitting coats and jackets with raised collars and a rainbow of colored caps and hats that each morning trudge through Fifth Avenue and all the other avenues making their way to the thousands of lit shops, offices, coffee shops and department stores; it's December with dark mornings and early dark evenings and rain and cold winds that blow through East Village and rip the last leaves from the plantains and ashes. Now in the evening they're bare in the narrow streets in the glow of the lights from flats, the small restaurants and boutiques and on such an evening he's meeting with Cartwright in the office on St. Mark's Place (a meeting he's postponed several times).

The week before, Eve returned to the flat on Second Avenue and he to a life that seems to have a future: Isn't she back in their rooms and bringing life to all its corners and giving him the impression the the flat is liveable and not a shadowy hiding place from the case and dusk without end? Even though she quickly tires and must lie down on the bed and rest and the burns on her arms and legs are still painful, she's rearranging the flat and already on the first day found an eight-armed Hanukkah menorah in a closet which she sets in the middle of the room, one candle burning, "a candle for each of the next eight days", as she says, and he buys potatoes, oil and flour in the kosher food store on the corner of Third and Second Avenue for the *latkes* and *sugabiots* she conjures up at the stove in the kitchen, which for months has been a darkroom for his exhausted condition until he was forced to flee from it. He can't stop touching and holding on to her, newly in love, and when they make love, standing in the kitchen or lying in bed, and his hands are electrified by her breasts or discovering new parts of her body, and they are at once happy and exhausted and, entwined in each other, fall softly asleep, they sleep for the first time in more than three months in a deep calm as if they'd gone into hibernation in each other's arms.

The long stay at the Memorial Hospital, where she several times alone in a temporary wakeful and clear state of mind in the midst of the numbing fog of fever, pain and morphine, the claw of death burned on her back had given Eve a greater gravity and at the same time a sinister humour. At one moment she's laughing over trivia, the next she's gloomy and insists on moving from New York, preferably to Jerusalem, and she surprises him by taking the threat that he and she must live with as long as Zawawi and Laban Mohammed are at large firmly.

"You've got to get us a gun," she says that evening when the first Hanukkah candle is lit, and her dark eyes glow in the light of the wavering blue-yellow flame on the dining table in the flat.

"You're not serious," he says.

"I've had time to think," she says, "and I can't only be dependent on your help."

"I don't like guns, never have …"

"No, but I know how to use a weapon," she says. "You learn that sort of thing in the Israeli army, and I'd feel a lot safer with a gun. It's about your safety, too."

"Mine?"

"Maybe you don't like the idea of a woman protecting you?"

"Sure, why not," he says. "I'm a beginner …, but guns mean trouble …"

"Don't you think there's been enough trouble already? You've been just *this far* from being shot; d'you think those killers will miss a second time given the chance?"

"Right now I think they're busy hiding from the police."

"But you don't know what they might do. In their eyes you've messed up plenty for them."

"I've thought about talking to Cartwright."

"He can't protect us 24 hours a day!"

"I was going to suggest that he moves in for a while …"

She shakes her head.

"I'm not having two men here, get me a gun."

"How?"

"Ask Cartwright, he knows."

And when he protests, she says.

"Be realistic. You haven't thought it through."

He had to admit she was right: he'd repressed the danger they were in, just couldn't think about it, and for the same reason there was an underlying vibrato in everything they did; he promises to talk to Cartwright.

But even though she reminded him of it for days on end, he succeeded in bringing her into an apparent carefree zone, until the fourth Hanukkah candle was lit and they were at a very delayed burial for Michelle's ashes at Greenwood cemetery in Brooklyn. Her husband, Paul Beauxchamp, who was stricken with food poisoning and was in a hospital in Shanghai when he got the news of Michelle's death, finally arrived in New York and the burial was set on a cold day beneath a clear blue sky in an area with many small headstones in the sweeping rolling terrane, with a view of the lake in the distance, the bright historical marble monuments, mausolea and the oriental chapel.

They're a small flock in dark dress around the urn, lowered into the ground in a small coffin and, according to Paul Beauxchamp's wishes, laid to rest by an older Catholic priest in frock. After casting earth on the coffin with a shovel and the appropriate words, the gray-haired priest with a marked face pauses and looks searchingly at their faces as if there's something he's forgotten. In the group is Cartwright, who's come at the last minute and stands there freezing, yet motionless beside the pale Beauxchamp, who stares with glassy eyes down into the grave. The priest has now found the words and says in a clear voice in the slight breeze:

"The Lord is my shepherd, I shall not want; He makes me lie down in green pastures. He leads me beside still waters; He restores my soul. He leads me in paths of righteousness for His name's sake. Even though I walk through the valley of the shadow of death, I fear no evil; for You are with me; Your rod and Your staff, they comfort me. ..."

Beauxchamp can no longer hold back his tears, he casts a red rose down to the coffin; one of those present, Michelle's mother, a slight woman totally in black, steps alone to the grave and stands there a moment looking down on the coffin. When she turns, she trips, about to fall. Cartwright quickly steps forward to help until Beauxchamp takes over. Eve and he also walk to the edge of the hole in the still green lawn and each cast a white lily; for some seconds, as the darkness of the hole captures his gaze and the brown coffin in the hole seems absurdly small to hold his feelings of sorrow and anger, the moments when Michelle was shot return to him. He again hears her voice and looks up to the cold, blue sky, which has no end.

Beauxchamp hosts a wine party in his flat on Park Avenue West, but Cartwright's declined; and when Jon and Eve arrive slightly late in a taxi, Michelle's mother has gone to lie down in one of the rooms and the other guests have already left. The slim, dark-haired and handsome Beauxchamp sorrowfully receives them and shows them to a table in the living room, where he promptly offers them a glass and thanks them for coming; but something's wrong, Jon senses it in his eyes and voice. Beauxchamp keeps working around the circumstances around Michelle's death and suddenly remarks:

"As I see it, her death could've been avoided."

"What d'you mean?" asks Jon.

"According to the police, it was you and not Michelle, they were after. Something to do with a tape, why didn't you just give it to them when they showed up?"

"I did, but I also tried getting away from them."

"Don't you see, your attempt at playing the hero cost my wife her life?" says Beauxchamp bitterly, staring at him.

"I don't think Jon was exactly tried playing hero," says Eve.

"You know nothing– you weren't there!" says Beauxchamp holding Jon's gaze.

"You don't know how you're going to act when a gun's aimed at you," he says. "I really tried covering Michelle, she stood right behind me, but I've regretted many times that I tried resisting."

Beauxchamp rolls the wine glass between his hands, as if it were a cognac glass and watches him. The sharp light from the lamp over the table on his pale face reveals fine wrinkles across his forehead and around his eyes, and that he's older than he immediately appears. At the other end of the room, the masks with their grotesque smiles and grimaces, which he'd brought back from his many journeys to the orient, seem alive in the semidarkness.

"I don't understand what you were doing with my wife when you must've known that those killers were on your heels," says Beauxchamp, leaning over towards him.

"I didn't know they were on my heels; and your wife invited me."

"That's hard to believe. Why should she? You've never had anything to do with her privately."

"It was an unusual situation," he says. "At the office, we all were affected by the case with Ifrahim Mohammed."

"And you came here to be 'comforted'?"

"I wasn't thinking clearly that evening," he says. "Maybe I just needed someone to talk to. And if it's any consolation, I feel responsible for her death."

"Responsible," says Beauxchamp tasting the word. "You had something going, didn't you? Just admit it. That's why you were here and why you didn't care about the consequences."

"We had nothing 'going'," he says. "I'm really sorry about what happened, but what difference does that make …?"

Beauxchamp empties his glass, puts it on the table with an outstretched arm, his gaze moves from the empty glass and up to him. A shadow glides across Beauxchamp's eyes, total silence between them, and he hears Eve's rapid breathing as she places her hand on his arm. It's clear that Beauxchamp's fighting with an inner wrath, even with something greater. It occurs to him that a man who'd once seen his mother shot in Saigon would have difficulty forgiving him any part he had in Michelle's death, and that Michelle's death had opened old wounds. Wasn't he ill in Shanghai around the time he got the message of Michelle's death? Maybe the message was the cause?

But Beauxchamp surprises them.

"Forgive me," he says smiling. "It's all been too much. I know that Michelle was happy being in your office and valued you …"

"Forget it," says Jon getting to his feet. "Don't give it another thought. In your situation, I probably would've flipped out, too."

"Flipped out?" says Beauxchamp smiling again. "Is that what I did?"

"Well, call it getting angry, whatever …"

"I *am* angry," says Beauxchamp also getting up from the table. "But what can I do …?"

"Hopefully the police'll get the two," says Eve. "Maybe that'll help?"

"They've probably gotten away; and even if they get them, it won't bring Michelle back, will it?"

They say good bye to Beauxchamp in the entrance, which is newly painted white and without a trace of what happened. Beauxchamp's hand trembles slightly as he shakes Jon's and in the yellow light of the subway on their way towards Lower Manhattan, among all the unknown faces, Beauxchamp's pained countenance stays with him, also in the lamps on the narrow streets in East Village and in the noise from Second Avenue, until they finally get up to their flat, when Eve starts asking him about his "relationship" to Michelle.

"There wasn't anything, we were just good colleagues," he says. "It was Beauxchamp who had affairs with other women."

"How do you know?"

"She told me so that evening," he says.

"Poor Michelle," says Eve.

And they go to bed early and wake up to the wind that's grown stronger and whistles through the cracks around the windows. In the course of the day, he confers with Johnson about Ifrahim Mohammed by phone, who with a vibrato voice tells him of his soon to be released on bail. He's barely digested the good news with Eve when he's called on his mobile by a secretary for Louise Black that Louise Black expects him at her office at New York Police Plaza One the next morning, but will not say what the meeting's about. Then he calls 'round to colleagues to hear about a replacement for Michelle at the office, but when Eve insists that she take her place and that she's prepared to step into his firm on equal footing with him, he accepts and in the evening darkness leaves down the windy Second Avenue to meet Cartwright and look through his list of clients. Brightly lit signs and Christmas decorations blow back and forth in front of shops and restaurants, paper flies through the air and the cold goes right through him.

When he opens the door to the darkened room with the empty desks and chairs and closed computer screens, the office seems like an empty scene. In the glass window to his office he looks like a ghost that's just gone by and the air is stale with a faint smell of soot, which he knows all too well. He opens a window and lets the door to the street stay open, the cool breeze rushes through the office, bringing with it some dried leaves. When he reaches for the light switch, with his back to the door, he hears the sound of footsteps behind him and jumps at the sight of a man in a dark coat and a hat shoved down over his forehead inside the door.

"Who's there?"

"Relax," says Cartwright taking off his hat.

"Oh, I forgot you wore a hat," he says turning on the lights.

"It's not just that, is it?" says Cartwright turning, closing the door and taking off his coat and looking at him with his guarded, weary eyes.

"No, it's the Tower, Michelle's death, Hamsal's death and now those madmen somewhere out there ..."

"I know what you mean," says Cartwright. "But d'you know that the police haven't a clue to where they are. They're puf! Gone."

"Have you talked to them?"

"Yeah, with Smith. He acts like he doesn't care, but it's obvious they don't have any idea what to do. The good news is that they might not be in New York, maybe Florida, maybe ..."

"The bad thing is that they just can't find them," he says lighting a cigarette.

Cartwright opens the refrigerator, takes out a beer and sits down in front of him.

"What was it you wanted?" he says with an echo of their hundreds of talks through the years. Jon's learned to count on him no matter what, but he's never really found out how Cartwright lives. Changing girlfriends, his sudden vacations in Miami, his two-room flat in New Jersey, his time in the army, his preference for whisky and The Doors and old Fords, his additional income, his rusty voice, all of this is ultimately a riddly for him just like the sense of a no-man's land around him where there's a kind of burn-out and solitude that he's only revealed a few times, but that could be read in his eyes. In the midst of it all is a surprising laughter that he in the last couple of months has heard less of.

He now asks Cartwright to pick up Ifrahim Mohammed from the "graves" the next day, where he'll be released on bail until they finally decide the fate of his case.

"Drive him home to his wife and kids in Brooklyn," he says. "I can't be there; I have a meeting with Louise Black at about the same time."

"It's a victory for you," says Cartwright, "about the same as they've given up running a case against him."

"Yeah," he says. "But I'm worried about him. Who knows what his brother and Zawawi could do?"

"You can't be everywhere."

"No, I've got enough problems with Eve."

"Eve?"

"She wants a gun."

"No problem," says Cartwright."

"But I don't want a gun in the flat."

"And what if it's a matter of seconds before you or Eve are shot?"

"I really can't imagine that happening ..."

"You're allowed to be naïve, but don't we agree that Eve has the right to protect herself?" says Cartwright with his rusty voice, who gets up, gets his coat, pulls a holster out of his inner pocket with a gun, takes it out and walks back to him.

"This is a 9 mm Browning, an excellent gun, you can borrow it. It weighs about a kilo, lays good in the hand, try it.

Reluctantly he takes the gun, it feels heavy in his hand and would give it back to Cartwright.

"No, feel it in your hand, there's a safety catch, no danger. Aim at the door over there.

He does as Cartwright says and aims the gun at the door.

"Pretend that you're going to shoot."

Reluctantly he presses the trigger, feeling only unease.

Cartwright takes the pistol and shows him how to release the safety, which he also tries and quickly gives it back.

Now Cartwright shows him how to remove the magazine and put it in again.

"There are 13 shots in the magazine, enough to kill several men and more than you or Eve need. When the safety's released and you press the trigger, it'll fire one shot after another automatically. A hellish instrument in the wrong hands."

But he's not convinced, neither when Cartwright tells him that the recoil is minimal and it's about staying calm and aiming at arms or legs at as close a range as possible to be sure to hit and not kill anyone.

"As cool as possible even at the time of fire with respect to the man in front of you," says Cartwright smiling slightly, when he sees how overwhelming it seems to him.

Cartwright repeats all his instructions and Jon thanks him ironically for the trouble.

"I hope I won't need it, I'd rather not."

When Cartwright goes soon after, he lets the gun lie on the desk that was Michelle's, Jon pretends not to see it and walks back behind the glass window to listen to his overfilled telephone answering machine and looks through his list of clients. A jolt runs through him when he hears Alice Carter's voice on the machine, he'd completely forgotten, jots her number down and will give it to Eve later. A theatre and film agent by the name of Goodman with offices on Fifth Avenue whose wife was murdered has in the past week sent several mails and a letter and pleads with him for a quick meeting, he's available every day this week. A woman who's been raped several times in the Bronx hasn't been able to get help from the police but has forgotten to leave her name and telephone number, in tears begs him to take her case. A man with a sad voice from Uptown Manhattan, whose bank account has been completely ripped off and is now acused of insurance fraud, asks meakly for help. There's no end to it. He decides to contact the theatre agent the next day, this time he needs the money. And then maybe the woman from the Bronx pro bono and …

He looks at his watch and discovers how late it is, it must be noon in Vienna and Sine must be at her office in the UNO building on Donau-Insel. On an impulse he rings her number and waits for the tone that the connection's gone through and it rings several times at the office on the other side of the Atlantic thousands of kilometers away.

Suddenly, almost unexpectedly she's on the line and he immediately asks about Tobias.

"He's fine," she says, "but he misses you."

"How d'you know?"

"He has a picture of you on the wall by his bed, every evening he lies there looking at it before he sleeps, but he doesn't say anything."

"Are you sure it's me and not the photo that interests him? When I visit him it takes days before I have the feeling he knows who I am."

"He knows that the man in the photo is his father, but he has trouble translating that to you when he finally sees you, and he doesn't very often, does he?"

"No," he says and avoids any explanations, that would sound like poor excuses anyway.

"Even though he's autistic, he connects something with his father; and, of the men I've known, you're the only one that can confirm that feeling with him. You have a special talent, and it's not just because you're his father. I just don't understand why you don't visit him more often."

"It's a long way between New York and Vienna," he says.

"You've chosen the distance."

"As far as I remember, we both chose to put some distance between us, and I have my job here in New York. I was the one who suggested that you come with me to New York, remember?"

There's silence an the other end.

"I also have my faults," she says.

"And your men …"

"Leave them out of this," she says.

"I'll visit Tobias as soon as I can. And longer. There's just a couple of things I have to clear up first."

"Aren't there always "a couple of things" you have to clear up?"

"Maybe, but right now there's no other way."

"I'm sure," she says.

"By the way, Eve wants me to go with her to Jerusalem."

" Jerusalem?"

"Yeah. It might be that we move …"

"To live …?" says Sine guardedly.

"Probably."

"Another city far away from Tobias," she says and says good bye in a voice with a twist of irony. He sits there with the receiver in his hand staring out into the deserted front office and then starts reviewing a couple of pending murder- and appeal cases that the Ifrahim Mohammed case has kept him from completing. In the UNO building, Sine replaces the receiver and walks over to the window looking out onto a winter gray Danube and Vienna's impressive buildings some distance in the haze. She regrets her irony, wasn't that what chased him out of Vienna seven years ago? Why didn't she then let him be who he was, with all his momentary distraction, as long as he was something for Tobias? Why didn't she leave with him then to New York? The void he left was too great, had she not spent so much energy in being angry with him, also in the years when he'd visited in Vienna and been with Tobias? A poorly disguised anger that kept her from seeing in him what she still loved and that she through a series of relationships to other men never found a replacement. Seven years with men who in one way or another wouldn't be "father" to Tobias, who didn't see more in him than a difficult, half crazy being that kept them from having a "complete and non-friction" relationship to her (as one of them directly put it). The feeling that the boy, whom she'd do and had done everything for, always came in the way, a kind of outcast, that one just accepted because he was, for good or bad, her child; that feeling had worn her out and isolated her more and more. Once in a while she found herself wishing that Tobias was far away with all his neurotic, habitual rituals that mustn't be broken or his occasional marked total lack of empathy and presence, and had she not occasionally seen Jon in Tobias' image, when she was trapped by a solitude in Tobias' presence? Those kinds of "forbidden feelings" and unreasonablenesses had brought her to a psychologist, who had given the green light that they weren't "outside the normal", her son suffered a chronic psychological illness that would be a burden for most, and on the contrary it was "beautiful" that she had managed to care for him so he lived an existence "close to normal", and even more: that she had strengthened his feeling of self by holding on to his special musical talents. But neither the psychologist nor anyone else could take her feeling of being trapped in Vienna and being left to herself with a task that was about to exceed her powers, and if she wasn't mistaken, there was only one who could share that task with her, one who saw Tobias with the same eyes as she. If he wouldn't come to her, then she must go to him.

As Sine's eyes, through the windows in the highly placed UNO building follow a gull that in the haze over the Danube gliding on a wind current, she makes a decision. In the office on St. Mark's Place Jon spends the next half hour running through the two cases until exhaustion overpowers him; but instead of getting up, he remains seated heavily by his desk staring through the glass window to the deserted front office. The echo of Sine's voice still rings in his ears and behind her irony he can also hear her longing for him. Or is he mistaken? Maybe it's his own longing for her that confuses him and gives him an unclear image of her? Why can't he just bury the thought of her once and for all? Why can't he even in the midst of the turbulence in New York and in the image of Eve lying and waiting for him in bed in the flat on Second Avenue, let go of the thought of the totally different life he could've had with Sine and his son in Vienna if he had stayed there and had tried to win over her reservations she'd had about him? Every time he hears her voice in the telephone his knees turn to jelly. The many times through the years he'd visited Tobias in her flat in Vienna, he'd searched for signs of sympathy from her, but they'd never been clear enough. Or were they? Hasn't she held back because she wanted him to come to her? Wasn't it he that with a half promise to come back to Vienna left her and Tobias? And now it's too late. Or is it? How can he fool himself that he can love two women at the same time, if it means that he's living half-heartedly one place and half-heartedly the other? When will he ever be whole? When will he ever be whole for any of his clients?

He sighs and turns off the lamp over his desk and walks out into the front office and puts on his trenchcoat; only when he's about to turn off the light there does he again see Cartwright's black pistol on Michelle's desk. Typical of self-delusion, it's as if he sees it for the first time; but he recognizes Cartwright's gun, not just from the small demonstration a couple of hours ago; the last time he saw it in use was at the gas station by Long Island Sound.

He picks it up as by chance on his way out of the office and puts it in his pocket.

What is he now? A man with a gun on his way out into the night and the cold?

On the sidewalk on St. Mark's Place under the bare trees, it rests against his thigh like a rock. He'd never get used to the feeling …

*

The next morning, before he leaves for police headquarters on Park Row, and while Eve's still in bed asleep, he puts the gun and a card with Alice Carter's phone number and a short explanation on the bedside table and tiptoes out of the flat so not to wake her. She hears the door shut in a distant room with a floor that looks like a mosaic with a golden background and red and white colours on the rows of houses, the kind she on a summer's day had stood up-on at the Hebrew University in Jerusalem, but now it's her father, who with his back turned, is on the floor and embraces her brother, who's there no more. The brother, all in white stares at her at once accusingly and sorrowful, and as she walks towards them with an outstretched hand, they vanish like a violet mirage and she sleeps dreamless with the thought: "Why has my father turned his back?"

At the moment she awakes half an hour later surprised by the gun next to the bed and not understanding where Jon is, he's in the shiny metallic eleva-tor in the block-like red building on Park Row on the way up to his meeting with Louise Black. He has no great expectations for the meeting; maybe she'll just check him an extra time more making sure that he stays away from the two fugitives, maybe some other unanswered questions.

After waiting in an antechamber, Louise Black comes out personally and fetches him in the surprisingly bright office with a panorama view over East River. She's wearing a short dark jacket over her white blouse and a faint spicy scent of perfume reaches him as she stands close by, and with an al-most invisible smile in her closed, regular face introduces him to the 40 year-old, gray-jacketed Mark Denvers from the CIA. The not very tall, tanned and crewcut Denvers resolutely offers him his hand and studies his face with eyes that reveal a strange light color in his pupils; the color gives the impression of a smudged gaze which after his first words, where he states his rank, is in contrast to his choppy manner of speaking.

They sit down across from each other in a corner of the large paneled office; he wonders what Denvers wants.

Denvers efficiently opens his briefcase and produces two red dossiers, places them in front of him on the table, leafs through them and without further ado draws a profile of Ben Zawawi. With his staccato voice he connects Zawawi to both al-Qaeda, sheik Omar Abdul Rahmane and the founder of Hamas, Abdullah Azzam, with whom he's served his "apprenticeship", and there's reason to believe that - if he's not still in New York or USA – has sought refuge with his "comrades in arms" in Gaza or on the West Bank. But it's most likely, says Denvers directing his floating gaze at him, that he's still in New York and is planning a new attack on a subway station *á la* the first one not yet carried out.

"The man is mortally dangerous just as his associate, Laban Mohammed, who has the knack of changing identities like others change their shirts, we know almost nothing about him apart from his prior status as imam in London and his possible prior connections with sheik Omar Abdul Rahmane during a stay in New York. We figure you can give us and the anti-terror corps with the NY Police more information."

"I'd be more than happy to tell you and Mrs. Black what I know, it's not much more than you've already told me," he says, "but what is the real purpose of this meeting?"

"We'd like to see you start working for us," says Louise Black with her drawling voice not moving in her chair. "We've looked at you, your many cases in Criminal Court as prosecutor and defense attorney, your work in Vienna in tracking down the war criminal Menken and other things. We think you possess the analytical and legal potential to be part of our team."

"Whose team?" he asks in surprise.

"You could work undercover for us as long as you're in New York and an agent for the CIA on certain "trips" outside the country. In that connection, you have an Israeli girlfriend very likely with an ill father in Jerusalem …"

"How d'you know?"

Instead of answering, Louise Black turns her pale face to Denvers, who says: "Sometime in the near future, we think it would be a good idea if you and your Israeli girlfriend went to Israel and you went on as a 'tourist' to the West Bank and helped us solve the riddle about Zawawi. With the talent you have in tracking folk down, we have no doubt that you could find him or get valuable information about him. The first place you should look is in Hebron."

"Now listen," says Jon, "you're wrong about my 'profile', thanks for the offer, but it's not for me. I'm a lawyer in a small office in East Village, that's enough. Right now my girlfriend and I just want peace and quiet. And I don't like you collecting all this information about me. Where'd you get it?"

"It's our job to know," says Louise Black pressing her thin knuckles together.

"Not so long ago, two of your people were convinced that my assistant and I "slept with the enemy". I don't understand …"

"That was a test, and you passed!"

He looks at the two: Louise Black with her street-smart clothing and spotless face with its intelligent but cool eyes, and Denvers, in his spotless smooth, gray suit, and who seems not to be there. A small ray of sunlight over East River shines through the windows behind them, shining faintly in their hair. Don't they look like two, grown up obedient children who've gotten lost in the woods without having the faintest idea where they are?

"Not alone do you 'test' me for something I've no interest in," he says, "but you tap me, too. Who's given you the right?"

"Who said anything about tapping?" says Louise Black.

"How else would you have so much information about me?"

"I'm not at liberty to say, but trust me, it's all legal."

"I don't."

"I can't go into detail, just refer you to the Patriot Act," says Louise Black cooly, "but I'll remind you that you owe us something:"

"How so?"

"Why d'you think it was so easy to get Ifrahim Mohammed released?"

"We had an agreement, you got information from me and you agreed to help my client, who wasn't guilty of anything."

"That address you gave us in New Jersey was a decoy; and remember, your client is out on bail!"

"Is that a threat on my client's liberty or ..."

"Think about it," says Louise Black holding his gaze.

"And look at it as a moral obligation to do something for the USA who's given you shelter for at least 14 years," says Denvers,who for some time has remained silent but whose nods seconded Louise Black.

"What 'moral obligation'?" he asks, sensing what was coming.

"The times call for unity," continues Denvers striking out with his hand. "What was it that President Bush said: 'Either you're for us or against us in the war against terror'? Right now, nine out of ten Americans are with us, there's a new patriotism in the country, a sense of new greatness. Rumsfeld will rebuild our defenses and with this administration we'll break through the axis of evil and show who's carrying the flag of freedom. That's what we're talking about. How can you say no to being a part of it?"

"My many years as a lawyer have taught me that the world can't be divided into black and white, good and bad. Right now your government is waging war in Afghanistan, where thousands of civilians are being killed with the sole purpose of capturing bin Laden and combating terrorism. Where is the 'good' in that?"

Denvers for a moment looks at him in disappointment, around the lips in his smooth-shaven face forms a goading smile as if thinking, 'What am I doing here with a man who understands nothing?', but says:

"You're from Europe, Europeans are too soft. I thought you'd be smarter being in this country so long. Here we don't turn the other cheek, but react, tear the evil up at its roots."

"Sorry," he says with an ironic smile, getting up from the table, "but I have my own plans."

Louise Black and Denvers also get to their feet, together they walk towards the door, out to the gray over-lit hallway, where Denver's tanned skin suddenly seems faded. He mutely shakes Denver's hand good-bye, his hand's sweaty.

"I don't understand people like you, you have everything in the palm of your hand, but throw it away," says Denvers stingingly quickly turning his back on him and continuing down the hall. Also Louise Black shakes his hand in the hallway, and he for the moment can't quite figure out how she's taken his no; she purses her lips, and for a few seconds her tired eyes shine from somewhere outside of her, and she says:

"If I were you, I'd reconsider my no."

"And if I still say no?"

"This isn't just about your client; we can always get you thrown out of the country."

"Throw me out, use that bizarre law, do what you want, but let my client alone, d'you hear!" he says and walks down the hall and waits for the elevator as several men in uniform pass him by, one of them laughing loudly. She stands there a moment staring at him, again he doesn't know what's going on in her head, and suddenly she's gone.

Minutes later he passes through the check points in front of the massive red building without difficulty and decides to walk down Park Avenue and through the streets to Mr. Goodman and his office on Fifth Avenue. Beneath the hazy sky, from which the sun occasionally shines and casts a bright veil down over the city's grey and brown buildings, he takes out his mobile and rings to Goodman to let him know he's on his way.

A half hour later, in the midst of the busy traffic, he's on his way across Fifth Avenue somewhere outside the pedestrian crossing and with the Empire State Building with its art deco façade and thousands of windows scraping the sky in front of him, he sees in the faint shadows a man he thinks he recognizes. At first it seems hallucinatory, like something out of a dream, but the man's face, which he's only seen from the side and the way he moves in his anonymous brown winter coat and dark trousers in the rush of pedestrians pulls him along, and as he from afar starts following him and at the same time afraid of losing him from sight, he wonders how sure he is: Is it Laban Mohammed or Ifrahim Mohammed walking in front of him? But Ifrahim must be with his family now in Brooklyn, or …

A short distance ahead of him the person apparently turns in to a door in a small portal and is gone, he speeds up and edges his way past the many pedestrians and is soon at a branch of the Chase Manhattan Bank. Here, in its cold wall he finds a window and cautiously looks in on a large, long, high-ceilinged room with many customers in rows in front of the various manned counters. At both ends of the room, which is discreetly decorated for Christmas with electrically lit stars and boughs of holly, walk two armed guards, one of them setting his watch, the other opening the door for new customers on their way in. His eyes search the crowd of customers on their way in and out and those standing still, and he's ready to accept disappointment when the man with the brown coat, black hair and black trousers appears. The man's standing with his back to him and has pulled some papers out of the inside pocket of his coat; it takes a while before he gets to the counter with a female bank assistant; and now what looks like negotiations between them: the bank assistant is unsure about something in the papers he's handed her, wildly gesticulating he tries explaining, the young assistant calls a supervisor, a man in a gray suit and red tie who quickly glances over the papers and nods with an apologizing look towards the man. Then he professionally opens a drawer under the counter, takes out a large bundle of notes and hands them to him, who quickly stuffs them in the coat's inside pocket, turns and walks towards the exit.

At that moment he quickly steps back away from the window on the pavement not to be seen and is now certain: The weak, staring glance, the brisk, elastic movements, that nervous and yet self-promoting bearing is Laban Mohammed's.

Everything that this man has done and has caused returns to him in the cold outside the bank, he turns his back to the wall and looks for his mobile phone to call Louise Black; but when he finally finds it, it's dead and in the corner of his eye he sees Laban Mohammed farther down Fifth Avenue, where the top of his black hair dances among other pedestrians who with large plastic bags are doing their Christmas shopping.

He starts walking and walks even faster, Mohammed ahead of him apparently is in a hurry, all the while trying to keep his distance. They pass street after street, building after building, sometimes he stops, pretending to look into shops with expensive goods or sometimes directly into a department store's vacuous world when Mohammed stops at a pedestrian crossing, impatiently waiting for the green light. His pulse tops as he around 47th Street, he's come too close to Mohammed; when he suddenly stops and pulls something out of his brown coat pocket, Jon has to walk past him and around the corner on 47th Street and somewhat farther ahead to a busy café. He pretends to enter the café, but turns in the doorway and scouts after Mohammed, seeing him stop for a red light at the intersection between 47th Street and Fifth Avenue with a map in hand. Mohammed looks up from his map and turns his face in Jon's direction, a second before turning his back, their eyes meet, and Jon goes farther down 47th Street. He agains turns around and quickly crosses between two cars and runs back to the intersection, where Mohammed is no longer to be seen; he turns the corner to Fifth Avenue and walks quickly to the sidewalk with a view to Rockefeller Center and the GE building and St. Patrick Church's neogothic spire. Strangely Mohammed's already far ahead of him, he recognizes his easy stride and his brown coat even though there are hundreds of people between them, and walks even faster. But before he reaches the Banana Republic and Sephora's windows with their show of expensive bags and perfume in an orgie of Christmas lights, Mohammed's vanished to the left, and when he's passed the stores and also turns left, he has the sunken skating rink in Rockefeller Center with its many skaters and the golden statue of Prometheus with the Christmas tree and its red lights in front of him. He stops, a rush of voices reaches his ears, the skaters' movements on the shining icy surface confuses him as he tries to find a focus; is Mohammed not there, no, he is; now he sees a man with Mohammed's coat and light step walk past him farther away and continue up Fifth Avenue with St.

Patrick Church's spiderweb-like towers ahead and turn down the street. Has Mohammed seen him, or is his merely in doubt about geography?

A moment later he's reached the sidewalk on Fifth Avenue and pursues Mohammed as he turns the corner to 50th Street. On the narrow street there are few pedestrians, but several trucks that drive slowly and block the view. Mohammed crosses from the right sidewalk behind one of the trucks and vanishes from sight. Out of breath he goes faster and would go the same way, but a truck has driven up from behind, all the way up to the vehicle in front and blocks his path; he must run around the next one coming to a deserted street. Mohammed's vanished.

Thirty meters in front of him a stairway leads down into darkness, on the railing around the stairs, printed on a faded sign: 47-50 Sts. Rockefeller Center.

Jon rummages around in his pockets for his subway pass and goes down the stairs, on the steps he becomes dizzy and is forced to stop, but he pushes himself on, down into a triangular recess covered with white tiles and garish lighting. He puts his card in the automatic access lock and quickly comes through to a corridor and another stone stairway when the stagnant, sucking noise and the harsh artificial lighting from the low-vaulted station with two tracks on each side of the platform hits him. Between the red-black painted pillars on both sides stand folk waiting – either singly or in small groups – for the next train. As he slowly moves forward he scans the platform, but there's no trace of him. His eyes fall upon a large posted chart over the railway lines; he then turns his gaze to a sign listing the B train's stations Uptown and Downtown. A train noisily rumbles in from behind, he turns and makes note of all boarding and disembarking passengers, but he's not among them. Soon after the train departs and leaves the station, with only a few waiting for B train's arrival on the other side of the platform.

He wasn't able to stay with Mohammed, he has to face it, that all his efforts were wasted, and he's stood up a new client, Mr. Goodman.

Worn out, but senses still sharp, he yet again scouts all sides for Mohammed, but at the almost deserted station there's no one to see apart from two older men in front of a pillar close by and a younger woman farther away.

Disappointed but also relieved he prepares to take the B train Downtown and
steps towards the edge of the platform by the tracks.

He looks at his watch, the familiar rumbling in the subway tunnel close to
the station from an arriving train roars in his ears, the platform vibrates beneath him, and as if it all happens beyond his consciousness and with movements that are merely reflex and defensive, he suddenly turns half way to the
left and reaches out towards a person who, like a shadow from the pillar behind his head has taken a few steps forward to push him from the side down
into the darkness on the tracks; but he's snatched the flurry of the shadow
which is Mohammed, and is now standing on the edge of the darkness and
before Mohammed's staring black eyes and is fighting hand-to-hand with
him, where in split second a bejeweled ring is revealed on Mohammed's little
finger. For seconds it seems as if he's the weakest, his heel is already out
over the platform's edge when Mohammed with a shout and with both hands
would give him the final shove. At that moment he succeeds in stepping to
the side, and it's Mohammed who crashes down on the tracks; Mohammed
tries getting up, but it's too late, the B train with screeching brakes and a
thump from his body is already on its way over him.

*

A person's sudden death is tragic, even if that person is a fanatic who, coldly
exulted, has moved into a darkness where other's lives have no meaning, are
even obstacles on the path to an unreal goal. And even though Mohammed's
death is a release for Jon and Eve and those closest to them, it leaves them,
after several days' of police enquiries and visible satisfaction on the part of
Louise Black, in a strange quivering void in which they seriously question
their continued existence in New York. This void becomes more intense
through the sadness that still hangs over what on the surface appears to be an
again dynamic city, and occasionally reaches all the way to their nostrils in
the sulphuric pong from Ground Zero as they move around the streets on
Manhattan.

For months the smoke hasn't completely dissipated, small fires continue to ignite in the thousands of tons of stones, bricks and wreckage, a fire that won't die. It's as if the wound after the attack on the city's riches, values and self-esteem won't heal, even though the country's politicians with their hefty rhetoric and a grandiose armed initiative turned against the country's new external enemies in a still more agitated mood of being in a permanent "war against terror" does what they can to cross over to the other side of point zero and create new horizons. Hard against hard, and a new even more comprehensive war – now against Iraq – is lurking on the horizon. Here, the Middle Eastern dictator Saddam Hussein and his violently repressive regime in an impoverished land will become the very symbol of the evil and the demonic threat against America and freedom that must be combated. Already in December 2001, through implications in the media, the connection is made between this symbol, bin Laden and al-Qaeda, and the time is not – as Jon can see – for firm proofs or "smoking guns", when it has to do with this case, where large interests are at stake. And it scares him.

For Eve, the death of Laban Mohammed is even more unreal than Hamsal's and Edelstein's, she'd never stood face to face with any of them and has in her submerged condition at the Memorial Hospital been so set on survival that she's shoved their names and identities from her; but now she's uneasy with the thought of what these events have done to Jon and by the intangible feeling of still hovering in continued danger in the flat on Second Avenue. Wasn't it just this angst-ridden vibrato she fled when she left Jerusalem for New York, and now doesn't she feel the need of a gun nearby to feel safe? Isn't it as if the conflicts in her own country repeat themself in New York, but with many intermediate steps and in a shockingly new way? And when she already misses her family in Jerusalem, why not break camp in New York and go back? The phone calls she's made to Alice Carter and Mary Betermann up to Christmas convince her that the grief from what happened to her and so many others in the South Tower will continue to live, might even only now break the surface as the world around them is busy and occupied by other things. She connects this with a city that has changed and has been twisted out of joint that she no longer knows, ignited as it is by daily rumours of poisoning by mail and new terrorist attacks. Yet another reason to convince Jon that he must come with her to Jerusalem, which he's never seen, but only dreamed of.

Christmas Eve, December 24th, all the candles in the Hanukkah menoral are lit and also a small tree which he's bought at an outdoors market nearby. They give each other gifts, they eat spicy soup, latkes and special cakes with jelly and drink red wine, they dance to klezmer music and Leonard Cohen's first songs, and finally they find each other in bed. That evening in their own festive circle, it's as if nothing can reach them beyond their own thirst to melt together and hover on their senses, and even though she wakes in the middle of the night with a feeling that it's burning somewhere nearby and goes out to the kitchen and drink water and look at her almost healed burns, she again falls asleep in his arms as he mumbles her name, in a way only he can. She's at complete peace with a lightness as if she's walking unhindered on a tight-rope over a soft forest floor or were lying in the sun on Tel Aviv's white beach. But when he the next morning, even before he's gotten dressed, calls his son in Vienna to wish him merry Christmas and is completely lost in his joy over talking to him and Sine, and she questions him about the conversa-tion, she doesn't believe what she hears: Two days ago, Sine quit her job in the UNO building in Vienna and together with Tobias is on their way to a six-month stay in Jerusalem.

"Jerusalem ... what's she doing there?" flies out of her.

"She isn't doing anything, it's my son. She's just good at getting things to-gether," he says, lighting a cigarette, going over to the window and standing bare-chested and looking down on Second Avenue. There's that hazy glance she knows all to well when there's something he's hiding and that he's not quite ready to share with her.

"How 'get things together'?"

"Somehow she's managed to get Tobias a scholarship to a music school in Jerusalem where they have experience with specially talented autistic chil-dre," he says not looking at her. "And Tobias' talent on the piano is unique ..."

"But why Jerusalem, there're other places …"

"Because," he says turning towards her, "she can combine it with getting back to her old job, archaeology, and be part of the excavations in Jerusalem …"

"Where?"

"I don't know Jerusalem," he says smiling weakly when he sees how it affects her.

"No, but I do."

He walks over to her and sits down on the edge of the bed.

"She said something about Hinnom Valley and an excavation of what some Israeli archaeologists think could be King David's palace."

"And of course now you want to go to Jerusalem?!" she says not able to hide her agitation.

"First of all I want to get away from New York and the calamity here and be with you," he says taking her hand. "But I like this city and it's here I have my work, so it's not that easy for me."

"No, you want to be with her again, don't you?" she says freeing herself of his hand.

"Not her, I miss my son."

"And that's why you'd go to Jerusalem?!" she says sitting up in bed, turning her face away.

"If we go to Jerusalem, it's to put all of this behind us and live together there. It's because we'll be together in your city. And then I'll have to find out how to be a lawyer there. Maybe I could work for an American-related firm, maybe I could write, who know, I miss writing, just as I did in Vienna …"

"Do you think you're ready for that?" she says.

"Yes, but you'll have to understand that I also want to be with my son."

Sure, sure she understands, isn't she extremely good at putting herself into his needs, she thinks, because he had that son, whom she'd only seen photos of on his pc screen and whose piano playing she'd heard on tape, and because he was more absorbed with his work, so there wasn't room for another child?

Hasn't she lied to herself when she's given him the impression that having a child didn't mean that much and that she, too, was absorbed in her work?

"You want to be together with your son, but I want a child with you," she says looking him straight in the eyes.

"Does the one cancel out the other?" he asks, getting up to put on his shirt and trousers.

"That depends on you."

"What d'you mean?" he says without looking at her.

"Do you want to have a child with me?"

"Yes," he says, "but right now I'm too exhausted to think about it."

"If I'm going to have a child, it'll have to be soon."

"When is 'soon'?"

"When we go to Jerusalem and live there."

He sighs and buttons his shirt.

"*If* we go to Jerusalem and live there," he says and turns his back to her to put on his overcoat and leave for his office on St. Mark's Place to get yet an overview of his cases and economy. She leaves him in peace regarding that question the next few days.

But she's caught in pendulum-like changes of mind and mood and can suddenly as she stands in the kitchen slicing bread, feel her legs disappear out from under her and she lacks a railing to grab. In these states that roll in like waves or soft blows to the back of her head, whether sleeping or awake, she's back on the smoke-filled stairs in the South Tower or by the window of her office looking out on the falling shadows from the panoramic burning North Tower and doesn't know what to do with herself, even though she can't logically explain what it is that happens. The days' early darkness also hits her like something coming from within, and she finds herself literally thirsting for the sun. The Hanukkah candles and the music she continuously plays and the many phone calls to her family in Jerusalem are not enough to numb her reactions (not even her father's voice), nor does she speak to Jon about it; in his own way, he, too, is affected and has gone into a sort of inner hibernation and listens with half an ear. One day he can sit and stare out into space and later vanish into the city, and when he returns to the flat, it's not clear to her what he's done; another day they take a walk in Tompkins Square Park, where under the bare trees he talks about closing his office, but when she catches the gist, it becomes some vague suggestions of 'sometime early next year', and when she hugs him his gaze is chilly in the bright daylight. One night he woke perspiring, had seen himself bound to a chair as monstrous things took place around him.

They know they've got to break camp, but lack the energy.

Every day she starts to pack, everyday she stops halfway, and now there are two half-filled suitcases and a bag waiting for her when she awakes.

*

New Year's Eve they've invited Cartwright, Johnson and his girlfriend from Chicago for a small party in the flat and have decorated with balloons and flags and garlands, just after midnight they all empty their glasses of champagne and hug each other and go down to Second Avenue in high spirits to shoot fireworks. The illuminated street has its groups of people, drunk and sober, greetings to all sides and across the street, horns honk from the passing cars, shouts and howls fly to the heavens, that are coloured by the rockets giving echos of booms and roars. The loud music from cafés and restaurants and flats is different from other New Year's Eves in New York, the very heart of this New Year's Eve pumps more weakly, but the group is set on putting the old year behind them, and Jon and Cartwright have bought an extra large supply of rockets.

A bit away from the others and in the middle of the cold night, Eve's getting cold and moves towards the street door, a small rowdy group walks by her on the sidewalk. The last one in the group, a stocky, not very tall man in a dark coat, turns silently towards her, from a photograph she recognizes Zawawi, their eyes meet, with a movement of his finger over his throat he marks what he's planned for her, then abruptly continues down the street. She's momentarily paralyzed, then a shout from deep within finds its way to her throat and her shrill voice echos throughout the street. Jon and Cartwright are there in a flash, in her fragmented speech, the name 'Zawawi' and her gestures sets Cartwright galloping down the street in Zawawi's tracks, and Jon calls Smith at once on his mobile and then takes her up to the flat, where he vainly tries to calm her.

The group dissolves, depressed and worried, Johnson and his girlfriend leave them in the flat and after some time Cartwright returns empty handed.

"There's at least twenty of Smith's men on the street," he says, "but no sign of Zawawi. They're fine combing the neighbourhood, Smith is raving, talking about a 'false alarm' and misuse of his precious time."

"False alarm!?" says Eve. "I saw the man; he was standing two metres away, threatening to kill me."

"You're positive?" says Cartwright not knowing what to believe.

"Sure she is," says Jon holding Eve close.

Cartwright sighs, leaving them again to take part in the search, and returns an hour later to tell them that the search's been abandoned without result, and they find their way to bed and try to sleep.

But sleep and quiet won't come, outside the windows is a maddening quiet, seldom has silence been so insistent at two in the morning new year's night in East Village as that night, and they both are deep down in their own shell with never ending pandemonium from their own imaginations.

In their frustration they keep circling around Eve's confrontation with Zawawi, "didn't it happen so fast that it could've been someone else just teasing you?" he says; but the more doubts he produces with what she's seen the more she insists that it was Zawawi who stood in front of her on the street. She goes even farther. She releases the safety catch of the gun that's still lying on the bedside table and starts pacing, fists clenched, back and forth in front of the bed, blaming him that they hadn't left New York long ago. Hasn't he been so fascinated with his own role in his client's case and everything that's happened after September 11th to see anything to do with her and their relationship? There've been days where she's had no idea who or what he was.

"Do *you* know?" she asks stopping in the midst of her torrent.

"How many really know how they'd react when they've gone through what we have?"

"A good deal is your own doing and you're good at talking around it," she says.

"No," he says. "I don't always know myself and especially these past three months I've been like Bambi on ice."

"Do you think you'll ever get off that ice?"

"Yeah," he says reaching out for her in the darkness. "It'll be together with you - in Jerusalem."

"Are you sure?" she says hesitating, standing in front of their bed.

He nods and smiles and she comes towards him in the bed. They undress each other and start making love, he deep within her, she senses his sweat and his scent and he vanishes into her eyes, a door opens into a blue room that he'd long forgotten but will never leave. It's as if a membrane bursts in their unified rhythm that they both rediscover and again all is possible. Tired, quiet and smiling they lie in each other's arms staring into the darkness.

When he's long ago fallen asleep and she feels his heartbeat against her skin, and noise from the streets outside again reaches her, she, too, is in restless doubt about whom it was she saw on Second Avenue shortly after midnight.

Thus marks the end of Jon's and Eve's many years in New York.

2002

In the Eliahu synagogue in Jerusalem's old city, there's an empty chair, that the prophet Elijah occupied and then left one Yom Kippur, before he vanished; by night drops of dew cover the hyssop and capers bushes in the carved blocks of the Western Wall of the city, they say that the wall grieves over Israel's calamities and the Temple's destruction in the year 70; in the Omar mosque with its gilded dome and marble columns and circular red floor around the cliff that's said to be the centre of the world, there's a print of Prophet Muhammed's foot and of the Angel Gabriel's hand.

Jerusalem is the city of dusk and shadows, but also of sun, water and hope and around the Shrine of the Book with its white "lid" that's cooled by fountains and houses the Dead Sea scrolls, is a black wall to tell the eye the story of the fight between the sons of light and darkness. In the grotto under the Omar mosque, in the Well of Souls, the dead sojourn before journeying on to paradise, everywhere the dead rummage among the living and the living among the dead, and just as the living are weighted down by the dead, so is Jerusalem buried between its mountains some place where the Gidon spring has its source. And is it not because of its fecundity that the almond trees are still in bloom that clear winter day in February when Jon and Eve are met at Ben Gurion Airport by Eve's parents and before anything else are driven out to Jerusalem's woods to walk among the cedars and cypresses and enjoy the view from the cliffs above the city?

On that crisp day in February with its blue sky, the old and new Jerusalem in the distance lie spread out at their feet with its yellow limestone buildings, highrises, business streets, domed mosques, churches, walls, valleys and clusters of terraced houses stretching as far as the eye can see towards Bethlehem to the south and around most of the hilly city. Jerusalem in its pockets of mountains was a surprise for all that traveled there by camel, or by horseback or as pilgrims on foot. Was it an image of paradise or hell, Gehenna, twenty times laid waste and twenty times resurrected on its own ruins, a city in constant change and pangs of birth and fights for existence, a state with a soul four-fold divided, that spawned and spawns unrest, longings and dreams to the point of confrontation, walls, armed battle? Everyone would have part in its fleeting image, here lived the Jewish prophets, Jesus of Nazareth came here riding on the back of a donkey surrounded by thousands of followers and later the prophet Mohammed came to it flying.

In the Hurva synagogue's lonely stone arch and in the drop-like mosaics beneath the dome of the Omar mosque and in the shards on Golgatha, time beats against a kind of endlessness, but in the suq behind the Damascus Port, the air around the crowds at the stalls and shops is heavy with scents of carnations, cumin, alba tree, muscat, ambra and oil. The cacophony of voices and movement here is repeated, but muffled, on the walking street Ben Yehuda with its streamlined businesses and cafés in the western Jerusalem and diminishes to a hush in the picturesque Yimin Moshe quarter with stone stairways and the narrow passages or in the orthodox Mea Shearim's crooked alleys where Jerusalemitic or Hasidic men on foot with striped, high necked silk cloaks or with brown cloaks and *spidic streimel* are seen beside broad-hipped women in brown sweaters, colorful scarves and dark stocking carrying heavy shopping bags.

The past and present meet; it's the noisy traffic; it's the suddenly established check points and military vehicles on Jaffa Street and roads out of the city and many young people in uniform around Zion Square; it's the armed guards at the entrances to restaurants in West Jerusalem and the silence around Zion Square after 10 PM – in February alone 12 Israelis have been killed by Palestinian suicide bombers – and the dilapidated buildings in East Jerusalem, where almost no Jewish Israelis come, and the darkness hanging heavily and weakly illuminated after 9 PM, and even though Jon even before his departure for Jerusalem was driven by one thought, he loses his footing these first days when Eve leads him around in what is her city and he forgets for some time what it was that occupied him and his life, when he landed in Jerusalem.

First the gentle hospitality from Eve's parents, who from the first day installed them in the house's well furnished basement floor, then the city and on the fourth day the inevitable visit to Yad Vashem, where stone blocks seem taken from the earth and out of obs-curity, engraved with the names of 5000 Jewish communities in Europe that no longer exist because their citizens were annihilated in nazi camps during the Second World War or vanished. In Children's Memorial Hall, five candles for 1.5 million murdered children in the Holocaust in a black mirrorer room becomes an endless number of candles; in the inner dome of the Hall of Names, faces are set to names through photographs of a large number of murdered, and when he together with Eve leave, moved, he's mute and standing on a hillside looking out over Jerusalem in the hazy light of day without being able to contain what he's seen. He thinks about his Jewish grandmother whom he'd never met – only in dreams – and of the concrete covers he stood on in the wooded hills near Weimar that hid the bodies of thousands murdered in the concentration camp Buchenwald and his tracking down of the Nazi doctor Jürgen Menkin in Vienna. All that in flashbacks. Isn't there a connection? Isn't it as if he's come home, but to an infathomable city, where the impression of a photo from an exhibit of a boy in striped Auschwitz 'pyjamas' with his shaved head, smooth face and half-extinguished, half-contrary eyes keeps on hanging in his memory and blocking the view?

"Home," says Eve as they walk among the bright buildings and evergreens towards the parking lot to drive back to her parents' house on Zealot Street.

"Yeah, is that so strange?" he says holding her close.

"Aren't you a bit hasty, d'you really think that Jerusalem can become your city?"

"Isn't that what you wanted?"

"Only if it's what you really feel."

He holds her at arm's length and looks deeply into her dark eyes. Behind them drive cars in and out of the parking lot, a bus with blue-uniformed school children has stopped twenty metres behind them and the first kids are chattering on the path in a long line. High above them a glides a hawk and opens the sky.

"Are you afraid that it'll never happen?" he says smiling faintly.

Not answering, she frees herself and walks to the car, unlocks it and gets into the driver's seat and sits. He wonders what's happening and follows after getting in next to her. Spread out in the landscape before them are large and small trees under the overpoweringly bright sky, all planted to commemorate the non-Jews who'd risked their lives to save Jews.

"When you first start your search for Zawawi on the West Bank, you're sure to change your attitude to Jerusalem and Israel," she says as her gaze is buried in the verdancy and contour of a pyramid cedar far away.

"It sounds like you don't think I should go there?"

"You know I don't."

"After what's happened in New York, I thought you understood why I've got to try finding him."

"It's too dangerous," she says looking at him. "I'm afraid something will happen to you. You don't know the rules, you'll be alone there ..."

"I've done that before, it has its advantages ..."

"Being alone in Vienna is something else than being alone on the West Bank ..."

He's silent and waiting for her to start the car, but she doesn't; she just sits there shaking her head at him.

"Don't you care whether I find the man who murdered Michelle and would've done the same to you if he'd had the chance?" he says in the emptiness of the car.

She angrily clutches the steering wheel:

"Of course I care, but no one's asked you to."

"I'm doing it for you, Michelle and me. No one's paid me, I'm doing it on my own ..."

"For how long?"

"Until I find him."

"Maybe he's not in the West Bank:"

"According to Denvers, it's possible that he's in Hebron, he's pretty sure, he was there two weeks ago, he says."

"Are you in contact with him?" she asks in amazement.

"Just before we left ..."

"I thought you wouldn't work for the CIA!"

"I won't, but why not take advantage of his information?"

She turns to him.

"Can't you see? You won't work for the CIA, but you'll do their job. Why don't you just leave it to them to find the man, they're much better at it than you!"

"I'm not so sure, otherwise, why would they ask me?"

"And you're going to play tourist on the West Bank, there are no tourists on the West Bank at the moment!"

"There're hotels and boarding houses on the West Bank and many of them are still open despite the intifada," he says calmly.

"How'd you know?"

"I've checked."

She's stunned.

"Why haven't you told me?"

"Because I knew you wouldn't like it."

She starts the car and they drive the twisted road down to the quiet neighbourhood where Eve's parents live. On the ways through the alternating bare and woody landscape they're silent, as they both brood over how to break the sudden ice that's come between them. But an unpleasant surprise is awaiting them in the house on Zealot Street. There they're received by Eve's mother with a worried look on her face who lets them into the living room, where Eve's father Moishe sits bent in front of the TV following a special broadcast. They see glimpses of tanks in movement, soldiers in battle dress at a roadblock and closed tanks at the edge of something that looks like a small village and the Israeli Prime Minister Sharon, who in the following clip explains something that Jon doesn't understand; but Moishe turns to him and says in English:

"They've started their offensive on the West Bank in Gaza; I hope they'll at least get hold of some of those murderers in the al Aqsa brigade and Hamas."

The moist eyes in his open, aged face capture Jon's gaze. There's no trace of either aggression or smile in Moishe's countenance, nor when he leans back in his chair and clutches his heart, a gesture Jon has seen him make the last couple of days, and each time Eve's mother Dalia is on her guard; but this time, as she places her hand on his shoulder, she says:

"Don't wish for more war, Moishe, your heart can't take it."

"Who's talking about war?" he says. "When the Palestinians can't clean up their own lines, when they keep on sending folk here to kill civilians, then there's no other way than to go into action."

"We've occupied their land, Dad, how long must this go on?" says Eve sitting down on a chair in front of him.

"Don't you think I want peace?" says Moishe. "Haven't I wanted peace all my life, but we're no longer sheep at the slaughter. We had enough of that in Europe, in Lodz your grandmother, grandfather and uncle and me were taken six o'clock in the morning by the Germans, and look what happened. They're no longer here, they vanished in the ashes of chimneys in Auschwitz. You never knew them, now we have our own land, our own military and strike again when anyone threatens our life."

"The Palestinians aren't German Nazis, we're the ones who've occupied them and not the other way around …"

Moishe thrashes out his arms.

"You still don't understand," he says. "We're surrounded by Arabs on all sides. Not long ago they wouldn't even recognize as a state. After the Six Days War in 1967 we offered them the conquered areas in exchange for recognition of our state and for peace, but they rejected us, we have to think about our own security. Most Arabs would like to see us driven into the sea."

"You're wrong," says Dalia. "There are many Palestinians who want peace with us. Things have changed and we can't keep on waging war with our neighbors. People get sick at heart."

Moishe clutches his heart and looks accusingly at his wife.

"I can't take it. You're a psychologist and you know something about people's hearts, but you've also lost a son and you're still naïve. If the Palestinians really wanted peace with us, why didn't they grab the chance when Barak reached his hand out to them and offered them practically everything they'd always said they wanted?"

"Because Arafat wasn't up to the task and got frightened at the last minute," says Dalia. "But that doesn't mean that many Palestinians don't want peace with us."

"That was also the big question that wasn't solved in the peace plan that Clinton with Barak's acceptance finally proposed to Arafat," says Jon, who until then had remained silent from his seat on the sofa.

They all look at him. It's not the first time since Eve's and his arrival from New York that Eve and her parents discuss the inflamed conflict while he's kept quiet. Until now the happy reunion between Eve and her parents and his own curiosity with Jerusalem occupied him, and isn't he a guest in a new home in a foreign country, which he first must learn to know?

"What question?" asks Moishe and he senses that the old man wants to test him.

"The refugee question and the question of Jerusalem's division," he replies with a vague smile.

"Oh yes, of course you've followed it in the newspapers, in New York they read newspapers, too, but in negotiations between two conflicting parties, the one part can't get it all. They must be willing to compromise, and Mr. Arafat was not."

"If he was, it was under all circumstances a compromise where East Jerusalem was a part," he says.

"But he wasn't," Moishe insists. "He stood with an olive branch in one hand and holding a rifle in the other."

"Are you sure it wasn't the same with Barak?"

Moishe looks at him, as if he's trying to hold his glance and reach a quick conclusion of who he was and what he thought of him. He sighs and moves forward in his chair.

"You rescued my daughter from a burning tower, it was a miracle, and because of this will you always hold a special place with Dalia and me; but don't try telling me about the situation in our conflicts with the Palestinians. I've seen too much and know too much about what we're up against. I've lost my son in this conflict, and I'll never forgive them."

"Jon's a guest here and he has a right to have an opinion about this conflict," says Eve getting up and suddenly standing between them.

"He doesn't know what he's talking about. Four days ago he arrived in Jerusalem and now he's an expert on something we've fought with all our lives."

"I'm no expert," says Jon, "but from my many years in the legal system I know that a conflict always has at least two sides."

"This here is beyond all legal systems," says Moishe wearily. "It's much greater than you think."

"Maybe," says Jon, "I'll soon find out what it's all about."

"What d'you mean?" asks Dalia.

He tells them about Zawawi and his plans to track him down. Dalia and Moishe are silent; Dalia reaches out for Eve's hand. It comes as a shock, not in their wildest dreams had they imagined that Eve in New York had been a possible target for an al-Qaeda inspired terrorist whose base was on the West Bank; and he doesn't regret a second bringing it up.

"I don't think Jon should go, especially not now, where the Israeli army has gone into action," says Eve to her father.

"If there's something he feels he must do, then I'd be the last to talk him out of it," says Moishe clenching his jaws.

"It's not the best way of starting a new life here," says Dalia holding her head. "I don't understand why you haven't told us about this, how you could live with those threats in New York?"

"We couldn't either," says Jon. "We've walked a fine line between leaving the city and bringing an end to the matter."

"And now it just keeps on here?" says Dali shaking her head and looking stonily at him.

"I can't see I have a choice. As long as Zawawi is free, it's just a question of time before he's involved in a new plan for terror. My client in New York, Ifrahim Mohammed, and his family can't be sure of what'll happen to them, my colleague was shot in front of my eyes, Eve could've been the next …"

He runs out of words, Dalia lets go of Eve's hand, she holds her hands up to her gray hair and sighs. Her wise, dark eyes in the olive skin with the slightly hooked nose and high cheekbones are again worried, and she searches for Moishe's gaze. Moishe silently clenches his fist, a moment later he's stroking his brow. Eve's eyes ask him to stop, but too late. The light in the white-walled room with the many linoleum etchings by Polish artists contrast with the dense darkness of the garden behind the house. He suddenly feels that he's on another planet.

"And what about our safety?" says Dalia.

"I've already thought about that," he says.

"How?"

"As long as I'm working on the case, it's best that there's no connection between you and me. I figure I'll find a room or other anonymous place in Jerusalem while I prepare to leave."

"You can't..." says Eve.

"Why not?"

"We've come to Jerusalem to be together, you can't just leave me!"

"Dalia's right, just to be safe, I'd better leave."

She'd protest, but Moishe clutches his heart for the third time and is pale. They help Dalia get him to bed on his wobbling legs that won't bare him, and once he's gotten some water to drink and his pills and has fallen asleep in their bedroom and they've let the door remain ajar, it takes them a long time to calm her. She's been alone so long with the unrest of his weak heart that sometimes seems to stop entirely and his respiratory problems and pains; the doctors have several times suggested a by-pass operation, but in vain. Moishe will live and die with his own heart without surgery of any kind and he's already lived longer than predicted.

Although they're tired, Dalia won't let them go, there are so many large and small episodes with Moishe the past years that must be aired. She found him lying or sitting on the floor in the entrance, even in the garden or out on the sidewalk in front of the house and had several times heard Death sing over him, but each time he'd stubbornly get up without greater after-effect. She can't imagine from where his will to live comes, a will that is greater than his health, and was against all logic established in the camps during the war, where every day Death was breathing down his neck. He was only seventeen and starving when he escaped Auschwitz, rescued by his talents for mathematics and drawing and worked periodically as "teacher in residence" for two children of a camp's doctor living in the camp. The same doctor forced him twice to assist in medical experiments, and since then has not been able to trust doctors. He's seen things, impossible to describe, with his mind intact; even for her, Dalia, he's kept quiet about some things. They're locked away by day, but break out as nightmares, and only after 40 years of working on him has she been able to get him to open up for one of her colleagues at their clinic in Jerusalem and has found some peace at night. Darkness and stubbornness have lived side by side in his body without knowing the other's face other than through soft knocking and slurred, slightly hollow voices as with a neightbour, whose back, neck and top of the hair are the only things seen on the stairs, and whose existence one can only guess. "Isn't this also a picture of the way Israel has lived with itself?" asks Dalia, and they don't know how to answer; Eve, because no matter how she's connected her father with Israel and in her childhood has seen him as a bit of an outsider, and Jon, because he has the feeling that the image falls short of the whole truth and that he knows so little of the country. With a view from the kitchen to a remote and scintillatingly bright Jerusalem, that amidst the massive darkness resembles a mirage, both Dalia and Eve try to convince him to forgo his trip to the West Bank, and he promises to reconsider (at least until the conclusion of the Israeli action). But when the mood of the night has vanished and he's slept and the light breaks in to him as he wakes next to Eve in bed in the basement room under the house, a feeling emerges within him that there's something he must do to find peace with himself.

But first there's something else he's driven towards.

*

On Straus road not far from Mea Sharim lies a plain two-storey yellow limestone building is tucked in between two office buildings. It's raining. He takes a taxi from Zealot Street, asks the driver to let him off some house numbers farther down the street and walks the rest of the way. He senses his own anxiety when in the building's roomy vestibule with a stairway up to the second floor notices Sine and her short, blond hair before she sees him; she's sitting with some others along a wall and is waiting for him, studying some papers that look like drawings. From rooms different places in the building the sounds of music and loud voices in a strange echo are heard, as if the entire house's subconscious was speaking at once.

Even before he left New York, he'd agreed to see Sine and his son that day, but for whatever reason, a reason he himself doesn't know, he's surprised to see her. Maybe it's Eve's many questions about his relationship to her that's brought him in doubt; while he and Eve sat belted in their seats in the plane en route to Jerusalem 12 kilometres above the earth and they had a vast, sunny landscape of mountainous white clouds around them, questions rained over him, he denied that she had any grounds for worry. Wasn't it absurd that he should travel with her to Jerusalem just to start something new with his ex?

But at the moment she sees him, with that smile he knows so well, and she with her usual abrupt movements folds the drawings away as he's on his way towards her on a floor that creaks beneath his feet, he's caught in a déjà vu of their life together in the flat in Billrothstrasse in Vienna and of an altered gaze in her brown eyes, as if asking him "Have you come to be together with me now? Isn't it about time?"

But she asks him nothing, when he gets up to her and gives her a little hug, he senses the elasticity of her back and a new scent that he'd never connected with her before. Here on this foreign spot, it's for some moments as if their previous love for each other with all that's been withheld in the intervening years, also something that's bathed in a kind of awkwardness and bitterness, is suddenly a refuge and a fixed point, where neither of them are able to express it to themselves or the other.

On the surface, they're two travellers who, after many years have met again in this restless and beautiful city, and they speak with slightly unsteady voices about their son and his progress, as she leads him up the stairs to the first floor and in to a small practice room where Tobias is seated at a shiny black grand piano and playing a waltz by Chopin. Stunned, he just stands inside the doorway as Sine with a nod sits down beside a middle aged man in a row of otherwise empty chairs, whom he guesses must be his son's teacher.

The tones flow melodically and rhythmically in a quiet cascade from the piano as Tobias' fingers dance across the keys. Although Tobias is sitting with eyes wide open with his face towards him, his somnambulent gaze keeps him from recognizing his father, and even when Tobias finishes the piece with a soft coda and Jon claps and walks towards him to give him a hug, it's as if his first eye contact and embrace is with a stranger, and with an aching heart he must say his name and call himself father for Tobias to wake up and discover who he is, but yet is unsure.

But he's done this so many times before and compliments him for his playing and begins talking about his life in Jerusalem trying to hold his attention. With his blond hair and lanky 14-year-old body, Tobias now looks like him at the same age, even his eyes. His language has developed since he last saw him in Vienna nine months ago, but his replies are still abrupt and gaze distant, under-scored by a smile that makes Jon doubt that he's listening. He notices all this in the few minutes they're together, when Tobias without warning suddenly turns from him and sits back down at the piano and starts playing and the teacher with a polite gesture interrupts Tobias and with a few notes on the piano shows him how he can improve his technique.

Jon sits down next to Sine to watch the teaching that is not so much with words as by the teacher's demonstrations that Tobias quickly copies, and when he repeats the piece has already added his own style. He's amazed that Tobias has found his own tone in his playing and plays more articulate than ever as an individual (he'd from the beginning in Vienna thought that his autism would freeze him into something mechanical); but most of all, until muteness took over, seemed to be in the same space as he. It's as if the last six months' shadows here in this small rehearsal hall with its acoustic resonance and with his own son as the midpoint has evaporated and he can't understand that he'd for so long accepted the physical distance between them. What was he thinking?

Later on in the day, that's just what Sine tries finding out when he leaves the music school with her and they sit and eat in a small restaurant with a few other diners in Nahalat Shiva and the gray wintry light streams in over them through the windows revealing that small, fine wrinkles have also invaded

their faces around the eyes and he doesn't attempt to explain away his neglect. Instead he says:

"I don't know how we can do it, but I'm not letting him go again."

"You might have to. We're not in Jerusalem forever. Tobias' stay at the
school is only until summer, and then I'm also finished with the excavation."

"And then what?"

"I figure that we'll go back to Copenhagen. If I try I can probably get a job
in the Foreign Office."

"You're done with Vienna?"

"Yes," she says looking him in his eyes without him exactly knowing what
she's thinking. Her look is both vulnerable and acusing, and he's thrown
back to the thousands of times in Vienna where they were close. The question on the tip of his tongue, whether there's another man in her life, doesn't
reach his lips nor does she talk about it; instead she becomes increasingly uncomfortable when she asks him about his time in New York and he in a diffuse and terse version of the events during and after the terrorist attack on the
World Trade Center can't avoid describing the state of angst that both he and
Eve have lived in. She's dumbfounded whe he discloses his plans of going to
Hebron to track Zawawi and when she finally comments on it, she says mat-
ter-of-factly:

"I know you. Probably something you feel you've got to do even though
everything speaks against it. I won't try talking you out of it, but think about
Tobias ..."

"What d'you mean?"

"You know what I mean."

"No, not really."

"I mean that your many activities and your involvement that I like so much
in you has a price. I know better than anyone that you think very little about
yourself; but seen from afar you sometimes seem selfish. And the price
shouldn't be that Tobias totally loses his father."

"Totally, you say. You're blaming me for not being around enough for
him?"

"Yes, I do," she says. "When you admit that you've neglected him by not visiting for longer periods, then I think you really should do something about it."

"And how can that happen if you and he leave as soon as it's summer"

She stops eating, knife and fork in mid-air, looking at something behind him. His eyes study her still lovely face, fine teint with the high cheekbones and shadow across her cheek. For some seconds he tries to imagine what she's thinking when she's digging in the earth for artifacts that haven't seen the light of day for thousands of years. Has she not always been closer to earth than he?

"Come back to us," she says finding his eyes.

"You're not serious!?" he says amazed.

"Yeah, come home with us."

"After all these years. Is that really what you want?"

"Why'd you think I'm in Jerusalem?"

"For Tobias!"

"Not just him, I could've chosen Toronto instead, there's a similar music school there."

"There're no excavations!"

"Excavation in Hinnom's Valley is exciting, but that's not why I'm here."

He's speechless, looks at her, senses her courage and at the same time her nervousness; many thoughts race through him: His desire to be with her and go in a door that she's unexpectedly opened; his commitment to Eve; an unease at being disturbed in his gearing up for the trip to the West Bank; somewhere in the back of his mind Eve's warnings about just this situation. He leans back in his chair at the white-clothed table with the still half-full dishes and glasses.

"You know I'm with Eve," he says. "I've come to Jerusalem to live here with her."

"What you have with Eve is your affair," she says getting ready to leave. "I don't know where you are emotionally; but now you know where I am."

"Leaving already?"

"Yeah," she says getting up from the table. "I've got to pick up Tobias. Today he's spending the night with me, other times he sleeps at the school, but mostly with me. He still has trouble being alonge."

"I need some time …," he says.

"You've had at least seven years, and now you have the spring …," she says bitterly, picking up her coat from a chair and starts putting it on.

"Why haven't you said anything before now?"

"I've had my own doubts, and I was waiting for you to come to me. You were the one who left, I didn't?"

She has her coat on and stands in the middle of the floor among the few guests and waits for him to say or do something that would make it easier for her to leave.

He gets up, puts on his trenchcoat, calls for the waiter, quickly paying the bill and silently follows her out.

Outside they walk some metres down the narrow road with shiny windows from the second floor apartments that reflect the sky. As on signal they both stop among the pedestrians, he puts his hand on her shoulder.

"I don't know yet when I'll be leaving, but I'll probably move to a room in East Jerusalem," he says. "I'll call when I get back."

She gives him a card with her telephone number and address.

"Think about that with Tobias," she says.

He nods and holds her close, and he controls his emotions when he again smells her scent. Like two strangers who once had known each other to the farthest corners of their drems, they part, and he's at once exaulted and divided within himself as he goes by foot towards the eastern half of the city.

*

That night he has a dream as he restlessly lies next to Eve, tossing and turning in the darkness: He crawls up a ladder towards the sky, the ladder, made of rope, ends abruptly and as he, under the sensation of a vast blue celestial dome that has no beginning nor end, becomes dizzy and starts crawling down

again, he realizes that the ladder isn't anchored to the ground and he's floating freely.

*

After a couple of extra days in her parents' house, where they lay plans for
the time after his return to Jerusalem (he, now in a more split state of mind,
which he tries unsuccessfully to hide from her), he moves, despite Eve's protests, to a room at the YMCA's large worn down hotel on Nablus Road in
East Jerusalem. From here he'd continue to Bethlehem and from there to
Hebron, but something holds him back, and it's not just Eve's and Sine's arguments against the trip, but also the daily reports on TV and in the new-
papers on the escalated conflict in Gaza and on the West Bank in the wake of
the Israeli army's activities in the region. Photos of the demolished and
bombed out houses in Gaza, tanks at the ready, angry and mourning Palestinians and Israeli officers that explain themselves, roll across the TV screen in
the hotel's cool, broad lounge where he, late in the evening apart from a few
other guests that come and go, sits alone and is sometimes able to get the
connection to cable or CNN to work. The feeling of being so close to the
dramatic events and yet far away gives the images an unreal quality, and the
large, dimly lit hotel corridors and rooms that particularly in the evenings are
practically deserted enhances his sense of being in a ghost-like zone that is
removed from all the possibilities of the wealthier part of the city. It's also in
this room that, on March 2nd, still undecided, after a visit from Eve, is ap-
palled by pictures from the orthodox Beit Yisrael in Jerusalem, where a
bomb was placed by the Al-Aqsa martyr brigade and detonated near a group
of women who'd been standing and waiting with their baby carriages as their
husbands left the synagogue near by. The bomb killed 12 and wounded more
than fifty, and the TV pictures project the inferno of chaos, sorrow, grief,
broken bodies, faces in shock and howling ambulances that the bomb's explosion from one minute to the next produced in the heart of Jerusalem.

   At night he has trouble falling asleep in his isolated room with the creeking
bed on the second floor. His irritation finally decides for him: he'll leave the

next day; but when in the morning he's sent to an office on the fourth floor by the young porter because of a technical problem with the print-out of his bill from a computer and gets there in his coat, he's unexpectedly invited to coffee by an older, well-dressed woman. He silently accepts the invitation; in a calm and cultivated voice and in English with a slight Arab accent, she introduces herself as the hotel's director and leaves to fetch the coffee from a small kitchen out in the hall. He sets his bag aside, takes off his coat and sits down by a small table in the corner of her large, dim office, where light can barely get through. Behind a thin curtain the Omar Mosque and the churches appear as blurred silhouettes and seem like a ghost of the past night's massacre on unarmed men, women and children.

The woman returns with a tray filled with coffee cups and a plate of cakes and even before she's poured a steaming cup of coffee for him and puts it in front of him, she says:

"I've heard you're on your way to Bethlehem…"

"Where've you heard that?"

"From the porter, you ordered a taxi to Bethlehem, didn't you?"

"Yeah?" he says mystified meeting her dark eyes.

"As the situation is right now, it's difficult getting mail through from here, maybe you'll do me a favour and take a package from me to an important person in Beit Jala just outside Bethlehem. The package just contains some brochures for the YMCA, a sphygmomanometer for measuring blood pressure and some medicine that can't be gotten in Bethlehem, but you don't have to."

"That's OK," he says. "I'm already booked in a small hotel in Beit Jala."

"How lucky!" she says happily. "In return you don't have to pay for your stay here, and I can get Amer Saleh to meet you at one of the road blocks and show you to the hotel."

"I don't mind paying," he says. "But who's Amer Saleh?"

"The man who's to get the package. He's the head of YMCA's rehabilitation centre in Beit Jala, where they treat Palestinian children and youths who are either physically or mentally traumatized by the conflict."

They continue talking as they drink their coffee and he expresses his outrage at the bombing the previous night.

"Yes it's terrible," she says. "That sort of thing shouldn't happen and when it does one's powerless. It's as if fanatics in both camps devour each other and grow even more blind. There once were many Christian Palestinians on the West Bank; now there's only about 3 per cent. The rest have left. You're brave to travel there now. You must have an important errand ..."

"Yes," he says, but says no more and when she sees he'd rather not talk about it, she gets up, turns and walks over to her desk to telephone. He gets up, puts on his trenchcoat and listens with half an ear, but can't understand her Arabic.

She finishes her call, writes something on a small note, takes the package from the floor under the desk, turns and gives it to him with a smile.

"Here's the package to Amer Saleh, I've just talked to him, he'll meet you. Just give this note to the driver and he'll get you to the right place."

He stands there a moment and observes her friendly yet tense attitude. Who is she? Where's she from? It's as if he's not only leaving her, but also Jerusalem.

"Take care," she says, "and for God's sake don't lose your temper no matter what the Israeli soldiers at the checkpoints do."

He leaves with the package and his bag down the long hallway and stairs down to the lobby and out into the cool air with a high, clear sky above the driveway to the building. The taxi's already waiting, he gets into the backseat; the driver with his unshaven face turns to him and offers a brief "Hello, sir" and takes his note.

A moment later, he's on his way.

*

The driver leaves Nablus Road and by many small streets and reaches a concrete drive onto a multi-laned highway surrounded by desert. A larger convoy of military vehicles is on its way south, but before they get onto the highway they're stopped by an armed soldier who's stepped out onto the road and waved them to the side at an intermistic checkpoint of three soldiers and a military jeep. The driver drives a bit forward, rolls down his window as a soldier approaches from ahead with his rifle swinging in front of him from side to side. In silence the driver presents his papers and driver's license, which the 20 year-old soldier studies closely and slowly, then knocks on Jon's window, who also rolls it down and hands him his passport. The soldier's eyes fall on the package and asks him in broken English about its contents and his errand on the West Bank. Apparently not satisfied with his reply, he takes the driver's papers and his passport back to the jeep and gets in. In the jeep the soldiers discuss amongst themselves, one of them laughs, another phones and it's not clear what's happening. His driver watches him in the rearview mirror and suddenly remarks:

"They're testing you. It could take ten minutes, a half an hour, maybe they'll try something, maybe not, just stay calm."

Behind them three cars are waiting. They wait, but don't know what they're waiting for; the soldier slowly walks back to their car and gives the driver all the papers and nonchalantly waves them through.

They drive along the broad highway and have barely gone four kilometers on the little trafficked road with a view of several clusters of new, white red-roofed houses rising above the desert landscape before they again must slow down and almost run into the back end of a line in front of a new, stationary, concrete checkpoint. The line is mainly comprised of military vehicles, that they'd seen earlier on the road, armoured tanks slowly passing the cage of the checkpoint with its dusty windows. From open shutes in the tanks, soldiers in battle dress greet the young soldiers in and around the cage, but as the last military vehicle passes the checkpoint, a large, heavy barrier is lowered in front of a battered white car in front of theirs, and they're forced to stop their car five metres from them.

Two soldiers, one with his rifle raised, immediately approaches the car and orders the driver and his passenger out. Standing on the road the two show their papers as the barrel of the soldier's rifle is pointed at them. Suddenly the other soldier grabs the driver's arm, a 40 year-old Palestinian in a dark, wrinkled jacket, and drags him towards the cage, whose opening he practically falls through. In the cage, three soldiers shout at him gesticulating, and when he comes back to the road led with a firm grasp on his right arm by one of the young soldiers, his cheek is bleeding and is shoved towards a closed military jeep; the other Palestinian, a younger man in a brown jacket, who's been standing on the road, is ordered in to the driver's seat of the white car. The man stalls in front of the open door, shouts something as he points towards his friend, who at that moment is shoved into the back of the jeep.

"What's happening?" Jon asks his driver and notices the palms of his hands becoming moist.

"I don't know, best to keep quiet and make like nothing," answers the man quietly and with a quick glance at him in the rearview mirror.

Two soldiers force the Palestinian in the brown jacket into the car, and with nervously awkward movements starts the car and drives forward, the barricade is raised and the white car continues out on the road to the other side of the checkpoint.

Now it's their turn.

They're waved forward in the car; the same two soldiers come towards them and wave them out of the car, the driver shows his papers, he his passport. The young soldier, with his smooth, pale face and curly dark hair looks like an overgrown child; he keeps the passport and orders him to remain standing on the road as he looks into the car, where he notices the package, which with a shout pulls up from the backseat as if he's found something dangerous.

He's shoved from behind, both soldiers leave the driver standing on the road, one of them shouts at him in broken English that he's to come to the cage. He does as they say and walks the six-seven metres to the cage with the greasy windows and nervously stands there in front of the closed door and waits to be called in, but they let him wait until they've opened the package and searched it and checked his passport. When he's called in with a bark in Hebrew by a soldier of about 25 who appears to be in charge, the contents of the package are spread over a table and the YMCA brochures thrown on the floor of the small, smoke-filled room.

The 25 year-old soldier, without helmet, pistol in his belt measures him quickly with his eyes and in English machine guns questions to him about the package; before he's answered one question, he fires the next, where Jon finally gives up answering.

"Then you won't answer?!" says the soldier with a voice almost breaking and that has now gotten the other soldiers' attention. As he holds the soldier's glare, he tries to see through his ultimate goal: will he be arrested, will he be denied passage, will he merely humiliate the driver and himself?

"I've answered as best I can," he says calmly, hiding his anger.

"You want me to believe that you're a tourist and at the same time delivering a package to a suspicious Palestinian organization!"

"It's just a package and the YMCA is an internationally recognized organization!"

"Do you know that the receiver of this package has been arrested several times for subversive activities?"

"I don't know Amer Saleh personally," he says, "but as far as I know he's the head of an aid programme for youths and children on the West Bank."

"He's a dangerous and untrustworthy person; stay away from him!"

He nods faintly, not answering.

As the three soldiers keep him in check with their eyes, one of them with a slightly raised rifle, he's again asked to account for the addresses and duration of his stay on the West Bank, and just as he's certain they'll deny him passage, the helmetless soldier gives him his passport, warns him about the Palestinians and with a pointed finger ordered to collect the package as fast as possible and get out.

"Does that mean that we can drive on?" he asks.

The soldier smiles stiffly, his young face grimacing, despite the absence of visible threat and the apparent security of two colleagues nearby, his eyes reflect a strange form of angst. For some seconds he registers that he's been caught on the wrong foot and builds himself up:

"We're at war with the Palestinians, but if you absolutely will go there and get your ass shot off, just drive!"

He gathers the items from the package in his arms and leaves the cage and is soon out in the sun. Another three cars wait in line behind the taxi and the driver's still standing away from the car, shivering in his thin nylon jacket awaiting permission to get into the car.

A soldier waves the driver into the car, and a moment later Jon is seated in the back with the blood pressure metre and the package of brochures and medicine.

The barricade's raised and they drive.

Only when they've driven some kilometres and the contours of Bethlehem with its grayish Church of the Nativity and mosque and bright houses on the hilltop come into view in the rolling landscape that alternates between moss green and rocky that he puts the things down beside him on the seat and breathes easier.

Because of the many roadblocks they must drive halfway around the city. Soon they see occasional gray flat-roofed houses on a dry and barren soil in the broad valley that on the horizon leads up to hills with colonies of clustered white houses of the settlers that hover over the landscape. They continue up the steep, narrow road to Mount Gilo until they're met by a massive concrete crossbar enclosed in barbed wire and cannot come farther. The driver stops the car and calls Amer Saleh on his mobile, then turns to Jon saying:

"This is the edge of Beit Jala, your hotel is farther on, Amer Saleh will be here soon, on the other side of the barrier, to meet you."

He pays the driver, puts the things from the package in his bag, thanks him and gets out of the car. With a wave of his hand, the driver backs the car, turns and quickly drives away and vanishes.

Behind the concrete barrier, the road continues into a neighborhood of ramshackle flat-roofed gray and white painted houses, rolls of barbed wire lay spread out on the path, he heaves up his bag and walks down the road and waits. A mangy stray dog crosses the path and sniffs around in a heap of garbage on a plot with beams for a house that's either not been finished or has collapsed. A boy bicycles out of a driveway of one of the houses and when he sees him stops and stands and stares. He sends him a faint smile, but the boy turns and bicycles back to the house.

He's alone on a slope in Beit Jala, a frontier that seems to be thrown years back and abandoned. From a minaret some distance away, the call of the muaddhin is suddenly heard, amplified by a primitive loud speaker that gives the voice a screeching, nasal character. Down in the valley on a road that winds through the bare and millennial landscape, an Israeli military column is on the move slowly and ominously with an inevitability that has long since caught up with the territory. What's its destination? What's going to happen?

Farther down the road beneath the increasingly grayer sky is a darkish man in a suede jacket on his way towards him. He looks to be in his mid-40's. His step is brisk, he raises his hand in greeting, it must be Amer Saleh. Jon works his way around the barbed wire, gives him his hand and meets his warm, but weary, brown eyes, Amer Saleh bids him welcome to Beit Jala in perfect English and offers to take his bag. He declines and they walk to Saleh's car that's parked some distance behind another but smaller roadblock.

In the car, Amer Saleh turns to him with a faint smile and says, as if they'd known each other long:

"You got through, everything okay?"

He tells about the experiences at the two checkpoints.

A shadow crosses Amer's face.

"That's what we have to live with. You've come at a bad time."

"How so?"

"Not only has Arafat's headquarters in Ramallah been bombed as well as a larger building here, many Palestinians killed, also women and children, but we expect that the Israelis return with a larger force and in a new wave on top of the senseless terrorist killings yesterday in Jerusalem ..."

Jon tells him of the convoys of Israeli military vehicles he's already seen.

"There you see, I fear the worst."

Amer starts the car and he steers silently along the sloping narrow road towards Hebron to the hotel. En route they pass several flat-roofed houses, a church with an eroded façade, isolated concrete apartment houses that appear to be semi-vacated and some few shops with vegetables and fruit; here and there appear heaps of ruins or bare stony ground and he wonders how Amer keeps his spirit in the face of all this.

When they reach the main road, Amer turns right and drives some distance; they pass an abandoned gas station and pumps, red with rust, and arrives at a wide, open space filled with rocks, weeds and a windowless wreck of a car to the left. Single cars drive towards them, one of them a yellow Mercedes of older vintage packed with passengers; Amer stops the car on the other side of the vacant ground and points to a well-cared for, bright building of several stories.

"Your hotel!" he says with a smile, and they get out.

Before they part on the sidewalk, he'd give Amer the things he's brought for him, but at that moment Amer's phone calls him to an urgent matter and asks him to come to his home that evening and bring them with him. Amer hastily gives him his card, hurries to his car and drives off, and he walks along a tiled walk to the small hotel.

He opens the heavy, screeching door with a glass pane into a vestibule that once certainly had been filled with guests, but now apart from some dusty tall cacti and green plants in white pots, is deserted. With his bag he walks up the stairs in the centre of the vestibule to the first floor, where he finds another deserted room with a TV, chairs and a table in the center and a row of doors to rooms out to the sides.

The stairway leads up to a new floor with yet more doors and rooms, but before he, slightly mystified, decides again to take the stairs, a door behind him opens and a tall, slim, red-haired, pale woman of about 60, agilely approaches him with an outstretched hand and introduces herself in English with a distinct German accent as Trude Wachmann and director of the place.

"You must be Jon Baeksgaard, our new guest," she says smiling. "It's a surprise for us every time there's someone who dares come here, on 'the other side'."

When she's shown him to his room and he's deposited his bag and removed his trenchcoat, she makes him a cup of tea and they sit down by the table in the space between the rooms where their voices echo under the ceiling. She wants to know what's made him visit Beit Jala, but he avoids telling her his real errand, without her really noticing, and he quickly senses that in reality it's she who's in need of confiding in someone.

"I'm sort of stranded here," she says. "I came here a year ago to pray at the Church of the Nativity, but before I knew it, I landed here at the Bible University's hotel. Then there were many guests, mostly from Europe, despite the intifada, the atmosphere was good and they needed a director. Now there's hardly anyone except Professor Said, who teaches the few young people at the Bible University and I'm still the director. Directing in the midst of Purgatory, as I usually say.

She laughs, but her laughter has a vibrato of sadness and solitude. He wonders what it was in Germany that made her flee to this time trap and this hotel to be director for shadows from the past. As if reading his thoughts, she says:

"There was nothing more for me in Germany. In Germany they think only of money, the Palestinians are a people in need, I wanted to give them a helping hand."

"And can you?"

"Oh yes, Professor Said is happy to spend the night here when there's curfew in the area or when they stop him at a checkpoint on his way home and he's forced to turn back. If I weren't here they'd have to close the hotel, it's a question of pride keeping it open, no one's yielding, neither Moslem nor Christian. Every time a hotel or shop or school closes, a small hope that's part of the greater hope is, as Professor Said says, snuffed out. In the end the greater hope is also extinguished. But you probably wouldn't understand."

"Yes, I think I do," he says and they continue speaking. He's so comfortable in her company that he several times is on the verge of revealing his real plan on the West Bank; when he the second time mentions his plans for visiting Hebron she looks at him in wonder:

"What do you want there? It's hell on earth, maybe I've misjudged you, maybe you're not what I think you are."

"Hell on earth, isn't that a bit strong?"

"Go there yourself, it's not far even though the journey seems endless. But don't go by bus, stick with the yellow taxis."

It's dusk, the light in the windows has faded, they look like shadows sitting across from each other at the table in the center of the space with their tea that's long gotten cold. Trude Wachmann gets up to turn on the lights over the table, but they don't work, 'it's the installations', she says and instead lights some candles as the darkness outside quickly takes over and gives him the feeling that they're on a lonely ship sailing through the night. He also gets up and thanks her for the conversation and her good advice, and as she shows him on a small map the way to Amer Saleh's house, she gives him yet another:

"Drop your trenchcoat and wear a dark jacket when you leave here. In the darkness all are cats gray, but here it's best to completely fuse with the darkness, you don't know who's got you in their sights."

"What d'you mean?"

"I'm talking about who and what might come and keep an eye on what moves here."

"Are you talking about Israeli snipers?" he asks worried.

"I don't go out after dark that much I can tell you."

"Has anyone here just been shot?"

"Yes," she says and the tense expression in her pale face with the vibrant, slightly staring eyes tells him that she'd rather not talk about it."

*

Some lamps burn over the Bible University's white buildings to the right of the hotel, as he fifteen minutes later leaves the darkened vestibule and locks the front door. Some distance down the street, to the right, around a large concrete building there are also lights, a car pulls out, it must be the local police station; the space across the street is dark and deserted, only a couple of the many street lights work on the road to the left, in the distance, the dim lights of Bethlehem.

It's cool, and in the vast firmament the stars are aglow, he's seldom seen these constellations and the moon's disk so clearly. Carrying his bag and wearing a dark jacket he walks down the road to the left and turns onto a small side street, where an elderly man and a younger one in conversation pass him, the older man in a checkered kefije, the younger looking curiously in his direction. At the end of this road are two houses facing each other on each their side of the street: one, older and dark, the other white and spacious, illuminated by a lamp over the front door, in front of the white is an old, spreading eucalyptus with its knobby branches, and on the graveled driveway he recognizes Amer's car.

Amer receives him with a cordial handshake, but visibly affected by his visit that afternoon with a family in the village of Ya'bod whose 5-year-old son hadn't been able to sleep several nights after confrontations and shooting in the village between Hamas and the Israeli army; the boy shouts and cries for hours, when the shooting temporarily stops and wakes up every other second at night certain that he'd seen Israeli soldiers climbing through the windows, even though the family lives in a flat on the third floor.

"When there are problems like that, they call me," says Amer, "and I or one of my colleagues tries to talk to the traumatized child and get peace for the family. Sometimes we can offer to treat the child in our centre, but we lack resources and psychologists and already have 70 children from the area in treatment."

He greets Amer's wife, mother and two daughters and eats with them in a large, rectangular room with a framed photograph from the stalls in Old Jerusalem on their wall. Here he tells them about New York and the USA, but they've barely finished their meal with a short prayer before Amer with a discreet gesture signals him to follow to the adjoining room, which is a combination bedroom and study. Amer closes the door behind him and turns on the TV, where a local news broadcast has just started. On the screen are pictures of Israeli tanks, shooting Israeli soldiers and F-16 fighter jets, that from the evening sky are bombing houses in Gaza; there's a clip to the Israeli Prime Minister Ariel Sharon in a sequence taken from CNN. Sharon seems gloomily relentless as he delivers his message to the press after a crisis meeting in the Israeli government's Security Council. Sharon's words are translated simultaneously to Arabic, but as he only understands fragments of the Hebrew, Amer turns towards him:

"Sharon says directly, 'Palestineans will be hit and it'll hurt. We must cause them losses, sacrifices that will make them understand the great price they must pay.' You know what that means, don't you?"

"I think so," he says.

"It means that the Israelis have initiated a new offensive, they might already strike tonight."

"Here, too?"

"Most likely Gaza, but possibly also here, who knows?" says Amer, sagging in his chair, wiping his forehead with his hand and staring out into space."

"You probably want to be alone with your family right now?" he says, unsure what to make of Amer's prolonged silence.

"No, I just have to warn my wife, and we'll have to take some precautions in the house. Later I'll follow you back to your hotel."

"That's not necessary," he says. "I know the way."

But Amer ignores him and is caught in his own exhaustion:

"It's hard to keep going. We're in a permanent state of emergency. And my job is to keep up the spirits of my personnel and the children in our centre. We've got six offices spread over the entire West Bank with a stubborn core of people trying to do the same. But it's as if a whole population is traumatized, children live with the impression of violence and conflicts each and every day and their drawings are filled with F-16 fighter bombers and soldiers at war. Four times I've been arrested without reason and four times I've been tortured. The last time they tried to break me mentally. I've been hung for days with a black cover over my head and a guard sometimes opening the lid to the darkness in my cell and emphasizing each and every word: 'You're losing your mind; slowly you'll lose your mind.' Everything's topsy-turvy with the Israelis: It's not they who must prove your guilt, it's you who must prove your innocence."

"But the military part of Hamas, the Al Aqsa brigade and the others, kill freely in Israel?" he says hit by Amer Saleh's words.

"Yes," says Amer holding his glance, "but who do you think is the strongest, and who's the weakest and most desperate?"

"There's no excuse for killing civilians, no matter who does it," he says.

"No and I can't defend the terrorist killing of civilians under any circumstances either, but the Israelis have to stop occupying my land."

"I agree," he says and will get up to fetch his bag and give Amer his things, but Amer places a hand on his arm.

"I've heard that you want to go to Hebron, why …?"

"There's something I've got to find out in Hebron, maybe it's no longer possible …"

"What?"

"I'm looking for a man connected with the military branch of Hamas. I'm trying to find him. He's guilty of several murders and has planned a terrorist attack on a subway station in New York."

"Who're you working for?" asks a mystified Amer.

"No one," he says and taking a chance and tells Amer about Ben Zawawi and his reasons for looking for him.

Amer shakes his head.

"I understand what you're saying and what you've been through, but you're here at the wrong time and what you're thinking is very dangerous."

"I've got to try," he says.

"Are you completely sure?"

"Yes," he says but feels like a man with his back to the wall.

"Then I might be able to help you. Call me tomorrow. I've got some connections in Hebron who should be able to help you."

Soon after he gives Amer the long-awaited medicine and blood pressure gauge, and Amer follows him to the ground in front of the house in the late evening darkness. Here they silently take leave of each other and he walks under a starry sky back to the road and hotel along deserted narrow streets.

The hotel is still in darkness and without electricity, but Trude Wachmann has left some candles burning on the first floor. He finds his way to his room, quickly removes his trousers, lies down on the bed in the rest of his clothing under the covers on the cool sheet and immediately falls asleep.

He glides into a timeless dream.

A young man in a linen coat with unruly long hair, curls at his ears and pale face is led into a high-ceilinged room by two armed guards. The room is large, cool and damp and with its gray stone walls, floor and ceiling resembles a room in a fort; the murky room is illuminated by burning torches set in iron holders along the walls, the man is led forward to a podium. On a chair on the podium sits a ruddy, slightly obese older man in a white toga, a meaty face and intelligent eyes. He puts three fingers of his right hand to his temple, he appears to have a headache and wishes he were somewhere else. It's in the middle of the night, the older man calls the young man in the linen coat to him, and the position is clear: He sits on top and the young man on the bottom. He orders the guards to retreat. The young man's tired face is half hidden in shadows as the older man starts questioning him, first with nonchalant gestures and a sharp voice, but that also jabs through himself because of his headache, then still more uncertain and doubting, as the young man's answers reach him as a soft, unexpected rain on his arid mind. He'd planned to judge the young man quickly as a rebel who with his sermons and earnest followers creates unrest in the city, and to return to his warm bed. No one's taken his defense, but now he trips over the man's words and keeps returning to one sentence.

"Say it again."

"What, Lord Procurator?" says the young man with the soft voice, wrenching of exhaustion."

"What you said before …"

"You shall love your enemies."

*

He awakes in the darkness to an enormous roar, the bed shakes under him, a small framed picture falls down from the wall, he's totally disoriented and at once afraid, and gets up and looks out the window: Farther down the road a building is in flames, but from where he's standing, he can see no people. He remains standing, trying to come to himself and understand what's happened;

but he hears a voice outside his door, and now a knock, he opens it. Trude
Wachmann is standing in the hallway with a frightened look:

"They've bombed the police station, it must've been one of their F-16's,
it's horrible …"

He jumps into his clothes and together they go down to the street in front
of the hotel. The building down the road is burning wildly and looks like an
enormous bonfire in the middle of the night, some cars stop some distance
from the burning ruin, people get out and keep their distance as they watch
the fire, but there's a long wait before an ambulance or fire engine arrives.
The hoses are rolled out, men in uniform move towards the violent fire, water
gushes out over the half-burned building. Despite Trude Wachmann's warning, he runs down the road towards the fire to offer his assistance, others
from the neighborhood have also come and he soon finds himself among a
small group of shocked and angry folk not able to do anything.

The fire slowly comes under control, a smoking pile of ruins remains, and
the anger and frustration in the group grows as the ambulance staff takes
turns searching among the hot bricks and retrieve two charred bodies. Two
women, the dead men's wives, who've arrived in cars driven by relatives, cry
loudly, one of them shouts her husband's name to the heavens. Both of them
are helped by the people near by into the ambulance, one of these is Amer,
who apparently was standing on the other side of the group nearby and has
now stepped forward with soothing words and an offer of help. Jon walks
over to him.

"They destroy our police station and murder our police, what'll be next?"
says Amer his eyes searching for an answer, but the fire has brought him one
step closer to darkness, and Jon quietly places a hand on his shoulder.

Together they walk down the dimly lit country road to his hotel. Before
they part Amer says:

"Women's mourning lasts hundreds of years, a fighter pilot's joy a few seconds."

Then he's gone.

*

The last hours of the night, he lies sleepless in his hotel room, several times considering whether there's meaning to continue, if this is the beginning, what awaits him ahead? And for the first time in a long time, he has the feeling that it would make no difference. He's stepped into a land with conflicts greater than mountains and what meaning does it have in the larger game that he tracks down a killer like Zawawi? There are many other killers in uniform walking around freely and are not bothered by anyone or anything because they're following orders. And what about the officers and generals that give these orders? And the politicians who sanction them?

But after an hour's sleep he awakes to the morning light and feels again that he has no choice and that it would be impossible for him to return to Jerusalem empty-handed. If he returns ...

He tries calling Eve, but the connection to Jerusalem is blocked; instead he calls Amer, who gives him a name and telephone number in Hebron.

"The man's worked for the police," says Amer. "He still has good connections there. He's promised to help you; but you have to tell him you 'job' yourself."

"Sure, of course."

"His son's been treated in our office in Hebron, so you can trust him."

He thanks Amer for his help.

"Be careful, there are sharks in the water."

He promises.

He packs his bag, leaves the room, eats a small breakfast in the kitchen on the second floor with a view to the vacant space across from the hotel, where some boys randomly throw stones at the wrecked car. He pays his bill to Trude Wachmann, who after the events of the night is very reluctant to let him leave, and walks down the road and further to the right. Here, near the bombed-out police station and another demolished structure he stands to wait for one of the yellow taxis.

It's still cold; he pulls his trenchcoat tightly closed in the long wait, as his eyes search after the few cars that pass him on the road. The smell from the burning ruin hangs in the air, but the light proclaims an early spring and the sky is blindingly clear and broken by faint rays of sun that cast pale shadows around the lampposts, trees and house walls. From a minaret farther up in the city again is heard the call of the muaddhins and reminds him that he's on foreign ground.

When a long, worn yellow Mercedes finally stops in front of him, it's packed. The driver in a thick jacket and a blue checked scarf across the his shoulders points to a small spot in the very back of the homemade backseat, the others move so that he can squeeze in and the car starts moving with noisy Arab music from the loud speakers in the doors.

The landscape alternates between the barren, rocky and hilly and the flat, fertile and cultivated; areas with the grayish-blue olive trees are replaced the closer they come to Hebron, by areas with fruit trees in bud and green grapevines. From time to time colonies of white settler houses with water towers enclosed by large fences and associated fenced-in roads up the hills. Not far from one of these, the car turns off the main road and continues on in a barren gravelly landscape with bulldozers, excavators and excavated soil and coughs its way up to an intermistic checkpoint where everyone must pay and get out.

They walk the last part of the way towards three armed soldiers and their armored military jeep and the lines of local men, women and children who are already on both sides of the checkpoint, whose invisible frontier is the soldiers' random pointing of it. Two women and a man with a crate of vegetables between them complain on the other side of the unmarked border that they can't come through, but with a rifle pointed at them, they're forced to the back of the line by one of the soldiers. No one appears to understand the rules for the soldiers' conduct and impatiently await a sudden change of mind so that they can carry on; but that doesn't happen.

Twenty minutes pass, a half hour, more and more get into the two lines, that at the same time are emptied of people who glide back or to the sides in the hilly landscape and vanish over the hilltops some distance from the checkpoint. A middle-aged man behind him taps him on the shoulder and says something to him in Arabic, which he doesn't understand, but when the man in his worn-out clothes starts to walk away from the line, he follows after and after some twenty minutes' walk at his heels he comes to a large cliff-like prominence which they both start to force. When the Palestinian almost reaches the top, he turns towards him and signals danger with his finger cutting over his throat. He ducks while the other creeps the last bit and cautiously lifts his head to get a view of the situation.

The man waves him up, he crawls the last metres with his bag over his shoulder and finds himself on a plateau in a wilderness of aromatic thyme, mint, gnarled pines and rocks before him. About 50 meters ahead, a narrow asphalted road runs around another hilltop and there wait two half-full yellow taxis.

The Palestinian looks guardedly over the landscape and turns towards him and says in broken English:

"No soldiers, if they see you, maybe shoot, no soldiers now."

They rush over to the cars and get into the one in front. Here they must wait another half hour before others coming the same way have found their way up to the cars and all the seats are occupied; in the meantime, the drivers keep a watchful eye on the surroundings and at any moment are ready to start the cars in case Israeli soldiers or Israeli police should suddenly appear.

Tension is chiselled in their faces, and when his car finally starts and drives and they're on their way down the high hill, his mute partner says to him in English:

"We're dead."

"Dead?" he says stunned meeting the man's dark eyes.

"We're locked in, no freedom ..."

The little man in the dusty overcoat and a melancholy smile turns out to be a lawyer with a small office in Hebron, where he tries helping women and fathers who've gotten stranded in the legal system that seldom functions.

"Don't ask me what I live on," he says, "I don't know."

"I'm also a lawyer, from New York."

The man looks at him in amazement.

"For me, New York could just as well be on the moon."

A panoramic rocky, rolling landscape, that in the distance works its way up, unfolds on one side of the road and on the other side olive groves glide past them. Still farther ahead appear the contours of the yellow-white city with minarets and high walls set down among large, mountainlike hills under a hazy sky.

He takes a chance and asks about the name Ben Zawawi.

"Don't know him, there are more than a hundred thousand Palestinians in the city," says the lawyer. "What does he do?"

"He's an important figure in Hamas here, as far as I know."

"There are many members of Hammas and many think they're important, but maybe's he's at the suq in the old town behind the Jewish quarter, Haret al-Yehud. Hamas has one of their offices there, but be careful; you never know what can happen around the Jewish settlement."

"Thanks."

"What d'you want with him?"

"Just a visit," says Jon in a hushed voice.

They get to a dilapidated, almost coulisse-like shop front, where there's a rush of local Palestinians on their way in or out of the city at the concrete barrier. Vendors in front of or in doors to the shops shout to the people, offers of bread, fruit and other goods. In front of the barrier are two personnel vehicles filled with armed Israeli soldiers, four of them have taken positions on either side of the small passage in the concrete block to check everyone coming in or going out, and a large line has formed in front of and behind the young soldiers who seemingly take their time with their inquisitorical task. Here among the other yellow taxis is their car, everyone gets out, he follows the lawyer over to the long line.

From Hebron the sudden sounds of exploding bombs and exchange of fire reach them; but from where he's standing he has only a view of a gravelled road towards a large parking lot with few cars and yet two more Israeli personnel vehicles. Unrest spreads in the lines, men and women, some with children in hand, turn anxiously to each other. It's as if the ominous sounds jolt the soldiers making them nervous, they start shouting and cutting folk out. More than before are denied passage and a small group of soldiers quickly move out of the personnel vehicles and with their rifles start herding those rejected passage back to the city or away from the opening to the gravelled road leading to the city. A woman falls and lies bleeding on the ground, and soldier angrily points at her with his rifle as two men rush to her aid and lead her away from the line.

The lawyer in front of him turns, saying:

"I've done this before. One false word and they'll open fire on all of us."

He feels his own fate in the palms of his hands as the line slowly moves forward. After a longer discussion between the lawyer and one of the soldiers in half Hebrew and half Arabic, where the lawyer several times points to him, the lawyer, with an irritated gesture, is ordered some metres through the passage and onto the path, where he stands and waits and the turn comes to him. The soldier, who's not more than 18-19 years old and has a handsome, closed face, that just like the rest of his body signals tension and distaste, looks at him closely and orders him in his school Egnlish to open his bag and show him his passport.

"You do business with him there?" says the soldier pointing with the barrel of his rifle to the lawyer.

"Yeah," he says slowly sensing what the lawyer has said to help him through.

"He says you're from New York, but your passport is from Denmark?"

"I've worked many years in New York," he says.

The young soldier suddenly comes close:

"Once I was in Denmark and Copenhagen, nice place."

He nods feeling the dryness in his throat.

"One of my friends was shot a couple of weeks ago by someone like him. You can't trust them, Arabs, they smile by day and are animals at night."

"I trust him," he says.

"That's because you haven't seen my friend's shot up face," insists the soldier as Jon feels the pressure from the line behind him.

"I'm sorry about your friend," he says as the soldier stares at him with an unfathomable glare that covers so many nights of undigested anger and re-pressed desperation. Then another soldier calls from the line nearby, bringing the soldier back to the noise and faces and chaos of that day, where the air's charged with aggression and the muaddhins voice calling weakly out to them from the high minaret in the fortress-like Cave of the Patriarchs, which serves as both mosque and synagogue and is like two chambers in a sharply divided heart. The soldier's body mechanically resumes his practiced routine with a wink to him that he's free to pass. Once those that went ahead of them stopped elsewhere in Hebron and the mosque in the Cave of the Patriarchs echoed with painful cries from the 24 worshippers during Friday's prayers, that were cut down by bullets from the settler Baruk Goldstein's automatic rifle; a hot August evening in 1929 67 Jews fell under Palestinian bullets in the city's houses and streets, and has it no end?

He follows the lawyer along the road, blocked at one end, towards the city. On their way, a massive control tower rises diagonally behind them to the left and at once he feels he's being watched from its glass that reflects the heavens and has been deposited in a prison camp. The lawyer points as they walk at a marbled wall to their right.

"See the bullet holes," he says. "Those missed their mark, but think of those that hit, one of them took a brother of one of my clients."

They continue to the parking lot with the few scattered cedars, parked cars, taxis and the two Israeli personnel vehicles, whose presence has clearly dampened the activity on the square and the road leading from it. Apart from a few taxi drivers with unoccupied vehicles and a small stream of people who with their packages and other things under arm are on their way to the path past the control tower, there's no one to be seen on the broad square.

The soldiers on the driver's seats of the vehicles watch them closely as they walk towards one of the taxis, which they both jump into after he's convinced the lawyer to drive with him part of the way.

"If you pay," says the lawyer with a weary smile.

"Of course," he says and just wants to get to his hotel as quickly as possible.

The pictoresque, but dilapidated, old houses that occasionally are followed by newly built white houses in concrete (some of them only half finished) close in on them on the relatively wide road, until they get closer to the heart of the city and to smaller streets. Suddenly they land in a narrow passage in a short line of cars and have to get out as the street is blocked farther ahead by two military jeeps and soldiers. He pays the annoyed driver and they get out, heading for the sidewalk. The lawyer suggests another route to the hotel and leads him down a side street, which in its narrownesss reminds him of an alley with recently condemned houses and many pedestrians. On the walls of houses hang posters with portraits of martyrs, young people, sometimes children; they turn the corner to another alleyway and soon after come to a larger, noisy street with many shops and a bank, and here beneath a colorful neon sign with the name 'Damascus' they find the entrance to his hotel.

In the deserted lobby with stone floor, where the walls are covered with blue tiles and a few framed photographs from Damascus, and a transistor radio from somewhere behind a door sends a mournful Arabic woman's voice singing out to them, they're immediately spotted by a dark-skinned young man in a dark jacket and tie, who from his chair behind a small consierge stand(with a running TV) with an eager gesture waves them over to him. When the porter gets his name and passport, he recognizes him as the long-awaited guest from Jerusalem.

"Are you living in Jerusalem?" he asks with a smile and in excellent English.

"Yes, for the moment," he says.

"But you're not Israeli?"

"No, I've lived several years in New York."

Apparently satisfied with the answer, the porter quickly finds the key and is ready to show him his room upstairs, but first the lawyer takes him aside and gives him a card with his address and telephone number. The lawyer's eyes in his tired face rest on him a moment.

"As you see my name is Faisal. If you have any problems, call me, I don't live far away."

He gives him his hand, thanks him again and Faisal moves towards the exit and vanishes on the street. The porter now leads him upstairs to the deserted hallway of the first floor and unlocks a simple room with a bed, table, lamp, chair and closet and a yellowed framed drawing above the bed of the old Hebron resting in the hilly mountain landscape with its white minarets, church towers and houses with vaulted or flat roofs. He closes the door behind him, walks into the room and as he looks out the window and down on the busy street in front of the hotel, where women in black or in modest over-frocks mix with older men with red checkered headscarves or young men in jackets and coats, he immediately phones Amer's contact.

The number is occupied, he stands some time in front of the window with his mobile in hand and gazes at two beautiful carpets with a distinct red color on display in the shop across the street, that light up the street. Just then a slightly distorted voice that he can't place reaches him and the pedestrians quickly vanish from the street; some rush back from whence they came, others seek into shops or stairways, others run forward along house walls, and soon after an Israeli military jeep drives down the already half-deserted street. From its loudspeakers sounds a nasal voice with warnings in Arabic.

When the jeep has passed there's a minute when the street is completely empty, as if a strong gust has swept through and blown all life away.

Is he dreaming or is he awake?

An open personnel vehicle with armed soldiers noisily drives through the deserted street, and shots are heard some distance away, a moment later the street is ghostly vacant.

He gets nervous and doesn't know where he should go and hurries out to the hall and down the stairs to seek advice from the young porter, but the small lobby is also deserted; he goes back to his room and again phones Amer's friend. This time he gets through, a voice answers in Arabic, and he catches the name Hussein and introduces himself in English. The voice switches over to English with a distinct Arab accent.

"You're Amer's friend?"

"Yes."

"Are you in Hebron now?"

"Yes at the hotel Damascus."

"I can't meet you now, Israelis are in the streets and there's curfew."

"I know," he says.

There's a moment of silence in the phone, he hears Hussein breathing.

"It's important?"

"Yes," he says.

"I'll come this evening."

"Don't put yourself at risk for my sake."

"Here, we're always at risk, and after dark I can easily get to you."

Hussein hangs up before he can protest. He stands a while looking down on the still deserted street. Yet another Israeli personnel vehicle passes, this time slowly, as if it's reconnoitering the street. A woman's face enframed in a wave of dark hair can be seen between two light curtains in a flat on the first floor across the street, their eyes meet then the curtains are closed tightly; the shadowy contours behind the curtains reveal three adults and three children.

Imprisoned just like himself.

*

He looks at his watch, but the hands and numbers on its face blur before his eyes when he lies on the bed. Exhausted he immediately falls asleep in the light from the street outside, and his unruly thoughts move towards a darkness in something that looks like a garden. Around him stand olive trees, the firmament above is filled with stars, the scents of flowers reach his nostrils, cicadas sing and behind him a small bonfire is lit, where John and Jacob sit praying. All twelve have broken up from their tent encampment on the Mount of Olives, Rabbi Joshua ben Jacob has led them to the Garden of Gethsemane, but one of them has vanished and the rabbi has appointed John, Jacob and him to go deeper into the garden, he saw how sad the rabbi was, but why? Why did he talk to them about their betrayal? He could never betray him. In the last days up to Passover, the rabbi has gathered many more followers than before on the Temple square and spoke and healed with great power, they ate their Passover meal together; there, too, he spoke of betrayal, but who would abandon everything they had and follow him for years only to betray him?

Before the rabbi left them in the garden, he asked them to watch and pray, his face was gray, stiff, he said, "I am despairing to death," but how can he, who's come with light and is Messiah for them and so many others be afraid?

Has he lost the faith? Is he not really the son of God? He walks farther among the olive trees and watches his steps; now he sees the rabbi farther ahead, he's lying in his linen coat between some trees with his face against the earth. His pleading voice reaches him, he says: "My father, if it is possible, so let this cup pass me by." He hears no more, he will hear no more, he hurries back to John and Jacob who both have fallen asleep. He sits down by the fire; he, too, dozes off, and knows not how much time has passed, he doesn't hear Joshua come. Suddenly he stands there and says to him: "Could you not hold vigil even an hour with me?" "It's the middle of the night, Rabbi," he replies, "we're all weary." "Get up," says Joshua. "Let us go, the time has come, they are on their way." "Who is on the way?" he asks in surprise, but even before he's gotten up, Judas appears among the trees followed by Roman soldiers, men from the Temple Guard with swords and cudgels and many of the elders from the Temple Council, he can also see most of the disciples and women who follow Joshua. Judas walks straight to Joshua; Judas seems gays yet at the same time nervous, says "Rabbi", takes hold of his hand and kisses it. "You have done yours", says Josua and gazes at him a moment without retracting his hand, but Judas glides away from his gaze, releases his hand and turns away with the face of a stranger.

Now the guards and the Roman soldiers grab Joshua, tie his hands and will immediately lead him out of the garden, but someone behind Joshua, someone he cannot see, draws his sword and hacks an ear off one of the guards. "Sheath your sword," says Joshua and with great strength tears his bound hands free of the Romans' grasp. In the next moment he places them up to the guard's bleeding wound and heals it through his touch.

The guard is speechless.

"For many days I've taught at the Temple square," says Joshua. "Why have you not touched me there? Now you come with your swords and cudgels and arrest me like a thief. Who are you afraid of since you need the help of darkness?"

"We fear only the gods, not Jewish nobodies and rebel rousers," says one of the Romans, a commander, and gags his mouth, another ties his arms tightly and binds him with a leather thong to himself. Most of them retreat;

the commander shoves Joshua in front of him between the trees and towards the garden's exit.

He doesn't know where the others have gone, maybe they've fled, but he follows the group of Roman soldiers, guards and the council elders around the rabbi through the night, along the Mount of Olives, across the Cedron Valley, in through Jerusalem's ports along the cobbled streets. They are only the small gathering around the silent Joshua when they reach a yard in front of the High Priest Kaifa's house. Here a port-like door is opened for Joshua and they pull him in. Like a dog.

He sees this at a distance. Now he's sitting with a cape around him, getting warm by a fire among the soldier guards and servants. The fire makes the faces glow, but he doesn't notice them, is totally absorbed by his imaginings of what's happening inside the house where Joshua, whom he's followed all the way from Galilee, is being interrogated. Only now does he discover that one of the servant girls is staring at him, and he moves away from the fire, farther into the darkness, but it's too late. She says, "Him there, he was also with him," pointing to him. He feels all eyes on him and his moist palms. "She's mistaken," he says. "I don't know him at all." Because of the cold he stays by the fire, but soon after there's another, an older man whose face he's never seen, who sits down beside him and whispers: "You're also one of them." "No I'm not, sire," he replies softly and gets up looking for a dark corner close to the house. From inside he hears angry voices, his hand trembles slightly, his thinks of leaving, but where should he go in this alien city? He freezes and is tired. Why has Joshua brought him in this situation? He thought Joshua was stronger, but when they came to get him, he just said, "This is your hour and the darkness is mighty." Now they're humiliating Joshua, and he, too, is humiliated. He comes closer to one of the windows the better to see, at that moment three men in capes, one of them the Temple guard, come towards him. One of them says: "He was also with him, he's also from Galilee." He stiffens, becomes angry, says: "Sire, I don't know what you're talking about" and hurries away from the yard and the fires. He walks through the deserted alleyways where shadows are. Where should he go? It's a labyrinth, where the scent of cinnamon, ambra and carnations still hang in the air and the echo of thousands of voices, and it suddenly becomes light, someone shouts at him from afar in the kashba. What has he done?

*

He awakes in the darkness, a voice calls to him through the door and now - knocking. Disoriented, he gets out of bed and takes time to smooth his wrinkled shirt and trousers before opening the door to the light in the hallway and to a tall, muscular dark-haired man in a dark, light-weight coat. The man's temples are gray, he looks at him with a penetrating gaze, gives him his hand and introduces himself as Hussein.

"I wasn't sure you were in your room," says Hussein somewhat surprised.

"Oh yeah, I fell asleep, thanks for coming," he says letting him in and turning on the lamp on the table.

Hussein limps slightly; probably as an old habit from the police, he immediately walks over to the window and looks down on the street, still void of people and practically no lights, except for those behind curtains in the flats above the shops. One neon sign for Falaffel blinks over a shop.

Not taking his eyes off the darkened street, Hussein says:

"D'you know what Hebron's called in Arabic?"

"No."

"Al-Khalil – You know what that means?"

"No."

"The Friend', that is, friend of the Lord, al-Khalil al Rahman, but there's not much friendship or hospitality here, is there? People are shot for a blink of an eye."

"It seems that way," says Jon closing the curtains and offering Hussein a chair; he sits down on the bed.

Hussein takes off his coat, lights a cigarette and looks at him closely, his left cheek in the shadows, in the semidarkness his eyes have a peculiar glow.

"If I'm to help you, you must know who I am. You're probably thinking, who is he, just a limping policeman, but I went to university in Bethlehem, wanted to be an architect, here we're always trying to get education. There just wasn't enough money for me to go there - you know why?"

He shakes his head.

"They took everything from us, my father and mother barely survived the massacre in Dir Jassin, west of Jerusalem in 1948; 250 civilian Arabs were killed and people fled their homes by the thousands. They came here, but were poor, and yet I dreamed of being an architect, I read and drew, naïve as I was."

Hussein takes a long drag on his cigarette.

"They shot a bullet into my leg some years ago when as a police officer I went to a checkpoint outside the Jewish quarter and insisted on talking with the settlers' leader about a boy who was beaten beyond recognition by one of the settlers. I don't know where the bullet came from, my son was frightened out of his mind. And yet I believe in peace. D'you understand what I'm saying? Not peace with those crazy settlers, but with Israelis."

"I think I understand," he says.

Hussein gets up abruptly, walks over to the small wash basin and puts out his cigarette, then turns to him.

"Amer speaks well of you, what can I do?"

"I'm looking for a man here," he says and tells him about Zawawi in detail. As he talks, Hussein sighs several times and lights another cigarette.

"We don't need that kind of people here," he says. "They're just as harmful as the settlers in the city; but I don't know him, even though I have some idea. Maybe his name isn't Zawawi, have you thought about that?"

"Yeah," he says. "That's one of the reasons I'm in Hebron."

"He must've hurt you badly?" says Hussein taking another drag off his cigarette.

"To the core," he says, getting up and taking a copy of a drawing from his bag, where it was hidden in a towel, and hands it to Hussein, who studies it carefully.

"Is this really the man?"

"It's a good likeness, except he was clean shaven when he threatened my girlfriend's life."

"Who made it?"

"The police in New York, on the basis of some still shots from a video that he didn't know he 'played a role' in."

"Are you working for them?"

"No," he says.

"With this here, I wouldn't mind."

"You sure?"

Hussein laughs.

"Surprised, huh? But neither our government nor Arafat nor Al-Fatah want anything to do with terrorists from al-Qaeda, nor the killing of civilian Americans or Europeans. If we find Zawawi or whatever he's called is a completely different problem."

"And that is?"

"Here we can only convict him for crimes he's committed in our territory, so what d'you have there?"

"Nothing concrete, I must admit," he says.

" I didn't think so."

Jon senses that it's all falling apart and for some seconds regrets ever coming.

"I shouldn't've come," he says. "It was stupid of me to involve Amer and you. I thought he could be handed over one way or another."

"An important, maybe 'secret' member of Hamas' military block? No, no way. Right now with the Israelis' action, things are so chaotic that one hand doesn't know what the other one's doing. Much is in ruins and people make war on each other. But I still might be able to help."

"How?"

"Give me a couple of days to think and make some contacts," says Hussein getting up from his chair. "First we've got to find and identify the man, if he's here in town."

Jon also gets up. They stand looking at each other, even though Hussein is the oldest of the two, he seems the least worn out, Jon has the feeling that even with his limp Hussein could get up and run through the night. Where he gets his energy is a mystery to him, he follows him out to the hall that's lit by a bare bulb in the ceiling, but maybe it's the strength of a survivor, who so many times has looked death in the face without being stung.

With their gray faces in the ceiling light, Hussein says:

"If the curfew's raised tomorrow, then look behind the Jewish quarter, you might find something there."

"You mean the suq?"

"Yes," says Hussein amazed. "I didn't think you knew the city."

"Someone's already told me."

"Who?"

"A lawyer from town."

"You know him well?"

"I met him on the way here."

"If I were you, I'd ask him to show you the way. Right now, nothing's safe."

Hebron is the city of drafts, the heat and the cold, it's the drafts from the grottos under the ground, called the Caves of the Patriarchs deep under the Mosque of Abraham, where the bones are, the munk Arnoul heard of it and found his way through a narrow passage and a rectangular stone path down to them. Once they went upright and were Abraham and Sarah, Isaak and Rebecca, Jacob and Leah or perhaps they only exist in the drafts of the mind or in the hot wind where the grapes, citrus fruits, figs in the summer send their scents through the streets; sweet, yes, great dreams now barricaded by barbed wire and encapsled in the kenotafs' cold, colored stones. Hebron is the city of clamour, voices, tanners and blown blue glass, but in the March winds from the Judean heights, angst is heard, that is what he awakens to.

The next three days, where the one long or short curfew is followed by the next, he tries alone or with Faisal searching the colorful, but decaying quarters like Harat al-Quittun, the tanners' quarter and the suq with its stalls of handcrafts. Sometimes entire streets are closed and stalls and shops in the old stone houses are closed up with green or blue doors on hinges. Some places they pass stinking alleys with piles of dirt and rubbish in the corners, other places they run into portals to the Jewish settlements in the centre of the city. Barbed wire is stacked in huge rolls, behind bars there are surveillance cameras and from a narrow opening with metal detectors the armed soldiers stare out at them.

There's no trace of Zawawi among the many faces he alone or together with Faisal meet on their path criss-crossing the many quarters; he hears nothing from Hussein and thinks of giving up and returning to Jerusalem.

In frustration he goes out on the fourth day to the concrete apartment blocks at Hebron's periphery to give his search its last chance. He turns on to a road among so many others. The atmosphere is tense in a surrealistic way beneath the bright sky; battered cars pass, carpets and clothing hang from small balconies, women in scarves look out of windows, children run back and forth on the pot-holed plots in front of and behind the blocks that are up to four stories high. On a bench in front of a kiosk two old men have planted themselves, both bent over the canes they've placed between their legs, sometimes sending a tense glance down the street.

He walks along the houses with the many doors into stairways and first sees the armored personnel vehicles – at each end of the road – drive in towards one of the blocks in the middle of the street; at the same time he hears the first shots from a flat above his right shoulder. Several men in black caps are from one moment to the next firing on the soldiers in the tanks, the dry sound from the automatic machine guns hitting shattering windows. A man crashes bleeding from the third floor and lands with thud on the ground in front of the block. Screams and shouts cut through the street, cars stop, doors are bashed in and men flee headlong down side streets. The old men on the bench rush off the same way, one of them drops his cane and falls to the ground and crawls the last metres until he rounds the corner of a house. Children scatter in all directions searching for cover; he, too, seeks shelter in a stairway as a group from the vehicles storm the stairs next door. One of them falls, bullets from the machine guns intensify and shatter windows and doors in the entire house. Heart-rending cries mix with sounds of hundreds of recoiling shots faster than the ear can register and from shattering glass and hard surfaces from which the missiles ricochet. A boy of 5-6 years stands frozen on the spot somewhere on the pot-holed plot between the tanks and his door. The boy hides his face in his hands; not really deciding, but on re-flex, Jon opens the door to the shooting and runs, ducking as he runs the five meters to the boy, scoops him up in his arms, turns and moves back towards the stairway, but something hits him on the back of his thigh. He resists and continues a few steps until he suddenly loses control, falls to his knees and drops the boy out of his arms. The boy rolls on the ground, stops a moment in confusion and looks at him and runs crying on along the house walls.

Jon tries to get up, but falls sideways to the ground lying there, he touches the back of his thigh and when he looks, his hand is covered in blood, he's been hit. Pain from the leg shoots through his body, his throat's parched; it's as if his head sinks down in the ground, but with one eye he still can see the road and the soldiers and the tanks, but he hears nothing. Hacking like a film on old reels he sees the soldiers dragging two men from the stairway. One of them is beaten on the back of his head and trundles forward towards the opening in the vehicle, the other is shoved in the same direction, a wounded soldier is helped into the cabin, a soldier looks his way but turns and hops in to the others. The vehicles start and drive off.

There's total silence on the street, as if it's holding its breath.

Then two men in work clothes suddenly appear beside him, one of them bends down over him and starts speaking, his voice ringing in the distance in Arabic. Others rush over, children and women, one of them has two large towels and some bandage that she wraps around his thigh with movements that say she's done this before. The men lift him from the ground and carry him to a large truck parked down the street and lift him into the passenger seat. One gets in and holds on to him, the other takes the steering wheel and starts the car.

"Hospital, hospital," says the man at his right, but in the state he's in, he can't reply, and the man waves his hand in from of his eyes to see if he's conscious, at the same time the car leaves the curb. He crokes something and tries to stay erect despite the pain in his leg, but in vain, he sinks down.

The car drives and drives, the light vanishes and returns; it seems an eternity with the rumbling under him. He feels that the car's stopped that someone's pulling his arms and legs and he's looking vertically up into the blue sky that's transformed to a yellow ceiling that again becomes a white ceiling and then a bright light that blinds his eyes. Something sticks in his arm as Arabic voices surround him and shadowy faces look down on him. He has something on his mouth, inhales through a funnel. Then the lights go out, as if someone suddenly flipped a switch.

It's dark as in the center of the universe's mysterious black fiber and his frontiers to the world are annihilated; he floats, he laughs. Finally the pain's gone.

"Eve," he whispers, and then: "Sine."

But it's so low, almost silent, that none of the doctors or nurses nearby at the crescent hospital Almohtaseb's operating room in the old Hebron hear him.

*

A week passes, he recovers surprisingly quickly and after four days, with his bandages and a crutch, can carefully get out of his bed in the three-bed ward and walk back and forth in the hallway past the many wards and in the stream of visitors and patients. Both Faisal and Hussein visit him, the former calls Eve in Jerusalem for him, who's shocked over the news, but Faisal succeeds in calming her and promises that he'll soon be back in Jerusalem; the other is still making plans for arresting Zawawi, but Jon senses that he, like himself, hardly believes that Zawawi is in Hebron at all.

"Despite your wound, you look relieved," says Hussein with a smile on his second visit. "Is that because Zawawi isn't in Hebron, or that he doesn't exist?"

"Oh yeah, he exists," says Jon returning his smile.

"There're still a lot of Israelis in the city, their raids are scaring everyone, maybe even Zawawi, or whoever he is."

"Yeah, maybe even him," he says.

Also the family to the boy he rescued in front of the apartment block comes to thank him. He receives their sweets and again holds the boy as he shyly sits on the bed and lets them photograph him with the boy.

His condition swings from enormous fatigue to excitement. One evening as he lies exhausted in bed in the three-man ward and darkness has fallen and the door's open out to the dimly lit hall, the door to the ward on the other side of the hall opens. A short, thickset man in a black jacket and beard steps out and quickly turns toward a patient in the room he's about to leave with a few loud words in Arabic as farewell. At first he has only a glimpse of him, but as the bearded man closes the door behind him and is now out in the hall facing him, their eyes meet momentarily; it's as if he's seen a ghost.

The man, who the moment before was excited by the farewell, stiffens with an ice cold gaze, almost dead to the core. It's Zawawi, he has no doubt. The man continues down the hall, but has he, too, recognized him?

With difficulty he gets out of bed, grabs his crutch and walks to the hall, where he just sees him leaving the building.

He gets back to the ward, finds his mobile and walks back to the hall to call Hussein.

"Are you absolutely sure?" asks Hussein several times when he realizes what it's all about.

"Yes!" he answers each time and describes Zawawi exactly.

"Then let's hope he comes again. I'll send a man over, act as if you've no idea who he is and why he's there. His only job is to be ready if Zawawi shows up again. If he does, then we'll take him in one of the alleys when he leaves the hospital. Got it?"

"Yeah," he says already uneasy about the days he's to spend at the hospital until that might happen.

The following night he lies bathed in sweat and barely sleeps. Every time a door opens to the hall, he doesn't know what to do with himself and finally in the morning, when the light shines through the curtain and the two other patients lie talking to each other, he falls asleep, only to be abruptly wakened by two Israeli soldiers who without warning have walked into the hospital to ask him his 'role' in the 'shooting epidsode' in front of the blocks. They quickly herd the two Palestinian patients out of the room and are then alone with him.

His initial foggy condition together with his Danish passport and the American lawyer's card that he takes out of his bag that Faisal got for him from his hotel Damascus makes them even more suspicious. With the younger rifle-armed soldier behind him, the older soldier, an officer, who introduces himself as legal advisor and is seated in a chair in front of his bed, keeps inquiring into his explanations and asking him the same questions in varied form.

"What were you doing on Ibrahim Street, what business did you have there at all?"

"I told you," he says.

"So tell me again."

"I'm visiting the city, I'am a tourist …"

"There aren't any tourists in Hebron now."

"Yes, me."

"Tourists visit the sites, they don't run around on Ibrahim Street."

"Has the Israeli army written a special manual for tourists?" he asks and realizes he'd gone too far.

"Don't try that stuff here, I don't give a damn for your passport or your lawyer papers, here we make the rules and ask the questions. Got it?"

He doesn't answer, looks into the officer's narrow eyes, but they dissolve and he holds his head.

"We've had enough of foreign so-called friends of peace running around the city and taking part in subversive actions."

"I have an Israeli girlfriend and live in Jerusalem," he says.

"Sure you do, you've no Israeli papers, but if you're really so happy with Israel and Jerusalem then get yourself back!"

"I'd be more than happy to," he says, "when the wound in my leg, from an Israeli bullet, has healed."

The officer with an intelligent, light face and American diction that leads him to believe he originally was American and probably connected to one of the settlements in the area, breaks out in laughter.

"I really feel sorry for guys like you," he says. "You don't understand shit. You haven't a clue to what's happening. It would be funny if it wasn't so sad and you get in the way for us who have to do the dirty work."

"The word 'dirty' is probably very accurate," says Jon.

"He doesn't get it!?" says the officer turning to his colleague, the younger soldier, who as the minutes tick by seems utterly uninterested in what's happening. "What d'you think we should do with him?"

"Take him with us," says the dark young soldier in poor English and gazes lazily at him.

They switch over to Hebrew and he guesses they're discussing whether the military prison in Hebron isn't already overcrowded. The officer makes a quick phone call and as he checks things out keeps his eye pealed on Jon. He switches off his mobile and gets up, hands hanging in his belt and says sharply:

"You're lucky. We just don't have room for you."

"I'm not afraid of you or your prisons."

The officer again breaks out in laughter, but his face abruptly changes expression. With a brisk wave of his index finger, he signals the young soldier and leaves the room. The young soldier approaches his bed, pulls his rifle from his shoulder and rams its butt down onto his stomach.

*

A few days pass, the sun breaks through and if you walk around Hebron, you could already smell the scents of lemons, carnations, thyme and spring. Dogs bark, noise and shouting from traffic rises to the blue unprotected heavens. At night sudden, sporadic volleys of shots can be heard like a release from a wave of aggression and dismembered hope far into the night itself. The Israeli combat vehicles have retreated from the city and are on their way elsewhere.

He leaves the hospital with a crutch and his bag. After spending the night in Faisal's old and modest two-room flat, he's on his way with Faisal by taxi to the parking lot near the city limits with the imposing control tower and the

marbelized wall where impressions of bullets and small projectiles are im-
bedded as brutal souvenirs.

In the taxi he gets a call from Hussein who drily informs him that Zawawi
was captured the previous evening after another visit to the hospital. He's
been interrogated the entire night in one of the local Palestinian police stations and charged for his activities in New York, which by fax has been confirmed by the New York State Police; he denied everything, also his identity
under the name of Zawawi. A raid on his temporary address (at a friend's)
early the same morning produced seven passports, all with his photo: Syrian,
Egyptian, Iraqi, Iranian, Pakistani; and all with different names. At the moment he's being charged for falsification of passports, but as his pc's were
confiscated at the same time, and they're in the process of screening them,
these appear to contain solid evidence for a connection to the al-Qaeda network and direct conspiracy in terrorist activities in New York and Kenya, so
the case is water tight. There's still the problem of what to do with him long-
term, as apart from the fraudulent passports he hasn't done anything illegal
on Palestinian soil and they don't want to extradite him.

"You can hand the evidence over to Interpol," suggests Jon: "Then they
can take him as soon as he sets foot out of Palestinian territory."

"We might do something else," says Hussein on the choppy connection.

"Like what?"

"Here the sentence for fraud can sometimes be unusually severe."

The connection is lost; he tries to call Hussein to say good-bye, but without
luck. Then he sees that the battery in his phone is dead.

The taxi arrives at the large parking lot, strewn with old and battered cars
of every sort, now alive with people.

He pays the driver from the back seat and with the same gesture hands Faisal some large notes, which he won't accept.

"Consider it a professional courtesy to your office in Hebron," as he stuffs
them into Faisal's jacket pocket.

"Isn't that the same as saying you don't need them yourself?" smiles Faisal
pulling them out of his pocket.

"Not as much as you. I've sold my practice in New York, it gave me some money."

"You're sure to need them in Jerusalem when you get set up there."

"Who says I will?" he asks amazed.

"Your girlfriend Eve when I talked to her on the phone."

"Let's see what happens."

Faisal smiles faintly again and puts the notes back in his pocket.

They get out of the car and walk together down the sandy path past the wall and control tower towards the checkpoint and the facade-like buildings on the other side of the border, where the yellow cabs and a bus stand waiting. Midway they stop because of his unsteady steps with the crutch as others walk past. Faisal, who's holding his bag, looks anxiously up towards the control tower's shining windows and hurries him along.

"What's wrong?" he asks and limpingly starts moving.

"The guards are always uneasy when someone stops here on the path."

"And that worry is always yours?" he says.

"Yeah, as long as we're in the jaws of the monster."

They both get through the checkpoint without difficulty, are waved on by the soldiers. When the driver in the almost filled battered, green bus with a honk signals departure, they part with a long embrace in the midst of a crowd of vendors and taxi drivers and customers under a sun that for the first time in a long time bites into the skin and gets the blood in the temples moving. The last thing Faisal says to him as he climbs on board, in front of the bus is:

"Remember, with us, peace isn't a luxury."

The bus leaves Hebron and drives out into the deserted, hilly landscape. From his hard seat by a window, he looks long for an atoning sign and finds them in the appearance of the olive groves, the long rows of tough trees in the arid earth. As a mirage in the middle of the desert they draw his gaze and remind him of all things' impermanence.

He's on his way home, but where is home?

Jerusalem or Copenhagen?

Why not both places when he now has at least two hearts under his shirt?

Weary hearts, but still hearts.

What was it his father always said when he lost at cards and sat with some hearts in his hand?

"Hearts are wild in the city of thieves."

*

At the next checkpoint all the men are made to leave the bus, also he, and stand in the burning sun, half of them are sent back on foot to Hebron, the other half again take their place in the bus that starts and drives on.

He's again by the window. The journey continues to places still unveiled for him.

The sun is great.

* * *

Lightning Source UK Ltd.
Milton Keynes UK
177657UK00001BA/1/P

9 781906 791766